I0681773

My Ripper Hunting Days

BERNARD BOLEY

© 2016 Bernard Beaulé All Rights Reserved

All rights reserved. No part of this book may be reproduced, distributed, or transmitted in any form or by any means, including photocopying, recording, or other electronic or mechanical methods, without the prior written permission from the Author, except in the case of brief quotations embodied in critical reviews and certain other noncommercial uses permitted by copyright law. The book cover and the pen name, Bernard Boley, are equally covered by the author's copyright.

This book is a fiction. Characters are entirely fictitious. However, when characters have really existed, they have been presented in a fictious manner and do not reflect their actual behaviour or language nor situations they may have been involved in.

Copyrights registered under the Copyright Act (R.S.C., 1985, c. C-42).

Legal deposit:

Bibliothèque et Archives nationales du Québec, 2016. Library and Archives Canada, 2016.

ISBN 978-2-9816286-0-2 (Printed)

ISBN 978-2-9816286-1-9 (EPUB)

DEDICATION

For Danielle, my wife and soul-mate, and my family.

CONTENTS

ACKNOWLEDGMENTS

When I began writing this novel, like most of the people, I almost knew nothing about Jack the Ripper. So I needed to learn everything I could not only about the killer, but also the late Victorian era. These are the following authors I must thank for having provided me with the basics: Paul Begg, Neil R. A. Bell, John Bennett, Stewart Evans, Martin Fido, Trevor Marriott, Timothy B. Riordan, Donald Rumbelow, Keith Skinner, Philip Sugden and Simon Daryl Wood.

Of course, it goes without saying that forums such as Casebook and Jack the Ripper Forums provided me with this fascinating ambiance so many Ripper experts and fans share among themselves.

And then there's the bi-monthly Ripperologist magazine, the kind of reference one uses to meditate in a Zen fashion about the Ripper and everything surrounding this timeless personage. In the last days before publishing my novel and regardless of any comment he may eventually come up with, David Green, Ripperologist's JTR novel review expert, has provided me with a discreet, but unimaginable support, probably without even being aware of it. He deserves a special place in this acknowledgment. Thank you David.

PROLOGUE

"Prepare to drop the anchor."

Andrew was at it again, giving orders. It really didnt matter to us since we all knew how important it was for him to live the dream of his life any time he could, and commanding a ship was his dream. As far back as I could remember, he had always said he would, some day, sail the seven seas at the helm of his ship. Everyone who knew my brother not only was aware of his intentions, but also admired him for having such a fine and noble goal. Actually, the boat we were on belonged to all four of us, Vincent, Daniel, my brother Andrew and I. We had seen it floating on the Saint-Lawrence River for weeks. The current and tide had led it to the shore in front of our parents house. A total wreck as far as I was concerned. It measured some twenty feet and had a small cabin. However, for my brother, it was as if the Flying Dutchman had revealed itself to him with a restoration mission to accomplish. He took charge of the boats refurbishing, although our parents paid for all that was needed, including a new motor. Still, in his mind, it was his. A year later, although it had a peculiar look and was hard to maneuver, it allowed us to explore the small world surrounding Orleans Island. We kindly let him pretend, one more time, that he was the captain.

We were no older than fifteen or sixteen. So one

could easily imagine how we felt each time we took it out. Our travels, even the shortest, became opportunities to improve our navigating skills, to begin a new series of adventures or whatever we set our mind to. However, there was one constant rule. Our parents always made it clear that Andrew, being the oldest of us four, would be responsible for all four of us reinforcing his wish to command. He never disappointed them nor did he abuse the authority he held. He took great pride in carrying out his role as a leader, and we respected him for that.

Our planned course would bring us to Grosse Isle, a small rocky island some twenty miles away from our home in Saint-Petronille, Orleans Island. When one would approach its West point, a Celtic cross would slowly reveal itself through the dense vegetation demanding from him to kneel down, bow his head and remember all those who had been buried there a century before. Five thousand, if not more, mostly Irish, hoped they would reach the land of the free only to hear ravens greeting them to their death. It was an outcome they could expect from the moment they accepted crossing the sea aboard a coffin ship.

The elders had warned us not to go there without giving us any reason why we shouldn't. It only increased our desire to explore the island, even if we also could hear the ravens' kraas as we came closer to the shore.

It was a sunny and warm summer day in July. The sea was calm, and the incoming tide was almost on the turn. Andrew kept watching for those treacherous underwater rocks as we came close to the shore. He had read the charts and knew where a sandy bay would allow us to make land also offering us sufficient protection against the winds.

"Now!" he shouted. Once again, yelling his order so loud that it would remind us who was in command of the maneuvers.

"Yes Captain," I responded with a smile.

I dropped the anchor and let it drag along the bottom until it hung solidly, slowly spinning the boat around. Facing the current, Vincent stopped the motor while Daniel, rope in hand, jumped off on the shore to secure the boat from the rear onto a close by tree.

"Good," said Andrew.

Minutes later, the boat was set for the day.

"Come on guys," said Andrew, "let's see what we can find."

"Are you sure there's nobody on the island?" Vincent asked as he turned his head toward the bushes trying to detect any human presence.

"Not really, so we'd better be careful," insisted Andrew.

"There's a rusted signpost over here," said Daniel. He had already climbed the hill at the end of the beach and pointed at it for us to see. "Let's see if I can get what's written." 'Strictly prohibited…', '…passers', '…trespassers will…,', '… will be prosecuted.'

"There's nothing like a good word from the welcome committee," I added, looking toward the shore then back at the boat where I was still standing. "Maybe we should leave."

"We've already trespassed," Andrew pointed out, "So we might as well get into trouble for something seriously worth it."

I looked around us to better evaluate the situation. Id rather stay aboard the boat. The tide will be coming down soon. One of us should stay here just in case we need to leave quickly or prevent the boat from running aground.

Andrew agreed, certainly admitting to himself that he, as a captain, should have required one of us to do exactly what I, as a fearful young boy, wished to do. Andrew jumped off the boat, and all three quickly disappeared behind the bushes at the top of the hill.

Thirty minutes had already past. I was getting bored and felt stupid for not having gone with them. I jumped into the water and swam under the boat. I looked at the keel then at the sandy bottom, and figured nothing could compromise the hull's integrity. As I got back on board, I decided to add a mooring so the boat would settle safely until the outgoing tide was down. I could now leave and walk the shore.

The beach was maybe a hundred feet wide and lined with boulders. Tall and thick bushes would hide it from those who would stroll on top of the hill.

"Seaweed, driftwood, more seaweed, rubbish... How exciting! The guys are certainly on to something more interesting than what I've got around me."

I headed toward the left and slowly moved away from the boat, daydreaming. Minutes later, I noticed what seemed to be a glossy piece of metal between piled rocks but kept going. I didn't give much importance to it, but some fifty feet further down; I suddenly stopped.

"Hey. Wait a minute," I thought. "Normally, metal rusts, especially when it's trapped by rocks close to water. This can't be an ordinary piece of metal. Got to go back and have a better look."

I turned around and walked back following in on my tracks.

"Where was it again? Hmm! The old maple tree, the grey and white boulders, the rock pile, there it is. How did that get here? It couldn't have slid between the rocks with the help of the tide; it's packed too tight. Maybe the rocks tumbled over it or... Nah!"

As I came closer, what seemed rather unthinkable became obvious. It was more than a piece of metal. I knelt down to get a better look. I was more curious than intrigued by my discovery, which could, after all, still be some rubbish. However, it seemed to me someone had carefully placed this object between some well-chosen rocks. They offered a good protection against the elements and kept the box from the view of passers-by. One large slab covered it; another one served as a front panel, which had probably slipped or had been misplaced, revealing a portion of a box. Smaller rocks were arranged in such a manner that they would avoid suspicion. I wasn't foolish enough to believe I was about to find a treasure. But then, who knows what actually happened while these immigrants in quarantine and travellers stayed on the island. Maybe one of them temporarily placed some of his possessions here while he was treated in the barracks. I carefully moved the rocks away. The box was set against a boulder. After clearing the area, I managed to pull it out.

It was a small, thin copper box but rather heavy for its size. One side had oxidized while the rest of it presented a weathered patina. Otherwise, it was intact. No exterior sign could help me determine its origin or ownership. Brass corners gave me the impression they may be holding a cover made of material. What had attracted my attention turned out to be a flap-lock still having portions of shining gold plating. I shook it with great precaution, and felt it held something bulky inside. I tried to open it, but the lid refused to yield. Was it locked or had time cemented the hinges? I couldn't tell. This would not stop me. Unlocking doors, unblocking windows, picking locks were no secret for me. As a teenager, after losing or forgetting the house keys so many times, I had learned to get in without anyone noticing it, particularly when I would come back home late at night. One of my uncles had given me one of those famous Swiss pocket knives, which I always carried and often used to break into our home. One of its blades would certainly do the job. I inserted a thin blade under the lid, running it around the box.

"Slowly," I instructed myself, "you don't want to break anything."

Something stuck to the blade. I pulled it out and looked at the tip. "Wax, it's sealed with wax... probably candle wax."

I couldn't help thinking that by making the box watertight, the owner certainly valued its contents. Even so, then why go to such an extent. Usually, people stay on the island for a short period. Perhaps it belonged to someone who lived at Grosse Isle. The owner may have forgotten it.

"Stop thinking and open the damn box!"

I went on removing the wax sticking to the lid. It still wouldn't open. The box was certainly locked. I pulled out the metal toothpick from the handle of the Swiss knife.

"This should work."

As I turned it in the box's keyhole, I felt a resistance but maintaining the pressure against the lock, it began to move. I spit in the keyhole, hoping my saliva would lubricate its parts, turned the toothpick in the other direction. It moved even more. I pushed it a little further in, twisting it in both directions and managed to give it a full turn. The lock finally gave in.

"Got it."

I was trembling with excitement. Whatever the box contained, it would now be mine. I looked around, nobody. I saw our boat; no one had come back yet. They were still exploring.

I took a deep breath and swung the lid open. No gold, no jewels or silver. What a disappointment. Just a brownish piece of canvas covered with grains of rice. Mother, I remembered, used rice in her powdered garlic and onion bottles to absorb any forming humidity.

"The owner is a woman," I hastily concluded.

Brilliant, but all this only to preserve a piece of sail,

ridiculous. Well, at least, it doesn't have that moldy smell so common to old fabrics.

There had to be something else. I noticed a string holding the canvas tightly packed. I pulled the canvas out of the box. I looked at it from all angles as if something would suddenly reveal itself to me and help me understand the nature of my newly found possession. Nothing in particular came to my eyes. I carefully started to untie the string and unfold the canvas. To my surprise, I discovered it served as a wrapping for some sort of book.

I looked around again. No one had yet returned to the boat. At this point, I didn't mind at all what they could be doing or even cared if they were in trouble. I had just found what seemed in my mind to be a valuable treasure. Nothing else could matter more.

The book cover had nothing written on it. I opened it. In the middle of the first page, it simply read: Woodrow Reily, 1889.

This book was almost a century old. Its backing was of worn tan coloured leather. I rapidly went through the pages. The paper was of poor quality. It was the kind of book one can use for many purposes: notes, daily thoughts or doodles. It had neither lines nor page numbers. It was handwritten and had dates on many pages. Attached to the interior of the back cover was a sealed letter marked with two words only, 'To Woodrow'. I didn't pay much attention to it at that moment, but it would become my Ariadne's thread weeks later.

My God, its a diary.

I was mesmerized. I sat on the slab and started reading it. After a few pages, I was horrified by its content. My stomach almost turned. I swiftly closed it, wrapped it back in the canvas. My hands were shaking as I put it in the copper box. I ran to the boat as fast as I could where I hid it in my backpack. I wouldn't dare tell anybody what I had just found. As a child, we all knew the bogeyman. Our parents would warn us of him if we didn't obey them. He was just a personage who could scare you until you cried. However, this diary had to do with someone who had really existed and was known to cut his victims in pieces. From September to November 1888, he had butchered five or six women living in London's ill reputed East End, in a place better known as Whitechapel. The description given in the diary of his way of doing, to this day, makes me sick. It mentioned all those directly involved in the Whitechapel murders, its author, Woodrow Reily, being one of them. I didn't even know this person ever existed. As for the man responsible for all these deaths, he was known to all as Jack the Ripper.

It took me fifty years to decide whether I would let you share in it with me or destroy it. By writing these words, you now know the decision I have made. By doing so, I transfer, upon you, the burden of all these years of secrecy and hope to finally be at peace.

Woodrow Reily
1889
GROSSE ISLE

1 THE EVENTS OF JANUARY 1889

SUNDAY, JANUARY 13, 1889

Almost three months have now passed since those
dreadful events occurred in Whitechapel. By now,
Londoners have certainly returned to their usual
occupations, daily headlines feeding them with
worthless matters for them to worry about. As for East-
Enders, they may now be finding comfort in their
miseries slowly forgetting the death of so many women
said to be of ill repute. For most of them, their fate shall,
however, remain precarious whilst that of the Ripper's
victims may appear to have been a better one, deserved
or not. Many a word pertaining to those deaths and to the
conditions of women of lesser means have been spread
around to feed the mind of the feeble with ludicrous
causes and simplistic remedies. This need to force
people into bringing about necessary changes or have
others abide by a given set of rules imposes strongly

upon them the building up of a reality quite different to what is and to what actually was. Such has been the doing of the papers during the fall of 1888. Then there are those who willingly ignore every single circumstance beyond their own world. It is not becoming of them to step outside of it, for their understanding of society is that it is something, which shall degrade them, hence something to distance themselves from.

Sadly, they had not learned from the events that happened at Trafalgar Square on November 13, 1887. For them, Bloody Sunday was strictly a mob riot or a political uprising, which had to be contained. A year later, the events of Whitechapel could not be anything more for them than a background again set by elements of the mob and to be dealt with accordingly. Sure enough, women have died. Bodies were cut open. Blood has flowed. A terrible mess, I must admit. However, the gap between what was written, spoken or perceived and what really took place is so wide, I truly wonder if it is possible for me to fully describe what actually happened during the autumn of 1888. It's not that bad shall now become good, nor wrong become right. Wrong, was the way of the undertaking of all these events; good, was undoubtedly the intention those who were responsible for them were seeking, at least in my mind. Many years ago, I had decided to flee whatever and whoever surrounded me, unless I deemed it necessary for my survival. I must admit I have more than survived. For once, I have lived. Maybe I should have spoken out sooner. Nevertheless, I consider myself as one who would mind his own business and limit himself into strictly doing whatever was asked as long as it was legally, socially or professionally required of me to do.

Had the man I now became existed at the time of these events, the situation would have evolved differently. Had I gone through the profound humane experience Grosse Isle offers to all, I, Woodrow Reily, would have risen up to this outrageous and manipulative man I met during the Whitechapel events and whom I believed to be Jack the Ripper. Enough said. Though my mind shall never free itself from the events I was involved in, directly or allowed by the position I held at the London Hospital, I have this unbearable need to exorcise myself by writing them down. At the time they occurred, many situations, in which I was involved were like viewing the peak of an iceberg. Only a portion was revealed to me leaving me unaware of what was actually happening sometimes merely a few feet from me. Had I known the outcome, I never would have let myself be caught in the chain of events I am about to reveal. I shall, however, make it my best to describe what I have experienced during these dreadful months of 1888. You may ask why one would undergo such a recollection of those terrible events? Justice and maybe revenge. One has to allow the truth to come out if he expects some form of justice to prevail or seeks vengeance for those concerned by the Whitechapel murders. I shall not be that person having been contaminated by typhus and pneumonia and possibly doomed to die soon. May the finder of these pages decide by himself the proper manner to conduct a task I regretfully leave unfinished. Enough has been said. May these notes speak for themselves.

BERNARD BOLEY

2 THE EVENTS OF AUGUST 1888

THURSDAY, AUGUST 2, 1888

Early in August, the London Hospital's pathology laboratory received a rather unusual guest. He was tall, close to six feet I estimated. Such a stature would set him out in any crowd. But then he also had this flowing mustache stemming from each side of his pale face. The long waxed tips pointing straight out on both sides of his face would attract even more attention. He wore a black velvet coat and held a matching cap in his right hand. A loosely hanging gold watch chain was attached to his waistcoat. Shiny cavalry boots fortunately without spurs completed his outfit. Professor Fillmore, one of the Faculty's most prominent members walked him through our facilities. His name was Francis Tumblety. Fillmore was my superior. He was neither tall or small, thin or fat. In fact, he appeared to be the perfect average man who could easily blend in with whatever or whoever surrounded him. However, the sound of his voice was nasty, the kind a baby would make when preparing to scream. One would always see him holding his eyeglass, which I never saw him wear, swirling it around his index. The faster the swirl, the more nervous he was, the rest of his body totally maintaining its composure. With Tumblety's visit, his eyeglass was swinging faster than I ever saw. I had to be very careful.

I could hear him giving elaborate details on the recent improvements brought to our pathology room. The visitor, however, did not seem to attach any importance to what was said, preferring looking at the display cabinet set against the back end wall. Whenever Professor Fillmore turned away from him, the visitor would again look in that direction. There, behind glass doors, human organs were contained in well arranged jars and kept for teaching purposes. He glanced at me then suddenly stopped. Until then, I could observe him discretely hoping, unsuccessfully as it turned out, to remain unnoticed. Heaven knows how badly I would underestimate an encounter with such a fascinating yet intriguing person such as the one I was about to meet! For at that precise moment, an irreversible course of events linking our fatal destiny had just begun.

"Good morning, young man," said he, staring at me, as if I were a prized museum artifact.

From his accent, I concluded he was from overseas, Canada or perhaps the United States.

I simply nodded, expecting to be briefly introduced considering my position. Professor Fillmore turned, looked at me then at his guest and came to a halt. Foreseeing being less the main subject of interest than I had unwillingly become, he gave me an obviously irritated frown.

"Still here, Mister Reily?"

Fillmore's words were clearly intended to belittle me as he did with all those surrounding him.

"Doctor," he worded, attempting to regain his guest's interest, "let me show you what you expressly asked to see?"

"Give me a minute, if I may, professor." Still looking at me, he added, "What a contrast your youth brings to this morbid place! Would you care to join us?"

I felt embarrassed but even more surprised by his highly pitched almost effeminate voice. One would expect it would sound differently for a man of his build.

"Mister Reily has to prepare the amphitheater for a lecture I shall be giving this afternoon? Am I wrong, Reily?"

Again, he wanted the visitor to understand our respective importance in the Institute.

"Now there, professor. You and I know there is so much to learn from your conferences on the dead, the dying as well as the sick. Yesterday's reaction from the audience and your reputation abroad speak for themselves. Shouldn't we allow one of your attendants also to benefit from your brilliant explanations?"

His ego so cleverly addressed, Fillmore had no choice but to abide by his guest's wishes.

"Why not," said he, trying to figure out a way to prepare for whatever role this visitor would let him play. "Let me first introduce him. Mister Woodrow Reily is one of our younger and quite promising assistants. Do not underestimate him. He memorizes precisely every pathology and forensic term or procedure he comes in contact with not to mention his keen sense of observation. I'm sure he shall eventually find a way to apply his knowledge should he become a full member of our staff."

Never had the professor spoken of me in such terms. It was undoubtedly a way for him to outwit the visitor. "Pleased to meet you, Mister Reily," said the visitor as he shook my hand.

"Doctor Francis Tumblety is a thoroughly experienced American physician," continued the professor. "The devastation of the civil war rapidly brought him to our common profession. He afterwards integrated, into his treatment of diseases, a still young but very much needed understanding of various chemicals found in plants. He practised also in Canada, in the provinces of Quebec and New Brunswick, if I'm correct."

"Professor, you certainly have a way of focusing on the essentials of my career," commented Tumblety. "I have always learned a lot from every person who shares the goals of our profession. I have a hunch that Mister Reily won't be an exception."

"I'm honoured, sir," I timidly replied as I tried to pull out my hand from his.

"Now let's put an end to all unnecessary formalities.

May I simply call you Woodrow?"

"If you wish," I said, seeking, however, an expression of approval from Fillmore, which came when he simply mumbled, "…think we should move … more important matters."

The next hour or so revealed itself to be my first experience with a conversation amongst equals not necessarily having the same expertise, but the same concerns. Tumblety constantly expected an opinion from me.

"You certainly have something to add, Woodrow," he would say, "Let's hear it."

As we came closer to the display cases, Doctor Tumblety, who had been in a good mood up till now, slightly opened his lips revealing clinched teeth. His look became strongly fixed revealing himself in a strange manner. It intensified as if it could pierce every object placed behind the windows in front of him. His right hand tightened onto his waistcoat pocket. The man had changed in a matter of seconds.

"Is there something wrong?" I asked rather surprised by his reaction in front of the female organs.

Tumblety stopped pointing at the showcase and caught up with me.

"No, not really," he replied, quickly pulling himself together. "It's just that examining some of these female organs reminds me of the intense suffering and torments those surrounding the deceased go through."

"Yes, but the same goes for these people before they died," Fillmore pointed out.

"Maybe," Tumblety added,"but death ended their torment while the living often keep carrying it. It then nurtures itself, grows and eventually takes control of the person's existence. The more violent or gruesome the death and its associated pain, the greater the impact bestowed upon those close to the dead. In times of war, generals learn quickly how to achieve this effect on the enemy."

"Quite frankly," Fillmore said,"I admire your interest in human behaviour."

I felt that Tumblety was rather relating to his own experience and not to that of others. It was preferable for me not to comment, but I couldn't resist asking: "Are there any professional explanations behind your remarks and female organs?" I asked as we continued walking along the display cases.

"I warned you about Mister Reily's sense of observation," said Fillmore, smiling at Tumblety.

"You did, indeed." He paused, smiled at both of us as if he had expected such a question and went on.

"Let me give you two situations. Take a family coping with the disease of one of its members, the mother, for instance. Imagine a serious infection of her uterus after she gave birth. As the disease evolves, the family adapts to it, each member supporting each other. When death comes, their suffering vanishes as time goes by. Now, consider a prostitute's organs infected by a venereal disease and a client she contaminated while he was only expecting a moment of pleasure. The latter wouldn't dare to talk of his bad condition with others if he has a minimal sense of decency. As his life evolves, so does his torment. All this also caused by an infection, which could kill him. Believe me, Woodrow, these women should be taken care of, and I am committed into doing exactly that."

"Are you under the impression that women are exclusively responsible for the spreading of venereal diseases." I quickly pointed out.

"Not at all," Tumblety added, "I was strictly trying to focus on my concerns with the female side of the problem."

"O'Reily, how dare you challenge Doctor Tumblety's intentions?" said Fillmore.

"Please forgive him," Tumblety said.

"If we can be of any help Doctor, do ask us," said Fillmore.

"Now, as for the female organs, they are precisely the reason for my presence her. I have studied them in the past and need to pursue my work. You can easily understand the need for me to add more specimens to my existing collection."

"Mister Reily," Fillmore asked, "Do you think you can provide him with whatever he requires that wouldn't deprive us seriously."

Usually, Fillmore would command me to do whatever he deemed necessary no matter how useless or ridiculous it could seem. It was his way of demonstrating his importance, and I would do nothing more than obey. This time he instead asked me if it was possible, obviously to give Tumblety the impression he was in excellent terms with his staff.

"I'll do the necessary. Should I report to you before proceeding?"

"Just fill in the forms for Doctor Tumblety and us to conform with the Anatomy Act, and I shall sign them whenever I have a moment."

"Maybe Woodrow and I should meet at another time and examine all the options," added Tumblety.

"I shall make him available at your convenience," promised Fillmore.

"I'm quite sure Woodrow's skills will improve my sometimes clumsy ways of handling things. Maybe we should schedule this meeting right now. What would you say, Woodrow, if we had dinner together this Saturday? Let's say at eight. I'll send you my card giving the address of the establishment. Of course, you'll be my guest"

"I can assure you he shall be available," added Fillmore imposing upon me a quick and positive answer.

I quickly agreed and felt a certain pride in what was asked of me by Fillmore and, above all, by Tumblety. I would make all necessary arrangements for them not be disappointed. I did my best as to remain flexible to any wish they would have during the rest of the visit. At one moment, he expressed his views on what he believed to be a serious flaw in forensic procedures. Again, he solicited my point of view.

"I was really surprised," he said, " to read in the press that examinations conducted in a murder case are not always carried in a fully equipped pathology facility such as the London's hospital but usually in premises close to the scene."

"You would even be more surprised," replied Fillmore, "if I told you our establishment is unable to respond to our daily needs. The overall situation is intolerable for all our medical staff should they be working in our premises or elsewhere."

"Oh really? How then can one expect to find the real cause of deaths if only superficial evidence is taken into account?"

"Our situation, we hope, should improve and eventually allow for a better solving not only of crime cases, but all those where the cause of death has to be determined. Mister Sydney Holland, one of our administrators is doing a remarkable job in doing so."

"And you, Woodrow, what do you think of all this?"

"Letting each District deal with these cases without having them overseen not only deprives the public of a complete and thorough process it should be entitled to, but also provides murderers with loopholes so wide they can easily walk through them with impunity."

"That's exactly the point I was about to make, my good fellow," Tumblety said. "One day soon enough,

London will be the victim of medical vagueness, incertitude caused by these inadequate conditions physicians are forced to accept."

Tumblety ended his visit with those stunning words. Seconds before leaving, he asked us to consider our meeting as one held between men sworn to professional secrecy. He made us promise that the conversation we just had including his presence would strictly stay between us.

Meeting Doctor Tumblety left me with the impression of a man who gave a great deal of importance to those surrounding him. He made quite a difference with all those I knew who had the responsibility of guiding me, by their example, into doing what was good and becoming good as well. My experience of teachers and members of the clergy, amongst others, is that they fail to adapt their rules to the changing reality in front of them. They prefer imposing their own limited and biased reality. Parents were quite often even worst. They had no rules. Many were angry frustrated people who had children and dealt with them as if they were their enemies.

One event comes clearly to my mind. One day, a neighbour came to our flat yelling at our mother that my brother and I had broken one of her dear possessions. She demanded compensation. Mother slapped us both in the face and promised the neighbour that his man would take care of it when he would get back. Later that evening and drunk as usual, he arrived swearing at our mother for not having a meal ready to serve. She avoided her daily beating by telling what had happened with the neighbour. His toolbox still in hand, he pulled out a long screwdriver. Lost in his rage, he hit us with it, inflicting a severe cut on the back of my head and breaking my brother's arm. Mother not only did not stop him, but observed the scene with a sinister smile.

"That'll teach ye," she screamed. It was their way of letting us know what was bad.

Tumblety, as I would afterwards discover, never imposed himself. He rather approached people from their side. It was easy for him to have us come out with an idea, transforming it into a shared interest and being thankful for our contribution. If we added his kindness, we morally felt compelled afterwards to assist him as best as we could. Was this the expression of a weakness on my behalf or did he know exactly how to call upon some hidden desire inside me? I couldn't tell, but either way, I would help him.

SATURDAY, AUGUST 4, 1888

The day was young. The sun still had not risen, nevertheless letting its light slowly introduce proof of its existence. Yet, I was already heading for the hospital. The mere fact that Tumblety and I would again meet could transform the continuation of an otherwise endless routine, one would call a job, into a highly significant moment in my life. Not that I did not appreciate working at the hospital's lab, quite to the contrary. I consider myself to be one of the lucky few in the East End to have the means to support himself. Even better, I managed to save some money just in case the winds turns in an unfavourable direction. Once inside the lab, I expected to receive his card at any moment. Throughout the day, my mind kept thoroughly scrutinizing numerous topics from every possible angle for I did not want to embarrass him in any way as I might have already done. I left by eight o'clock, Tumblety showing no sign.

MONDAY, AUGUST 6, 1888

Still disappointed and wondering what could have happened to prevent Tumblety and I from meeting on Saturday, I made my way through the usual morning crowd. The first opportunity for me to be of some help to Tumblety came soon after our initial meeting. To-day during the morning, he had a note delivered to me by a cabdriver. It read:

> *Dear friend,*
> *I'm extremely sorry for having been unable to meet you Saturday. It was impossible for me to get in contact with you. I absolutely need to see you to-day concerning matters we have discussed. Would Whitechapel Station suit you at seven? Give the cabdriver your answer or write me your preferences as to where and when. However, it must be before night.*
> *Francis Tumblety*

Whitechapel Station is to the left of the hospital just minutes away from my workplace. Should it rain, I wouldn't have a long way to walk. My work ends at seven o'clock but I have grown the habit of leaving around eight or nine. This usually gave me sufficient time, after my work, to read any piece of medical literature lying around in the lab. I would prefer the College's books, but they were reserved exclusively to the registered students and teaching staff. As for the books on Whitechapel Street's free library, they were of no interest to me.

Given the circumstances, I would settle for seven o'oclock and told the driver so.

After he left, I kept wondering what could be so important that we had to meet with such short a notice.

We covered many topics during his two-hour visit. No one in particular seemed it would require of me to do anything so soon. Haven't we all participated in passionate conversations on the need to change the world the next day and agree upon a set of actions each one will accomplish only to realize that we never do anything after all? I thought our meeting was one of those. Three words in his note, however, struck my attention: "...to day... before night". I couldn't figure out the urgency of any situation involving both of us that had to be dealt before night would fall Fillmore having guaranteed my availability, I wouldn't deceive him.

As promised, Tumblety was waiting for me at the station. Tall as he was, I could easily distinguish amongst the people around him at the corner of East Mount and Whitechapel Street. I waved at him.

"Walk with me," he said after we shook hands. "I prefer not having people overhearing any word I might say."

We headed West on Whitechapel Road.

"What are your projects for the future? Fillmore led me to believe that you were talented enough to become a physician. Is that part of your plans?"

"Even if it was, my chances are slim. I don't have the means nor do I have a family history I can rely upon.

I admit I have tried, but failed to be accepted as a student. The committee had the nerve to tell me that my results from the tests were more than needed, yet they rejected my application. I remember precisely what one of them told me. Young man, have you looked at the way you present yourself before us? A man of your kind would not fit with our school's tradition."

"Damn fools. In America, things would have been different, trust me. Maybe I could lend you a hand. I have excellent relations with many influential members of the medical corps. Tell me, what would you have liked to do? Set yourself up as a medical practitioner, teach?"

"I'm not at sufficiently at ease with people to become either one. Medical research is where I would have felt comfortable."

"That explains finding you in the pathology lab." Do you assist in any way in the examination of bodies, in dissections?

"I prepare the bodies, clean them, bring the instruments, put aside the organs for further examination…"

"But do you observe how it's done?"

"Of course. Some examiners even insist on having their own style and take great pride in carefully demonstrating it to me. One often amused those assisting him by dissecting with his eyes closed, walking his left hand fingers over the body to locate, with a fascinating degree of precision, the place to cut with the knife held in his right hand. I noticed he always had specific parts of the body he would use as an initial reference, such as the navel. I quickly figured out that the constant gap between his fingers served as a unit of measurement, which, given the dimension of the body, led him where he wanted, down, up or sideways."

"Good, very good. I knew I had the right person," he added with a rather scary laughter.

The right person for what, I thought.

He stopped and breathed deeply. "I'll never get used to London's East End smell, you know. Even if rain cleans the air, the odour of filth comes back minutes later only to cling to your clothes. It's like some people. Whatever you do to get rid of them, either they manage to cling or, within minutes, others appear and replace them. Don't you agree, Woodrow?"

"About the smell or the people?" I answered with a smile as I looked strait in front of me, intentionally avoiding the expression I suspected he would have on his face. "Just joking," I said. "I agree."

"Wherever you may find yourself, there's a great probability of also finding there many kinds of people that you immediately dislike or even hate. Knowingly or not, they often remember you of someone of your past."

"Fortunately, it goes both ways," I said. "You also meet people you appreciate from the moment you meet them."

"Are you relating to us?"

I didn't answer. I figured it would be better for Tumblety not to know how much our highly pleasant conversation could be influential in any way on my current or future behaviour towards him.

"I may be wrong, Doctor, but I feel you didn't express an urgent need to see me only to tell me that."

"I did, for some part at least. Do you remember when I mentioned I would take care of a certain kind of women?"

"The sick?"

"Amongst others. Some, in particular, are doomed without knowing it. They have not only placed themselves on a road offering no possibility of turning back, but even worse, they have widened it to trap others."

"Quite frankly, Doctor, I don't follow you."

"Whores dammit, Woodrow, prostitutes," he almost screamed out. He came to a complete halt knocking his boot heels onto the side-walk "I'm talking about those women well aware of their condition, nevertheless condemning men to share their deadly fate."

Again, the expression on his face left me wondering.

Was it pure hatred or was he showing me his determination in curing these people?

"You want to take care of prostitutes. Are you serious? Other women deserve more attention, I believe."

"Don't tell me you're one of those Brits separating those surrounding you into the deserving and the undeserving people. So much needs to be done. There are very efficient ways of taking care of someone's miserable condition. Sometimes, you can solve the problem, but other times you just can't. It's too late. You watch their situation deteriorate until they die unless you put an end to their suffering. During the civil War, I swear to you, many wounded soldiers asked physicians to do exactly that. Many field physicians made arrangements for that to happen as did some of their comrades-in-arms on the battle field."

"You're talking about killing people. You must be out of your mind?"

"Calm down," he said quickly scanning around us to see if my words had drawn any unwanted reaction from people close-by. "Let's move on, if you please," he added crossing the street.

We went on without saying a word. Then he suddenly spoke out. "What I said has nothing to do with killing or murdering people." His tone let me clearly understand how infuriated he was by my choice of words.

"It has everything to do with coping with one's agony and irreversible destiny. My profession requires nothing less of me."

"It demands that you heal them."

"Watching them die passively is not healing. If you aspire to become one of us, you will learn that stopping a treatment, refusing a medical procedure or even better, accelerating the achievement of the predictable outcome are the only solutions in many cases."

"I can understand that healing has its limits. Given that, your approach has a certain logic. I admit I never gave much consideration to questions of ethics. My job made me understand that dead people didn't mind what happens to them. What you're saying is one way for you of taking care of sick prostitutes is ending their lives. I'm I correct?"

"Helping them, Woodrow, helping them bring to an end their miserable lives. By the same token, they can provide me with organs I need for my own research."

"Have you ever done this before?"

"I think I've already answered that question."

"I mean with prostitutes?" He gave no response, simply looking at me as if it should be implied from the general meaning of our conversation. It became clear to me that whatever I would come out with wouldn't change his mind. My questions even started to upset him. It was preferable for me to tone down my remarks.

"And how do I fit in all this? Don't misunderstand me. I do not mean to say I would agree in advance on anything you would ask of me."

"If I had organs of a deceased person, would you accept preserving them using the facilities of the lab until I have time to have a better look at them before bringing them to America?"

"Would that be all?"

"For the moment, let's say that would be it. Eventually, there could be more. It all depends on you.

You could assist me in my studies of diseases and remedies in America, if you wished so. It would be much easier for me then to help you obtain your diploma. What do you say?"

Research assistant, diploma, I couldn't believe it. He was offering me the sky, but my attitude and remarks were almost destroying exactly the kind of relation I was so much in need of.

"I shall take care of everything you bring me," I answered looking strait at him so my expression would leave him with no doubt. "I suppose you had someone already in mind."

"Yes. I've learned of this woman, a prostitute. Her name is not important, and I won't annoy you with unnecessary details. It could be even done to night. If so,

I will let you know one way or another." "I'll be ready."

"Don't worry. If anything goes wrong, I'll take full responsibility. Now if you don't mind, I have to leave you and get prepared."

I watched him continue at a faster pace on Whitechapel Street. Although our conversation left me with certain doubts, I felt he was still worthy of my trust.

WEDNESDAY, AUGUST 8, 1888

Very early in the morning, the news vendors near the hospital were screaming their hearts out to sell the latest edition of the press.

"Read about it, Read all about it, murder in Whitechapel," one said whilst another yelled over him, "Get the News, the Daily News, women stabbed to death on George Yard." It wasn't front-page news, but the boys always had a way of selling ink to the locals. I gave a halfpenny, folded the paper under my arm and rushed to the laboratory. No one had arrived yet. I didn't take the time to change and went directly for the article.

SUPPOSED MURDER IN WHITECHAPEL
About ten minutes to five o'clock yesterday morning, John Reeves, who lives at 37 George yard buildings, Whitechapel, was coming downstairs to go to work, when he discovered the body of a

woman lying in a pool of blood on the first floor landing. Reeves at once called Constable Barrett, 26 H, who was on his beat in the vicinity of George yard, and Dr. Keeling, of Brick lane, was communicated with and promptly arrived. He made an examination of the woman, and pronounced life extinct. Giving it as his opinion that she had been murdered, there being knife wounds on her breast and abdomen. The body, which was that of a woman apparently between 35 and 40 years of age, about 5 ft 3 in in height, complexion and hair dark, wore a dark green skirt, a brown petticoat, a long black jacket with a matching coloured bonnet. The woman is unknown to any of the occupants of the tenements on the landing, on which the deceased was found, and no disturbance of any kind was heard during the night. The circumstances are therefore mysterious, the body has been removed to Whitechapel Mortuary, and Inspector Elliston, of the Commercial Street Police Station, has placed the case in the hands of Inspector Reid, of the Criminal Investigation Department.

The crime had been committed on George Yard Street, only a few blocks away from where Tumblety and I parted the evening before. He had mentioned the possibility, that same night, of doing something for a woman. The paper now reports that some bad has been done to a woman, quite a disturbing difference, I thought. My body shivered at the very thought of Tumblety possibly being involved. At that instant, Fillmore entered. Trying to fold back the paper as fast as I could, I placed it in a drawer of my desk.

"You seem to be in a hurry, this morning," he noted. For once I was glad it was him and not a messenger

Tumblety would have sent one if organs were to be

delivered to me.

"Get me my reports, Reily. The board wishes to see me."

As I prepared them, he looked at me, surprised. "You could at least take time to dress properly." I was so troubled by what I had read I totally forgot changing clothes and was still wearing my raincoat.

"I'm terribly sorry Professor," I responded without believing a single word I just told him.

"Don't be sorry, fool, go change immediately. I'll take care of my notes myself. By the way, have you heard from Doctor Tumblety?"

"He sent me a note asking me to meet him." I dared not say more.

"Don't have him wait. I was quite clear on what I expected from you," he said as he left the room.

The day passed without any word from Tumblety. To be of any use, organs have to be dealt with as soon as possible. As a physician, Tumblety was well aware of such requirements and would not have jeopardized his clear intention of examining them. Having received no organs during the day meant the absence of a link between him and the woman's death. I felt reassured. The proximity of the location stayed however unresolved in my mind.

THURSDAY, AUGUST 9, 1888

I arrived at the lab earlier than usual, but still no news from Tumblety. On my way to the Medical College carrying some material to be given out to the students, I heard some members of the staff mention that the Coroner would hold an inquiry on the woman's death. It would take place at the Working Lads' Institute right across the hospital during the afternoon of that same day. I couldn't resist attending it. However, as a precaution, I left a note informing Fillmore I was preparing for a meeting with Tumblety.

The hall was already crowded thirty minutes prior to the beginning of Martha Tabram's inquest. Obviously, the more horrendous the crime, the more curious it attracts. The atmosphere was the same one would experience at a circus. Only the refreshments and the smell of the animals were missing.

Of the five witnesses giving their testimony that afternoon, two caught my attention, John S. Reeves, a labourer living on George Yard and Deputy Coroner, Dr. T. R. Killeen.

Reeves identified himself as the person who found the body around a quarter to five on Tuesday morning.

He noticed the body of the victim lying on its back whilst he was coming down the stairs. It had shed all of its blood on the landing of the first-floor. The crowd oohed and ahed at such a point the Coroner demanded to restrain from commenting in any manner. Reeves continued. He indicated that he immediately went for the police. From the way her clothes had been messed up, he believed she had struggled with her attacker.

As for Dr. Killeen, he had been called to the scene of the crime by police-constable Thomas Barrett. He arrived at 5:30 am only to notice her death, which he estimated had occurred some three hours previously. His post-mortem examination of the body revealed no less than thirty-nine stabs, one through her heart causing her death. He gave the coroner some details: the left lung stabbed in five places, the right lung, in two places, the liver, five. The spleen had two stabbings and the stomach six. He counted nine wounds on the victim's throat. "Butchered, she was butchered," cried out loud a woman sitting in front of me, resulting in the Coroner admonishing her. According to the witness, more than one instrument could have been used, including possibly a dagger. The victim, whilst a little plump perhaps, seemed otherwise to have been healthy.

The body having not been identified yet, the Coroner adjourned the case.

I approached Dr. Killeen as he left the hall hoping to obtain additional details of the post-mortem examination. Small groups had formed in the narrow corridor, each one soaking up as many interpretations as they could from the witnesses.

"Doctor, Doctor Killeen, could you grant me a moment?"

"And who might you be, may I ask?" said he, staring at me as if I was someone who didn't deserve the attention of a well-known physician.

"I'm part of London Hospital's Pathology staff. Reily is my name, Woodrow Reily. I only have one question."

The moment I identified myself as a member of the Hospital's staff, people started to gather around me as if two men of great importance were about to exchange thoughts. Killeen wasn't pleased with the possibility of me causing a commotion.

"Be quick about it."

"Were any organs removed from the body by the killer or killers?"

"What a silly question. Why on earth would someone commit such an act?"

Those surrounding us laughed. Killeen started making it through the small group of people still remaining in the room.

"Sir, if you please." I said desperately trying to gain back his attention.

"No," he responded almost annoyed, "no part of the body was removed, partially or totally. Now if you are done, I have more serious matters to attend to."

"You have no idea how important your answer is. I am so grateful for your time and thank you."

The facts brought out by those two witnesses relieved me immensely. It couldn't be Tumblety's woman. First of all, she had not been the subject of a medical procedure but stabbed. Secondly, the testimony led me to think she had not been affected by a deadly disease, quite to the contrary. Tumblety was not medically interested in a healthy woman. Finally, although viciously stabbed, the body was left whole. Tumblety did not benefit from her death with some of her organs.

I still had work to finish at the laboratory. Once there, I was glad my note was exactly where I had left it and proceeded to destroy it immediately. Nothing had been disturbed. Professor Fillmore had probably not shown up, and my absence, most likely, the note went unnoticed. Given the circumstances, I didn't expect a message from Tumblety either and left early. The past days had drained all my energy away. I remember sleeping well that night.

THURSDAY, AUGUST 23, 1888

On August 23, two weeks later, the George Yard Street murder inquiry resumed. The victim was identified as Martha Tabram. Known as a woman selling trinkets, she also prostituted herself. To make things even more complicated, she was in the habit of drinking most of her earnings. The Coroner's jury came to the standard and laconic formulation of the verdict for these cases: wilful murder against some person or persons unknown.

SATURDAY, AUGUST 25, 1888

Each Saturday, I had a few unpleasant tasks to do such as a thorough clean-up of the lab, the dissection room and the sterilization of instruments. Students were still on holiday, and therefore, it demanded me very little time. But as soon as a session begins, it would cause me to clean more in a day than a road-sweeper would do in a week. Each student is usually assigned to a given place and rapidly reveals the kind of physician he would eventually turn into by the care he gave to his equipment. Some were unacceptably negligent with whatever they handled and yet would never doubt their claim in becoming a surgeon. I would prefer ending my own life rather than entrust them with it not even for a moment. Fillmore, for his part, had a tendency to keep chipped phials until they broke in a student's hand. By blaming the replacement on their clumsiness, he was convinced he would be in a better position to explain any shortfall of our budget to the board. Since no student could be accused at this time of the year, I would throw away those I found. Saturday is also the day I draw up an inventory of materials and equipment and make sure we would not be short of anything. Every Monday morning Fillmore would blindly sign each requisition form I would prepare. So was his trust in me. During the past weeks, I had progressively built up a reserve of jars, wax to seal them as well as formaldehyde just in case Tumblety would come up with more organs than I expected. My efforts could turn out to be pointless for he had had given neither me nor anyone else the slightest sign of him still being in London.

Once this dreary routine had finished, so would be another day at work.

It had been impossible for me to enjoy Bank Holiday earlier that month, an illness probably caused by the food I ate the day before kept me to my bed. Fortunately for me, it was a dull day. No sun, only clouds with and on and off rain benefiting those who offered a sheltered form of amusement. I, however, decided to indulge myself this Saturday after my work and make up for the pleasurable moments I had visiting Kew Gardens each year. There, I would usually sit close to the ponds and admire the water lilies and lotuses. The carps would often jump out the water and feed on the insects flying inches above the surface. There would always be someone to spare pieces of their bread with them resulting in an amusing struggle amongst the fish for the slightest crumb. This Saturday, instead, considering the late hour I left the hospital, I would settle for a pint at a pub, something I would not ordinarily allow myself. The cruel and continuous experience of my parents not being at their best with liquor showed I should keep a distance from its use.

London's East End has proven itself to be nothing less than a city within the City for as long as one could remember. Countless occurrences of the worst this world offers should have convinced everyone with a mind of his own to name this place the 'End' rather than the East End. For beyond whatever one could imagine, one can only find himself in hell. However, good people coexisted with the bad and the evil, all struggling each day to survive. Sooner or later, all those living in East End learn to distinguish one from the other. Their safety depended on East End's many unwritten rules, and striving to survive was one of them. So was finding out the places where you would be well advised not to go alone by night. There, such as the Wicked Quarter Mile on Commercial Street, you would foolishly endanger your life yet one single road away, you were in a safe haven.

As I walked on Whitechapel Road, East End revealed even more of itself to me than it had in the past. A Saturday evening in a soon to end summer would often do this to you, if you lived here. There were those, such as I, who had ended their day's work and those who would begin it, all of them outnumbered by those who had neither beginning nor end to their day. Many of these only measured time by counting the number of days since their last meal, others by the last time they slept in a bed. You could read their hunger, their exhaustion or their distress on their faces as easy as if it were the two or three words of a title printed on a book's cover. Even though it would surely be unsettling for an outsider, the story behind one's despair was just another tale those around would refuse to hear for it could be also theirs on the following day. Keeping things to yourself was another unwritten rule. You glanced at a man standing on the corner of a street and immediately knew he had just arrived from the country simply by the stamina he still showed but would lose unless he found some work. All were too late for a workhouse to offer them a shelter or did not spare the money for a doss house. They would wander through the night looking for a doorway, a bench or some grass to sleep on for a couple of hours, a bobby, by then, asking them to move along. They would go further and start over. For most of these people, not having skills was the least of their problems; living in East End amongst so many offering the same was worse. Whilst the latter would fight for a job, the former would kill for half of the job for which they all had the similar skills.

And then there were the merchants, the street peddlers and hawkers carrying on with their usual business. Children with their trinkets held high in their little hands were as common as rats in a cellar. "A penny for a box o' matches," one shouted out across the street. Many a good woman, one time or another, had no other choice but to join with prostitutes and offer their body often for less than a shilling. The next day, it was as if nothing irreproachable had happened to them. At the bottom of the scale of these people of unlikely trades were the beggars. They could only show an empty hand, which, sadly, would stay that way for hours. Offering something and its corollary, knowing to whom it could be offered, were two other basic rules.

These people living on the same streets I'd lay my feet on each day were the East Enders. I was one of them and knew all the rules.

Someone I was well acquainted with in my home town once worked at the White Hart, the pub where I would have my pale. This man was the only remaining link to my past and had slowly tamed me into meeting him there to share the very few good memories our village had left us. He is dead now, crushed, ironically, under a broken wheel and axle of a brewer's carriage in front of the pub. The establishment was located on a safe section on Whitechapel Road near the flat I shared on King Edward Street. Unlike many pubs, the White Hart was known to be well run hence it introduced you to a slightly different crowd. Its owners would examine you from the bar and decide if you were deemed worthy of becoming one of their patrons. Once inside, the rules of the street ceased to apply and were replaced by more appropriate ones. If you heard a quarrel going on over a wager, the owners would make sure it never turned into a fight. The evening was still young, but in a few hours, and as people would fill the place, the atmosphere would darken. Alcohol would make them forget, remember, smile, laugh, talk, come to tears, and if one had too much, bring him suddenly to a silence. Its odour would progressively cover any smell, god or bad.

I wasn't in a hurry to drink nor was I in a mood to mingle with others. Paying for my pint was to me as it would be for a traveler paying for a train ticket or a poor for a bed in a doss house. It gave the purchaser the right to sit or sleep wherever the price entailed him to, and I would always choose to sit far from the bar in a less noisy corner, but close to a lamp where I could read.

I had barely begun enjoying my brew when an elegantly dressed man in his sixties entered. He quickly surveyed the interior and made his way towards my table. From his felt to his gaiter covered boots, one could not be otherwise prevented from concluding to his better condition. Everyone's eyes went for him. Some commented on his appearance then went back to their own affairs. He unbuttoned his overcoat revealing a perfectly cut three-piece suit, removed his hat and sat both hands clenched to the gilded knob of his cane. "Way too overdressed. Didn't buy his tweeds on Petticoat-lane," I thought as I glanced at him.

"And what may the kind man wish to drink?" asked one of the owners quickly coming to him before any waiter could.

"A fine cognac would do me some good."

"I'd rather ye 'ave a pint o' bitter, cause cognac 'ere 'as only the name. It ain't fit for a decent man o' yer liken."

"So be it." It took only seconds for him to be served. Before he was even told the price of his beverage, the man placed a shilling in the owner's hand folding it, making him understand he needed not to bring back his change. He held the glass up, pulled out a handkerchief from a pocket and cleaned its rim then wiped off the foam from his lips after taking a sip.

He was one of these higher class persons whose lifestyle and wealth you would envy but would also hate for their haughty manners. I would not allow him more consideration and opened my book to read. Moments later, I heard him starting to speak without addressing anyone.

"I'm fascinated to see how much a person can define himself by what he is saying or doing. Take that man in the corner to my right, for instance. He is blind drunk, yet the woman at his side continues to show him great interest."

I couldn't resist turning my head in that direction. I indeed noticed a fine-looking woman talking to a man just about to drop his head to the table and fall asleep. "Others, on the contrary," he continued, "shall stay silent or remain motionless even though the place where they are, such as this pub, commands otherwise. You, my good fellow, why are you here? It's obviously not the best place to read a book. Don't you agree?" he added now directly facing me.

It was me he was addressing since the beginning. His remarks astounded me. My face was turning red out of embarrassment. I closed my book with a noise almost decided to leave the pub. I felt as a child caught doing something wrong and wanting to flee before getting into more trouble. I decided to leave.

He could do nothing but understand the state he had just put me and how much I was irritated. As I passed by the table where he sat, he grabbed my arm.

"I beg your forgiveness," he quickly said. "It was never my intention to interfere with your privacy. I know no one here and would be delighted to converse with someone. With no disrespect to the others in these premises, you seemed like a respectable young man. I'm I wrong?"

"Because of my book?" I asked. "I don't believe to be the only one here able to read," I added still upset by his familiarity.

"No, it's that I am not at my best when spontaneously engaging a conversation with people I do not know. I am truly sorry and hope you can return to your reading and forget all this. Don't leave because of the mistake of a silly old man such as me. Please..."

His expression took a radical turn; he now looked miserable. I had to stop him from breaking down further.

I pulled a chair behind me, brought it close to his

table and sat.

"It is I who should learn to be less touchy," I said. "I must admit I was listening to every one of your words," I said with a smile. "The women you were referring to over there, I would bet she is more interested in his money than in his looks, which leads me to believe she is a lady of the street trying to bring him out."

"If he does, that's probably the only thing he shall be able to do. The man's rag will require a lot of starch for him to make some use of it."

We both laughed.

"My name is Gordon Fitzgerald. I'm from Dublin but have a place here in London."

"Certainly not in the East End if I consider your dress up but then, it's none of my business knowing where. I am Woodrow Reily and work at the London Hospital. Mind me if I ask you what a person like you is doing at this time of the day on Whitechapel Road. Are you aware you're at great risk in this area?"

"I have people who know my whereabouts, and my driver is waiting outside for me."

I looked through the front window. True enough, a coach was at the corner, and a tall wide shouldered man, its driver, stood waiting at the door. Who is this, I thought? Fitzgerald, if my memory was clear seemed to be a name of importance in Ireland. It then hit me.

"Are you related to the Fitzgeralds of Kildare? The Duke of Leinster's family to be more precise?" I whispered so my words would not draw attention and compromise his presence."

"The Duke is a distant cousin. He and I are not in good terms. Decisions made by the family have tremendously affected the estate and the wealth of all the family. Fortunately, my side of the family managed to preserve the little we had and make it fructify. I rather not say more. And you, may I ask?"

"Woodrow Reily, originally from Derry and currently living in Whitechapel for the past eight years. Tell me, what brings a man of your condition in this area? Are you not aware that such a deployment of wealth is an invitation you are openly sending to everything bad East End hides?"

"I was warned against coming here but decided to ignore any advice. All my life I have done what was expected of me from my family. I went for a higher education at Eton and Cambridge, served as an officer in India, married into a good and well moneyed family, greatly increased its financial situation. In short, I gave all that was possible of me but in return received far less. I consider it fair now to allow myself some freedom in whatever form I desire."

"Thieves and murderers could put an end to more than your freedom in a matter of seconds. Even the police avoid many streets when patrolling alone at night."

"You do not seem afraid of walking around alone here."

"It's not in my nature, but I can give quite a hard time to anyone who attempts to reduce me to submission."

"Then maybe you can help me. There is so much to be done and so little time for me to accomplish it alone."

"What is it with people of your kind? You keep imposing yourselves upon others and then, give no sign. No less than three weeks ago, the same has been asked of me. Games, it seems that all you can do is involve others in your selfish games."

"I swear this would not be a game," said he as he knocked on the window and signed his driver to come to him. "Would you agree on having dinner with me at my place to-morrow evening? I have this little town-house on Campden Square. I am sure you shall easily understand my situation once there. If you accept, my driver shall pick you up at eight. All he needs to know is where."

"A meal in a rich man's house! Why not?" I thought and accepted. "I'd rather have your driver come and pick me at the hospital at the main entrance around half past seven, if you don't mind," I added, "A coach at my door would cause me too many questions, and I'm not into giving explanations in my neighbourhood."

"Then I shall see you at eight," he said whilst putting on his overcoat. "Do you wish for me to have you driven to your place to-night?"

"That's very kind of you, but I still have some reading to do." As he left the pub, I couldn't help to notice his glass was almost full, only the sip he had taken was missing. I went for it before any drunk would have, allowing me to stay even later than I ordinary would.

SUNDAY, AUGUST 26, 1888

Fitzgerald's driver was on time. I waived at him to stop and wait for me to approach for it deemed preferable for me to ride a cab unnoticed by the regulars of the hospital. Soon after, we arrived on Campden Square. Despite the fog, the street was still well lit. The driver stopped, came to the front of the cab and brought down the running-board to ease my way out. "It's here," he paused. "Just knock at the door. Someone will let you in."

Fitzgerald's town-house was anything but the small one he said he owned. It was a three-story building, cellar excluded, and judging from its width, it could probably lodge a hundred poor in East End. I slowly walked up the stairs and admired the vibrant effect the lights behind the door gave to its stained-glass window. It puictured a young woman playing a Celtic harp. The door itself was made of sculpted oak and held by polished brass hinges. I raised the lion face knocker but hesitated before letting it fall down. Dressed in my best clothes, nevertheless, still looking like a shabby commoner, I felt embarrassed to be the guest of someone related to a well-known Irish family.

A man opened the door, bowed down. "Good evening Mister Reily," he said. "Do come in."

I entered and took my hat off. He held a hand out for me to respond by giving it him, which I did with extreme nervousness, amazed by the beauty of the interior. A crystal chandelier lit the large hallway. On the left side, a half-opened door revealed an immense library room with shelves up to the ceiling filled with so many books, a rolling ladder was installed allowing the reader to reach them. In the middle, a stairway led to the upper floors. Paintings of various sizes covered the wall, portraits presumably of members of his family, landscapes, horses and dogs. In front of me, hanging high up against the wall, were the family coat of arms surrounded with swords, pikes and pistols. A large corridor leading to the back of the house showed two double openings on its right.

"Do follow me," the man said as he showed me the way to the drawing room. Fitzgerald was seated near the fireplace, reading the papers. He rose as I came in.

"Mister Reily, I'm so happy to have you here."

"Good evening, sir" I said as I offered my hand to shake. I looked around and was even more amazed by the beauty of the room. In the midst, a heavy table, on which were placed two vases of summer's last roses.

In a corner were a harp and a piano. In between, a small table held a pile of musical scores leading me to believe the family enjoyed music. Red wine coloured draperies framed four tall windows overlooking the driveway. However, what struck my attention was a very large rug hanging on one of the walls and representing a unicorn kicking its front legs high in the sky. I was speechless. Fitzgerald laughed. I was about to ask him if his was laughing at me or amused by my wonderment when he opened.

"My dear fellow, you have the same expression I had when my wife's people installed that rug on the wall. I asked her why she was putting a rug on a wall instead of on the floor. 'Why you silly man', she said, 'this is a tapestry not a rug. Don't you know the difference?' That was more than twenty years ago, and to-day I still call it a rug, which exasperates her."

His remarks revealed a simple man in spite of his apparent wealth.

"Winston, bring us some sherry unless our guest prefers some Scotch. I've just received an excellent Glenlivet and have not tasted it yet. We should try it."

"I must admit having never tasted either one, so I shall follow you."

"Make those two glens, Winston. He's a fine man, you know. He has been with the family since I was young, very young. He showed me how to fish and the art of casting. His wife also worked for us. She died two years ago after a long illness. It broke his heart. You have already met Timothy, my driver." Winston came back holding a tray with a bottle and two glasses, which he served us. "

"Did you know Americans serve scotch over ice cubes? It destroys the flavour. A real abomination, if you want my opinion."

"Sir," Winston said, "Madame Padoue told me to inform you that dinner shall be ready whenever you wish." "Very well, Winston, that will be all. Our cook, Madame Padoue, is from Bordeaux in France. I asked her to surprise us and can't wait to see what she shall come out with. Enough with the household, let us sit and enjoy this elixir."

I was pleased to discover a drink soft on the tongue but showing its strength when swallowed. "What an interesting feeling it leaves," said I as I sat on an armchair.

"You haven't told me what you do for a living."

"I work as a clerk and assistant at the London Hospital pathology department."

"Are you well paid?"

"I believe seven pounds a week to be quite acceptable."

"Married?"

"No. Bringing up a family in Whitechapel is the last thing a man would do if he considers himself sane.

Whatever the angle you examine it from, it's stays unhealthy if you are not built strong"

"What angers me the most about districts such as Whitechapel, Spitalfields and Hoxton, along with Stepney, Bethnal Green and Limehouse, is the fact that so many people are living on the poor. It would not surprise me to learn that dwellings in the East End can bring more money to their owners than the rent of the same space would elsewhere."

"Are you serious?"

"Think of it for a moment. A bed in Whitechapel or Spitalfields room can easily be rented three times a day for 4d each. Consider three to four beds in a 10 by 8 feet room with an original rent of 2s per week. I'll let you do the calculations."

"Don't expect to see things change. It has always been this way."

"It simply means that those who administer London profit by the overcrowding of East End and the housing contracts they might be linked to. If one cannot pay the price of his rent, another will come by instants later with the money and take his place. Why would an owner want any other way of earning his living? It demands no effort; the investment is without risks and immigrants as well as people coming in from the country keep on adding to the existing supply."

"Father, you have done it again?"

A female voice came from the corridor followed by loud footsteps of a person in a hurry.

"Is it true you were in Whitechapel last night and invited a complete stranger for dinner?"

A young elegant woman wearing a blue satin dress with delicate embroideries appeared at the door of the drawing room. Seeing me, she immediately came to a halt. "Who is this man?" she asked.

"I suggest a change in your tone, darling. He is the guest of this house and deserves to be addressed as such."

"You know what mother thinks of your... how should I say it?... your adventures in the East End."

"Whatever your mother thinks of my life is strictly business between her and me. What matters more is what you think, Elizabeth."

"You should be careful," she expressed with loving tenderness. "You know how much it would destroy me if something happened to you."

"Now that's a little better. Come and meet Mister Woodrow Reily, a charming young man, if I may say. He works at the pathology lab of the London Hospital.

Mister Reily, this is my older daughter Elizabeth."

"Glad to meet you Miss Fitzgerald."

"Forgive my rudeness, Mister Reily. You must understand my concern. Father often invites vagrants at our home for a meal. One of them has even stolen the fork and knife he used directly under father's nose."

Under different circumstances, I would have been insulted by her attitude and immediately respond but the peach colour of her skin, her unbelievable green eyes and the fairness of her Auburn hair calmed me. Loose waves arranged around her head with two long curls coming down over each shoulder framed her face and neck as if they composed an artist's painting.

"I promise to ask you personally the permission before stealing anything. I shall even start immediately by asking the permission to steal a smile from you."

She couldn't resist and offered me one.

"Well said, Mister Reily." Fitzgerald tapped my shoulder then kissed her daughter on her left cheek.

"Look at what you have done now. You made an allied of my father, and both of you are against me. Maybe I should still be angry."

However, she was not.

"Let's move along to the dinning room," Fitzgerald paused, "or else Madame Padoue will serve our meal to the dogs and give us the spoon."

I offered my arm to his daughter, but she preferred her father's.

As I walked in, I was hard for me to imagine a dinning room showing such richness. The table, covered with silverware, could hold twelve people well apart from each other. Each seated person would have in front of him three glasses undoubtedly made of crystal, a serviette rolled into a sterling ring, more forks, knives and spoons one could need to eat. Four silver chandeliers completed the one hanging from the ceiling. Fitzgerald was lucky his robber only took a fork and a knife. Fitzgerald sat at one end of the table, his daughter on his right, I, facing her.

I had never tasted food so good. First, came a soup Madame Padoue said to be a slightly peered cream of cauliflower. Then, followed veal scallops in a creamy sauce, in which she revealed she had added Madeira wine. Brussels sprouts and potatoes accompanied the meat.

Fitzgerald watched me eat, discreetly pointing at the appropriate utensil I should use. His Daughter, at one moment, noticed his maneuver and bent her head to cover her smile.

"What do you say of this Bordeaux wine, Mister Reily?" asked Fitzgerald.

"I know very little about wine. All I can say is that no wine I ever drank had the taste or the colour of this one."

"Each year brings a different wine even if it is from the exact same piece of land or what the French call a vineyard," added his daughter Elizabeth.

"I shall forever remember your teachings," said I with a bit of sarcasm.

"Since we are talking of the French," commented Fitzgerald, "I read in the papers that their government is currently working on measures to improve the conditions of the poor and the homeless. From what I learned, they will go well beyond what our own administration is prepared to do."

"If you permit me to say so, despite all the richness the British Empire claims to possess, the larger part of the social responsibility relies on the goodwill of private organizations."

"I would add to that certain individuals," said Elizabeth looking at her father. "They should concentrate on the neediest instead of spreading money without distinction. But then, finding them could also endanger their lives. Maybe you could be of some help. Don't you think so father?"

"I was just about to ask him the same thing. Let us first enjoy this "crème brûlée". We could talk this over after."

We finished desert with a different wine, a Sauterne if I remember correctly the kind Fitzgerald mentioned.

He invited me back to the drawing room for us to enjoy a cigar.

"A delightful meal, Madame," Fitzgerald said as she was returning to the kitchen. "Once again, your French inspiration has tickled our senses."

French cuisine served to Irishmen in the midst of London. I found it to be a rather amusing combination.

"I shall let you go on by yourselves, if you don't mind? I may share many of my father's opinions, but not his liking for the odour of a cigar after dinner. Mother withstands it even less," she added with a tease in her expression. "It was nice meeting you, Mister Reily."

She slowly walked up the stair holding her dress and disappeared. Fitzgerald noticed my disappointment in her leaving.

"She and I have a lot in common. Quite the opposite of her mother and my other daughter, Audrey, I must admit. I believe she sometimes tries to protect me from the grip they wish to impose upon me."

"No sons?" I inquired.

"Only one, William. He died accidentally four years ago whilst breaking one of the wild horses I bought in the United States." His deep breath was one of a man still sorrowed by his loss. "Even though he was an excellent horseman, the family, led by my dear wife, instead blamed it on me. He was about your age and height as a matter of fact. Enough said, we must examine how I could improve my way of helping out."

We spent the rest of the evening discussing not only about those in need, but particularly those who best deserved a helping hand. Cognac and Cuban cigars made us quickly come to agree that I would serve as an intermediary between them and Fitzgerald. He gave me some money to cover the cost of communicating with him by telegram. He mentioned his daughter's concern about desperate Irish families living in London and invited me to learn more of her intentions by asking her. I quickly suspected he had noticed my interest in her daughter, and that he was expressing some sort of approval in me seeing her again.

I couldn't avoid talking of my meeting with Francis Tumblety, what was asked of me by the Hospital and the offer he made me about becoming his assistant and attending a medical school. I could read a certain doubt on his face. "Did you ask yourself why he made you that offer? I'd be careful if I were you," were the only words he said to which I didn't pay much attention probably having drunk a bit to much.

Around one o'clock, Timothy drove me back to King Edward Street wondering if I would be able, the next morning, to accomplish everything that is expected from my work.

THURSDAY, AUGUST 30, 1888

For the past three days, I spent most of my available time walking in Whitechapel and Spitalfields trying to separate the wheat from the chaff as the Bible would put it. If only there had been some wheat in the heap, things would have been easy. I spoke with many people working at the district's parochial relief-officer whose position would help me pinpoint those seriously in need on the combined grounds of health, family and work problems. It demanded of me the difficult task of eliminating many, proving what Tumblety had told me to be true. I was making out a preliminary list when someone opened the door of the lab. Thinking of the devil, it was actually him.

"How is my young friend?" he asked with a large smile on his face.

"Doctor Tumblety? Well, I'm fine thank you and you?"

"I am in great shape."

"I was without news of you for almost three weeks

and truly believed you had gone back to America. Where have you been all this time, if I'm not too indiscreet?"

"I told you I would get back to you, although I agree I expected it would be much sooner. What can I say for my defense? There are so many exciting people in London. They almost made me lose my mind if not my time."

"Are you still in search of organs?"

"Of course, I am. There are many opportunities, particularly in the East End. But the right time and moment do not favour me as much as I would like. Tell me, are you still willing to help?"

"I gave my word both to you and Professor Fillmore and have gathered all that could be needed to preserve various organs."

"You remember when I told you how improvised most of the dissection premises were. What if the tools were to be inappropriate? It could compromise everything, don't you think?"

"Indeed, it could."

"Do you have any suggestions?" he asked as he walked by the wall cabinets containing organs.

"Let me see. I could lend you a bag with various dissection instruments, just in case they need them."

I was surprised to notice again how he seemed fascinated by them, in particular female organs. "As for the organs, do you have any idea, which one they would provide you with?"

"It all depends on the time of the death and the premises."

"Maybe I can make you a small sealed bag for you to carry them. It would keep the bodily fluids from messing up your clothes."

"I couldn't ask for a better treatment. I shall owe you."

"Tumblety followed me all around the dissection

room as I prepared what I taught would be needed, admiring all the instruments, particularly the dissection knives.

"You have a Liston," he said picking up one of them and looking at it closely. "It's an excellent tool. This one is rather old, but its blade is still sharp. It has LH stamped on the handle."

"It is from an old set," I answered without looking at him.

"Back then, the hospital could order those knives with or without initials for the same price."

I went on placing everything in a black leather brass-handled bag Fillmore once used as a practicing physician. He closed the drawer and came back to me showing the same state of excitement as the last time we met, probably even more, which left me quite perplexed. He left immediately after I had finished, only waving at me sending me these somewhat chilling words, "I'll return with organs, trust me."

FRIDAY, AUGUST 31, 1888

Around thirty minutes past six, I left my flat and headed for the Hospital. I had barely reached the corner of the street I live on and Old Montague Street when I came upon Tumblety. He looked extremely nervous, turning his head in all directions as if everyone was staring at him. Something in his usual appearance had changed; it was the tips of his mustache now curled up.

"Good morning, Doctor," said I. "Quick, quick Woodrow, take the bag."

"Did you obtain what you wished for?"

"Not enough time."

"Then why such a hurry?"

"It's too complicated to explain here."

"Why don't you come with me at the lab? It would be

much quieter, and Professor Fillmore will certainly be delighted to see you."

"I can't. I really must leave you."

Without even saying good-bye, he left almost running away from me. I did not know what to make of his behaviour, which I considered rather strange to say the least. Bag in hand, I headed for the Hospital's lab and noticed people coming in and out. There were more than the usual, but I paid no attention. Most likely, a street fight was attracting its normal crowd of onlookers not yet asked to move on by the Bobbies.

I was in the lab by seven. Since I was under the impression that Tumblety had not used the instruments, therefore, there was no need for me of provoking unnecessary questions or remarks coming from Fillmore. Hence, I nonchalantly put the instruments back to their place before his arrival, which occurred an hour later. He was seemingly ending a conversation in the corridor. "… extremely embarrassing for the hospital," I heard him say. Then he added, "I totally agree with you on the urgency of doing something about it."

"I cannot believe it," he said as he closed the door behind him. "Whilst we try to save peoples lives in our hospital, others are killing them right in front of us."

"What?"

"Haven't you heard what happened only hours ago on Buck's Row? A woman had her throat slit and her abdomen cut open. I just finished speaking with Dr. Llewellyn, the police surgeon who performed the preliminary examination. Didn't you hear us?"

"Maybe the last words, but nothing more."

"How can we expect to raise money for the hospital if we are now surrounded by murderers not to mention all the other criminals? I must talk to the director immediately and come up with a solution for our board of administrators. Reily, I expect you to handle all you can of my work during my absence."

"I shall do my best," I told Fillmore before seeing him leave.

He was more annoyed by the negative impact of the recent murders could have on fund raising than by the loss of a victim's life. Quite typical of the real bastard I always saw in him. As for me, I was struck by certain disturbing coincidences occurring with the death of this woman and the one on George Yard Street three weeks before. On both occasions, Tumblety and I met on the preceding evening. Each time, he had mentioned the possibility of obtaining organs although, I must admit, it never materialized. The next day, a woman would have been found murdered.

It was much too early in the morning for the papers to have come out with more information. I would have to wait. In the meantime, I tried as much as I could to concentrate on my work and not disappoint Fillmore but was more anxious of getting my hands on the papers. The day was endless, leaving me deeply troubled. I ran to buy the last edition of the Evening News and The Star almost tearing the pages open in order to get to the event. I looked for the keywords that constantly came to my mind all the day. They were all there printed before my eyes.

The Star's title resumed my fears.

A Policeman Discovers a Woman Lying in the Gutter with Her Throat Cut - After she has been removed to the Hospital she is found to be disemboweled.

...The throat is cut in two gashes, the instrument having been a sharp one, but used in a most ferocious and reckless way...

The ghastliness of this cut, however, pales into insignificance alongside the other. No murder was ever more ferociously and more brutally done. The knife, which must have been a large and sharp one, was jobbed into the deceased at the lower part of the abdomen, and then drawn upward, not once but twice. The first cut veered to the right, slitting up the groin, and passing over the left hip, but the second cut went straight upward, along the center of the body, and reaching to the breast-bone. Such horrible work could only be the deed of a maniac.

The other murder, in which the woman received 30 stabs, must also have been the work of a maniac. This murder occurred on Bank Holiday. On the Bank Holiday preceding another woman was murdered in equally brutal but even more barbarous fashion by being stabbed with a stick. She died without being able to tell anything of her murderer. All this leads to the conclusion, that the police have now formed, that there is a maniac haunting Whitechapel, and that the three woman were all victims of his murderous frenzy.

The article in The Evening News gave more details pertaining to the stabbings.

...besides the wound in the throat, the lower part of the abdomen was completely ripped open, with the bowels protruding. The wound extends nearly to her breast, and must have been effected with a large knife...

... the only articles found on the body were a broken comb and a piece of looking glass. This fact leads the police to think that the unfortunate woman belongs to the class known as "unfortunates" and that she spent her nights in common lodging-houses where such articles are necessary. The wounds, of which there are five, could only have been committed with a dagger or a long sharp knife...

I suspected that this unfortunate woman on the streets in the midst of the night would most likely be a prostitute, the exact kind of person Tumblety said being interested in. Although no mention of any removal of organs was made in either article, I still had doubts. Only the findings of the complete examination and the testimony brought at the inquest could help erasing them. If the Star was to be trusted, the proceedings would shed more light by Monday morning.

3 THE EVENTS OF SEPTEMBER 1888

SATURDAY, SEPTEMBER 1, 1888

The news of a murder so close to the hospital's location was spreading around. Here and there, small groups were sharing information obtained in the papers, keeping their voices low not to generate panic amongst the patients.

"Woodrow, Woodrow did you hear about yesterday's mur...," she paused, "...death on Buck's Row?" It was Miss Layton, a nurse I knew quite well, coming to me from behind. "Did you read this morning's papers?" she added as I turned.

"Yes Nancy, I learned of it yesterday."

"Do you know where it happened?"

"Right across at the Working Lads' Institute, this afternoon at one. Here, read it yourself," she said handing me a newspaper.

I went through the article searching for more than what was printed the day before.

"They're bringing in the big guns," I said. "Scotland Yard has designated someone to come over, and the Coroner for the South-East Middlesex district himself will be leading the hearings."

But Nancy wasn't listening to what I had just said.

"Are you still hiding yourself in the laboratory and the dissection room?" she asked. "We don't see much of you."

"And who 'we' might be?" I asked her. "Am I needed elsewhere?"

"Does everything only have to do with work?" "For me, it does."

"Then go back to your creepy basement and your 'master' Fillmore before you make me angry," she said grabbing the newspaper out of my hands. "I prefer the living to the dead, good bye."

She turned on her heels, her loud footsteps signaling me her disappointment. She obviously had more in her mind than the news of the day, which was quite the contrary for me.

As I entered the lab, Fillmore was already there waiting for me, arms crossed.

"Good morning Reily. Come quick. I need for you to do something normally not requested of you. Mister Holland and I met, and both of us expect comments from the inquest that can create an opportunity for the hospital. However, we don't know how it will come out, but it clearly appeared to us that someone from the hospital should listen to every word spoken during the hearings."

"Are you thinking of me?"

"Precisely. Our personal presence at the inquest shall certainly draw too much attention and therefore, could be misinterpreted. You, on the other hand, could easily mix in with the others. Your excellent memory would also be of great help to us."

"What about my work?"

"It's already been taken care of at the request of Mister Holland. Someone will replace you. The only thing we demand is for you to report to me at the end of each session."

"It shall last more than a day?"

"At least two if we consider the likelihood of having many witnesses appear. One last thing. I'm well aware of your inquisitive nature. However, this time, you do not ask questions nor speak to anyone and no notes. Is that clear?"

"Quite clear, Professor."

"Now finish your morning's work."

I went about with my usual occupations keeping to myself the excitement of being ordered to attend the inquest instead of chancing my presence, which otherwise, I would have done. I, nevertheless, sent a telegram to Fitzgerald informing him of the preliminary list I had drawn up the day before and asked if he wished to look it over.

The Coroner began the inquest by reminding everyone of its purpose. He indicated that, contrary to a trial, no witness is sworn in, only the jury. Their testimony strictly serves to better understand the circumstances of the death, the evidence, its causes and to formulate the appropriate recommendations and conclusions. He invited the members of the jury to ask for any precision they would deem necessary.

The victim was identified as Mary Ann Nichols by her father Edward Walker, the first witness to give a deposition. He had not seen her in three years. She was forty-two years of age and had been married twenty- two years to a William Nichols but they were living apart for the past seven or eight years. They had five children, the eldest being twenty-one years old and the youngest eight or nine years, none living with their mother. Walker admitted she drank at times, probably more since her husband took up with a young woman.

John Neil, police-constable came second. He

indicated that the deceased was lying lengthwise along the street, her left hand touching the gate. He examined the body with the aid of his lamp and noticed blood oozing from a wound in the throat. She was lying on her back, with her clothes disarranged. He felt her arm, which was quite warm from the joints upwards. Her eyes were wide open.

"Did you notice any blood where she was found?" asked the Coroner.

"There was a pool of blood just where her neck was lying. It was running from the wound in her neck." "Did you hear any noise that night?"

"No; I heard nothing. The farthest I had been that night was just through the Whitechapel road and up Baker's-row I was never far away from the spot."

"Whitechapel road is busy early in the morning, I believe. Could anybody have escaped that way?"

"Oh yes, sir. I saw a number of women in the main road going home. At that time, anyone could have got away."

Asked by a juryman if the body could just have been laid there, the woman having been killed elsewhere, the constable was quite clear.

"I examined the road," he answered, "but did not see the mark of wheels. The first to arrive on the scene after I had discovered the body were two men who work at a slaughterhouse opposite. They said they knew nothing of the affair and that they had not heard any screams."

The last witness on that day was Doctor Henry Llewellyn, a police-surgeon, who lived very close to the murder scene. By far, the testimony he was about to give was the most important for it could shed some light on the possible involvement of Tumblety.

"Under normal circumstances, said the Coroner, the jury would have been given a full written report following your post-mortem examination. We all agree this case is everything but normal including poor quality of the premises of the examination and did not allow for such a report."

Tumblety's words concerning the 'inadequate conditions physicians are forced to accept' came back to my mind. I could at least give him credit once again for the accuracy of his predictions.

"I am also aware," he continued, "of the extreme severity of the wounds inflicted to the victim and the discomfort the public will experience with their description. I shall, however, ask you to give a complete deposition as to their nature and their relation with the cause of death."

"Very well. On Friday morning," started Llewellyn, "I was called to Buck's Row about four o'clock. The constable told me what I was wanted for. On reaching Buck's Row I found the deceased woman lying flat on her back in the pathway, her legs extended. I found she was dead and that she had severe injuries to her throat. Her hands and wrists were cold, but the body and lower extremities were warm. I examined her chest and felt the heart. It was dark at the time. I believe she had not been dead more than half-an-hour. I am quite certain that the injuries to her neck were not self-inflicted. There was very little blood round the neck. There were no marks of any struggle or of blood, as if the body had been dragged. I told the police to take her to the mortuary where I would make another examination."

He paused a moment, looked at the jury then pursued with his testimony.

"About an hour later I was sent for by the Inspector to see the injuries he had discovered on the body. I went and saw that the abdomen was cut very extensively. I have this morning made a post-mortem examination of the body. I found it to be that of a female about forty or forty-five years. Five of the teeth are missing, and there is a slight laceration of the tongue. On the right side of the face, there is a bruise running along the lower part of the jaw. It might have been caused by a blow with the fist or pressure by the thumb. On the left side of the face, there was a circular bruise, which also might have been done by the pressure of the fingers. On the left side of the neck, about an inch below the jaw, there was an incision about four inches long and running from a point immediately below the ear. An inch below on the same side, and commencing about an inch in front of it, was a circular incision terminating at a point about three inches below the right jaw. This incision completely severs all the tissues down to the vertebrae. The large vessels of the neck on both sides were severed. The incision is about eight inches long. These cuts must have been caused with a long-bladed knife, moderately sharp, and used with great violence. No blood at all was found on the breast either of the body or clothes."

Again, he stopped, pulled out a handkerchief, wiped the drops of sweat from his forehead and went on.

"There were no injuries about the body till just about the lower part of the abdomen. Two or three inches from the left side was a wound running in a jagged manner. It was a very deep wound, and the tissues were cut through. There were several incisions running across the abdomen. On the right side there were also three or four similar cuts running downwards. All these had been caused by a knife, which had been used violently and been used downwards. The wounds were from left to right and might have been done by a left-handed person. All the injuries had been done by the same instrument."

No mention was made as to the removal of organs. At this point, Tumblety remained innocent of any wrongdoing whatsoever.

Feeling that the courtroom couldn't bear the weight of any additional testimony after such horrors were revealed, the Coroner decided to adjourn the inquiry till Monday morning.

On my way back to the hospital, it occurred to me that many aspects of Mary Ann Nichols death remembered me of how Martha Tabram also an ill-fated woman from the East End had been violently knifed.

Both could have been victims of the same brute.

Once at Fillmore's office, I reported to him as requested. He was delighted by the comments made by the Coroner regarding the mortuary.

"You are absolutely sure of what the Coroner said?" he asked.

"Positively, Professor."

"Repeat what he said, word-for-word. Then I want you to write them down for me to bring to Holland as soon as possible."

"How can these remarks provide an opportunity to the hospital?" I asked.

"Don't you see? We are already a stronghold in matters related to forensics. Not only would it would cost less for the government to expand our facilities than starting from scratch elsewhere but our actual expertise would reassure everyone."

He had a point in favour of the hospital, although he would certainly arrange for him to benefit first from any investment. Minutes later, we parted; he, to meet with

Holland, and I, to see if everything was under control at the laboratory. A reply-paid telegram had been left on my desk for me to easily see it. It was Fitzgerald answering mine.

Absent til Monday. Would appreciate examining your list whilst dinning at eight, Monday. My coach shall pick you up at your convenience.

Gordon Fitzgerald

I responded by informing him of my availability and gave indications as to where his driver would find me.

MONDAY, SEPTEMBER 3, 1888

Monday's hearing brought no answers to my questions. I would have to wait until the resuming of the inquest on September 17 before learning more. On the whole, the proceedings were hard to follow for everyone, none of the testimonies being introduced chronologically. Most witnesses confirmed what had been said previously by others. Police patrolling the area heard no one cry for help whilst two horse-slaughterers said they would have heard any noise a vehicle would have made had one passed on the street. However, I was surprised to learn that Dr. Henry Llewellyn, the police-surgeon, when at the scene of the crime, omitted to see that the victim's abdomen was cut very extensively and even more by an inspector's statement indicating the surgeon's examination of the body at the mortuary on Old Montague Street had lasted about ten minutes only. Autopsies carried at the Pathology Department usually take an hour, which made me doubt whether it was caused by Llewellyn's lack of professionalism or the premises. When I reported back to Fillmore, he favoured the latter and asked me to write a note, to that effect, for him to sign. As far as I was concerned, he was no more no less covering up for his colleague.

When I was afterwards alone in the laboratory, certain of Dr. Llewellyn's words suddenly came back to me and struck my mind. He had mentioned the cuts being caused with a long-bladed knife. Even the papers had reported it. How could I have been so dumb in overlooking that detail twice mentioned? I had provided Tumblety with an instrument capable of inflicting the same wounds. Luckily, I also remembered I hadn't cleaned the instruments he had returned to me, taking for granted they had not been used. Had he used them, given the number of hours between the victim's death and the moment he met me, he would not have had the time to clean them thoroughly as much as I do. If so, maybe they still had blood stains. I opened the drawers where I had placed them and examined all of them very closely, one by one. Surely enough one had a small trace of blood on the handle. It was the seven-inch-bladed amputation knife. An extremely sharp tool similar to the ones he had most certainly learned to use as a physician during the Civil War. It was almost as if my heart had stopped. He had lied to me, but I could not prove it no more. Three days had already past, and he could now argue that it could have been anyone's blood.

The odds seemed turning against him. He was in the area shortly after the murder. He had the necessary tool.

What about the motive behind this crime? Police were clueless, robbery and jealousy having been eliminated at the inquest. Years ago body-snatching from graveyards for the purpose of providing body parts to hospitals could turn a quick profit. Some were even willing to kill to obtain specifically diseased organs requested by hospitals and medical schools. Such was not the case for Tumblety who did not appear to be in need of money. I was told he had made a fortune in Canada and in the United States. Furthermore, no organs were removed from Polly Nichols. It couldn't cross my mind that he would kill people just for the purpose of removing organs needed for his research. Death constantly surrounding us could provide all he wanted with our assistance, and he spoke only of persons already doomed, which was clearly not the case of the two murdered women. If he was the killer, what could then be his motive?

As Timothy drove me to Fitzgerald's home, the

events of the past weeks tumbled against each other in my mind over and over and began imposing their toll upon me. Fatigue, nervousness and anxiety were unmistakably building up, leaving me completely baffled and with no other option than passively watching them occur. Confronting Tumblety without any proof of his involvement could compromise the promise he had made to help in my admission in a medical school. Fillmore, completely absorbed by his fund-raising scheme would wash his hands of it claiming he had given me full and entire responsibility of all matters pertaining to Tumblety. I couldn't question the police-surgeons any further or try to obtain details from the investigators either without arousing suspicion as to my own involvement in the deaths.

Although the evening dinner would have normally let me anticipate some sort of comfort, I was without a smile when I arrived. It was Fitzgerald himself who opened me the door.

"Good evening, sir."

"Come in, Woodrow," said Fitzgerald.

I slowly entered, almost dragging my feet.

"Good God! Have you seen yourself? You really seem troubled. Is everything all right? Winston, quick, take care of his hat and overcoat."

"Oh! Yes," I said trying to pull myself together.

"You need a drink, believe me. Winston, bring Mister Reily a cognac and for me, a scotch. Come now, let's go sit and examine the situation more closely. The cigar room shall do fine."

We entered the room, which did not offer anything that could have rejoiced me. Shades hid all the windows blocking any daylight. Wooden cases containing hundreds of artefacts covered the walls. The dark colour of the furniture, obviously mahogany, added to the heavy atmosphere of the master's den. I walked towards the center of the room and melted down on an armchair, its soft leather almost wrapping me in it.

Winston had already returned with the drinks.

"There is nothing better than a cognac to bring someone's spirits back. Now young man, drink it up, all of it."

I obeyed and immediately swallowed it in a single gulp sending shivers down my spine.

"A slap in the face would have had the same result," he added with a grin. "But I see you as a man rather able to handle the kick of liquor. Now tell me what is going on."

"I have this strange feeling of being once again trapped in a endless tunnel," said I, mindlessly facing forward. I took a deep breath before adding, "And the only way out would be for me to turn back, which would be even worst."

I turned towards Fitzgerald still standing up and trying to figure out what I was saying. I decided to approach the matter differently. "Have you ever had the impression you were reliving something you swore you had buried deep inside of you in your past?"

"Déjà vu."

"What?"

"It's a French expression meaning some familiar aspects of your past suddenly happening again. It could either be a person, a place, a door, actually almost anything could trigger that feeling."

"Exactly."

"When you say trapped, I tend to believe you are experiencing a rather unpleasant sensation. Am I wrong?"

"Again, you guessed right. Someone is using my position at the hospital to achieve his own questionable intentions. This person has managed to leave bread crumbs on a trail leading certain people, namely the

Yard, to believe I am responsible for these recent events."

"Obviously, that person would be Tumblety and the events, the Whitechapel murders," said Fitzgerald as he sat on the armchair facing me.

"Damn that man!"

"You might want to loosen up your teeth and unclench your hand from that glass, or you will break it."

"You have no idea how angry this makes me..."

"And if you do nothing about it, whatever options you may have will suddenly disappear hence leaving you even more trapped in this tunnel you have probably dug yourself into."

"I dug this tunnel? Are you joking?"

"Not at all. At the risk of upsetting you even more, you may have unwillingly put yourself in a delicate position and make Tumblety responsible for your own doing."

"But he manipulated me."

"No. You accepted being manipulated by paying more attention to his propositions than what was really at stake. That, my friend, is the price for expecting too much from someone you don't know."

"Damn me for being so foolish."

"Almost everyone went through a similar experience; so you shouldn't feel bad about yourself. But I agree. Damn you, if you accept being fooled again."

Fitzgerald stood up, walked towards one of the windows, spread open the curtains and looking back at me went on. "If I understand correctly, in your past you probably have experienced similar circumstances of persons deceiving you in whatever expectations you had. These persons being bad, hence the current one, Tumblety, is also bad. You turned these people into adversaries and are now trying to get even with them.

Tumblety has become a substitute, although you have nothing against him to prove your right. The murders seem to have given you a convenient way of resolving this issue."

"This all seems so easy for you," said I, taping my fingers against the armchair and wondering how he came to such a conclusion.

"You gave me the dots. All I had to do was connect them together and show you the resulting outline. Having met Tumblety only weeks ago, it seems impossible that he could be the sole responsible for such an intense reaction on your behalf. So it has to something that happened quite a while ago, most probably during your childhood."

"Did you mean to say that Tumblety is not the murderer but only a pretext?"

"I didn't say that. You could be absolutely right or totally wrong. What I should have stressed out is that you should preserve the same determination with Tumblety as you have with those persons of your past but not for the same reasons. Not to get even with someone who has nothing to do with your past but to find out if he is the actual perpetrator of those crimes."

He returned to his seat, laid back with a smile of satisfaction having demonstrated what seemed obvious to him. "Oh! One last thing. The faster you acknowledge this, the easier it shall be for you to go on with your life."

"It was my father," I whispered.

"What, I didn't hear you."

"I said that person of my past was my father. I was too young to fight him then and preferred to leave what you would call a home. He is probably dead now... out of drunkenness."

"Ghosts are hard to defeat, don't you think?"

"Maybe."

"Should he still be alive, and you met him, what would happen?"

"I'd make him pay for everything he has done to us." I paused for a moment, took a sip of cognac, wondering if I could speak out the words I had in my mind, and looking at Fiztgerald, added, "I'd kill him."

"Tumblety has taken your father's place in some respect, triggering an occasion for you to get even with him. He probably hasn't been the first one towards whom you expressed such anger, and each time you are doing that, my friend, you are digging yourself deeper in this tunnel of yours. It's up to you to decide to dig yourself out of it. Then again, you could sit and wait for the tunnel to collapse feeling sorry for yourself and expecting all of us to pity you."

"That's easy for you to say." I kept my head down and dared not to look at him anticipating very well the expression his face would carry. "You have all the means to make all the changes you desire and become whoever it pleases you or do whatever you want at any given moment."

"Is that how you see me?"

"Yes and that is what your damned status has given you." My last remarks left him silent for a moment that seemed endless. I had no doubt gone too far.

He stood up and picked up from a small but beautiful table set against the wall the bottle of cognac Winston had earlier left there. "That, my dear friend, is a poor excuse for doing nothing."

Coming close to me, he poured cognac in my glass as well as in his, emptying it in a single gulp.

"We too often take for granted that the status we inherit at our birth or what made us who we are cannot be changed. One always has a choice regardless of the situation he may find himself in. Many people are not really aware of their existence, even less their condition, for they have known nothing else by reason of their isolation. Hence, their past justifies their poor condition. However, some, nevertheless, manage to find a way, even minimal, to maneuver. Others will break their mold only to cast themselves in another one as tightly fitted as the previous one. But then, it reflects who they aspired to become. I have decided long ago not to be moulded and to destroy each one that would slowly cover me. That has been my choice beyond and above every mean this earth ever granted me. One can always choose to see, judge and appreciate himself in a different manner and, again, choose subsequently how to act upon it."

He filled his glass one more time and sat on the armchair facing me. He contemplated his glass obviously satisfied with what he had just said. Nevertheless, he went on. "Now what is your reason for not doing the same? And don't try to tell me that deciding not to choose is also a choice. Only politicians with no backbone use that kind of rhetoric once elected."

If cognac hadn't begun stirring me up, his harsh words did.

"I probably deserved that," said I.

"Had we been fencing, you would have touched me in the heart area and won."

"Only your pride has been touched. If it was your weakness, from this day forwards, it can become your strength as well. It all depends on you, in which case I haven't won at all, at least not yet. Do you understand what I am saying, my young friend?"

"I do indeed. I still have options."

"There shall always be options."

"That's what I meant."

"Good. Then let's go over your list of Irish families whilst eating. Madame Padoue has another culinary surprise for both of us."

"Your daughter Elizabeth will not join us?"

"Not to-night. She is spending some time at our country home with her mother."

"Oh!"

"You seem disappointed. You shouldn't. If you thought I was a little rough on you, consider yourself lucky not having dealt with her. She has a special way of handling people she considers worthy of her time."

"Am I one of those people?"

"You shall have to ask her yourself," he answered with an intriguing smile."

"I probably will."

Had I not written down the menu Madame Padoue prepared for us, I would be unable to describe it. It consisted of Crème de Crécy, Quails in raisins served with a Riesling and a Soufflé for dessert. Porto and an assortment of cheese, French of course, completed the feast.

My list was more than preliminary from Fitzgerald's perspective. It was important for him to 'invest', were his exact words 'in their gaining a level of autonomy that would fulfil the lives of those selected'. He strongly believed handing them money would only bring a short term improvement and result in them returning to their initial state. He had a precise plan in mind but preferred us working out its foundation before revealing it to me. He only told me I was to supervise its implementation by those actually concerned.

I returned home much more confident as to the way I could cope with upcoming events no matter the direction they would take for I knew I could now influence their outcome. It fascinated me how such a person succeeds in turning you inside out in a matter of minutes only to offer you a full and non judgmental view of who you actually are.

WEDNESDAY, SEPTEMBER 5, 1888

In the midst of the afternoon, one of the hospital's runners came to the Lab informing me that a gentleman wanted to see me in the front lobby.

"Did he give you his name?" I asked although I had an idea who that person might have been.

"No, but says ye know 'im, 'e's been 'ere before. The tall man with the mustache."

"Tumblety! Tell him I absolutely need to meet me here instead. Go and make it fast."

I had a surprise in mind for him and needed for him to be on my own ground. A few minutes later, he was entering the lab.

"Good afternoon Woodrow. How are you to-day?"

"Very good and you?"

"I'm in a splendid shape. I see you are quite busy, so I won't disturb you very long. I came to ask if I could borrow the same instruments you had gathered for me the other day."

"Have you found someone with organs for you?"

"There are always people about to die. The question for me is finding a person corresponding to the object of my research, and I have one at this moment.

Unfortunately, she is going to die in a few hours, so I don't have much time to discuss her medical situation, even if I would like to."

"I see. Have you heard of the recent murders in Whitechapel?"

"Who hasn't? It's in every paper. Why are you bringing this up just when I have so little time to spare?"

"The hospital is very worried particularly since the last murder happened almost across the street. Police may come at their convenience and verify our records and instrument's inventory. You know how they can become inquisitive under pressure. If some are missing, they shall certainly require an explanation. If it depended only on me, I wouldn't hesitate in letting you leave with the bag, but my superiors could differ."

"I really don't know how I can reassure you." I could read his embarrassment in his face. I was of course inventing every word I was saying, but he did not know it or even suspected it.

"There is only one way to get round this."

"I'm all ears."

"The hospital trusts me. If I were to accompany you with the instruments, there would be no questions at all on their behalf. That would prevent the police from wasting their time."

He looked totally surprised by my proposition, which I was convinced he would refuse preventing him from having the potential murder tools hence avoiding the death of another woman.

"Then let's do it. Get the bag ready. I'll fill you in with the details as we reach the woman's home. I'm warning you. It could be dangerous for your own health."

"What?"

"I said 'let's do it'. Quick now."

I had perfectly heard what he had said the first time. I was completely flabbergasted for it never came to my mind he would accept my proposal. I was now the one caught off guard. My foolishness forces me to become his accomplice, I thought, as I silently prepared the bag.

On the street, I kept racking my brains only minutes away of becoming a murderer. I had to come out with a solution.

"We must take a cab, or else we shall be too late," signaling a driver with his hand raised high up. "The woman lives on Flower and Dean Street. We won't make it in time if we go by foot."

He jumped into the hansom almost pulling me with

him.

"The White House on 56 Flower and Dean and make it fast," he yelled at the driver. "She's at a lodging-house with her husband and the physician I called for. The poor man is going to pieces. She has a terminal case of tuberculosis and will die in the coming hours. I've paid for everything, including the funeral arrangements."

"She's not alone on the street?"

"Why should she? I found this place for her where her husband can spend her last days at her side. A priest should be there by now. We gave her absinthe and laudanum to case the suffering."

"You went through all these means for her organs?"
"Correction, I paid for her lungs, heart and a couple of other organs. Why all these questions? I thought we had covered all this on our first meeting. After her death, she will be brought to the mortuary. The physician will proceed with the post-exam, attest to the cause of death for the death certificate, and then we will remove the organs the way your Anatomy Act requires. Maybe we will need what's in the bag, maybe not. We will soon find out. The poor husband will have enough money to buy his way to the States or Canada and start a new life. I even gave him names of people I know in Montreal."

Was I hearing what he just said or was I imagining it still under the shock of my presence with him? This man was showing a tremendous respect and compassion towards a woman and his husband, and I had already judged him to be a murderer. How can I have been so wrong? I was speechless.

"Since you are with me, maybe you can show me how your famous physician dissected with his eyes closed."

He had no idea what was going through my mind and hardly heard what he had said. "I'm so sorry, I said shaking my head to clear my distracted mind. I must be exhausted and did not hear all of what you said."

"I was talking about the surgeon you knew who sometimes dissected blindfolded. You could show me how it's done."

"I'll see if I can repeat what he did," I said trying to smile.

When we arrived at the lodging-house, the woman had already died in the presence of the priest. Her body had been moved to the mortuary where the physician was waiting for Tumblety to arrive. We proceeded with the post-mortem, including the demonstration of what I presented as a 'blind man's dissection technique'. I had a preliminary look at the body, its size, proportions. Once blindfolded, I counted 'One, two, three' whilst measuring the distance from the navel with my fingers to a specific point where I announced, "The left kidney is underneath my index." I asked Tumblety to cut some two inches through the skin and fat and carefully move around the bowels for him to reach for the kidney.

"Fascinated, I'm fascinated. It is exactly where you told me," he said whilst I removed the cloth from my eyes.

The sequence of events went as he had said it would and brought sufficient facts to end my suspicions against him. I had been wrong all the time and swore to myself that in the future I would not come to such hasty conclusions making me look like a fool.

"You see, my dear friend, how simple it is to add some decency in one's death and make things easier for those surviving," he said as we were walking back on Whitechapel Road. "No one has to hide away as if getting the organs I need was wrong. Hadn't it been for the unfortunate death, I would have invited you to accompany me at this fine little place I found on Cleveland Street. There are many young boys of your age who would be excited to meet you. I often go there to enjoy the presence of younger men. Maybe another day we could go together, but now I bid you good night and hope you learned from this experience as much as I from your demonstration."

"You cannot imagine how much I have. Have a very good night, Doctor Tumblety."

I still had to work to do at the laboratory with the organs he entrusted me with. Cleaning them, placing them in the appropriate jars, writing labels took me at least an hour. Fortunately, the organs having not been removed from our dissecting room, there was no need to fill in a report for Fillmore. However, although I rinsed the instruments at the mortuary, I made sure all traces of blood from the instruments had disappeared.

FRIDAY, SEPTEMBER 7, 1888

To-day's Daily News mentioned that Mary Ann Nichols was interred at the City of London Cemetery.

Around nine in the evening, I was about to return to the laboratory when someone knocked on the door and immediately entered without leaving me the time to answer. It was Tumblety, quite excited. Two well-dressed young men entered behind him.

"Doctor Tumblety, how nice it is to see you again."
"Good evening Woodrow. Leaving already?"

"Only minutes to go before my day is ended. The organs are ready for you to pick up."

"Good. I have a carriage waiting for me. These men will take care of everything if you don't mind?"

Men! I thought. They appeared quite young to me maybe even in their late teens and gave off an odour, which had more to do with the fragrances used by women than the sweat of virile dockers.

"Not at all," I answered. "Is there anything else I can do for you?"

"As a matter of fact, there is. Hey, be careful with those jars," he yelled at one of his young helpers who almost dropped a large one. "My friend here and I went through a lot of trouble to get what's in there. And don't forget to separate them carefully with a lot of straw," he hollered at them. "I don't want them to break while we're on the road like the last time. Sorry Woodrow, you were saying? Oh yes, I remember I also came for the instruments. Are they still available?"

"Why of course. Let me prepare the bag." As I gathered what he wanted, it took me only seconds to realize he could ask me if I were to accompany him again for the benefit of the hospital's reputation and quickly improvised, "I have excellent news for you."

"You do."

"It will be unnecessary for me or anyone else from the hospital to accompany you this time. Who would dare to challenge the deeds of a good man such as you?"

"I must admit I expected something more or less along that line."

"What makes you say that?"

"I don't believe your administrators would appreciate putting a hospital such as the London on a soft ground if proof has already been given to them as to what I actually do."

"I should be back quite early to-morrow morning."

"Is seven o'clock too late for me to be here?"

"Make it six, just in case, if it's no problem for you."

"Six it shall be."

SATURDAY, SEPTEMBER 8, 1888

It had rained for the past two days, but to-day the sun showed its strength one more time before the coming fall season would decide whether it would let it warm us or not. To make the most out of it, I would certainly go one more time to Kew's gardens. I got up early knowing I had to be at the hospital in case Tumblety would have organs to preserve. It was also clear to me how everyone would fight for a seat on outgoing tramways and omnibuses on a bright Sunday. I gulped down a boiled egg and a cup of tea and quickly left my home. It would take me only minutes get to the hospital, an hour to process the organs and estimated being able to catch a tram by a quarter past seven.

A Swiss watchmaker couldn't have wished a better timing between both Tumblety's arrival and mine, six o'clock on the dot.

"Doctor, how did things go," I asked. "Good and bad all together."

"No organs?"

"I have but one organ, a uterus, when there was a possibility for much more. Can you imagine removing organs in the dark? I hoped for the bladder and the vagina, but my unfamiliarity with the blindfolded dissecting technique did not suffice. What a mess."

"Really," I said scratching my head as I tried to picture the conditions he encountered working on a dead body in the dark. "And the family, how did they take it?"

"They were absent. I'm still mad about the whole affair."

"Don't be so hard on yourself. There shall be several other occasions for you to accomplish your mission.

Give me what you have, and I shall take care of everything. What you need now is to rest. You look completely exhausted."

"I shall follow your advice, my good Woodrow. I wonder what I would do without a young man such as you and cherish your friendship, you know." It was with these kind words that he left me.

I was rather glad he only had one organ requiring very little time to preserve for many were already waiting for the tram at the news-stand lurking behind the morning edition of the dailies. I glanced at the front-page headlines, which hardly offered a reason for me to spend a penny. Lloyd's weekly had its usual crowd of readers huddling together over the most horrendous event it dared put to print and this week's edition had certainly brewed something for me. The title and first lines hit me like a rock thrown at the back of my head.

YESTERDAY'S WHITECHAPEL TRAGEDY.
LATEST PARTICULARS.
Down to an early hour this (Sunday) morning, the police had not succeeded in tracing the murderer of the woman Chapman, whose body was found shockingly mutilated under the circumstances reported in our seventh page.

I picked a copy of the paper and threw a penny at the vendor's waiting hand before embarking on the tramcar. One hour later, I was enjoying the refreshing views of what I considered as 'my own', Kew's garden. Many tree leaves were already changing their colours bringing out even more the flamboyance of the tall oaks. The understandably great number of visitors felt the coming of the saddest season of all. Women of the fortunate class had dressed up in matching shades almost as if they were mourning the ending summer. One could see them absorbing the last fragrances of the summer flowers and finding some comfort in the freshly opened Chrysanthemums. From the bench I was sitting on, I admired the carps and goldfish catching insects before the being slowed down into hibernation by the cold water of the pond by the garden's museum. It was still summer for all those surrounding me, but it had been the final season in another unfortunate woman's life that being the one mentioned in the paper I had bought.

Her name was Annie Chapman, and she had been murdered on Hanbury Street. It was said the wife of the Prince Albert public-house could identify the man who most likely had committed the crime him being seen, as the reporter wrote it, 'early yesterday morning with marks of blood upon him'. There were hopes that the enigma of the recent slaying of women would be solved clearing once for all the man I had wrongfully considered as their killer. I went for details on page 7 of Lloyd's Weekly expecting a good description of the suspect. This man, of 'rough appearance…had a brown stiff hat, a dark coat and no waistcoat. He came in with his hat down over his eyes, and with his face partly concealed, asked for half a pint of four' ale'. What struck the witness, a Mrs. Fiddymont, 'was the fact that there were blood spots on the back of his right hand. This, taken in connection with his appearance, caused her uneasiness. She also noticed that his shirt was torn'. I almost burst out laughing, the testimony quite obviously being unbelievable. The man to my right, peeking at the article I was reading, noticed my reaction.

"Not that it could be any of my business, but do you think such horror is amusing?" he asked.

"Not the crime, the testimony of one of the witnesses," I responded. "A man having just killed this poor woman would immediately after come for a drink in a pub with his hands full of blood. Unless he intentionally wanted to be arrested or worst lynched, such behaviour is utterly ridiculous."

"Oh, I hadn't read that information. I daresay you have a good point."

I went back reading. For me anyway, it had no importance, the paper indicating further down that he 'wore a ginger-coloured mustache and had short sandy hair', which did not fit Tumblety's description.

I was, however, horrified by the blunt description the

paper gave of the discovery of the victim.

'The victim was lying on her back with her legs outstretched close up to the flight of steps leading into the yard. The throat was cut open in a fearful manner - so deep, in fact, that the murderer, evidently thinking that he had severed the head from the body, tied a handkerchief round it so as to keep it on. It was also found that the body had been ripped open and disemboweled, the heart and abdominal viscera lying by the side. The fiendish work was completed by the murderer tying a portion of the entrails round the victim's neck '.

I folded the paper bringing it down on my knees and caught the deepest breath I could. The only thing that could be worst to me would be Fillmore forcing me to attend another inquest and hear the witnesses repeating each one in their own words what they had seen.

MONDAY, SEPTEMBER 10, 1888

I had barely started to work when Fillmore came in the lab. "The papers' only interest is this rubbish," he said throwing the stack of newspapers in his hands on my desk. "This is becoming intolerable. I assume you know what I am talking about and what I am about to ask you."

"I have a pretty good idea of what awaits me."

"Then get ready, the inquest starts in two hours.

However, before you leave, I want you to read all the articles and see if there is something in there for us. I also want a written report from you."

My personal reason for attending Polly Nichols' inquest had vanished with the proof of Tumblety's innocence clearly demonstrated by his humane behaviour. Now I had no choice but to comply with Fillmore's instructions even if his own motivations only served his personal ambition.

THURSDAY, SEPTEMBER 13, 1888

Although three hearing days were scheduled for the week, Fillmore had to wait until the third day of the inquiry before he could capitalize on complaints expressed by Mr. Wynne E. Baxter, the same coroner responsible for Polly Nichols' case. His remarks pertaining to the mortuary where the post-mortem was carried would undoubtedly feed his quest for power.

The Coroner's opinion couldn't be clearer. "The fact is that Whitechapel does not possess a mortuary," said he. "The place is not a mortuary at all. We have no right to take a body there. It is simply a shed belonging to the workhouse officials. Juries have over and over again reported the matter to the District Board of Works. The East End, which requires mortuaries more than anywhere else, is most deficient. Bodies drawn out of the river have to be put in boxes, and very often they are brought to this workhouse arrangement all the way from Wapping. A workhouse inmate is not the proper man to take care of a body in such an important matter as this."

As for the first two days, they confirmed the preliminary statements the press released during the weekend concerning the discovery of the body, the identification of the victim as well as her whereabouts. We would all learn that Annie Chapman was a widow and her husband, Frederick Chapman, a coachman from Windsor. They had three children, two of which, a boy and a girl, were still alive. They had been living apart for about four or five years. Since his death some eighteen months before, which coincided with the interruption of the weekly payment of 10s he would send her, she lived in various common lodging-houses in Spitalfields. She was known for drinking more than she could handle but otherwise presented herself as a very industrious woman. Timothy Donovan, the deputy of the common lodging house where she last stayed testified that, 'Generally on Saturdays, she was the worse for drink. She was very sociable in the kitchen. I said to her, "You can find money for your beer, and you can't find money for your bed." She said she had been only to the top of the street - where there is a public-house'.

She was last seen around a quarter to two in the morning of Saturday. As so many other unfortunate women, she had probably met her fate selling her body to make ends meet, covering by the same token the cost of her bed. Her body was found in the backyard of 29, Hanbury Street. No one had heard a sound of any dispute going on nor seen anyone walking away from the scene.

Mr. George Baxter Phillips, divisional-surgeon of police, who had attended Nichols' inquiry with Dr Llewellyn, gave a minute and astounding, if not brutal, description of what he had to submit himself to. At one point, he openly complained about the circumstances of the post-examination giving the Coroner the chance to add more to his previous comments, which were validated by the jury's foreman. Fillmore would be exhilarated. It would, however, give rise to a series of suspicions hovering over the medical profession and all those working nearby, including me. I even kept the article the Daily Telegraph had printed and considering the importance I give to the preservation of its accuracy, transcribed it with my own notes.

"On Saturday last," Phillips said, "I was called by the police at 6.20 am. to 29, Hanbury Street, and arrived at half-past six. I found the body of the deceased lying in the yard on her back, on the left hand of the steps that lead from the passage. The head was about 6 in front of the level of the bottom step, and the feet were towards a shed at the end of the yard. The left arm was across the left breast, and the legs were drawn up, the feet resting on the ground, and the knees turned outwards. The face was swollen and turned on the right side, and the tongue protruded between the front teeth, but not beyond the lips; it was much swollen. The small intestines and other portions were lying on the right side of the body on the ground above the right shoulder, but attached. There was a large quantity of blood, with a part of the stomach above the left shoulder. I searched the yard and found a small piece of coarse muslin, a small-tooth comb, and a pocket-comb, in a paper case, near the railing. They had apparently been arranged there. I also discovered various other articles, which I handed to the police. The body was cold, except that there was a certain remaining heat, under the intestines, in the body. Stiffness of the limbs was not marked, but it was commencing. The throat was dissevered deeply. I noticed that the incision of the skin was jagged, and reached right round the neck. On the back wall of the house, between the steps and the palings, on the left side, about 18 inches from the ground, there were about six patches of blood, varying in size from a sixpenny piece to a small point, and on the wooden fence, there were smears of blood, corresponding to where the head of the deceased laid, and immediately above the part where the blood had mainly flowed from the neck, which was well clotted. Having received instructions soon after two o'clock on Saturday afternoon, I went to the labour-yard of the Whitechapel Union for the purpose of further examining the body and making the usual post-mortem investigation. I was surprised to find that the body had been stripped and was laying ready on the table. It was under great disadvantage I made my examination. As on many occasions I have met with the same difficulty, I lowingnow raise my protest, as I have before, that members of my profession should be called upon to perform their duties under these inadequate circumstances."

"The mortuary is not fitted for a post-mortem examination," pointed out the Coroner. "It is only a shed. There is no adequate convenience, and nothing fit, and at certain seasons of the year, it is dangerous to the operator."

"I think we can all endorse the doctor's view of it," added their foreman.

"As a matter of fact" continued the Coroner, "there is no public mortuary from the City of London up to Bow. There is one at Mile-end, but it belongs to the workhouse, and is not used for general purposes. I must apologize for these interruptions, but you shall certainly agree there are limits to what is asked of our profession. If it pleases you, I would ask for you to resume."

"The body had been attended to since its removal to the mortuary, and probably partially washed," said the surgeon. "I noticed a bruise over the right temple. There was a bruise under the clavicle, and there were two distinct bruises, each the size of a man's thumb, on the fore part of the chest. The stiffness of the limbs was then well-marked. The finger nails were turgid. There was an old scar of long standing on the left of the frontal bone. On the left side, the stiffness was more noticeable, and especially in the fingers, which were partly closed. There was an abrasion over the bend of the first joint of the ring finger, and there were distinct markings of a ring or rings - probably the latter. There were small sores on the fingers. The head being opened showed that the membranes of the brain were opaque and the veins loaded with blood of a dark character. There was a large quantity of fluid between the membranes and the substance of the brain. The brain substance was unusually firm, and its cavities also contained a large amount of fluid. The throat had been severed. The incisions of the skin indicated that they had been made from the left side of the neck on a line with the angle of the jaw, carried entirely round and again in front of the neck, and ending at a point about midway between the jaw and the sternum or breast bone on the right hand. There were two distinct clean cuts on the body of the vertebrae on the left side of the spine. They were parallel to each other, and separated by about half an inch. The muscular structures between the side processes of bone of the vertebrae had an appearance as if an attempt had been made to separate the bones of the neck. There are various other mutilations of the body, but I am of opinion that they occurred subsequently to the death of the woman and to the large escape of blood from the neck." The witness, pausing, said, "I am entirely in your hands, sir, but is it necessary that I should describe the further mutilations? From what I have said I can state the cause of death."

"The object of the inquiry is not only to ascertain the cause of death, but the means by which it occurred. Any mutilation, which took place afterwards, may suggest the character of the man who did it. Possibly, you can give us the conclusions to which you have come respecting the instrument used."

"You don't wish for details," stated Doctor Philips. "I think if it is possible to escape the details it would be advisable. The cause of death is visible from injuries I have described."

"You have kept a record of them?"

"I have."

"Supposing anyone is charged with the offence, they would have to come out then, and it might be a matter of comment that the same evidence was not given at the inquest."

"I am entirely in your hands," he again said.

"We will postpone that for the present. Can you give your opinion as to how the death was caused?"

"From these appearances, I am of opinion that the breathing was interfered with previous to death, and that death arose from syncope, or failure of the heart's action, in consequence of the loss of blood caused by the severance of the throat."

"Was the instrument used at the throat the same as that used at the abdomen?"

"Very probably. It must have been a very sharp knife, probably with a thin, narrow blade, and at least six to eight inches in length, and perhaps longer."

"Is it possible that any instrument used by a military man, such as a bayonet, would have done it?"

"No; it would not be a bayonet."

"Would it have been such an instrument as a medical man uses for post-mortem examinations?"

"The ordinary post-mortem case perhaps does not contain such a weapon," said the physician obviously trying to protect the medical corps.

However, this case was anything but an ordinary one, not even close to a usual post-mortem examination.

Doctor Phillips' observation reminded me that the exact content of the leather bag I had lent Tumblety provided for every organ removal situation he could have encountered. Any physician having experienced the inadequacies of a local mortuary would have done the same and carried amongst other instruments, similar to the one he described, "a very sharp knife, probably with a thin, narrow blade, and at least six to eight inches in length."

"Would any instrument that slaughterers employ have caused the injuries?"

"Yes; well ground down."

"Would the knife of a cobbler or of any person in the leather trades have done?"

"I think the knife used in those trades would not be long enough in the blade."

"Was there any anatomical knowledge displayed?" "I think there was. There were indications of it. My own impression is that anatomical knowledge was only less displayed or indicated in consequence of haste. The person evidently was hindered from making a more complete dissection in consequence of the haste."

"Was the whole of the body there?"

"No; the absent portions being from the abdomen."

If my attention grew with the Coroner's question despite any reference to a specific organ, the answer almost threw me off my seat.

"Are those portions such as would require anatomical knowledge to extract?"

"I think the mode in which they were extracted did show some anatomical knowledge."

The Coroner as well as the witness once more referred to the medical domain as if it were unthinkable for a physician to turn his skills against a human being. The police would certainly widen their area of investigation and visit all the establishments related directly or not to that domain particularly in Whitechapel. I had to get prepared in order to avoid being caught between a rock and a hard place with the assistance I gave Tumblety.

"You were shown some staining on the wall of number 25 Hanbury Street?" continued the Coroner.

"Yes; that was yesterday morning."

"To the eye of a novice, I have no doubt it looks like blood."

"I have not been able to trace any signs of it. I have not been able to finish my investigation. I am almost convinced I shall not find any blood."

"We have not had any result of your examination of the internal organs. Was there any disease?"

"Yes. It was not important as regards the cause of death. Disease of the lungs was of long standing, and there was disease of the membranes of the brain. The stomach contained a little food."

"Was there any appearance of the deceased having taken much alcohol?"

Was Baxter opening a dangerous line of question trying to present the victim as a drunk prostitute leading the public to think she got what she deserved? I hope I was wrong, but paid more attention to what was said.

"No. There were probably signs of great privation. I am convinced she had not taken any strong alcohol for some hours before her death."

"Were any of these injuries self-inflicted?"

"The injuries, which were the immediate cause of death were not self-inflicted."

"Was the bruising you mentioned recent?"

"The marks on the face were recent, especially about the chin and sides of the jaw. The bruise upon the temple and the bruises in front of the chest were of longer standing, probably of days. I am of opinion that the person who cut the deceased's throat took hold of her by the chin, and then commenced the incision from left to right."

"Could that be done so instantaneously that a person could not cry out?"

"By pressure on the throat no doubt it would be possible."

"There would probably be suffocation."

"The thickening of the tongue would be one of the signs of suffocation?"

"Yes. My impression is that she was partially strangled. A handkerchief found amongst the clothing was saturated with blood. A similar article was round the throat of the deceased when I saw her early in the morning at Hanbury Street."

"It had not the appearance of having been tied on afterwards?"

"No. Sarah Simonds, a resident nurse at the Whitechapel Infirmary, stated that, in company of the senior nurse, she went to the mortuary on Saturday, and found the body of the deceased on the ambulance in the yard. It was afterwards taken into the shed, and placed on the table. She was directed by Inspector Chandler to undress it, and she placed the clothes in a corner. She left the handkerchief round the neck. She was sure of this. They washed stains of blood from the body. It seemed to have run down from the throat. She found the pocket tied round the waist. The strings were not torn. There were no tears or cuts in the clothes."

After Phillips testimony, the Coroner adjourned the inquiry until September 19. Later that evening, Fillmore was in his office seated at his desk reading the report I had just finished writing.

"Every doctor walking on the street carrying a bag or a case will now be followed by a police, an undercover investigator or an ignorant crowd ready to lynch him on the first sign of any questionable behaviour," he said swirling his eyeglasses around his finger. "Every medical instrument they shall have in their hands will be perceived as a potential weapon. Not only that, everyone who has ever held a knife and is working or studying here will be interrogated. I am more than outraged; I am furious."

It was better for me to stand still until he would calm down. He stood up with such suddenness that his chair tipped back almost falling back on it. He went on blowing off more steam.

"Even Baxter's comments on the shortcomings of the post examination in mortuaries, which would have helped us grandly in our fund-raising are superseded by the presumption of guilt for now on hanging over our heads. Damn fools, Baxter, Phillips, all of them. I should have sent someone with no memory at all instead of you, Reily. At least, it would have delayed me from getting the news a day or so. Damn you. Now leave, I have to find a way to arrange all this mess for the Board."

That was his way of thanking me for doing precisely what he had ordered me to do.

Walking down the stairway, my own questions came at once, for God knows I was in no way under better conditions than Fillmore. What should I do with the equipment inventory records? They indicate the use of every jar, the lending of each instrument. My name appeared under every item Tumblety needed, not his.

What explanation would I give for each of these entries? Should I add his name, bleach out the ink or keep everything as is, offering them to the police as a potential trail of evidence? No sooner had these last words came to my mind than I realized that somewhere, deep down inside me, I still had traces of doubts concerning Tumblety. I had to keep the records intact even better I could avoid being suspected and hide them temporarily since they resulted from a personal initiative. Nobody, I thought, knew about their existence.

That same day, I started bringing my inventory books to my place.

MONDAY, SEPTEMBER 17, 1888

The papers reported that the very private interment of Annie Chapman took place this past Friday at the City of London Cemetery. A marker contained these words: 'Within this Area lie the Mutilated Remains of Annie Chapman, who was interred here in Grave 78 on the 14th of September in the year 1888'. In a few years henceforth, I suspect no one will ever know she even existed.

WEDNESDAY, SEPTEMBER 19, 1888

To-day's' hearing almost led Coroner Wayne Baxter to express his anger against Dr. Phillips. To say the least, it started as a struggle of minds regarding the disclosure of details about the examination. Already on the hearing of the 13th, Phillips felt ill at ease with certain aspects of it being made public. The Coroner had postponed for that portion of his testimony but expected it to be delivered on this occasion. He probably suspected more objections would come from the surgeon hence the presence of his deputy, Mr. George Collier, as a visual reinforcement for Phillips to face up to.

"Whatever may be your opinion and objections," Baxter warned him, "it appears to me essential that all the evidence that you ascertained from the post-mortem examination should be on the records of the Court for various reasons, which I need not enumerate. However painful it may be, it is necessary in the interests of justice."

"I have not had any notice of that. I should have been glad if notice had been given me, because I should have been better prepared to give the evidence; however, I shall do my best."

It was as if he had never delivered a post-mortem examination report to a coroner. What the bloody hell was he trying to do?

"Would you like to postpone it?"

"Oh, no. I shall do my best. I still think that it is a very great pity to make this evidence public. Of course, I bow to your decision; but there are matters, which have come to light now, which show the wisdom of the course pursued on the last occasion, and I cannot help reiterating my regret that you have come to a different conclusion. On the last occasion, just before I left the court, I mentioned to you that there were reasons why I thought the perpetrator of the act upon the woman's throat had caught hold of her chin. These reasons were that just below the lobe of the left ear were three scratches, and there was also a bruise on the right cheek. When I come to speak of the wounds on the lower part of the body, I must again repeat my opinion that it is highly injudicious to make the results of my examination public. These details are fit only for yourself, sir, and the jury, but to make them public would simply be disgusting."

"We are here in the interests of justice, and must have all the evidence before us. I see, however, that there are several ladies and boys in the room, and I think they might retire."

"If their presence here is the sole reason restraining you from pursuing, so be it." Facing the crowd, he then said, "I appeal to the understanding of the two ladies and ask them to kindly leave the room. As for all you messenger boys, I need not telling you more, the rules of this court preventing me from saying those lesser words I would normally use with you."

But Dr. Phillips still had an objection. "In giving the details to the public, I believe you are thwarting the ends of justice."

"We are bound to take all the evidence in the case," the Coroner said, clearly insisting on the word 'all'. "Whether it be made public or not is a matter for the responsibility of the press."

"We are of opinion," the jury Foreman intervened, "that the evidence the doctor on the last occasion wished to keep back should be heard." Several Jurymen outspokenly expressed their support with their 'Hear, hear', which caused the Coroner to politely calm them down with the movement of his hand.

"I have carefully considered the matter," he then added, "and have never before heard of any evidence requested being kept back."

"I have not kept it back; I have only suggested whether it should be given or not."

"We have delayed taking this evidence as long as possible, because you said the interests of justice might be served by keeping it back. But it is now a fortnight since this occurred, and I do not see why it should be kept back from the jury any longer."

"I am of opinion that what I am about to describe took place after death, so that it could not affect the cause of death, which you are inquiring into."

"That is only your opinion, and might be repudiated by other medical opinion," said the coroner who was about to lose his patience if I judged his tone of voice.

"Very well. I will give you the results of my post-mortem examination but first need to refer to my previous testimony."

Again, he was trying to win some time. The Coroner accepted and had it read over at a quick pace suggesting Phillips to indicate any misunderstanding of a word pronounced by the clerk. Dr. Phillips dared not stop the clerk, having understood by now the limits to Baxter's patience. He gave further details on the parts of the body which the perpetrator of the murder had carried away with him.

"The abdominal wall has been removed in three parts, two from the anterior part. There was a greater portion of skin removed on the right side than on the left.

On adjusting these three flaps it was evident that a portion surrounding and constituting the navel was wanting. The womb itself and two-thirds of the bladder were absent from the body. I have nowhere found traces of them."

The bladder, the bladder, I thought. Phillips had identified one of the organs, which, with the vagina, Tumblety told me he had almost removed but missed because of the darkness.

"I am of opinion," Phillips added, "that the length of the weapon with which the incisions were inflicted was at least five to six inches in length - probably more – and must have been very sharp. The manner in which they had been done indicated a certain amount of anatomical knowledge as did the cutting in three portions of the abdominal wall, and the non cutting of the intestine. Also the way in which the womb was removed showed this in a more marked degree."

The rest of the crowd, although now only composed of men, reacted to the appalling description Phillips wished to avoid. Some left, the majority, however, stayed, still capable of more. As for me, I almost threw up. Not out of the same disgust the others demonstrated for I had been through much worst a view such as an opened decomposed body, but from imagining Tumblety using the blindfolded dissection technique I had taught him. Images of him cutting out body parts of his victim kept running in my mind.

"Order, Order or I shall clear the room," the Coroner said. "Can you give any idea how long it would take to perform the incisions found on the body? Doctor Phillips?"

"I think I can guide you by saying that I myself could not have performed all the injuries I saw on that woman, and effect them, even without a struggle, under a quarter of an hour. If I had done it in a deliberate way, such as would fall to the duties of a surgeon, it would probably have taken me the best part of an hour. The whole inference seems to me that the operation was performed to enable the perpetrator to obtain possession of these parts of the body."

"Have you anything further to add with reference to the stains on the wall?"

"I have not been able to obtain any further traces of blood on the wall."

"Is there anything to indicate that the crime in the case of the woman Nichols was perpetrated with the same object as this?"

"There is a difference in this respect, at all events," remarked the Coroner, "that the medical expert is of opinion that, in the case of Nichols, the mutilations were made first."

"Was any photograph of the eyes of the deceased taken," asked the Foreman, "in case they should retain any impression of the murderer?"

"I have no particular opinion upon that point myself. I was asked about it very early in the inquiry, and I gave my opinion that the operation would be useless, especially in this case. The use of a blood-hound was also suggested. It may be my ignorance, but the blood around was that of the murdered woman, and it would be more likely to be traced than the murderer. These questions were submitted to me by the police very early. I think within twenty-four hours of the murder of the woman."

"Were the injuries to the face and neck such as might have produced insensibility?"

"Yes; they were consistent with partial suffocation."

I would have been less stunned had a bomb exploded directly underneath me. The organs mentioned, the anatomical knowledge, even the use of a long blade knife, it was all brought out and presented as evidence. As for his motives, I still couldn't say if helping in ending lives was his first motivation, or if it was simply a way for him to obtain their organs, this being his real reason. Nevertheless, from his own admission, both were intimately connected but did not exclude other deeper motives. The only thing missing was a name and that name could have easily been Tumblety's. For now on, if I were to make the wrong choices, it could instead be mine.

Immediately after, a Mrs. Elizabeth Long testified. On the morning of the murder, she passed in front of 29, Hanbury Street at about half past five o'clock. On the right-hand side, the same side as the house, she saw a man and a woman standing on the pavement talking. The man's back was turned towards Brick-lane Road, and the woman's was towards the market. They were standing only a few yards nearer Brick Lane from 29, Hanbury Street. She noticed the woman's face and recognized her as the deceased she afterwards saw in the mortuary. She did not observe the man's face, but noticed he was dark and wore a brown low-crowned felt hat. He seemed to her a man over forty years of age, a little taller than the deceased.

SATURDAY, SEPTEMBER 22, 1888

September 22 would be the last day of Mary Anne Nichols' inquest. On Monday's hearing, one single piece of information given by Dr. Llewellyn was of interest to me. He had proceeded with a re-examination of the body, which confirmed the impression he left me of having hastily carried the first one he had done. Being called back, he now brought to light that no part of the viscera was missing. However, my relief would be short-lived, Wednesday's hearing having completely changed the perspective from which reality had to be examined.

On this Saturday afternoon, John Thail, the police-constable who had discovered the body 3:45 in the morning indicated he had passed every thirty minutes on the corner of Buck's Row and Brady Street and had noticed nothing on his previous run. It meant to me that the murderer disposed of only thirty minutes to commit his crime, including his arrival with the victim and departure from the scene. His testimony seemed to be in total contradiction with that of Doctor Phillips who said it would have taken him an hour or so to butcher the victim. Furthermore, I remembered the exact words Tumblety had said on the morning of August 31 when I asked him if he had any organs with him, "Not enough time." Either he had nothing to do with the death of the poor woman, or he was actually giving me the precise reason why he came empty handed. Hence, I disregarded Doctor Phillips' opinion regarding the duration of the crime. After killing her and under complete darkness, he only had time to begin the removal process by opening her with the amputation knife. It was still stained with blood when he returned me the bag, and I had destroyed this piece of evidence by cleaning it. I even repeated the same error the second time he borrowed the instruments.

The Coroner, Wynne   Baxter, could not figure out what possible motive could be behind Nichol's murder.

She was without money, hence robbery had to be excluded. As for other common motives, jealousy, revenge, or greed, they could not apply to this case, no disturbance, noise or cries being heard. The circumstances of the death of Polly Nichols and Anne Chapmen being similar in many respects, he suggested to the jury that these two women may have been murdered by the same man with the same object. The jury added a rider to its verdict of wilful murder against some person or persons unknown. They felt important to express their thanks to the Coroner for his remarks made on the need of a mortuary for Whitechapel.

The testimonies given in the three past cases deeply upset me. For in my mind, Tumblety and I were unmistakably at a crossroad, having used me as a shield. Little did I think the first time we met, that each word he would pronounce was part of a well-orchestrated plan he was laying out. Looking back, I came to the conclusion that every move he made or prepared us to make was carefully staged without raising any suspicion. A master puppeteer he was. Madness always finds its way out. But his had already gone way beyond. He was making it mine.

My ordeal was far from being over; it had only begun. Getting back at the laboratory, the latest edition of the British Medical Journal was lying on Fillmore's desk. I flipped through its pages and noticed a short article on the Whitechapel murders. It confirmed Baxter's testimony regarding the organs removed by the perpetrator of the crimes even adding details not disclosed.

> *British Medical Journal*
> *September 22, 1888*
> *The Whitechapel Murder DR. GEORGE BAXTER PHILLIPS gave some remarkable evidence at the adjourned inquiry respecting the mutilations found on the body of Mary Anne Chapman, who was found in the back yard of 29 Hanbury Street, Whitechapel, on the morning of September 8th. He expressed the opinion that the length of the weapon, which must have been very sharp, was at least five or six inches, probably more. The mode in which the knife had been used, he said, seemed to indicate some anatomical knowledge. The reposts published in the daily press are incomplete. It is there desirable to state that the parts removed were a certain portion of the abdominal wall, including the navel; two thirds of the bladder, posterior and upper portions; the upper third of the vagina and its connection with the uterus; and the whole of the uterus.*

Tumblety had used the word 'mess' to describe the conditions under which he had executed his work. Quite an understatement when one reads the magazine's medical description.

As I passed in front of the dissection room, I overheard Fillmore talking with Doctor Thomas Horrocks Openshaw, Curator of our Pathology Museum.

They were accompanied by two other men whom I believed to be late visitors.

"Oh, there you are Reily, come in. This is Inspector Frederick George Abberline from Scotland Yard and Sergeant William Thick of the Metropolitan Policc H Division. Inspector Abberline is in charge of the recent Whitechapel murders."

"Were you not at the Chapman inquiry this week?" Abberline asked.

"It was I who imposed upon him to attend the inquiries," said Fillmore before I had to open my mouth which was his habit of doing. "Frequent comments were made about inappropriate conditions police-surgeons have to live up to in most of the mortuaries."

"Yes, I am quite aware of what was said. It is not easier for us, but we can't do anything about it."

"Still, it bears a certain impact on the role of our establishment." Then turning at me, "Inspector Abberline was asking us if we had recently purchased organs. What would you answer to him, Reily?"

"Frankly, the death rate in the East End is terribly high. The laboratory can hardly deal with the bodies of the hospital's own patients."

"So you don't have a need for organs, if I understand you correctly," commented Thick.

"Precisely," I answered.

"Even more so, our museum already has a wide variety of specimens," remarked Openshaw. "What you saw in the Laboratory is only a small sample of our rather extensive collection."

"As a matter of fact," Fillmore added, "we are sometimes asked to provide organs for external research projects. The latest request having been made in the beginning of August. Isn't it so, Reily?"

"Yes Professor," I answered hoping he would not ask me to provide details of Tumblety's initial visit and his subsequent meetings with me.

"This confirms that the murder's motive is not body-snatching," pointed out Abberline. I presume you keep records of all those jars full of organs."

"Each jar is labeled with references in our record books. Organs donated for research are also recorded. Reily, show them an example."

"That won't be necessary," said Abberline as I was heading for my desk. "If needed, we shall come back and look into your control methods. I, however, would ask you to show us the various knives used in a dissection procedure. It will give us a better idea of the possible weapons this madman uses."

"Reily," said Fillmore noticing I wasn't paying attention.

"Yes Professor. If you gentlemen wish to follow me,

I shall show them to you," I said as I pointed the direction to them.

"Do you need anything more of us?" asked Openshaw.

"Not for the moment," replied Abberline. "Now Mister Reily, let's have a look at those knives."

I led them to the drawers where we kept all the dissection instruments. "I suggest you not limit yourselves to knives. This fool can decide to collect complete body parts of any future victim and could need to work with other kinds of instruments."

"Excellent idea, Mister Reily. However, tell me," Abberline asked, "what makes you believe there will be other murders?"

"The Coroner, Wayne Baxter, to-day said that neither robbery nor jealousy was, in his opinion, the motives for all the three killings. You were quite sure they were not body-snatching cases. Everything indicates this man simply has an itch for killing women, which is, if you permit me a metaphor, pathological. I would add that the violence of each aggression has escalated. If it has not climaxed with Chapman's mutilations, he shall search for another prey to convey to her his rage at its fullest. I dare not imagine what he could do to the next one."

"I like the way this man thinks," Abbcrlinc said turning to Sergeant Thick.

"Maybe he should consider a career in our division."

"And why should he choose to be with you instead of us at the Yard? You know where the best find themselves?" He added proudly pulling on the flaps of his vest. "Now let's get to business."

By humouring under extreme circumstances, they unknowingly brought my spirits back. "If the murderer only wants large body parts, he would probably use a saw. As you can see, they come in different sizes depending on the importance of the part to be sectioned off."

I let them examine the metacarpal saws for cutting hands, feet, fingers or smaller bones, tendons, then capital saws for large bones and even the hey saw to cut into the skull bone.

"My butcher only has one saw," Abberline said, "and does every bone cutting with it."

"Yes but I believe it's because he is not into selling fingers nor toes," Thick commented innocently.

I couldn't keep myself from laughing. "I think we should move on with the knives. We have double-sided amputation knives for cutting in both directions in only one motion of the hand and single-sided large amputation knives. They are…" I suddenly stopped giving explanations. The Liston amputation knife was missing.

"Is something wrong?" Abberline asked.

"No, no, everything is fine. I simply misplaced a knife." It was a pure lie, but I had to find a way out. "I was about to say they are of various lengths. Some have removable handles, which reduces the space normally needed to carry them."

"Or to conceal them," said Thick.

"Of course, but if a criminal used one of them, he would lose time in re-assembling it just before committing a crime."

"Excellent remark," said Abberline looking at Thick. "These drawers contain various scalpels and lancets,"

I said as I opened a couple of them. "You shall notice many curved lancets. They are used to dissect ligaments and tissue."

"One of them could have been used with Tabram," said Abberline.

"Maybe to cut but not necessarily to stab," I responded. "The blades are rather thin and could easily brake against a bone."

"You seem to know the instruments quite well," Thick noted.

"I have been working here for seven years now. Believe me, I have to anticipate what a pathologist intends to do and bring him the right instrument. Keeping my job depends on it. It's probably the same thing for you with all those firearms you lay your hands on."

"Quite true," Thick remarked. "Tell me, do you know how to use all of these?"

"I'm not a physician just an assistant hence I am not authorized to practice medicine nor do I have the skills required. I admit having frequently seen doctors use them. I would have to practice a lot before being at ease. May I continue showing you other instruments?"

"Please do."

I showed them the bone chisel and hammer used to trim bones, which gave in to another amusing comment from Abberline. "If this lunatic wants to nail a body part on a wall or sculpt a bone, we now know what tools he can use." He then added in a very serious tone, "One final question, Mister Reily. You probably are aware that we have to ask about your whereabouts on the night of the murders."

"I am at your service, Inspector," said I.

I answered all their questions. If certain periods could be corroborated, I was, however, alone most of my free time. Fortunately, the detailed description I gave of where I was, who I met and spoke seemed to satisfy both since they left. Nevertheless, I went to the door and made sure they had effectively done so then quickly headed towards the drawers. I had to find the missing knife, the one I was sure Tumblety had put back, having heard him close the drawer from which he had pulled it out. I opened it, completely emptied it and carefully examined the other drawers; it was nowhere to find. Either the clerk on supply assigned by Fillmore or Tumblety took it.

Early in the evening of that day, I leaned back on the chair in my room to rest before eating. My eyelids became heavy inviting me to let go. I remembered when I would walk in Whitechapel, although perilous for the unwise, it still offered me the view of men, women, young and old, hoping to better at least their material situation if not themselves. The means by which they would accomplish their quest involved a constant set of choices where one's gain inevitably meant another person's loss even if this other were to be a close one, husband, wife, daughter or son. As with the animals, it was the survival of the fittest, the only difference being animals shed no tears nor do they rejoice. I could see myself walking amongst them, seeing here a young boy playing with a piece of wood he had turned into a pirate's sword, there a mother breast-feeding her child. On the other side of the street a man was drinking water from the public fountain then shaking whatever drops remained in his hand onto his friend standing at his side, both laughing. At the corner of the road I was about to cross, a group of young women hid their giggles with their hands, probably teasing each other with the promises made to them by their boyfriends. People entering shops, others coming out with their purchases as well as men and women pushing or pulling carts of all sizes filled with goods proved to all the legitimacy of their human activity in the neighbourhood what say I, of their existence.

That was before, almost a long time ago in my measure of time.

Now, since the savage killing of three women, all I manage to see in their eyes is a foggy gleam. They all look at each other as if men and women ceased to exist only to be replaced by suspects and victims. I looked at the sky. It was almost as if the sun decided to let the clouds mark the dark moments of Whitechapel and the deadly nights reign over the light of the day. Voices and sounds of the street progressively merged into a fading out noise, leaving only my echoing footsteps to be heard. People began to vanish around me one by one in a ghostly ambiance. Streets were narrowing bringing the walls closer to me as if they were begging me not to venture myself further down the road. I had lost my direction but could still see a lamp post in front of me, and by it a man knelt under his large cape. I would ask him for some help and quickened my pace. As I was about to tap on his shoulder, he suddenly turned his head up showing me a horrifying mask covered with blood dripping on his clothes. His right hand held the stolen Liston knife. He stood up allowing me to discover the laid body of a woman whose wide opened abdomen was emptying itself of its last red fluids of life. As he was slowly removing his mask with the hand still holding the knife, the monster raised his other hand to my face. In it was the uterus he had just removed. The now visible face of the monster was that of Tumblety. "Here Woodrow, take it. I owe it to you," said he in a grotesque loud voice. I sat strait up in my chair, waking out of a nightmare, screaming. My body was shaken with unstoppable spasms of fear. I sprang up and walked for minutes in the room, breathing deeply to regain my calm.

I shall remember September 22 all my life for it was this day I became convinced Tumblety was the man who killed Tabram, Nichols and Chapman. I was decided to find him, force him to accomplish his promise regarding my potential medical career, and then end his life with my bare hands. I would let no one know about it but I.

WEDNESDAY, SEPTEMBER 26, 1888

This afternoon would be the last day of Chapman's inquest. The Coroner summed up her life and her death. Had she not have been murdered, his description would have fitted so many of the unfortunate class living in Whitechapel.

"The deceased," he said, "had evidently lived an immoral life for some time, and her habits and surroundings had become worse since her means had failed. She no longer visited her relations, and her brother had not seen her for five months, when she borrowed a small sum from him. She lived principally in the common lodging houses in the neighbourhood of

Spitalfields, where others, such as she, herded like cattle. She showed signs of deprivation, as if she had been badly fed. The glimpse of life in those dens, which the evidence in this case disclosed, was sufficient to make them feel there was much in the 19th century civilization of which they had small reason to be proud; but the jury, who were constantly called together to hear the sad tale of starvation, or semi-starvation, of misery, immorality, and wickedness, which some of the occupants of the 5,000 beds in that district had every week to relate at coroner's inquests, did not require to be reminded of what life in a Spitalfields lodging house meant. It was in one of those that the older bruises found on the temple and in front of the chest of the deceased were received, in a trumpery quarrel, a week before her death. It was in one of those that she was seen a few hours before her mangled remains were discovered."

"On the afternoon and evening of Friday, the 7th of September, also spent her time partly in such a place, at 35, Dorset Street, and partly in the Ringers public house, where she spent whatever money she had; so that between 1 and 2 o'clock on the morning of Saturday, when the money for her bed was demanded, she was obliged to admit that she was without means, and at once turned out into the street to find it. She left there at 1:45 a.m. She was seen off the premises by the night watchman, and was observed to turn down Little Paternoster-row into Brushfield Street, and not in the more direct direction of Hanbury Street. On her wedding finger she was wearing two or three rings, which appeared to have been palpably of base metal, as the witnesses were all clear about their material and value."

"They now lost sight of her for about four hours, but at half-past 5 o'clock, Mrs. Long was in Hanbury Street, on the way from her home in Church Street, Whitechapel, to Spitalfields Market. She walked on the northern side of the road, going westward, and remembered having seen a man and woman standing a few yards from the place where the deceased was afterwards found, and, although she did not know Annie Chapman, she was positive that the woman was the deceased. The two were talking loudly, but not sufficiently so to arouse her suspicions that there was anything wrong. The words she overheard were not calculated to do so. The laconic inquiry of the man, 'Will you?' and the simple assent of the woman, viewed in the light of the subsequent events, could be easily translated and explained. Mrs. Long passed on her way, and neither saw nor heard anything more of her, and that was the last time she was known to have been alive."

He necessarily referred to the testimonies of other witnesses and tried to reconcile certain discrepancies before giving his opinion on the manner Chapman was killed and mutilated. The words he would pronounce greatly mattered to me. I prepared myself to register as many details as I could, each element bearing a possible link with every word Tumblety had spoken since Fillmore and I had met him.

"The wretch," he continued, "must have then seized the deceased, perhaps with Judas-like approaches. He seized her by the chin. He pressed her throat, and whilst thus preventing the slightest cry, he at the same time produced insensibility and suffocation. There was no evidence of any struggle. The clothes were not torn. Even in those preliminaries, the wretch seems to have known how to carry out efficiently his nefarious work. The deceased was then lowered to the ground, and laid on her back; and although in doing so she may have fallen slightly against the fence, the movement was probably effected with care. Her throat was then cut in two places with savage determination, and the injuries to the abdomen commenced. All was done with cool impudence and reckless daring; but perhaps nothing was more noticeable than the emptying of her pockets, and the arrangement of their contents with business-like precision in order near her feet. The murder seemed, like the Buck's-row case, to have been carried out without any cry. None of the occupants of the houses by which the spot was surrounded heard anything suspicious. The brute who committed the offence did not even take the trouble to cover up his ghastly work, but left the body exposed to the view of the first comer. That accorded but little with the trouble taken with the rings, and suggested either that he had at length been disturbed, or that, as daylight broke, a sudden fear suggested the danger of detection that he was running. There were two things missing. Her rings had been wrenched from her fingers and had not since been found, and the uterus had been taken from the abdomen. The body had not been dissected, but the injuries had been made by someone who had considerable anatomical skill and knowledge. There were no meaningless cuts. The organ had been taken by one who knew where to find it, what difficulties he would have to contend against, and how he should used his knife so as to abstract the organ without injury to it. No unskilled person could have known where to find it or have recognized it when it was found. For instance, no mere slaughterer of animals could have carried out these operations. It must have been someone accustomed to the post-mortem room."

I suspected the Coroner of having recently learned from Abberline or Thick's visit to our hospital for he was referring to a more technical vocabulary.

"The conclusion that the desire was to possess the missing abdominal organ seemed overwhelming," he added. "If the object were robbery, the injuries to the viscera were meaningless, for death had previously resulted from the loss of blood at the neck. Moreover, when they found an easily accomplished theft of some paltry brass rings and an internal organ taken, after at least a quarter of an hour's work and by a skilled person, they were driven to the deduction that the abstraction of the missing portion of abdominal viscera was the object, and the theft of the rings was only a thin-veiled blind, an attempt to prevent the real intention being discovered. The amount missing would go into a breakfast cup, and had not the medical examination been of a thorough and searching character it might easily have been left unnoticed that there was any portion of the body which had been taken."

"The difficulty in believing that the purport of the murderer was the possession of the missing abdominal organ was natural. It was abhorrent to their feelings to conclude that a life should be taken for so slight an object; but when rightly considered the reasons for most murders were altogether out of proportion to their guilt. It had been suggested that the criminal was a lunatic with morbid feelings. That might or might not be the case, but the object of the murderer appeared palpably shown by the facts, and it was not necessary to assume lunacy, for it was clear there was a market for the missing organ. To show the jury that, I must mention a fact, which at the same time proved the assistance which publicity and the Press afforded in the detection of crime. Within a few hours of the issue of the morning papers containing a report of the medical evidence given at the last sitting of the Court I received a communication from an officer of one of our great medical schools that they had information, which might or might not have a distinct bearing on that inquiry. I attended at the first opportunity, and was informed by the sub-curator of the Pathological Museum that some months ago an American had called on him and asked him to procure a number of specimens of the organ that was missing in the deceased. He stated his willingness to give £ 20 apiece for each specimen. He stated that his object was to issue an actual specimen with each copy of a publication on which he was then engaged. He was told that his request was impossible to be complied with, but he still urged his request. He wished them preserved, not in spirits of wine, the usual medium, but glycerine, in order to preserve them in a flaccid condition, and he wished them sent to America direct. It was known that this request was repeated to another institution of similar character. Now was it not possible that the knowledge of this demand might have incited some abandoned wretch to possess himself of a specimen? It seemed beyond belief that such inhuman wickedness could enter into the mind of any man; but, unfortunately, our criminal annals proved that every crime was possible. I need hardly say that I at once communicated his information to the Detective Department at Scotland-yard. Of course, I did know what use had been made of it, but believed that publicity might further elucidate this fact, and therefore, had not withheld the information."

This seemed in complete contradiction not only with the conclusion we had all came up with during Abberline and Thick's visit but also with the facility in purchasing organs elsewhere than in hospitals as Tumblety himself demonstrated. I was not convinced by hearing what the Coroner had said in support of his revelation.

Then addressing the Jury, Baxter continued, "Gentlemen, I have endeavoured to suggest to you the object with which this crime was committed and the class of persons who must have committed it. The greatest deterrent from crime was the conviction that detection and punishment would follow with rapidity and certainty, and it might be that the impunity with which Mary Anne Nichols and Martha Tabram were murdered suggested the possibility of such horrid crimes as those, which you and another jury had been considering. It was therefore a great misfortune that nearly three weeks had already elapsed without the chief actor in this awful tragedy having been discovered. Surely, it was not too much even yet to hope that the ingenuity of our detective force would succeed in unearthing this monster. It was not as if there were no clue to the character of the criminal or the cause of his crime. His object was clearly divulged. His anatomical knowledge carried him out of the category of a common criminal, for that knowledge could only have been obtained by assisting at post-mortems or by frequenting the post-mortem room. Thus, the class in which search must be made, although a large one, is limited."

With such a precis profile, he almost could have given my name. Had Abberline or Thick been at the inquiry and seen me, they, for sure, would have asked me to follow them for further interrogation. The credibility of the deposition I gave Abberline could now be questioned at any moment. Catching and killing Tumblety were no more the sole options I could favour, the evidence still placing a person of my kind at the top of any list. I had to come up with a more cleaver and definitively more resistant solution, which had to exonerate me of any responsibility. I was quite certain Tumblety would not innocently present himself before me for he would have to explain his theft of the Liston knife from a man so eager to supply him with everything he would have needed.

THURSDAY, SEPTEMBER 27, 1888

To-day, I was glad to have a full day's work, which created a wall-effect against all the thoughts these crimes would have otherwise occupied my mind. Even if classes had already begun, the first-year students had by now gone through the embarrassments their second and third-year mates had them endure and started to become as cocky as they were. They would risk a prank or two particularly on the non-teaching staff such as I. However, they would learn at their expense I was not born as of yesterday and usually caught them at their own games. Each year, I would pick one who appeared to be the most naive and gullible of all and replace the blood of a freshly dead body with a thick blue liquid for him to examine. I would then let him know the deceased was probably of royal origin and ask my victim to cut him open. As soon as the blue 'blood' oozed, the poor student would usually panic or express his astonishment. I would request of him to immediately call upon Fillmore with all the predictable results it would entail.

Most of these younger ones would then understand the need of establishing mutually respectful relations whilst a few and rare others irritated themselves by seeing what they define as a person of lesser condition dare to react in the same manner as they had.

This year, however, I was in no mood for any amusement of this sort and if there had to be a victim of any gesture on my behalf it would be Tumblety. Preparing for an eventual and possibly deadly encounter would be the first step for me to cross. He had made Whitechapel his battle ground and women his enemies. It would now have to become mine also for me to fight efficiently against him and the battle field to be covered was immense. I had to provide for all contingencies. Where will he strike next, most obviously in an area still not soiled with oozing blood of his doing? Had he found an ally in the night, I would turn it into a caring brother as dawn and dusk become my new friends. Should rain or fog blind my eyes, I shall turn them into my guiding companions. He had chosen his weapons; I would have to find mine and learn to be as ease with them as he with his. He managed to dissimulate his height, his looks, his flamboyant dressing, by George even his mustache! I would make them known to all in all, their variations. There was only but one way to achieve my goal, and it was for me to carry the banner. It meant I would wander the streets by night as so many did, them looking for a place to sleep, I for a man to seize.

I could, nevertheless, foretell that my presence could attract the attention of   many and worsen my already fragile set of alibis. Should I inform Abberline? Perhaps,

I thought. However, I was not fully convinced this avenue would clear myself of any wrong doing. Fitzgerald seemed a better choice, and I decided to seek his advice by sending him a telegram, the conduct of our mission giving me the perfect introductory pretext. I hastily wrote down the message I would send at the earliest.

> *Sir,*
> *Need to seek your advice concerning recent matters that might hinder the success of our business.*
> *Woodrow Reily*

By five in the afternoon, a response arrived.

> *To-night at eight, Timothy shall be at your usual departure place.*
> *Gordon Fitzgerald.*

At the convened time, I was at Fitzgerald's place having, however, asked Timothy to slowly ride through Whitechapel Road and Aldgate High Street. This would allow me to survey part of the battle field unnoticed. Elizabeth greeted me at the door and to my dismay, informed me her father had been ill in his bed for the past two days.

"What is wrong?" I asked.

"Come in the drawing room. I must inform of his condition before you may see him for he is too proud to tell you himself."

I feared for the worst and followed her silently.

"First," she said whilst we sat, "you must promise me not to say a word about our conversation to my father."

"Why such a secrecy?"

"Promise me."

"I promise," said I, however, not knowing what to expect.

"Father is dying. He has only but a few months left his doctor told us. Since he has met you, everything seemed to have changed for the best. He had the energy of a young man. You could read from his eyes the enthusiasm of the gold digger about to hit the mother-load. You made him rediscover his appetite not only for fine food but also for life. The project of his life was not his estate but the caring of the poor of Irish origin. Since William has died, his heart wasn't in anything any more. Now, he is working with you and through you. What you have accomplished so far brought him a comfort not even he would have suspected. I envy you for having come so close to Father in such a short time. At the same time, I admire the sincerity and the absence of all self-interest in your actions. It remembers me of my brother William whom I loved so much. You are bringing to an end a deed, a dream with which Father and he had only dealt with words."

She paused, glancing tenderly at me.

"I was only sharing the same concerns he had and…"

"Please; it is hard for me to say these words. Do let me finish, then you may speak." She paused again.

"Father has asked me to help him set forward everything you deem necessary to fulfil his dream.

Money should never be a reason for you to slow down your pace. I also had a project. It concerned Irish orphans to be brought either to the United States or Canada where Catholic families would adopt them. If it pleases you, we can join our efforts, Father and you with your families and I, with my orphan children. Now what is it you wanted to say?"

"Nothing. I mean I am overwhelmed to say the least. I always considered being a solitary person, minding my own business and doing what I was told. Your father has introduced me to a different man hiding somewhere inside me. This new person was probably the real Woodrow after all, waiting only to breathe for the first time."

"You certainly did not know he had asked about you prior to your initial meeting."

"I was not aware of that."

"He was hospitalized at the London Hospital and frequently saw you in the hallways. He told me he had discovered a strange but quite intriguing little mouse coming in and out of his hole in a wall. You were this little mouse," she said bringing her head down to conceal her smile. "He wanted to befriend this little creature and managed to learn of you all he needed before engaging with you in a memorable conversation at the Crown pub."

"I almost lost my temper, and you knew all this before I came here the first time?"

"That night, I was not aware you were the person he had spoken of to me. I had never seen you before, but I figured it out. I must admit it was difficult for me not to let you see I was also involved in this taming operation." Now she was smiling openly whilst taking my hand in hers. "Father would often wink at me during the meal without you noticing anything. Do you forgive us?"

I did not know if I was to be angry or joyful for

having been so easily caught in their trap, her beauty and candour keeping me off guard. "There is nothing to forgive. Maybe this mouse was only waiting to be caught one day by someone like you."

I looked in her eyes but could say no more.

"Father told me you had something important to say to him. I must warn you he is very tired and needs to rest. If these news are seriously bad, I would suggest waiting a day or two till he improves or trust me with them for me to let him know at an appropriate moment. Feel free to decide what suits you better."

"No disrespect to you, but it concerns a personal matter, which bears upon our project. Consequently, I prefer telling him directly. I shall wait for you to tell me when I could meet him. In the meanwhile, I shall do whatever is deemed necessary. Now tell me more about your project with the orphans."

From dinner till ten in the evening, I listened to every word she would pronounce, completely subdued by her charm. She had gone through all the administrative requirements, raised funds, even investing the larger part of the sums needed from her own assets. She obtained the best prices and conditions for the transportation by train and boat, here and abroad. She had established many contacts in New York and in the province of Quebec where Catholic families were willing to adopt the young orphans. She had a strong preference towards Quebec given the beauty and immensity of the land and the kindness of its French-speaking people. She also had been told that the same two congregations involved the orphanage in London, the Sisters of The Holy Family of Bordeaux and the Missionary Oblates of Mary Immaculate, had close ties in Quebec City with their French-speaking counterpart. It would be easy for the young children to learn the language in exchange, they would find a place to preserve their religion amongst an almost exclusively Catholic population. No man could have done a better job. I could not refuse the invitation she had made of us joining forces. It would at least give me the possibility of seeing here again. These moments spent in her company turned out to be refreshing and well deserved considering the enormous stress I had been under in the past days.

On my way back, I asked Timothy to drop me at the corner of Commercial and Whitechapel where a very demanding schedule awaited me for the duration of my first night carrying the banner.

FRIDAY, SEPTEMBER 28, 1888

The night had been cold and fully justified the warm clothes I wore. The waning moon gave the little light it had preferred keeping for itself whatever heat it received from the sun. The people of the evening had ended their outing and left the streets. Those of the night were now crawling out from everywhere, joining the wretched who had neither day nor night at their advantage and who would constantly search for work, food and shelter.

In want of a weapon, I walked the 'Wicked Quarter Mile', and, on Dorset Street, easily found in a single person not only the provider of what I needed but the teacher of the art of knifing as well. Dunken was his name. He was standing on a street corner holding his hand out hoping someone would drop some coins in it. Life had drawn a great sadness on his face, which added to his obvious fatigue put him apart from the others surrounding us. He looked as if he had just fallen into this world of madness and despair not knowing yet how to cope with such a sudden change. I couldn't help but gave him some of the shillings I had in one of my pockets.

"Thank yea," he said looking at me. "If there's

something I can do in return, just say so."

I didn't respond and went on my way when suddenly I stopped, turned around and asked him : "Could you find me a good folding knife with a long blade."

"Just that? Sure!"

"When could it be done?"

He didn't answer. Instead, he smiled, put a hand in his trouser pocket and pulled out what must have been his own knife. He opened it. Holding the blade between his fingers, he presented it to me. "Like this one?"

I carefully took it and found its handle offering my hand an easy grip. The blade was extremely sharp, at least four inches, I thought. It had a lock, which prevented it from folding back over the fingers. "It's perfect," I said.

"Mind my saying but you don't seem to be looking just for something to peel an apple. Do you know how to use such a tool If I may ask?"

It was as if he had read my mind. The question for me was how to ask more of him without fueling any suspicion.

"I could show you some easy basic tricks for some more of those coins of yours," he quickly said.

"I...,I... Why yes it would certainly come in hand some day."

He fully deserved the meal and pint of ale I offered him in addition to his wages of one pound for the two hours it took him to share his deadly skills. I learned from him that one always overestimates his strength when a prey presents himself as defenseless. "Sizing-up your attacker is the first to do," he said. He suggested walking with my right hand in my pocket ready to pull out my knife, showed me how to grab it from inside my right pocket whilst removing my coat to shield me against my attacker. He made me understand that the view of blood drawn from a visible part of the aggressor's body either frightens or slows down even the boldest and would have to be my first concern. Any expression of hesitation detected in the attacker's eyes, body motion or voice were to become a signal for me to strike again, again and again until he fell to the ground. The decision would then belong to me to go for the kill or simply transfer my coat from left to right hiding my bloody knife and hand and slowly walk away as would any peaceful by-passer.

I promoted myself from an Irish fist-fighter to a potential knife-mugger.

Facing the front of Christ Church as its clock stroke three, I decided to rest for a while. Quite a strange place to find myself standing, I thought. Two victims having been killed within a two hundred yard range of where I was located. I sat on its doorsteps only to be warned by a policeman within minutes of closing my eyes to move along. I looked around me noticing that four other men had also stopped to rest and had been given the same order. I rose up with a grunt and went on. Some tea would help me stay alert. Right across the street, the welcoming doors of the Ten Bells could not have made me a better offer had I faced Heaven's gate. Having a hot drink never felt so good to me and brought me to ask for a second one. At a table close to the bar, I could hear some men and woman talking about a play they were practicing. The presence of actors came as a reminder of my need to learn how one can disguise himself. I had to find a way to be drawn into their conversation; so I listened carefully.

"It is completely ludicrous for the Director to ask each of us to play two roles," one said.

"Has he read the play or does he want us to return to the middle age?" a woman asked.

"Even there," said another, "I would have to play against myself in Act II."

A very tall man sitting with them hadn't spoken yet. He gave me an idea. I approached them and decided to make a move.

"Sorry if I interrupt you. I couldn't help but to hear your conversation. May I ask you a question?"

"It will cost you," the tall man said, "since you have imposed on yourself the status of a spectator, and we do not perform for free."

"Bring us all some gin," I asked the barman showing him a handful of shillings.

"You have just been promoted from spectator to actor," the woman commented. "Bring your chair and ask us what you desire." We all introduced ourselves and enjoyed the stinging taste of our common drink.

"I was wondering," I asked, "if your director demanded one of you to play the role of a small person. How would you bring down your height?"

"Show him George how you do it," said the older one named Lawrence.

George stood up backing off from the table.

"Pay attention. If you look at me from the front, you may not have noticed that my knees are slightly bent. Doing so, I took three inches off. If I turn sideways, you shall easily figure out my trickery, and I would then lose all credibility in my role as a smaller man. But if my trousers were larger, they would greatly hide my bending. The arms must also be kept bent otherwise you would have the looks more of an orangutan than an actor. I would also ease my walk wearing a long coat or a cape, and the audience would never suspect my real height."

"Fascinating," I said as I watched him change from a giant to a man of my size.

"That's not all", he added. "My shoes or boots would have no heels shortening me one more inch," which he would mimic by walking only in his socks. Finally, I would draw attention on other parts of my body such as my hands, my mouth."

"Now if you design your set efficiently," the woman said, "and have the lights in strategic places, you will increase the illusion created by the actor."

"But if I were outside," I asked Ginger, "what could I do?"

All laughed at my question.

"Haven't you ever walked on the street whilst others were on the side-walk just by you?"

"How stupid of me. I probably had one too much."

The last thirty minutes gave me all the time needed to learn the basic mechanics and materials used for theatrical make-up. "I greatly enjoyed your company but need to leave. Thank you so much."

"It was our pleasure to perform exclusively for you, Woodrow," said Lawrence. "If you need more on another day, and for the same price," he added lifting up his almost empty glass, "just come at the Lyceum Theater where we repeat until the Strange Case of Dr Jekyll and Mr Hyde play ends."

I pulled out my watch. It was twenty past four. Time had flown faster than I thought leaving me one hour to sleep before going to work.

The evening of that same day, again I jumped into the lion's den this time observing how women of the night would approach their potential clients. Listening to what they said taught me more than I desired, their vocabulary mostly made up of expressions and words my ears never heard. For the fair ones, it was quite easy regardless of their stench or filth. But even the old, the ugly, the toothless, the plump and the scaring thin, all had their way of stirring up some form of curiosity. Of course, I was also the subject of their attention wherever I set foot should it be in a pub or out on the street. My eyes would detect any suspicious move a man dared to make in presence of a woman or simply observing them as I was.

All night long I would go from one place to another, carrying the banner on streets, roads and lanes I never knew existed in Whitechapel and Spitalfields. Passing in front of the Synagogue on Brick Lane, the inscription of the sundial 'Umbra sumus' truly defined the shadow I meant to become in my hunt for Tumblety. In one of his poems, Diffugere Nives, Horace had expressed those sad words, Pulvis et umbra sumus, We are but dust and shadow, living dead.

I started recognizing some people I had seen the night before and kept my face hidden to avoid being recognized by them, even if I dressed differently. Had I any intention of committing a hideous crime such as those of the Ripper, I was now convinced I possessed all the means and the will a predator would have dreamed of. I was becoming a hawk, a nightjar in Whitechapel but Tumblety would be my first and only prey.

SATURDAY, SEPTEMBER 29, 1888

On the morning of Saturday, I was surprised to see Timothy driving close to me as I was hurrying on the side-walk. I was even more surprised when I noticed his passenger was none else but Elizabeth. She waved at me.

"Woodrow," she said. "I have news for you on behalf of my father."

"How is he?" I asked.

"Much better given the circumstances. I personally wanted to bring you the news. He wishes to know if you would accept having dinner with us to-night."

She had used the magic word 'us' meaning she would also be there. I immediately accepted trying as hard as I could to hide from her my excitement.

"Then would eight be convenient?"

"Of course," I said as they drove off.

That evening, on the cab, I felt totally exhausted and believed I slept almost all the way to Fitzgerald's home. Winston opened the door before I even had the chance to raise the knocker. Behind him was Fitzgerald.

"Come in my dear friend," he said in a soft voice.

Although his face was pale, he stood strong on his feet and his hand, rather firm as we shook, gave no impression of weakness. I was more than satisfied by his improved health and didn't mind letting it show.

"Sir," said I, "I am so…, you look really fine. What a great pleasure for me to meet you to-night. We have, I believe, so much to catch up with our project."

"You mean projects, if I understood Elizabeth correctly. Come. She is waiting in the drawing-room."

As we entered the room, Elizabeth stood up and walked towards us.

"Woodrow, my God, you look so tired! Come quick and have a seat."

"I was about to say the same," Fitzgerald added. Is that what you needed to tell me?"

"No, I've only been this way for a day or two." I said trying to reassure both.

"I think this shall be another cognac situation, Winston…"

"I'll be fine; I swear."

"Then would you care for a Glenlivet? I have an even better selection than the first time you had a taste of Scotland's finest."

"Yes, I might just be in serious need of a drink," I answered.

"Winston," again said Fitzgerald. "Make it two glens for us. And what will you have Elizabeth?"

"A sherry, as usual."

"Now," Fitzgerald said. What is bothering you?"

I raised my head up towards him then looked at Elizabeth, then again at her father. He understood my embarrassment but before he could say a word, I looked at again towards Elizabeth.

"Both of you need to hear exactly what is happening. I must ask you to trust me and believe every word I say.

You certainly have read and probably discussed about the Whitechapel murders."

They acknowledged with a sign of the head.

"There could now be very good reasons for the police to believe I killed all three women, Tabram, Nichols and Chapman. I am innocent of any wrong doing yet I cannot prove it beyond anyone's doubt."

Fitzgerald sat, his knees trembling. Elizabeth immediately came to him.

"Father, are you well?"

"Yes darling. I am doing fine. Woodrow, I am one who shall never doubt you. You must tell us what you can in order for us to provide you with all the help you may require."

"If this can better establish my credibility, I believe I know who committed these crimes but cannot prove it either."

I proceeded to tell them who I thought the murderer was, where and how we met. I mentioned the beginning friendship between him and I upon which he played to obtain various surgical instruments needed to kill Chapman and remove her organs. I explained how he stole the Liston knife he would probably use against his next victim. I gave them an overview of the Coroner's opinion regarding the suspect's profile and its potential damaging effect on me, which started with Inspector Abberline's visit at the London Hospital. They quickly understood my fatigue when I described what I had done during the past two nights and my decision to continue as long as Tumblety remains free.

"If I am arrested, you shall know why. Consequently, our projects shall certainly be compromised. Even if I am released, a certain degree of doubt shall still subsist affecting all relations we have already established and preventing us from building new ones. Now you know why I seek your advice."

"You are indeed in a delicate position," said Fitzgerald. "Let us suppose you went to the police and gave them all the information in your possession. What do you believe they may do if another woman is murdered whilst you are in custody? They will have to release you, don't you think?"

"Not necessarily. Some strongly believe the killings are the doing of more than one person. I would still be considered as an accomplice and kept in prison. Even in the best case, meaning by that if I am remanded on bail, I risk being lynched by the mob."

"You could leave the country until everything calms down," remarked Elizabeth.

"He would still fall under suspicion when he returns. He has to stay. Actually, the solution is quite simple.

You need a guardian angel."

"Father, you are not serious. Spirits can't help him." "Quite the contrary, I am very serious. What I meant is someone unseen constantly behind Woodrow who would provide him not only with an alibi but also with an extra pair of hands, in case he needs them." He looked at us with a large smile winking both eyes.

"I hope you're not considering yourself as a candidate for the job," said I.

"If I were younger, I would be delighted to join forces with you. No, I was thinking of Timothy. He could easily fold an opponent in four and put him in his back pocket to sit on. When would you want him to start?"

"I had planned covering another sector of Whitechapel this night. Am I asking him too much too soon?"

"If I know my people well, I'd say Winston has already begun taking care of that detail with Timothy. Starting to-night, you shall have your guardian angel."

"Great Scott, now we are talking business!"

"My dear Woodrow," Fitzgerald said, "we were already making business, and we've expanded with Elizabeth's project. Now we are consolidating. I must say your determination is unquestionably your strength and challenged me into getting in the action. Are you aware how much you have changed in the past month. It makes me proud to be your friend."

"I owe it to you, sir."

"If you keep talking like this, Father will charge you some interest. We'd better move on and have dinner. I must warn you our doctor has instructed Madame to go light on cream, butter and spices for Father's own good."

"Did he?" Fitzgerald replied. "Well then, my darling, I should have warned you I gave Madame Padoue a day off and asked her sister Beatrice to replace her? I'm quite sure she totally ignores any instruction her sister had and, of course, it's too late to do something about it."

From the smirk on his face, I could swear he knowingly substituted one French cook with another only to enjoy the pleasure of savouring what life offers him, perhaps for the last time.

The conversation during our meal concerned a new perspective we could integrate in our projects. Before, Fitzgerald and I had only thought of having families find a better place outside London. Now, the joining of our efforts gave us the possibility of having them considering another option, changing continents as the orphan children would.

"I shall meet each family and present them with this option," said I. "I deem it necessary to hear what each member has to say before they decide since they shall have to depend even more on each other to overcome the unforeseen situations their new country will reveal."

"Well spoken, Woodrow," Fitzgerald said.

"When will you find the time to accomplish all you have imposed upon yourself?" asked Elizabeth.

"To-morrow, I shall start visiting the families and intend to continue during the evenings. I shall keep my nights for Tumblety and be at the London Hospital during the day."

"May I accompany you whilst visiting your families," Elizabeth asked.

"If your father sees no objection, I would be delighted."

"Why would I object? Together, you would come to a fairly accurate opinion on how each family reacts to the options they have."

"When shall we begin?" Elizabeth asked. "I do not work to-morrow."

"Then I shall pick you up at your place round ten in the morning if it suits you."

"Perfect. That will give me enough time to catch some hours of sleep."

"If you excuse me, I need to rest a bit," Fitzgerald said. "I bid you good night."

"Good night sir. I also must leave you. A long night awaits me."

"Let me walk you to the door, Woodrow," Elizabeth said.

She took my arm offering me another of her loving smiles. As I was about to cross the doorstep, she looked at me, came closer and kissed me on my right cheek whilst holding both of my hands with hers. "Be careful."

Much too shy to even lay my lips on her forehead, I could only tell, "I shall, I promise," and left.

Timothy was by the horse, waiting for me. He had harnessed it to a peculiar looking costermonger's barrow instead of using the coach and was letting it feed itself some oats from one of his hands. "We won't look obnoxious with the cart," he said without taking his eyes off the horse. I approached him, having to speak to him before we left.

"You know, Timothy, don't feel insulted by what I will say, but if you prefer, I could manage on my own."

"A good man you really are, Mister Reily. It is not only Mister Fitzgerald's choice to have me with you but mine as well. This mad man has to be stopped, and I would be privileged to lend you a hand."

"I appreciate it, Timothy," I told him as I put a warm and thankful hand on his shoulder.

We jumped on the cart sitting side to side. "One last question before we leave. I know you only by your first name. What is your family name?"

"O'Conner, Timothy O'Conner. My friends call me Timmy."

"If I had friends, maybe one of them would call me Woody."

"If you let me become a friend of yours, I shall then call you Woody."

"Well Timmy, off we go."

He snapped his whip in the air making it crack and headed for Whitechapel under the rain.

SUNDAY, SEPTEMBER 30, 1888

It was almost midnight when I decided Timothy and I should split after having gone around together through the streets of Whitechapel. Oddly enough, we left the barrow at a stable on Buck's Row, the exact same stable in front of which Polly Nichols was found dead a month before.

"My brother, Brian, works here," Timothy told me.

"Ever since the murder, he finds it difficult to cross

the gate and hopes to find a job elsewhere."

"I feel sorry for him. I am still upset with that particular crime as well. Not only did it happen only streets away from where I work but also where I live."

"We've all been touched in a different manner by these events, haven't we? But now we have a direct and common concern."

"Just in case something goes wrong, how will you know?"

"You won't see me, but I will arrange for me to always have you in my sight. You can signal me when needed, and I shall come. Just tip your hat back and I shall understand."

"Fine with me. I think of going South of Commercial Road then up a little West past Spitalfields' Market."

"I'll be right near you."

I walked down on Cannon Street, and although it was slightly raining, there were still many people on the streets, most of them having no other choice.

Misfortunate women of the night at least had the chance of taking advantage of the rain, their clients quickly deciding to indulge themselves with whatever charms they were offered. Once I had reached James Street, I decided to start zigzagging up. At the corner Fairclough and Berner, I noticed a rather tall woman, standing alone. As with many others I met, I went to warn her of the danger of staying too far away from the protective light of the lamp posts. She obviously detected I was not a potential client and even asked if I were a disguised policeman, which I denied with a smile. She accepted my invitation to walk her closer to the lights on the corner of Berner Street. She told me her name was Elizabeth but was known as 'Long Liz' on the streets because of her height. We saw a shop still opened and had a look at the fruit on display in the window. Her eyes opened wide at the sight of fresh grapes.

"My dear man, how much for your grapes?" I asked.

"Six pence a pound the black 'uns, sir, and four the white 'uns," he responded.

"Which will you have," I asked, "black or white? I shall offer you whichever you like best."

She pointed at the dark red ones.

"Give us half a pound of those red ones."

He passed me the grapes through an opened half-window as I paid him. Crossing the street, I took a few and told her to keep the rest. Minutes later, I left her, knowing she would prefer the coppers of a client to my conversation. A constable walked by us on the other side of the street lending to believe she would be safe. I bid her good night.

Once on Hanbury Street, again I went up and down streets on both sides. Everything looked as normal Whitechapel could be. I turned left on Commercial Street until I reached Phoenix Street and came down on Norton Folgate where I felt we should stop and rest. It was way past two in the morning and I had been walking close to three hours, protected by Timothy, my invisible angel. I knew there were pubs near the market but decided to go on Widegate Street where it would be less crowded. I tipped my hat, and within seconds, Timothy was at my side.

I only had to look at the Kings Stores Pub's door to find out he had understood my intentions with a smile. We had barely started refreshing ourselves, I with a tea, Timmy preferring a gin when two men ran inside yelling.

"e's did it again," said the first one. "Two of 'em this time," said the other.

Questions were pouring out from everyone. "What, two? Where, when?" "Did someone see 'im?" No one could answer these questions. All the two men knew was that two other women were killed in Whitechapel.

Timothy and I looked at each other both feeling all we had done had been useless.

"Only one way to look at this," he told me face down and clenching his teeth. "We didn't do it." He raised his glass as a toast to the victims adding, "May their souls rest in peace," then emptied it in a single gulp. "We should go home now," I said.

BERNARD BOLEY

4 THE EVENTS OF OCTOBER 1888

MONDAY, OCTOBER 1, 1888

By ten this morning, I was outside my flat waiting for Elizabeth. The few hours I slept gave me some energy, but I still had a want for it. Minutes later, she arrived. I jumped in the coach and was so much marveled by her beauty, I almost knocked my head on the moulding of the coach's door.

"Woodrow, it's awful," she said. "Timothy told us about the two other victims. He managed to learn it was two women. You must be devastated."

"To say the least," said I, still contemplating her. "We'll get the London Daily News. It will give us more than we want to know."

Timothy drove by the first news-stand he knew where I picked the Daily. Its front page covered almost exclusively last night's crimes.

"Listen to this, Elizabeth. 'Two dreadful murders were committed yesterday morning in or near the East End. In one case a woman was found in a yard in Berner Street, Commercial-road, with her head nearly severed from her body. In the other case, a woman was found in Mitre-square, Aldgate, within the City jurisdiction, with her throat cut from ear to ear, and the body mutilated in a way that reproduced the worst features of the murder of Annie Chapman. Both the victims were women of low life. The body found in Berner Street has been identified as that of Elizabeth Stride. Late last night a man was arrested on suspicion at a lodging-house in the Borough.' My God! He killed her."

"Killed who?"

"The women I spoke to last night. Her name was Elizabeth Stride. Timothy and I were on Berner Street.

The murderer probably saw me talking to her while I was offering her some grapes. A constable also saw us together and will certainly consider me as the potential murderer. The same goes for the merchant from whom I bought the grapes. Now I'm in dire staits and probably the most serious suspect the police could ever find."

"Calm down. We know it's not you. You were with Timothy, your alibi."

I frantically went through all the articles trying to find more details. "I feel responsible for her death. I should have stayed with her. Now she's dead. Oh God!"

"What?"

I was struck dumb, and had difficulty in finding my words.

"When they found her body, they said that her right hand was tightly clasping the grapes I had just given her. It means it only happened minutes after we parted. I can't believe it; the murderer slipped through me and Timothy."

"Enough of this," she said taking the paper out of my hands and throwing it to the floor. "Not only will you ruin our day but even worse, you are about to lose your mind if you keep going on like this. Forget it for the moment, I beg you. You got a witness no one will challenge, and remember why we are here together. We have some fine families to meet, and I can't wait for you to present them to me."

I looked at her. She did not seem to be angry but rather reassuring. Preferring not to respond, I took a deep breath, and gave Timothy the address of the first family on our list we would visit. "Timmy, bring us to Pelham Street, 27."

Elizabeth smiled. Once arrived, I helped Elizabeth get out and gave the Weekly to Timothy.

"Have a look, Timmy. Your eyes won't believe what's written. Maybe we could talk about it later. We're here for an hour or so."

"Woodrow, please," said Elizabeth frowning at me.

"Well, someone has to keep the fire burning. Don't worry, I am totally devoted to our visit and to you."

It would be the first time Elizabeth would set foot in the living quarters of the people of London's East End.

The thirty children she was taking care of all came from a single orphanage, Saint Mary's to be precise. She did not know what was to be expected with a single family nevertheless, she believed it would be a scaled-down version of where she lived meaning smaller rooms, less furniture and accessories. The first family we would meet presented her with a vision of reality she could not even imagine existed. They had given up their youngest child at the orphanage for adoption and reclaimed her soon after. They lived only one street behind Hanbury Street where Annie Chapman had been killed. I dared not mention it to Elizabeth. I knocked on the door. Nobody answered. I knocked again, waited a moment and turning the knob I entered. She looked at me surprised by my rather intrusive behaviour.

"It's simply a signal letting all know someone is entering the building," I told her. "Follow me, you shall quickly understand."

Once the doorstep crossed, she noticed the peculiar arrangement of the interior. What came to her first was the corridor leading to what seemed an opened room at the end and a staircase to the upper floors on her left. On each side of the corridor were two closed doors.

"The kitchen is over there at the end of the corridor," said I. "The Skeet family lives in the second room to your right."

"One family in a single room!" she said.

"Yes, all five members of the family. There are four families on this floor, two on each of the others. Some fifteen to twenty people live in the other rooms but are not part of a family."

"No drawing room?"

"The main kitchen is the equivalent of a drawing room for all the tenants. I understand your uneasiness but try not to show you're in one of these places for the first time. They are very poor yet they still have their pride."

I knocked on the door of the room. A lovely little girl answered.

"Well if it isn't my darling Catherine. How are you, child?" I asked.

"Daddy, daddy, the nice man is back."

"Mister nice man," said Elizabeth with an evident mockery. "Isn't that charming!"

"Someone has to be the nice man from time to time,"

I said with a naughty smile. "I suppose it is my turn."

It definitely felt good to have a child say I was 'the nice man'. I glanced inside and saw her father lying on the only bed the room had. It was a typical Whitechapel house room measuring no more than nine by five feet. In the left side back corner, a young boy was sitting on a chair, sleeping with his head resting on one of its arms.

"Good day Desmond," I softly said not to awaken the boy.

"Mister Reily, come in," Desmond said as he rose from the small bed. "Welcome again to our home."

"Your wife Judith is not with you?"

"The missus is in the kitchen giving Sarah a bath."

I entered, Elizabeth following behind me. The room was rather dark, light coming only from a small window covered with soot.

"Desmond, may I introduce to you Miss Elizabeth Fitzgerald. She and I work together on the project we both spoke about last week. This is Mister Desmond Skeet, one of Spitalfields Market's finest fishmongers."

He was rather embarrassed to see her, nervously wiping his right hand on his trousers to clean it as a man of his trade would do before shaking hands but then put both hands behind his back pulling his shoulders back proud as a Yeoman Warder. Elizabeth came close to him and offered hers without hesitating.

"Mister Skeet, I am so pleased to meet you."

He had to respond to her move and gave his, which she immediately covered with her other making him feel more comfortable. Looking at the children she then said,

"What beautiful children you have." Even dressed as a lady, she wanted him to feel as if she was, in a certain way, part of the family.

"You've just met Kate," he said, "Over there is Henry. Henry, wake up. We've got visitors."

She went towards the boy who was slowly rubbing his eyes with his little closed fists. She bent down and offered him her hand. "Hello Henry. My name is Lizzy." He took her hand obviously shaking a lady's gloved hand for the first time in his life.

"We should all go in the kitchen; we'll have more room to sit," Desmond said.

As Elizabeth was leaving, she quickly looked one more time inside the room. Her eyes had become used to its darkness and could now notice the absence of any form of decoration on the walls. The colours had faded so much with time that one could hardly guess what they were originally. On a makeshift table in the opposite corner where the chair was, she saw an old pewter candlestick holding a half burned candle. The bed was placed between these two pieces of furniture, its mattress made of canvas probably filled with straw hosting more lice than the London Hospital could hold people. Looking down on the wooden stained floor, she caught a glimpse at what could be all their belongings hidden under the bed.

It was what they called 'home'.

We were lucky. Judith was alone in the kitchen with her youngest child wiping him dry with an old yet clean towel anyone else in Elizabeth's world would call a rag.

She smiled at us as we came in.

"Mister Reily, what brings you here?"

"We have a second proposition to make for the betterment of your family," I said, "and would like all of us have a look at it together."

As we all sat, I introduced Judith to Elizabeth, who took Sarah in her arms smelling the clean and soft skin of the baby as if it was a rose.

"May I hold her for a while?" she asked Judith.

"Of course you can. As long as you wish," she said.

I explained to Judith and Desmond the offer covering every possible aspect.

"I'm worried about the chances I would have of finding a job in my trade," Desmond pointed out explaining his current situation.

"Since the loss of two fingers on my left hand, not only I was never compensated, but I even lost my job.

And I am right-handed! Poor Nancy has to work as a part-time charwoman. How can it be different across the sea?"

"We would make sure before you leave that a job will be waiting for you as well as a real home for you to live in," I answered. "Someone over there shall be in contact with you and us to help you in any capacity."

"And we would not suffer from being Catholics," said Judith.

"May I?" Elizabeth asked me. I nodded. "Do not fear. You would be set up in a community composed of a majority of French Canadian and Irish Catholics. She looked at us then bringing her head down closer to the infant, and said, "You would be as safe there as Sarah is in my arms here."

Listening to her words, all of us could not help but notice Sarah had fallen into a deep sleep holding one of

Elizabeth's fingers with her hand. No more than five minutes later, they favoured the new offer giving

Elizabeth and I the signal to leave.

By the end of the day, we had visited five other families. With each one, Elizabeth had a way with a few simple words of making them more than comfortable with the proposition we had for them to decide upon. She was fascinating. She confessed to me that the only children she was involved with were the few she had met in an orphanage. Hence, her knowledge of poverty and distress came only through the words of Victor Hugo's Les Misérables. To-day, she had seen the children of the East End streets and became aware of the miserable condition of the families.

"Did you know that many outside the East End consider the death of those poor women murdered to be the normal and logical extension of the life conditions they implicitly agreed upon?" I asked her.

"How dare they say such stupidities? What you have shown me is nothing less than proof of their own responsibility. Their lack of understanding the unfortunates and their fear of them are the real cause. It has condemned these people to an existence we would refuse to live."

Once back at the coach, Timothy informed me that

police authorities decided to add more of their people patrolling the streets of Whitechapel some even disguised as women. Many were wearing boots with rubber soles and heels instead of hobnailed leather to avoid any noise their steps would make. We agreed that it would hence be unlikely for the killer to manifest himself this coming night and would have a full night to rest.

Elizabeth offered me dinner at her father's home, but completely knackered, I refused. However, I offered a compromise by riding back with her after which Timothy would bring me to my place.

Before she got off the coach, we looked at each other, but could not find a single word to wish us good-bye. I brought my lips slowly closer to hers and kissed them. I could feel her warm fingers reaching for the back of my neck expressing her tender response to my now daring embrace. It lasted only seconds but felt like this unreachable eternity one aspires to live with his loved one. I watched her climb the stairs, and as she opened the door, her head turned offering me again her lovely smile before disappearing inside.

TUESDAY, OCTOBER 2, 1888

The utmost urgent thing for me to do was getting an early edition of the papers to find more about the murders. The Daily News was the first one I could manage to grab from the paper boys on the streets. As I feared, the woman killed on Berner was the one to whom I had offered grapes, Elizabeth Stride, '… familiarly known as Long Lizzie', said the paper.

If Tumblety had seen me walking the streets, I thought, he would possibly have guessed I was hunting him. Perhaps he intentionally killed her only to signal his presence hence punishing me for doing so, and then went on to attack his next victim expecting to satisfy his morbid quest for female organs. Would he try to kill me if I insist on catching him? The odds were against me. I was one of the last persons, if not the last, who saw the victim alive, and a constable could possibly identify me. I could easily become a serious suspect providing Tumblety with a perfect alibi which would only require from him to report me to the police.

I kept reading without paying attention to where I was going and barely avoided a hurrying cab as I was crossing Whitechapel Road. Elizabeth was right; I was losing my mind, and these initial signs of paranoia were telling me that my blind stubbornness could even be a threat to my own life. I had to regain control and be as cunning as he was, for this mad man now had the nerve to send a letter to the Central News Agency. It had been sent on September 25 and forwarded to Scotland Yard who had refused to have it released to the public until this day. It bore the terrifying signature of 'Jack the Ripper'.

> *25th Sept.*
> *Dear Boss,*
> *I keep on hearing the police have caught me, but they won't fix me just yet. I have laughed when they look so clever and talk about being on the right track. That joke about Leather Apron gave me real fits. I am down on ---, and I shan't quit ripping them till I do get buckled. Grand work, the last job was. I gave the lady no time to squeal. How can they catch me now? I love my work, and want to start again. You will soon hear of me with my funny little games. I saved some of the properred stuff in a ginger-beer bottle over the last job, to write with, but it went thick like glue, and I can't use it. Red ink is fit enough, I hope. Ha! ha!The next job I do I shall clip the lady's ears off, and send to the police-officers, just for jolly,*

wouldn't you? Keep this letter back till I do a bit more work, then give it out straight. My knife's so nice, and sharp, I want to get to work right away if I get a chance. Good luck

Yours truly,

JACK THE RIPPER.

Don't mind me giving the trade name.

Wasn't good enough to post this before I got all the red ink off my hands; curse it. No luck yet. They say I'm a doctor now. Ha! Ha!

Hoax or real, this letter fed me with a new energy as it would probably henceforth do the same with sensational journalism. However, my failure to capture Tumblety during these past days indicated the need for me to reconsider my methods of laying hands on him. I would have to wait till the end of the day before exploring new possibilities. With these two additional deaths, Fillmore would obviously ask me to attend the inquiries which I dreaded to do for I was convinced it could compromise my chances of capturing Tumblety. If ever a person in the audience or even a witness such as the merchant from whom I bought the grapes recognized me as having been in the proximity of Berner Street, I would have to explain publicly my presence on the scene of the murder. If anyone suspected me of being the murderer, Timothy, my guardian angel, would obviously support my version of the facts. However, I believed Tumblety to be the kind of killer highly interested in reading every article in the press pertaining to the murders. He would learn from them how well he performed and infer any action the police or the public could take. I would not provide him with any advantage over me and had to remain out of the limelight.

Sure enough, when Fillmore entered the laboratory, he looked at me and only had to say these few words, "I imagine you know what you have to do."

"Professor, if I may?"

"What?" he said looking at me irritated by the mere fact I asked a question.

"Perhaps we should not distance ourselves from any insinuation or misleading opinion the voluble Baxter will undoubtedly express, and abstain from attending the inquest?" I said with my head down pretending I was looking for something on my desk.

"Normally, I would agree with you. We know how much he will invest on comments bringing him the attention of the public regardless of the soundness of their content. But when he met the sub-curator of the Pathology Museum after the Chapman inquiry regarding a request to purchase of organs, I was also present. I suggested him a certain degree of prudence in the wording of his remarks in such a way to avoid any form of witch hunting upon any specific group of persons. We should fear no more from him hence you shall attend the inquest. One last thing. From now on, I shall ask you to restrain from questioning my decisions. If there is someone constantly aware of the need to protect the Hospital's notoriety, it is surely me."

"I shall do as you wish, sir," I said picking up a pencil and pad from my desk and leaving for the inquest. I had to hurry for the inquiry was scheduled for eleven at the Vestry Hall in Cable Street. Fortunately for me, neither Inspector Abberline nor Sergeant Thick were attending. I was not sure, however, if the grape merchant would be called as a witness, or even if he was already sitting amongst the audience having only glanced at him on Berner Street. As a result, I took extreme precautions not to draw attention from anyone.

Although many have identified the body of the victim as that of Elizabeth Stride, it was not yet officialized. No relative had properly done so during this first session.

The testimonies of this day would bear nor impact on neither me nor the Hospital. The only witnesses heard from were those attending a meeting in a building next to the crime scene, including the man who had discovered the body.

I returned to the laboratory around five. I stayed unusually late. Not because of my work but to benefit from its rather isolated location more suitable than any other place for me to reflect on my eventual approach to capture Tumblety.

On a sheet of paper, I wrote down a two-column list, the first containing everything I knew about Tumblety, the second all the unanswered questions I had.

On the latter, I underlined what deemed important to me such as where he lived in London, how he spent his time, with whom. I, however, remembered him inviting me to a place on Cleveland Street but knew nothing more, and added this fact in the 'Known' column. He had never spoken a word concerning certain aspects a man of his age and condition would usually bring into a conversation, his family, the possibility for him of being married with children, his close friends amongst other subjects. I was still at a deadlock as to the motives triggering him into killing, but felt that choosing his victims amongst women who would say yes to any demand a client made surely reinforced a need he probably had to dominate, women in particular. They were not so much his targets as his instruments, the vectors of his power. Out of cleverness or pure luck, he was still free, which would no doubt fuel even more this power enticing him into killing again. What could he lose? Would he be hung differently if he committed ten murders and mutilated them all? "Certainly not," I thought. Then, there shall be more.

As for the former list, it could eventually provide me with clues. He had mentioned the Army during the Civil

War, his presence in field hospitals, his research with organs. His flamboyant dressing, height and other physical characteristics were provided him with a rather interesting personality but could as well be his way of hiding what he really was. Fillmore presented him as a man interested by chemicals found in plants, talked about his practice in Canada and in the United States. He seemed to have given a great importance to whores. I knew now what he meant by taking care of them, all his victims being low women. The mere fact he committed these crimes directly on the streets rather than in secluded areas letting everyone see how devastating his stabbings were illustrated the little importance, respect or value he gave to women.

I correlated together elements of both lists. It became clear to me that I should learn from his past by getting in contact with those who knew him and find if he behaves in a similar manner and in similar places in London. Once in these new places, I could seek for people who have seen him and try to track him down. I would again ask Fitzgerald for his advice and help.

The word 'organs' of my first list kept ringing to my ears without me being able to figure anything out of it. It angered me for almost every word heard or spoken close to me always evoked a series of references or souvenirs of sounds, images, doors or flavours but this time the word 'organs' left me completely cold. I circled it and let it rest hoping something would come to my mind in the upcoming days.

It was ten o'clock. I hadn't eaten yet and was tired but went home quite satisfied with my evening's work. To-morrow could be a day of promises and deceptions at the inquiry, but I hoped it would not make me regret being there.

WEDNESDAY, OCTOBER 3, 1888

Two days after Elizabeth Stride's death, Mary Malcolm, her sister, brought an end to the question of the victim's identity. She did not recognize the body as that of her sister the first time she saw it at the mortuary, only having a presentiment of her death by feeling a pressure on her breast and hearing three distinct kisses. An adder bite on her sister's right leg had left a black mark turned out to be a positive way for her to confirm her identity. She indicated her sister was regularly in want of money and obtained two shillings every visit she made to her on Sundays. She was also into drinking to such an extent she was arrested many times and fined.

Doctor Frederick William Blackwell, physician and surgeon, testified he was called to Berner Street by a policeman and arrived at 1.16 a.m. followed some twenty minutes later by Doctor George Baxter Phillips, the same examiner as in Chapman's death. No mention was made by Blackwell as to the possible removal of an organ from the victim's body.

Presuming Doctor Phillips would go further into the details of her injuries, Phillips, nevertheless, gave a blunt description sufficient enough to establish a link with the manner by which the four previous victims were murdered. He pointed out that, "In the neck, there was a long incision which exactly corresponded with the lower border of the scarf she wore. The border was slightly frayed, as if by a sharp knife. The incision commenced on the left side, two inches below the angle of the jaw, and almost in a direct line with it, nearly severing the vessels on that side, cutting the windpipe completely in two, and terminating on the opposite side one inch below the angle of the right jaw, but without severing the vessels on that side." His testimony ended the first day of inquiry at the end of which I wrote a short note to

Fillmore informing him that the Coroner seemed to have kept his word, not even coming within a hair's breadth of the subject of the hospital or its staff.

I stopped at a pub across the street from the hospital for a bite and some tea. My endeavour to find Tumblety, I now considered to be Jack the Ripper had taken much of my spare time to the detriment of the families and orphans the Fitzgeralds and I were concerned about. The Skeet family was only but one of those asking for guaranties before crossing over to Canada, and we considered it to be easily understandable. For if they were living in hell or close to its gates to say the least, the presence of the devils of Whitechapel was foreseeable even to them. They knew the streets, the people and managed to assume all the appropriate behaviours needed to survive. A new land meant a new city, town or borough and within this unknown place were new people and a new set of unwritten rules to abide by or suffer from. Here, the causes of sufferance were known whilst most of the remedies were within their scope. There, across the ocean, they would most likely have to start all over. We had placed all of them on a threshold beyond which their hell could seem to be a sweeter choice than that of another land. Waging their lives on an unknown future was the decision they had to make. The stories they had heard about the Irish immigrants in New York being considered no more no less than a pale but otherwise equally despicable version of the American nigger didn't help in its making.

It was now up to me to obtain these guaranties by sending telegrams to agencies, employers, vicars only to name a few describing the families, the skills they possessed, giving references and endorsements. I had thirty families for which I would muster up a quite different and more gratifying form of energy than what the Ripper required of me.

Many of the pub's patrons were engaged in animated if not emotional conversations on the recent murders. They all agreed on the ineptitude of the Commissioner of the Metropolitan Police, Sir Charles Warren, and his condescending attitude towards the East Enders who, in his mind, had fomented the previous year's bloody riot. From time to time, I glanced at them. No more than a month ago they were only people living around me. Now, they are as much my people as I belong to them. In what seems as a distant past, I used to experience a strong discomfort in sitting in a pub. It has yielded its place to a sentiment of personal pride by simply being in their presence. The words of my telegrams could never have been fed by a better source of inspiration than this East End pub. Westminster, with all its self-centered eloquence, could learn a great deal by holding its sessions in such a noble place for it is the place of the true people not only of Whitechapel or London but all over England.

On my way back at the laboratory, I started wondering if Fillmore would be asking me those silly questions strictly related to the hospital's image without expressing any concern about the victims. In the hallway, a young boy ran in front of me forcing me to stop.

"You're Mister Reily aren't ye?" the boy asked. "Yes," I said.

"I've been told to wait fo' ye all day if necessary and deliva this note personally to ye. The man said to wait for your answer."

His left hand held up the letter whilst the other was opened meaning the boy was expecting some sort of tip on my behalf.

I opened it and hadn't it been for the boy's presence, I would have almost run for my office as I had immediately recognized the sender's handwriting as

Tumblety's. I could not believe what was written.

My dear young friend,

Might you be interested in having dinner with me to-morrow? We have already postponed it but now seems a good time. Give your answer to the boy. If you accept my invitation, I will pick you up at six at the Hospital.

Francis Tumblety

I was astonished. I've been searching him for days without any luck, and he had the nerve of contacting me for some frivolous activity. If he was the Ripper, why was he doing this? He must be completely out of his mind. I could have him arrested or even finish it with him as I had promised myself to do. There was something I could not figure out.

"So?" said the boy.

"What?" I said.

"Yer answer?"

If I accepted, I could learn more, confront him, see how he reacts and then, decide what to do from there on.

"Tell him I accept. There you go young man," I said giving him some coins.

As he ran away, I looked around to see if Tumblety would have been foolish enough to watch my reaction from inside the Hospital. Nowhere could I recognized his distinguishable hat or mustache.

At the office, I wrote two notes before attending the continuation of Elizabeth Stride's inquest at Vestry Hall.

The first one I had sent by messenger to Fitzgerald informed him of the situation and of my planned whereabouts for the day. The other gave Fillmore the progression of the inquiry reassuring him, by the same token, that nothing to this day had tarnished the hospital's reputation.

On this third day, four witnesses confirmed Elizabeth Stride's identity, including Michael Kidney, a waterside labourer who lived with her on 38, Dorset Street, Spitalfields. He believed her disappearance four days prior to her death could have been another occurrence of her occasional absences, although he expected it to last no more than a few hours.

A young boy, Thomas Coram, had been called as a witness, him having found on Whitechapel Road a 9 to 10 inch long bladed knife the handle of which was wrapped in a blood-stained handkerchief. I was disappointed for he had not given any further description of the knife, its length being the sole aspect that could relate it to the knife Tumblety had stolen from the hospital.

Doctor George Baxter Phillips gave the jury his description of the way the body was positioned on the street.

"Her body was lying on its left side, the face being turned towards the wall, the head towards the yard, and the feet toward the street. The left arm was extended from elbow, and a packet of cachous was in the hand. Similar ones were in the gutter. I took them from the hand and gave them to Dr. Blackwell. The right arm was lying over the body, and the back of the hand and wrist had on them clotted blood. The legs were drawn up, feet close to wall, body still warm, face warm, hands cold, legs quite warm, silk handkerchief round throat, slightly torn. I produce the handkerchief. This corresponded to the right angle of the jaw. The throat was deeply gashed, and there was an abrasion of the skin, about an inch and a quarter in diameter, under the right clavicle. On October 1, at three p.m., at St. George's Mortuary, Dr. Blackwell and for part of the time Dr. Reigate and Dr. Blackwell's assistant, Dr. Blackwell and I made a post-mortem examination. Dr. Blackwell kindly consented to make the dissection, and I took the following note: 'Rigor mortis' still firmly marked. Mud on face and left side of the head. Matted on the hair and left side. We removed the clothes. We found the body fairly nourished. Over both shoulders, especially the right, from the front aspect under collar bones and in front of chest there is a bluish discolouration which I have watched and seen on two occasions since. On neck, from left to right, there is a clean cut incision six inches in length; incision commencing two and a half inches in a straight line below the angle of the jaw. Three-quarters of an inch over undivided muscle, then becoming deeper, about an inch dividing sheath and the vessels, ascending a little, and then grazing the muscle outside the cartilages on the left side of the neck. The carotid artery on the left side and the other vessels contained in the sheath were all cut through, save the posterior portion of the carotid, to a line about 1-12th of an inch in extent, which prevented the separation of the upper and lower portion of the artery. The cut through the tissues on the right side of the cartilages is more superficial, and tails off to about two inches below the right angle of the jaw. It is evident that the hemorrhage which produced death was caused through the partial severance of the left carotid artery."

He gave no indication regarding any extensive mutilation or removal of organs as it had occurred with the three previous deaths hence, at this point, the murderer could have been anybody.

Asked by the Coroner what the cause of death was, Phillips answered, "Undoubtedly the loss of blood from the left carotid artery and the division of the windpipe."

No other witness having been called, the inquiry was adjourned until Friday, at two o'clock. As I walked out, I couldn't avoid observing those who had probably attended the inquest out of mere boredom. If they expected it to be entertaining, the look on their faces revealed an otherwise obvious feeling of disgust. As promised, Tumblety was waiting for me.

"There you are," he said with is usual charming smile.

"Good day sir."

"Let me have a look at you," Tumblety said. "I don't want to seem rude, but we can't let you go dressed up like that. They won't let us in."

"Who won't let us in? Where? Why?" I was already pumped up by the potential outcome of our meeting, and now he was adding even more constraints.

"You'll understand later. In the meantime, we'll make a short stop and see what we can do. Trust me, It's not that your dress-up looks shabby, its more like a question of protocol or etiquette amongst those we may meet."
"But, but, I cannot afford such an expense and think we should forget about our dinner," I muttered.

"I'll personally take care of everything. I insist," was his answer.

His words left me with mixed feelings. A bit humiliated in showing Tumblety how destitute I was, but mostly upset in giving him the opportunity to impose himself upon me. He gave the cab driver an address and once there asked him to wait for us. It was a tailor's shop he knew. Some thirty minutes later, I came out wearing a new frock, waistcoat, shirt, collar and cuffs, trousers, shoes as well as some accessories deemed to be appropriate by Tumblety. It must have cost him well over 5 £. He took a rather unusual wallet from one of his pockets. It contained a small pouch section he emptied in his hand to pay the tailor. Out came coins and two small old brass rings which he quickly put back in looking up all around to see if anyone had noticed it. I turned my head away as if I didn't care about what he just had done but immediately remembered Chapman's two missing brass rings mentioned earlier during the day at the enquiry.

"Now we're ready," Tumblety said as he left the store, and he climbed up the cab. "The evening is ours to enjoy."

Minutes later, we quickly passed by what I believed to be Piccadilly Circus and went for some street behind it. Suddenly, the cab stopped.

"We'll walk the rest of the way," said Tumblety as he opened the door to let me out.

We went through a poorly lit courtyard. Nevertheless, the mere fact of being in the West End gave me a minimal sentiment of security. Well placed limestones in the recent brick masonry of some of the buildings showed me that the owners maintained their property in a more than an acceptable state. Still, nothing led me to expect the presence of a restaurant or any other commercial establishment for that matter. On the left side where Tumblety was heading, I noticed an arched cast iron gate at the entrance of one of the buildings. A small brass statue was set at the top of the arch. It was that of a naked man. I must admit I was somewhat chocked by such an ornament, which immediately drew a smile on Tumblety's face.

"It's a miniature reproduction of Michaelangelo's famous statue of David. You certainly remember the young man who triumphed over Goliath in the Ancient Testament don't you?"

"Oh! Not Really." I answered, my ignorance now adding to my embarrassment.

"Come, It's right here."

As we approached our meeting place, I noticed a rather surprising door knocker. The struck plate was a definite reminder of the arch's statue, a male's naked torso. The bottom portion of the plate was obviously missing, a more recent piece of brass having been added. Looking at the knocker itself, two extended arms whose joined hands were designed to hit the plate, I could easily imagine what the original plate offered to those metal hands and preferred not making any comment. He dropped them three times, waited a moment then again, twice this time. The door opened almost instantly. A tall remarkably well-dressed man facing us looked at Tumblety, smiled then at me and without pronouncing a single word let us in.

We gave our coats and hats to a rather young boy at the cloakroom.

The moment I entered what Tumblety had said to be a restaurant, it became quite obvious that there was more to it. The entrance hall was sober although intricately carved mahogany panelings covering all the walls revealed the refinement of its owners. Doors on both sides led to what I believed to be parlours. I only had a glimpse of their interiors since we hastily walked down the hallway. Their bright colours, however, contrasted with those we passed by. As for the hallway, the bottom section which I was later told to be designated as a wainscots were also made of mahogany. The colours of the wallpaper lightened the atmosphere and would soon introduce me to the more extravagant décor of the main hall.

It was as if we had entered a completely different world.

"What is this place?" I asked Tumblety. "You said we would have dinner in a restaurant but this..."

"I never mentioned a restaurant, my young friend, I said I'd have dinner with you, and we shall. It's much more than a restaurant. We are in a very private gentleman's club. Very few are accepted as members and I am one of these lucky ones."

"I heard someone mentioning the existence of these clubs, but I never expected them to be like this," I added looking all around me.

The main hall where I stood rose up all the height of

the three story building. The ceiling depicting a bright blue sky had clouds which added to the realism of its overall design. In the midst of the roof, a glass cupola would let the sun send its light in all directions. One ornament after another fascinated me. Gilded moldings and scagliola columns would have created a solemn atmosphere if it had not been for the statues set against the wall or in niches. They all represented young naked men and boys.

"Come, let us begin our evening by letting me offer you a drink," he added heading towards one of the two stairways. "Beware there is nothing more slippery than new leather soles on these marble stairs. I wouldn't want you to come down faster than you'd be going up," he added with a wink.

I held the handrail just in case, but I did not share his amusement given I was about to confront him. We entered the club's smoking room and sat at one of the tables. All the easy chairs were covered with a brown leather upholstery. I must say I never sat in something as comfortable as these. A servant immediately came to us addressing Tumblety.

"Good evening sir, may I offer you something?" "Certainly George, responded Tumblety. Woodrow my young friend, how about celebrating our common roots with a fine Irish whiskey?"

"As you wish. I probably need something strong enough to stir me up."

"Great. You may, however, be surprised by what our good Ireland can come up with. George do we still have some eighteen-year-old Irish elixir?"

"I believe we always keep some Bushmill or Jameson, sir."

"Bushmill it shall be, George."

I noticed the waiter going back to the bar paying more attention to those around us. As I glanced at them and listen to portions of their conversations, it became clear to me that this gentleman's club was private not because it would allow its members to share domains and issues which normally belonged to men, but to hide one questionable side of who they were. Many of them were expressing much more than the usual male friendship we generally observe. Some were dressed normally but would engage with others as if they were women. Some had high-pitched voices. Others kept gesticulating in a manner I considered to be exaggerated even annoying. Many older members left only minutes after their arrival accompanied by one of these boys. I believe one even said "Pick me instead" and felt disappointed by the member's refusal to do so. Again, I preferred restraining myself and making no comment regarding my observations. More urgent matters needed to be addressed.

"Is there something wrong? You seem worried. Did something happen? Tell me."

"Haven't you read the papers?"

"We all read the papers. Is there any particular topic disturbing you?"

"The Ripper murders."

"Oh! I'm not surprised at all by these events. Put too many rats in an enclosed space, reduce the food supply, and, soon enough, they shall start eating each other instead of protecting themselves as they normally do. Look at lemmings jumping off cliffs if there's an insufficient number of predators to regulate their population. Someone simply decided to take care in his own terms of the ongoing situation in the East End."

"Are you saying it's normal or acceptable for humans to act as animals?"

"I'm simply stating facts, my dear friend. You know as well as I do that everything concerning what is acceptable has always been decided by the strongest and imposed upon the weakest. Whatever domain you examine, family, military, religion or politics, history has taught us that and only that. There has never been any given as far back as I look."

"And you consider yourself amongst..."

"... the strongest," he replied before I even had the chance to place another word.

"Luckily, society catches up with the abusers and handles them appropriately," I replied determined to win this fencing duel we had just engaged in.

"Still the strongest manage to outwit them all," he said in a condescending tone.

"Is that what you are trying to do?"

"What are you insinuating?"

I could read anger in his eyes, but before he could let it out, we both noticed George, the waiter, coming back with our drinks. Although a truce implicitly took place, an end to a skirmish, what say I, a battle was to be expected.

"Thank you George. That will be all for the moment. Woodrow, I think this conversation is heading in the wrong and potentially dangerous direction. It would be better, even advisable for both of us to enjoy this fine whiskey. The least one can say about it is that you can't swallow it and talk at the same time. I choose not to talk so cheers!"

I had to admit there was something in this man that could simply throw you off in a second. He seemed used to this kind of situation and felt he was already savouring his victory. Convinced of the contrary and holding what I believed to be the high ground, I picked up my glass, brought to my nose and found it offered an odour no other whiskey ever gave. I took a sip and whilst I expected a sting announcing a form of resistance, it rather let itself be tamed and eased its way down my throat.

"I must agree it tastes good."

"Don't say I didn't warn you," he said offering me a friendly smile he probably hoped would calm me. "Now tell me. What's going on? Why this aggressive tone?"

"I believe I deserve some honest answers regarding your quest for female organs. Many disturbing coincidences and a missing surgical instrument at the laboratory are placing me in a more than delicate position."

"Really?"

"The day before the first woman was murdered, you told me you were about to obtain some organs. You even mentioned it would come from a prostitute. The following day, the papers come out with an article on a woman's horrible death and guess who, a prostitute. A little over a week later, another prostitute was murdered. Her uterus had been cut out. Hours later, you bring me a uterus after having asked me to be at the Hospital early to take care of organs you would bring me. Now add to this, Doctor Tumblety, that in the coroner's opinion, the murderer benefited from a great anatomical knowledge. Again, another prostitute is murdered with a long bladed knife. You remember the Liston amputation knife you were interested in when I prepared your bag in the dissecting room?"

"Let me see. I think so."

"A few days later, I noticed it was missing. No one else besides you and I have been there during that period. Doctor Phillips indicated to one of the coroners that he suspected the knife used in one case to have been a thin, narrow blade, at least six to eight inches in length. He also pointed out in his conclusion that a witness had said two brass rings were missing from Chapman's fingers, rings like the ones I noticed you had in your wallet. You certainly foresee the conclusions I am about to reach?"

"Please go on," he said maintaining a totally calm composure.

"To say the least, I believe the police could come to the conclusion I was an accomplice to the butchery. Someone is trying to set me up. By doing so, I would be forced to eventually help out the perpetrator of those crimes in any way it may suit him."

"I must admit you have quite an amusing imagination."

"Let me finish. This person would have managed to build a certain degree of trust, present himself as a charming, generous man without having to use many words. He must have used the same scheme with those poor women. Who do you think this man could be?" "The way you present it, it could only be me." He paused a second and looked strait to my eyes. "Are you accusing me of being the Ripper?"

"Prove me the contrary?"

Tumblety carefully looked around probably not to arouse any suspicion, sat way back in his seat and took another sip of whiskey.

"Don't you think that if I was the Ripper, I would have overseen the possibility of meeting someone as intelligent as he seems to be. Let's say someone like you for instance, who thinks he could figure out the whole puzzle after putting only a few pieces together. I would then have no other choice but to find a way to eliminate the threat he now had become knowing that he figured out everything. Do I need to add this would probably be carried out in the same manner the Ripper dealt with those women? I imagine you're already aware of this scenario."

"Go on," I told him.

"On the other hand, if you were totally wrong. You could easily imagine how insulted I would be in seeing someone attacking me in such a way. You would be compromising the true friendship I expected to see growing between us. All the career opportunities I could have offered you would never materialize. Don't you agree? One has to be either foolish or courageous to pursue the endeavour you have undertaken. Which one are you, my dear friend?"

"Time shall tell," I replied.

"In both cases, you could lose more than you think. Are you prepared to pay that high a price just to satisfy your curiosity?"

"I am well aware this could happen."

He looked at me, then added with a cynical smile, "Frankly, Woodrow, I wouldn't want to be walking in your shoes, however, new they may be."

"You think you can make fun of this? Real friends don't hide serious matters from each other. Yes, maybe I would lose someone I could have called a friend under other circumstances. Well let me stay in line with your words. At least, I would still be walking whereas if you murdered these women, you would be hanging. So tell me Doctor Tumblety, it's my turn to ask you. What shall it be, a lost friendship or a newly discovered murderer?"

My words infuriated him. He was about to respond when I noticed his eyes were aimed at something or someone behind me. The sound of footsteps heading towards us grew and also gained my attention. Suddenly before I could even turn my head to see who it might have been, I recognized Abberline's distinctive voice.

"Well, well, well, look who we have here Sergeant. If it isn't our young apprentice Reily and the famous Doctor Tumblety! I can't say I'm surprised to find you here Tumblety, but you, Woodrow. Its Woodrow isn't it?"

I turned my head and answered, "Yes inspector, Woodrow Reily."

Thick, his colleague, was with him. "Good evening

Sergeant," I added.

"Evening sir," said Thick tipping his hat.

"What are you doing here, Reily?" Abberline asked. "And with this man? You two know each other?"

"We met at the London Hospital and are currently working together on a research project of mine," Tumblety pointed out. "Aren't we Woodrow?"

"We are indeed," I replied.

"Do you know what kind of establishment this place is young man? What usually goes on here?" Abberline asked.

"I believe it's a private gentleman's club."

"One has to be bloody blind to use the word 'gentlemen'," he said. Looking at Sergeant Thick, he started laughing out loudly. "Gentle they may be, but men, I doubt it. Look at those two," he added pointing at two rather effeminate young boys holding hands by the bar.

I was shocked by what I saw.

"Do you mind telling me what brings you here Inspector?" I asked.

"Doing my job, Reily. In case you ignored it, the Whitechapel case isn't the only one I'm concerned with.

Overlooking morality issues is also part of my responsibilities, which is why I'm here."

"Oh I wasn't aware of all your tasks."

"Now when it comes to our common friend here, I'm also concerned with another kind of cases, the radicals of the Irish Republican Brotherhood. But then again, I haven't managed yet to find in which of these three categories he fits best, a person of interest in the Whitechapel murders, a perpetrator of illegal activities between men or an Irish conspirator."

"Woodrow, don't believe a word he says about me and the Fenian or about anything else for that matter.

Abberline and all the others of his kind know for a

fact that I'm innocent of any charge one would file against me."

"Since you helped out Thomas D'Arcy McGee, one of those 1848 Irish rebels," Abberline added looking at me but talking to Tumblety, "some thirty years ago in Canada, you managed to attract more attention than you expected didn't you Tumblety? Do you want me to remind you of all your past travels in various places in her Majesty's kingdom? Now isn't it a fact that you have been accused by mister Albert Fischer of... How should I put it? ...of misconducting yourself this past July and with other men in August."

"If you intend to charge us with anything or arrest us, do so, otherwise, I'll...,"

"Call in the police...," said Abberline bursting into laughter. "Thick, I believe Tumblety needs your help," he added moving back and sarcastically bowing to introduce his colleague.

"Don't worry yourself, we have no questions for either of you... at least for the moment." Thick said. "But since we enjoyed so much meeting you, maybe we should stay for a while with you."

"I think we should leave, Woodrow," Tumblety whispered to me. "We have some serious business to attend to. Don't you think?"

I hesitated before answering. It quickly came to me that both of us leaving at the same time presented an obvious risk of me being killed given the content of the conversation we had. He made it quite clear that I could represent a serious threat to him. Staying here alone with Abberline would even worsen the situation. Tumblety would certainly conclude I would reveal everything I knew. Abberline could also consider any word I'd say as a way for me to escape any suspicion, he or Thick could build up. Anger growing in me, brought to decide in favour of leaving. I stood up calmly; my right hand reached inside my trouser pocket and felt my pocket knife. Should the worst happen, I felt was ready to handle it.

"Let's leave," I told Tumblety looking at Abberline straight in the eyes.

Tumblety was just behind me. I made it quickly to the cloakroom. The young attendant had probably heard all the commotion since he had already my coat and hat in his hands ready for me to pick them up. I walked away from all three of them putting my hat on and quickly wrapping my coat on my left hand. I brought a sleeve closer to my neck to use it as a protection against any attack and went for the club's entrance door. I needed room to defend myself if it had to come to that. The courtyard would offer me better conditions to deal with Tumblety's intentions should he decide to act.

"Wait for me Woodrow," Tumblety yelled. "We need to finish our conversation."

But I had already crossed the club's door, pulled out my knife and unfolded its blade as fast as I could.

Suddenly, a voice shouted, "Over here." Was it someone calling Tumblety? An accomplice of his? Fighting against one was within my capacities, but two!

"We're over here at your left, It's us," the voice again called.

I examined the courtyard as I moved down the street. It was darker than when we arrived and couldn't figure where that voice came from. It seemed, however, familiar. Slowly, I began distinguishing the vague form of a coach and marched hastily in its direction. Looking behind me, I saw Tumblety still trying to catch up with me and increased my pace.

"Quick Woodrow, get in."

It was Timothy. Sitting at the driver's seat of Fitzgerald's coach, he held the door opened with one hand, firmly keeping the reins in the other. Without any hesitation, I jumped inside.

"Let's go, Timmy," I yelled closing the door. Taking my hat off, I glimpsed a human form sitting in front of me. It slowly moved towards me.

"Elizabeth!" I shouted whilst trying to catch my breath. "What are you doing here?"

"Now that's a silly question," she replied. "Would you prefer having me bring you back where you were?"

"It could have been dangerous for you."

"I presume that explains why you were running so fast unless you couldn't resist the idea of seeing me," she teased.

She hid her smile with both her hands hoping not to embarrass me, but her jumping shoulders gave her away.

I started laughing as well. Bringing down her hands to better hold them in mine, something different than her usual beautiful smile suddenly revealed itself to me.

"If something had happened to you..., I would,   I mean my father would have been in shambles," she muttered.

"And you?" I dared to demand.

She sighed but did not pronounce a word.

Timothy managed to have the galloping horses bring us quickly away throughout dark streets only he knew.

Minutes later, he slowed down letting us understand we were now safe. I told Elizabeth what had happened during my meeting with Tumblety, the exchange with inspector Abberline.

"The odds were against me," I told her. "I felt either Tumblety would try to get more out of me or Abberline possibly bring me in for interrogation."

"It would be better for you not to go back to your room to-night," she said. "You shall spend the night at our place."

"But..."

"Father was well aware this eventuality could occur

and would not consider any refusal from your part."

She mentioned Fitzgerald had shown her the note I had sent him. I understood from her that Timothy would stand close by just in case I had needed some help or a safe place to stay. However, she had managed to convince Timothy to let her accompany him without her father knowing it.

I decided to sit by her side and even took the risk of placing my arm around her shoulders. She offered no resistance and let her head down against mine. I wouldn't have minded if Timothy had driven the remaining of the night allowing Elizabeth and I to share these comforting silent moments.

Once back at Fitzgerald's home, Elizabeth led me to the room they had provided for me on the second floor.

It was at least three or four times the side of my own and well furnished. The bed was a large one with a high carved headboard. On one side of it stood a writing desk with all the accessories one would need, inkstand, pens, pencils and paper. On the other side, I noticed a white and blue porcelain basin and pitcher, a mug, a complete shaving set, a soap dish; all set on a marble top toilet cabinet. At its foot were a chamber and slop jar. Clean towels and chamber clothes had been placed on the rods of the table. A bevelled mirror held in a beautiful wooden frame had been set against the wall. Opposite to the bed, two gentleman's easy chairs separated by a small table invited the visitor to quietly read his daily paper or preferred books before going to bed. At the right of the chairs, a large mahogany wardrobe stood against the wall. I opened and found It containing a variety of suits, shirts, collars and shoes, all of very high quality. A night shirt had been laid out on the bed, most likely by one of the servants.

I undressed, freshened up before dropping on the bed for the night.

FRIDAY, OCTOBER 5, 1888

Around five o'clock, the repeating sound of someone knocking on my room door awakened me. I quickly got up put on a night robe and went to see who was making such commotion in the hallway. It was Fitzgerald, all dressed up and smiling.

"Sir, is everything alright?" I asked.

"Of course. And you? It seems you had quite an encounter last night. Tumblety and inspector Abberline. You're becoming popular."

"Maybe more than I can handle, I think"

"Trust me; you would be surprised to learn what you can accomplish if you gave yourself the chance. It took quite some courage to confront someone who could actually be Jack the Ripper."

"You seem to have some doubts concerning Tumblety being the murderer."

"Actually, based on what you came up with, I believe you have serious reasons of suspecting him. What I'm saying is that should he had been the murderer, he would not have hesitated to use on you the same methods the

Ripper is known for having used on his victims."

"I was ready and quite prepared to defend myself but Abberline still being close by would have given him

good reasons to believe I had something to do with all this."

"By now, he probably has. Hence, you must prepare yourselves consequently. I'll wait for you downstairs whilst you put something on."

Fifteen minutes later, a warm cup of tea was waiting for me.

"Taste some of this and tell me what you think of it," Fitzgerald said to me offering a dish. "Its called kedgeree."

"It has a curry flavour in it."

"It's made with flaked fish, rice, eggs and butter."
"This will feed me for the day."

"Now, we must examine our options. Tumblety has managed to avoid the police's attention. Why, do you think?"

"If, as Abberline mentioned last night, Tumblety is involved one way or the other with the radical branch of the Fenian movement, he may be presenting a greater threat to the nation. On the other hand, when I consider those who attended his club, the least I can say is that he is a man of questionable morality."

"What do you mean."

"What I'm suggesting is that he seems to have a strong preference towards men. The kind we express towards women. I doubt the Fenian would accept him if they knew about this."

"That, my friend, could become the best way to eliminate the threat he may be imposing upon you."

"One thing still leaves me wondering." "And what would that be, if I may ask?"

"Based on what you just revealed, why would he even bother killing women?"

"Perhaps he is intentionally trying to mislead everyone with his Fenian connection and the other people he meets at his club. It offers him the possibility to give way to his monstrous behaviour."

"I have to find out exactly who this Tumblety really is."

"You should then accept the idea of following each and every trail he leaves. You understand, don't you, that you might have to move around beyond the limits of London?"

"I know."

"At this point, I believe you should do the same he seems to have been doing, misleading the curious. Avoid bringing up the Whitechapel murders in any conversation. It otherwise might result in having others attempting to establish a link between you and these events. If Abberline tries to get in contact with you in order to discuss these matters, give him, however, an honest answer. But don't feed him with more than is asked."

"After my fleeing last night from the club, I believe it would be better for me not to wait for Abberline. I must meet him as soon as possible some time to-day but my job and my presence at the murder inquiries make it rather complicated."

"Let me take care of that for you. I know precisely who to contact at the hospital."

"I can easily imagine how Fillmore will react when I get back."

"Remember, it would not be advisable to provide Abberline with reasons to suspect you by telling everything you know. Don't worry to much about Tumblety. I asked Timothy to keep an eye on you which he gladly accepted. You must have made a good impression on him since it takes quite some time before he accepts those he usually considers as strangers."

"Normally, I should be attending the opening of the inquest on the death of Catherine Eddowes, considering it may become a question of interest for the Hospital. However, I believe meeting Abberline to be more important. Anyway, I'll find whatever could be pertinent in the papers in a day or two."

Minutes later, Timothy was waiting for me on the cab and drove me close to my place where I changed into something more appropriate. I then went to work realizing that my boring occupations would now relieve the tensions. Nevertheless, I was still in for surprises. Someone had delivered the package containing the clothes I had left at the club. An envelope was attached to it. The note inside read:

> *My dear young friend,*
>
> *There was no reason for you to run away like you did last evening. I would never have harmed you.*
>
> *However, at the present moment, I am in no position to give you any specific reason for you to think otherwise. A complex chess game is what you are engaged in and you have only discovered a few of the pieces on the board.*
>
> *Francis Tumblety*

Was he misleading me again? His note indicating something higher could be at stake convinced me even more into pursuing the truth. Meeting Abberline would certainly help me achieving that goal of mine. As I came out of the Hospital, I noticed, to my surprise, Timothy was still there.

"Ready to go to the Yard, sir... I mean Woodrow?" he asked.

"You were waiting for me?"

"Mister Fitzgerald wanted me to help you in any way you would deem necessary, and I must add it pleases me to do so."

"Well Timothy, bring us to Scotland Yard."

Timothy drove the three miles separating us from the Yard as fast as he could. It would be the first time I've been in the new Metropolitan Police building. Coming out of the cab, I had a better view of the building and was a bit amused by its architecture. It looked like layers of chocolate cake, each one separated from the other with whipped cream.

"I don't know how long this could take so it would be better for you not to wait for me Timothy," I told him.

"As you wish. However, I still have to look out for Doctor Tumblety."

"Then take good care. I'll get in contact with

Fitzgerald later to-day."

Once inside, by simply identifying myself as working at the Hospital and having information of great importance to give to Abberline, a constable immediately took me to his office. He opened the door and led me in.

"He's here inspector," the constable said. "Who?" Abberline asked.

"The man you were talking about earlier this morning," he replied.

His comment clearly meant that I was expected, which rather caught me by surprise.

"Well, well. Come in mister Reily. Ask Thick to come and join us," Abberline told to the constable. "You expected me?"

"Not really," Abberline answered. "We were just going through yesterday's main events, and people we had met. What brings you here?"

"I wanted to clarify certain aspects of your encounter yesterday with me and Tumblety, and by the same token, ask for your advice."

"Are you here to defend Tumblety."

"Is he suspected or accused of any crime?" "Not for the moment."

"If I understand correctly what you are telling me is that you placed him under observation."

"You might say that. The same goes for many others but I am not allowed to give any details. Hell, half of East-Enders are accusing the other half of being the Ripper!"

"Then allow me to explain why we were together last night."

The growing noise of footsteps led me to believe someone was approaching the office. Moreover, the squeaking sound of hinges and of a door opening and closing behind confirmed my impression. I hastily turned my head and recognized Abberline's assistant, Sergeant Thick.

"Oh, Mister Reily. So you're the reason Abberline wanted me here? Isn't he, inspector?"

Abberline stood up and walked towards me. "Yes.

Do sit down Mister Reily," he added pointing a chair close to his desk.

I sat followed by the sergeant who simply went to sit on the corner of the desk.

"Mister Reily here is paying us a friendly visit just to tell us what he was doing with Tumblety. Please go on."

"Firstly, I would like to mention that I've never been to his club before. You can't imagine how I was deeply shocked by the behaviour of those who were present around us. I had heard of men having a questionable way of conducting themselves together, but I never went for details."

"Let us say they were simply involved in preliminary introductions. You wouldn't want to know what usually happens afterwards elsewhere," Abberline pointed out.

"Oh God! Secondly, Doctor Tumblety invited me at his club probably as a way to thank me for the help I gave him at the Hospital."

"What kind of help?" Thick asked.

"Actually, it was Doctor Fillmore whom you already met who formally requested of me that I provide him with everything his medical research demanded."

"Did you hear this Thick? Tumblety is now into medical research," Abberline laughed out. "What is he going to come out with the next time?" he added. "Tell me, what kind of research is he involved in?"

"Neither Fillmore nor Tumblety gave me any specific details on this project. I was however told to provide him with whatever he deemed necessary."

"But you probably have an idea of what he was working on, don't you?" asked Thick.

"What I understood is that it had something to do with the health of women. Tumblety was concerned with diseases they carried, in particular, prostitutes, and the opinion he had of them spreading them out to men."

"Can you imagine this?" Abberline mentioned. "He calls himself a doctor but considers women to be responsible for those diseases. If I remember how it works," he added with a smile, "it takes two to play that game!"

"May I ask you a question concerning something you mentioned last night about Tumblety?"

"Don't expect me to say more than what is publicly known already."

"Quite understandable. You said he had certain relations with the Fenian Brotherhood. What kind of relations?"

"He says he is simply helping out Irish families thanks to his presumed great wealth. But there is more to it than what meets the eye."

"Is there a way for me to find out? It's something quite personal."

Abberline looked at me with a rather surprised expression on his face. "An Irish who ignores how to obtain by himself information on the brotherhood! Somewhat unusual, don't you agree Thick?"

His remark irritated me, but I preferred not letting it show. I had to quickly find a way for him to give me at least a hint if not a name. I stood up, walked towards the door as if I intended to leave and turned around towards both of them. "Oh by the way, did I mention he is searching for female organs."

"What the bloody hell did you just say? Female organs?"

"Given your response, I believe I didn't. Sorry about that," I added whilst directing myself closer to the door.

"Maybe the next time we could talk about it."

"Why didn't you start by giving us this information?" Abberline said with a loud voice.

I looked back at him, his colleague and couldn't resist. "A Yard's inspector who ignores these facts concerning Tumblety! Somewhat unusual, don't you agree, Thick?" I was surprised to hear myself pronouncing almost the exact words he had used against me, and added to this savouring moment of revenge, a cynical smile.

"Don't play games with me Reily," Abberline shouted. "Come right back here and sit down."

"Am I to understand you are willing to share the information I requested? How kind of you," I said quite happy with the new outcome.

"Don't push it, Reily. As I have already mentioned, I am not in a position to talk about these matters to anybody. However, given the unexpected information you just brought up, I believe there is an option."

"An option?" said Thick, surprised by Abberline's remark.

"Commissioner Warren forbade us to say anything.

However, he didn't mention anything about writing down some of it, did he?" Abberline asked Thick with an obvious quest of approval from his partner.

"Not a word," answered Thick with a wink in his eye letting us both understand he did not mind at all.

"I knew something could be done to help me, and appreciate it."

He pulled out a pad from his jacket pocket, picked up a pen from his desk, sunk it in the ink bottle and wrote down something. Tearing the page from the pad, he handed it to me. Still, I noticed some resistance from his expression.

"Take this, and don't read it out. Walls have ears. You are aware, aren't you, that the Fenian may feel threatened by any question you ask them and could act in an unpredictable manner."

"Now that you've told me, I am."

I almost had to pull the paper from Abberline hand so much was the resistance I felt from his fingers.

"Is there a problem?" I asked.

"Don't come back complaining things went wrong. You are on your own from now on. By the way, this conversation never occurred; you hear me?"

As I nodded, he freed his hand leaving me with the paper. Before putting it my pocket, I noticed three names and cities.

"Don't worry, I believe I can manage the situation. Thank you for the information."

"Good. Now what's the deal with those organs?"
"The Hospital's directors agreed to provide him with female organs needed for his research on the treatment of diseases with herbs and plants from America which we did."

"Is that it? Where's the bloody problem?" Abberline asked obviously disappointed by the information I provided him with.

"It didn't seem to satisfy him completely so he started looking for dying women whose family would accept to have him remove the organs he needed. Again, the Hospital accepted to do what was necessary for him to carry them back overseas. Now, that may still seem acceptable although unusual for most of the people but strange coincidences began at that moment."

I told them about the fact that every murder happened the same day Tumblety had told me to expect organs on the following morning, that an amputation knife had disappeared from our lab during that period. I also mentioned the organs he brought to me on one of these occasions which I processed as requested. I ended with the two brass rings I noticed Tumblety had in his wallet; the kind Chapman could have worn the day of her death, and were said to be missing.

Thick became overexcited. "He's our man, Inspector. We've got to lock the bastard up before he does it again."

"Just a minute William. I can understand you would have, I might say, personal reasons to move quickly but we need to see the complete picture before buying it." Abberline looked at me hoping for more. "Reily, does the Hospital still have organs to give him?"

"Not for the moment. He's already picked everything we had for him. And considering last night's events, I seriously doubt he'll hurry back to ask me for more organs."

"You know what to do if he tries to get in contact with you, don't you?"

"I presume it would be to let you know as soon as possible."

"Exactly. Now if you have no other questions or information to share, I hope you wouldn't mind letting me get back to my job. Your collaboration was appreciated. I wish you good luck," said Abberline. "Some day soon, I hope, we could have a pint together after this sordid case is over," added Thick. "At least one," I concluded with a smile.

On my way out, I pulled out the paper Abberline had given me, slowed my pace and examined more closely the names and places he had written down. One, Derrick O'Connell, could be contacted in Manchester. The second, a certain Russell Sweeney, was to be found in Liverpool. As for the third man, David Flanagan, it seems he lived in Dublin. I entertained serious doubts as to the authenticity of the names Abberline had given me but had no other choice to begin with what I had. Once outside, I was surprised to see Timothy still waiting for me and waiving for me to join him.

"Did it all go as you wished, if I may ask?"

"It could not have gone better. Have you been

waiting all that time for me?"

"I had a couple of things to do close by and came in case you needed a ride back."

"That's very kind of you. Since, you are there, would it be possible for you to drop me at the hospital. I would only take minutes for me to take care of some important business."

"To the hospital it shall be."

As we moved, I had this absent minded feeling which I appreciated given the turbulence imposed on me during the past weeks. I looked through the cab's window. The weather was rather muggy with cloudy skies. Add to that the absence of wind, the smell of the streets would sink down and remain under our noses even more. No doubt that an unpleasant rain was to be expected. It would not however be a surprise for any Londoner at this period of the year nor for any other period for that matter.

At the hospital. I jumped out, waved at Timothy who responded with a nod. I felt the need to move in haste keeping my head down in order for me not to attract any attention or respond to any regard in my direction.

A quick glance allowed me to conclude that nothing had changed since my last visit to the lab. I decided to write Fillmore a note who, by now, had certainly good reasons to require some explanations on my behalf.

Sir,

Recent events occurring during the past weeks lead me to believe the Hospital's reputation and that of its medical staff could seriously be threatened. Even my own security could be compromised. All my energies and resources are actually aimed at resolving this situation in favour of us all. Unfortunately, it is impossible for me to provide you with more details at the moment, and I deeply apologize for not being able to do so. Under such circumstances, it is easy for me to understand that the

*disappointment and even a certain degree of anger
you could experience as to my conduct would
normally bring you to put an end to my employment.
Although I would logically adopt a similar conduct,
had I been in your position, allow me to propose an
alternative.*

*I could offer to resign, which could alleviate the
burden on your shoulders or the Hospital's, or you
could grant me a leave of absence without pay. Since
my intentions are to keep you informed on the
progression of these matters, in either case, I would
still attend the inquiries, and contact you should they
reveal any pertinent information related to the
Hospital.*

*My signature on this note gives you the option to
decide on the manner you consider appropriate to
handle the situation.*

Respectfully yours,
Woodrow Reily

I directed myself towards Fillmore's desk where I left
the note only to hear him almost shouting.

"There you are!"

I turned around to look at him and almost smiled at
his familiar way of addressing me with his swirling
eyeglass. I would probably miss him should my relation
with the hospital be brought to an end. In a certain way,
he helped me build a mental wall surrounding me and
protecting me against undeserved disrespectful
observations.

"What were you doing?"

"I was leaving you a note offering some sort of
explanation. Here, read it if it pleases you." I said as I
picked up the note from his desk and offered it to him.

Without saying a word, he pulled it out of my hand,
brought his eyeglass closer to his eyes and began

reading.

"What the bloody hell do you think you'll be accomplishing by resigning? It's the Ripper you're after? Damn you!"

I stood silent.

"You can easily figure out what my preferred decision would be," he added, his eyes staring at me. "But that would probably not be in my best interest to do so, if I understand what little there is to be understood, and the mere fact that you are totally aware of it irritates me even more."

"Trust me sir. The decision is entirely yours and would not be challenged."

"At least, you have the courage for once to face me. I was told that you are determined to take control of an issue involving our institution for obscure reasons and I should allow you some leeway. It seems only you can resolve this deadlock we have been placed in. If you have the keys, let us hope you shan't open one of those Pandora's boxes."

"A what?"

"Never mind! You must be aware you are compromising everything you have achieved during these what, seven, eight years with us?"

"Eight, sir. Eight years and three months to be exact, sir."

"Why would you go ahead with this senseless quest."

"I still can't explain all of it to myself, sir."

"I must admit a man embarked on such a quest deserves some respect for doing so." He began walking around in his office. "Quite a pleasant change."

"Thank you sir."

"Don't thank me. I was strictly thinking out loud rather than addressing you, young man."

I understood by these words that it was the only way for him to express indirectly a form of affection or at least empathy towards someone.

"Now, what we shall do? A leave of absence would give me a certain degree of control over the situation. To what extent, for the moment, I ignore it. However, I shall recommend it to our board. Should the situation evolve in an unfavourable manner, it still leaves me with two options."

"I believe it to be a wise decision, sir."

"Probably because it's the one you expected me to take. Considering we've been working together many years, you somehow learned to know me more than I figured. I'd even add you may have begun thinking as I would, which is not necessarily a sign of improvement."

We both smiled.

"Has Tumblety tried to get in contact with you recently?" I dared to ask Fillmore.

"Not that I know of. Does he have anything to do with your note?"

I did not respond.

"I know, I know. Don't look at me that way. You can't give me any details. However, we must stay in contact with each other just in case something unexpected came up. The Hospital deserves all our loyalty and attention."

"I agree. Communicating by telegram or courier seems to be the fastest way to proceed."

"Excellent."

"Now, I shall have to find a way to explain all this to the board and find your replacement. But then, it's my problem, and it may seem somewhat out of scale with yours."

We both looked at each other. He seemed worried to say the least. Or was it a certain sadness? I extended my hand which he also did and both shook hands.

"I'm aware you will be missing your favorite scapegoat." I said with the rapid look of an accomplice.

"But you should not worry. I expect to return soon, I hope, and give better reasons to complain."

We could not hold our laughs. A first for both of us.

"I can always count on you for that," he added.

"Good luck in whatever foolish endeavour you have chosen. And don't forget to inform me on the progression of the inquiries."

A few minutes later, I was back on the cab. Deeming it necessary to have various ways of dressing up minimizing the chances of having people being suspicious of my presence amongst them, Timothy suggested I make a stop on Petticoat Lane to pick up some clothes. He felt it would be of some help to me by easily blending with the shabby clothed people I could eventually meet on my way to Ireland.

Although, the lane is the poor man's clothes market, one could find a rather wide variety of garments in different degrees of wear, from boots and shoes to trousers, waistcoats and dress-coats without forgetting collars, cuffs and hats. You could also find women's clothes, lace, muslins, kerchiefs but, surprisingly, female buyers were scarce. Unsafe for them? Not at all. It would not be different from walking somewhere else in Whitechapel. For me, their absence reflected simply the fact that it was the man of the house who held the money and made the decisions concerning acquisitions of goods. Every square foot of the lane is occupied by either an item, a buyer or a seller who would ask for bids from those surrounding him or claiming to anyone who showed the slightest interest that his items could fit as a glove. It would be hard for any newcomer to imagine the abundance of clothes. Piles and piles stretched out all along the streets and alleys. Any attempt to find someone on Petticoat Lane is doomed. At least, such was my understanding of this market place until right in front of me stood Elizabeth smiling at me.

"What the bloody hell are you doing here?"

"I had to see you somewhere else than at father's home."

"You could have asked me to meet you in a more convenient place. Don't you think?"

"Perhaps, but I had no other choice." What is going on?

"I learned that you were preparing to go to Manchester and probably Dublin. I'm I correct?" "Yes, maybe even to-day."

"I had to warn you before you would have met with father prior to your departure."

"How did you know I would be here? How did you get here?"

"Timothy arranged everything after I spoke to him. He brought me here where it would be safe for me to wait for you."

"So that's why he insisted on me stopping on Petticoat Lane. He dropped me knowing precisely I could not avoid meeting you."

"He is waiting for us. It would be better if we went somewhere I could speak with you alone."

"Let's go in here," said I, pointing to the Bell pub at our right.

I opened the door letting her in and looked around to make sure no one was following us. As I glanced inside to guess what kind of characters we could expect, I was relieved to see that the atmosphere was rather quiet.

Each East End pub has its own look, but they all had the same odour brought in through the years by the same kind of people drinking for the same reasons and sharing the same and often hopeless dreams. We sat at a table near the window. In a matter of seconds, a waiter stood at our table staring at Elizabeth.

"What will the missy have?" he asked.

My eyes fixed him directly letting him understand I

would not tolerate any wrongful behaviour from him or anyone else.

"A pint of ale for me... and what will you have Elizabeth?"

"Some tea would be perfect"

"Tea and ale it'll be," he said as he directed himself to the bar.

"Now, what is it you needed to inform me of?"

"If I understood correctly what father told me, the wild pursuit of Tumblety you have engaged yourself in has reached a new level. It's now having you search for him across the country."

"Three cities, to be more precise, not the whole kingdom. I need to now who this person is really. I recently obtained some rather intriguing information."

I quickly gave her the elements of the discussion I had with his father concerning Tumblety 's questionable interest for younger men and the Fenian connection.

"You want to get in contact with the Fenian! Have you lost your mind? What does all this have to do with the murders?"

"Look at it this way. If your behaviour turns you into a suspect of different crimes, you are either totally mad or possibly using one crime to dissipate any attempt made to pin another even more serious one on you. Which is the worst? Where does the police focus its attention? On a man possibly murdering women, on someone perhaps involved in terrorism or on an adult male interested in young men? I believe that's what Tumblety is doing and he is attempting to have it all pointed in my direction."

"But you could also be guilty of none because it is rather unlikely for a person to place himself in such an awkward predicament."

"Precisely. In either case, the police would let you free...to continue whatever criminal activity you had initiated."

"All three could be linked."

"And maybe to the same person, Tumblety. I'm convinced that following one trail while keeping in mind the two others will give me the overall portrait."

"Or get you killed."

"Simply walking in the East End can get you killed. I rather take control of my actions than being a random victim. But tell me. You didn't want to see me only to share what we already know. I am somehow under the impression you had something different to say. Now, what would that be?"

"You and father have discussed all of this on many occasions. I believe both of you take great pleasure in meeting together and sharing thoughts on these murders. I must warn you that father enjoys, as mother would say, playing mind games with those surrounding him. Particularly setting them up as pawns in a chess game. She hated it when he engaged in these games with her. It sometimes became cruel and dangerous. At one point, she decided to stay away from him when my brother had his accident and died."

"Maybe this explains why I have never seen her at your father's place. Was he playing mind games with your brother resulting in his death?"

Elizabeth looked at me making me quickly understand she didn't wish to go further into what I had just said.

"I dearly love father but also needed to warn you. I wouldn't want something even remotely similar happening to you."

"You care that much for me?" I said staring up at the ceiling to avoid embarrassing her.

"Do I have to spell everything out, silly," she added with her beautiful smile and eyes reflecting the unspoken words I hoped she had pronounced. "We should go find something suitable for your journey."

Some thirty to forty minutes later, we were at the coach, Timothy looking at me seemingly delighted by my own expression.

A rather enthusiastic Fitzgerald welcomed me back at his place.

"Elizabeth, Woodrow! What a pleasant surprise to see you together."

"I helped him find some clothes for his upcoming travels."

"My God," said he, almost laughing when he saw Timothy coming behind us, both hands full of wrapped packages. "Are you planing a trip around the world?"

"I prefer not taking any chances of being perceived as an outsider. I even plan on letting my beard and moustache grow as I move from one city to another."

"If you don't mind, I'll let both of you conspire against the whole world, while I rest before dinner," said Elizabeth smiling at us as if we were two young boys preparing some mischievous prank.

She could not have been more descriptive of our intentions. We looked back at her feeling caught with our hands in a cookie jar and went on.

"What cities are you talking about, Woodrow?" Fitzgerald asked me as he directed me to the library.

I gave him an update, explaining my visit with Abberline and Fillmore.

"By the way, I understood from what Fillmore told me that you were the one who contacted the authorities of the hospital and having them accept my leave of absence. I am grateful for your magical intervention."
"I'm glad I was of some help. Did he mention my name?"

"Not at all. Would it have been a problem, had he known it was you?"

"Sometimes it is a matter of the utmost importance to

stay anonymous, but it wouldn't have bothered me, had he mentioned my name for reasons which I consider irrelevant."

I gave him the three names Abberline wrote down and the cities where I would have to go to find them.

"I shan't bore you with the details, but maybe I can wire some people I know. It may prevent you from spending time looking for these persons. In Manchester, you might want to go in what may be left of the Little Ireland area near Oxford Road. The Brotherhood was quite active over there years ago."

"I really appreciate your help, sir."

"May I suggest you start in Manchester and once there, decide on continuing towards Liverpool or Dublin depending on your findings. You might obtain all the information you need without having to go elsewhere. When would wish to leave?"

"Not knowing what I should expect, leaving as soon as possible will give me more time."

"You have been quite active these past days. I believe it would be recommendable for you to rest a little before departing for an unknown period. How does leaving on Monday seem to you?"

"In three days!"

"Remember, my dear friend, that you still have other matters pending. Does the question of the families Elizabeth is working on ring a bell?"

"Oh! You're right. So that brings me to stay until Sunday."

"I'll ask Timothy to get the train tickets you will be needing. As for your expenses, you should not worry about them. It will also give you more time to prepare yourself. Then again, who knows what might happen during the weekend. The Ripper could be arrested."

"Or strike once more."

"So you're forced to stay in London and help me with

some Irish families, are you?"

I immediately recognized Elizabeth's voice. Fitzgerald and I hadn't notice that she had returned and was standing against the door frame. I have never felt so embarrassed in my life and backed off as much as I could in my armchair. "Huh...!" Wordless, I could only offer her a ridiculous smile.

She laughed at my reaction. "That will teach you," she said. "Now Father, if you don't mind, it's my turn to discuss with Woodrow about those families. It shouldn't take long. We simply need to plan a visit of more families during the coming days."

"Then I'll set in for the night."

Fitzgerald walked towards Elizabeth, kissed her on the cheek and left for his room.

"Thank you again, sir", I said as I stood up, went close to Elizabeth took her hand and brought her to sit on the Chesterfield.

"We won't be able to visit any family until Sunday," I said. "If I remember correctly, the continuation of one of the inquiries is scheduled for to-morrow. I promised Fillmore I would do my best to attend them, and report back to him any situation potentially related to the hospital."

"Then Sunday morning, around ten." She paused a moment. "There are families, I believe, we should consider before others. They live on Fashion Street close to Spitalfields Markets. Timmy would bring me to your place and from there we would go and meet them."

"Excellent. Don't feel insulted, but it would be preferable for you to avoid drawing attention from East-Enders by wearing something you would only find in wealthy parts of London. It would also be a good idea to ask Timothy to drop us off a few blocks away from the first home we would visit. This way, we would blend much easier with the people on the street."

"It shouldn't be a problem for me to find something convenient."

"That said, if you don't mind, I believe I should leave."

"Timothy will drive you back."

She walked me to the door. I opened it looked at her wondering if I could kiss her, hesitated but considered it inappropriate.

"Sleep well I," I told her.

"You to," she responded, and to my great surprise, kissed me on my cheek. I raised my right arm and brought it to her shoulder gently holding it to prolong this moment of tenderness.

Off I went, feeling a bit embarrassed for not having taken the initiative of the kiss.

SATURDAY, OCTOBER 6, 1888

As I woke up, the events of the past weeks went through my mind. I had to admit to myself I was dispersing my energies in three different directions. Two had a certain connection between them : attending the Whitechapel murder inquiries and pursuing a person I believed to be the murderer, Tumblety. The third one was helping Elizabeth select families who would start a new life overseas. For someone like me who preferred minimizing his contacts with people and now finds himself constantly amongst others, this, to say the least, was quite unexpected. Finding an explanation for such a change was not an immediate concern of mine probably because deep inside, I knew I had to finish what I had already started.

On my way to Stride's inquest, I picked up to-day's paper. The Daily Telegraph had published a transcription of the inquest on Eddowes death held the day before. Some of the family members and close friends were called as witnesses describing Eddowes as not having the habit of staying out late and except for the three-four past weeks returning to her usual lodging house with her man, John Kelly. Constable Edward Watkins revealed that he had not noticed anything out of the ordinary while patrolling his beat covering Mitre-Square, the murder having been committed between his 1.30 and 1.44 walks in the square area.

'I next came into Mitre-square at 1.44, when I discovered the body lying on the right as I entered the square. The woman was on her back, with her feet towards the square. Her clothes were thrown up. I saw her throat was cut and the stomach ripped open. She was lying in a pool of blood. I did not touch the body. I ran across to [Kearley & Tonge's warehouse. The door was ajar, and I pushed it open, and called on the watchman Morris, who was inside. He came out. I remained with the body until the arrival of Police-constable Holland. No one else was there before that but myself. Holland was followed by Dr. Sequeira. Inspector Collard arrived about two o'clock, and also Dr. Brown, surgeon to the police force.'

Dr. Frederick Gordon Brown surgeon to the City of London Police then came and provided the jury with the results of the post-mortem examination he conducted the following day. The gruesome details he offered whitened the face of almost all those attending it.

'The body was on its back, the head turned to left shoulder. The arms by the side of the body as if they had fallen there. Both palms upwards, the fingers slightly bent. The left leg extended in a line with the body. The abdomen was exposed. Right leg bent at the thigh and knee. The throat cut across.

The intestines were drawn out to a large extent

and placed over the right shoulder -- they were smeared over with some feculent matter. A piece of about two feet was quite detached from the body and placed between the body and the left arm, apparently by design. The lobe and auricle of the right ear were cut obliquely through.

The face was very much mutilated. There was a cut about a quarter of an inch through the lower left eyelid, dividing the structures completely through. The upper eyelid on that side, there was a scratch through the skin on the left upper eyelid, near to the angle of the nose. The right eyelid was cut through to about half an inch.

There was a deep cut over the bridge of the nose, extending from the left border of the nasal bone down near the angle of the jaw on the right side of the cheek. This cut went into the bone and divided all the structures of the cheek except the mucous membrane of the mouth.

The tip of the nose was quite detached by an oblique cut from the bottom of the nasal bone to where the wings of the nose join on to the face. A cut from this divided the upper lip and extended through the substance of the gum over the right upper lateral incisor tooth.

About half an inch from the top of the nose was another oblique cut. There was a cut on the right angle of the mouth as if the cut of a point of a knife.

The cut extended an inch and a half, parallel with the lower lip.

There was on each side of cheek a cut which peeled up the skin, forming a triangular flap about an inch and a half. On the left cheek there were two abrasions of the epithelium under the left ear.

The throat was cut across to the extent of about six or seven inches. A superficial cut commenced about an inch and a half below the lobe below, and about two and a half inches behind the left ear, and extended across the throat to about three inches below the lobe of the right ear.

The big muscle across the throat was divided through on the left side. The large vessels on the left side of the neck were severed. The larynx was severed below the vocal chord. All the deep structures were severed to the bone, the knife marking intervertebral cartilages. The sheath of the vessels on the right side was just opened

The carotid artery had a fine hole opening, the internal jugular vein was opened about an inch and a half -- not divided. The blood vessels contained clot. All these injuries were performed by a sharp instrument like a knife, and pointed.

The cause of death was haemorrhage from the left common carotid artery. The death was immediate and the mutilations were inflicted after death.

We examined the abdomen. The front walls were laid open from the breast bones to the pubes. The cut commenced opposite the enciform cartilage. The incision went upwards, not penetrating the skin that was over the sternum. It then divided the enciform cartilage. The knife must have cut obliquely at the expense of that cartilage.

Behind this, the liver was stabbed as if by the point of a sharp instrument. Below this was another incision into the liver of about two and a half inches, and below this the left lobe of the liver was slit through by a vertical cut. Two cuts were shewn by a jagging of the skin on the left side.

The abdominal walls were divided in the middle line to within a quarter of an inch of the navel. The cut then took a horizontal course for two inches and a half towards the right side. It then divided round the navel on the left side, and made a parallel incision to the former horizontal incision, leaving the navel on a tongue of skin. Attached to the navel was two and a half inches of the lower part of the rectus muscle on the left side of the abdomen. The incision then took an oblique direction to the right and was shelving. The incision went down the right side of the vagina and rectum for half an inch behind the rectum.

There was a stab of about an inch on the left groin. This was done by a pointed instrument. Below this was a cut of three inches going through all tissues making a wound of the peritoneum about the same extent.

An inch below the crease of the thigh was a cut extending from the anterior spine of the ilium obliquely down the inner side of the left thigh and separating the left labium, forming a flap of skin up to the groin. The left rectus muscle was not detached.

There was a flap of skin formed by the right thigh, attaching the right labium, and extending up to the spine of the ilium. The muscles on the right side inserted into the frontal ligaments were cut through.

The skin was retracted through the whole of the cut through the abdomen, but the vessels were not clotted. Nor had there been any appreciable bleeding from the vessels. I draw the conclusion that the act was made after death, and there would not have been much blood on the murderer. The cut was made by someone on the right side of the body, kneeling below the middle of the body.

The intestines had been detached to a large extent from the mesentery. About two feet of the colon was cut away. The sigmoid flexure was invaginated into the rectum very tightly.

Right kidney was pale, bloodless with slight

congestion of the base of the pyramids.

There was a cut from the upper part of the slit on the under surface of the liver to the left side, and another cut at right angles to this, which were about an inch and a half deep and two and a half inches long. Liver itself was healthy.

The gall bladder contained bile. The pancreas was cut, but not through, on the left side of the spinal column. Three and a half inches of the lower border of the spleen by half an inch was attached only to the peritoneum.

The peritoneal lining was cut through on the left side and the left kidney carefully taken out and removed. The left renal artery was cut through. I would say that someone who knew the position of the kidney must have done it.

The lining membrane over the uterus was cut through. The womb was cut through horizontally, leaving a stump of three quarters of an inch. The rest of the womb had been taken away with some of the ligaments. The vagina and cervix of the womb was uninjured.

The wounds on the face and abdomen prove that they were inflicted by a sharp, pointed knife, and that in the abdomen by one six inches or longer.

I believe the perpetrator of the act must have had considerable knowledge of the position of the organs in the abdominal cavity and the way of removing them. It required a great deal of medical knowledge to have removed the kidney and to know where it was placed. The parts removed would be of no use for any professional purpose.

I think the perpetrator of this act had sufficient time, or he would not have nicked the lower eyelids. It would take at least five minutes.

The throat had been so instantly severed that no

noise could have been emitted. I should not expect much blood to have been found on the person who had inflicted these wounds.

The inquest was then adjourned until next Thursday.

I expected to-day's inquest concerning Elizabeth Stride's death would reveal valuable information clearing me of any involvement in this murder. The mere fact that I had met her during the last evening she was alive convinced me of remaining discreet during the hearings. I decided to let many others enter before me and found a place to sit in the rear.

The divisional-surgeon of police, Dr. Phillips, entered minutes later. He was asked to give certain precisions regarding an injury the victim was said to have in the palette which served to identify her as being Elizabeth Stride. It also gave him the possibility of putting an end to what was considered by many as only a 'rumour' that a grape stalk was found in a sink in Dutfield's Yard by two private detectives. I was stunned but not displeased at all to hear that my gift of fruit to Elizabeth Stride was now considered a rumour. What had happened to the merchant who sold them to me, I wondered?

"I examined the two handkerchiefs which were found on the deceased" Phillips said. "I did not discover any blood on them, and I believe that the stains on the larger handkerchief are those of fruit." There we go again, he mentioned the damaging word 'fruit'.

"Neither on the hands nor about the body of the deceased did I find grapes, or connection with them. I am convinced that the deceased had not swallowed either the skin or seed of a grape within many hours of her death."

"What?" said I, in a low voice which seemed to upset

those sitting by my side.

Phillips' words came as a surprise considering the facts I was now the only one who could testify to the veracity of this information. I felt it would be better for me not to challenge his testimony at this moment. Doing so would place me in a delicate position. What he stated afterwards was now only a sound in the background as obvious questions came to my mind. Had Tumblety taken them from her or did she give them to someone before meeting him? I was anxious to hear more on this issue from other possible witnesses.

"I have stated that the neckerchief which she had on was not torn, but cut," he continued. "The abrasion which I spoke of on the right side of the neck was only apparently an abrasion, for on washing it, it was removed, and the skin found to be uninjured. The knife produced on the last occasion was delivered to me, properly secured, by a constable, and on examination I found it to be such a knife as is used in a chandler's shop, and is called a slicing knife. It has blood upon it, which has characteristics similar to the blood of a human being. It has been recently blunted, and its edge apparently turned by rubbing on a stone such as a kerb-stone. It evidently was before a very sharp knife."

"Is it such a knife that could have caused the injuries which were inflicted upon the deceased?" the Coroner asked.

"Such a knife could have produced the incision and injuries to the neck, but it is not such a weapon as I should have fixed upon as having caused the injuries in this case; and if my opinion as regards the position of the body is correct, the knife in question would become an improbable instrument as having caused the incision."

"I have seen several self-inflicted wounds more extensive than this one, but then they have not usually involved the carotid artery. In this case, as in some others, there seems to have been some knowledge where to cut the throat to cause a fatal result."

"Is there any similarity between this case and Annie Chapman's case?"

"There is very great dissimilarity between the two. In Chapman's case the neck was severed all round down to the vertebral column, the vertebral bones being marked with two sharp cuts, and there had been an evident attempt to separate the bones."

"From the position you assume the perpetrator to have been in, would he have been likely to get bloodstained?"

"Not necessarily, for the commencement of the wound and the injury to the vessels would be away from him, and the stream of blood - for stream it was – would be directed away from him, and towards the gutter in the yard."

"Was there any appearance of an opiate or any smell of chloroform?"

"There was no perceptible trace of any anesthetic or narcotic. The absence of noise is a difficult question under the circumstances of this case to account for, but it must not be taken for granted that there was not any noise. If there was an absence of noise I cannot account for it."

"That means that the woman might cry out after the cut," remarked the Foreman.

"Not after the cut."

"But why did she not cry out whilst she was being put on the ground?," asked the Coroner.

"She was in a yard, and in a locality where she might cry out very loudly and no notice be taken of her. It was possible for the woman to draw up her legs after the wound, but she could not have turned over. The wound was inflicted by drawing the knife across the throat. A short knife, such as a shoemaker's well-ground knife, would do the same thing. My reason for believing that deceased was injured when on the ground was partly on account of the absence of blood anywhere on the left side of the body and between it and the wall."

Dr. Blackwell came back to the stand adding that he had removed the cachous from the left hand of the deceased, which was nearly open. The packet was lodged between the thumb and the first finger, and was partially hidden from view but made no mention about grapes.

"With respect to the knife which was found, I should like to say that I concur with Dr. Phillips in his opinion that, although it might have inflicted the injury, it is an extremely unlikely instrument to have been used. It appears to me that a murderer, in using a round-pointed instrument, would seriously handicap himself, as he would be only able to use it in one particular way. I am told that slaughterers always use a sharp-pointed instrument."

"No one has suggested that this crime was committed by a slaughterer," insisted the Coroner.

"I simply intended to point out the inconvenience that might arise from using a blunt-pointed weapon."

"Did you notice any marks or bruises about the shoulders?" asked the Foreman.

"They were what we call pressure marks. At first they were very obscure, but subsequently they became very evident. They were not what are ordinarily called bruises; neither is there any abrasion. Each shoulder was about equally marked."

To the coroner's question whether he had noticed any grapes near the body in the yard, Dr Blackwell gave a clear "No" for an answer.

"Did you hear any person say that they had seen grapes there?"

"I did not."

The testimony of the three following witnesses would make me quiver with every word brought out by them or question given to them for I was convinced it was me they were talking about.

William Marshall, a resident at No. 64, Berner Street, and labourer at an indigo warehouse had seen the deceased on the night of the murder.

"Where?" asked the Coroner.

"In our street, three doors from my house, about a quarter to twelve o'clock. She was on the pavement, opposite number 58, between Fairclough Street and Boyd Street."

It was precisely the time I was with Elizabeth Stride.

"What was she doing?"

"She was standing talking to a man."

"How do you know this was the same woman?"

"I recognize her both by her face and dress. She did not then have a flower in her breast."

"Were the man and woman whom you saw talking quietly?"

"They were talking together."

"Can you describe the man at all?"

"There was no gas-lamp near. The nearest was at the corner, about twenty feet off. I did not see the face of the man distinctly."

"Did you notice how he was dressed?"

"In a black cut-away coat and dark trousers."

"Was he young or old?"

"Middle-aged he seemed to be."

All cats are grey in the midst of the night, explaining to myself his error.

"Was he wearing a hat?"

"No, a cap."

Again another ill perceived but how relieving image of what I always wore, my good old felt fedora.

"What sort of a cap?"

"A round cap, with a small peak."

"It was something like what a sailor would wear."

I was wondering if this man was sober when he had noticed me.

"What height was he?"

"About 5ft. 6in."

"Was he thin or stout?"

"Rather stout."

Until now, and excluding my stoutness of course, only half of what he had said corresponded to the actual facts.

"Did he look well dressed?"

"Decently dressed."

"What class of man did he appear to be?"

"I should say he was in business, and did nothing like hard work."

"Not like a dock labourer?"

"No."

"Nor a sailor?"

"No."

"Nor a butcher?"

"No."

"A clerk?"

"He had more the appearance of a clerk."

"Is that the best suggestion you can make?"

"It is."

"You did not see his face. Had he any whiskers?"

"I cannot say. I do not think he had."

"Was he wearing gloves?"

"No."

"Was he carrying a stick or umbrella in his hands?"

"He had nothing in his hands that I am aware of."

"You are quite sure that the deceased is the woman you saw?"

"Quite. I did not take much notice whether she was carrying anything in her hands."

"What first attracted your attention to the couple?"

"By their standing there for some time, and he was kissing her."

Kissing her! I certainly would not have kissed although I remember having once whispered some words to her ear.

"Did you overhear anything they said?"

"I heard him say, 'You would say anything but your prayers.'"

I remember saying those exact words to her after she candidly lied to me. She had mentioned her humble Swedish origins to mc thcn addcd she nevertheless had direct family ties with the royal family.

"Different people talk in a different tone and in a different way. Did his voice give you the idea of a clerk?"

"Yes, he was mild speaking."

"Did he speak like an educated man?"

"I thought so. I did not hear them say anything more. They went away after that. I did not hear the woman say anything, but after the man made that observation she laughed. They went away down the street, towards Ellen Street. They would not then pass number 40."

"How was the woman dressed?"

"In a black jacket and skirt."

"Was either the worse for drink?"

"No, I thought not."

"When did you go indoors?"

"About twelve o'clock."

"Did you hear anything more that night?"

"Not till I heard that the murder had taken place, just after one o'clock, whilst I was standing at my door, from half-past eleven to twelve, there was no rain at all. The deceased had on a small black bonnet. The couple were standing between my house and the club for about ten minutes."

Detective-Inspector Reid asked if the couple had then passed him.

"Yes," he answered.

A member of the Jury asked if Marshall had seen the man's face as he passed.

"No," Marshall answered, "he was looking towards the woman, and had his arm round her neck. There is a gas lamp at the corner of Boyd Street. It was not closing time when they passed me."

The man was certainly the worse for drink or wasn't really paying attention to what was going on. For when I bought the grapes, we stood close to the merchant's window taking cover against the walls from the pouring rain. Minutes later, I left her and never saw anyone we could have ever walked in front of.

The two next witnesses, James Brown, a dock labourer and Constable William Smith saw what could have been me. With both simply saying they had seen us at a quarter to one on Sunday morning last, me carrying a parcel wrapped in a newspaper in my hand wearing a dark felt deerstalker's hat and a long cutaway coat, meant it was some else, probably Stride's killer.

Once these testimonies ended, the inquiry was adjourned to Tuesday fortnight, at two o'clock. As I left the building, I heard someone mention that Stride would be buried to-morrow at East London Cemetery. Minutes later, I entered the hospital and quickly wrote a note to Fillmore and gave it to one of the runners for him to deliver it as soon as possible.

SUNDAY, OCTOBER 7, 1888

As promised, Elizabeth and Timothy were at my place at 10 o'clock. I asked Timothy to drop us once we would get at the corner of Whitechapel and Commercial Street. Entering the cab, I noticed that she was dressed in a sober but still elegant manner. She wore a traveling navy blue jacket with matching gabardine skirt both decorated with a discreet black trim. Her loosely plaited hair was brought back up under a straw hat trimmed with a wide white ribbon on which was placed an ivory decorative braid. Her gloved hands held a small purse, also blue.

Looking through the door window, I noticed we were about to arrive. Timothy brought the cab to a halt, came down to open the door and helped us out.

"I should be back here around three. Would that be too carly?" Timothy askcd us.

"I believe three should be fine," I answered as I offered my arm to Elizabeth, and we both headed towards Fashion Street.

"We're entering a part of London full of contradictions you would never imagine could exist," I said. "Should anyone threaten us in any form, I shall warn you. Do whatever I demand without saying a word or reacting openly. So don't be surprised."

"Are you under the impression I don't have an idea of what I can expect," she answered.

"Having an idea is one thing, being in contact with the real thing is quite another. For a newcomer like you, each street would appear to be like any other. However, you would soon find out, sometimes too late, the existence of territories having their own set of unwritten rules. Ignore them and you put your life at risk. But then, if you abide by all of them, you cease to own yourself."

"What kind of rules," she asked.

"The way you dress, the words you may use with certain people, the places you buy your food, the situations you must ignore as if they have never happened, just to name a few."

She looked around noticing the people coming and going, glanced at her apparel. "Oh," she went. "I may be a little overdressed."

"We are at the limit of what is acceptable, but you must not worry yourself."

"It must be terrifying for some who has just arrived here."

"One doesn't appear here suddenly. Most of the poor, the hopeless you see here were like that before. They moved in from the country as I did, expecting to improve their lives only to fall into this quicksand pit.

To survive, they have to quickly learn to read what and who surrounds them and make the appropriate adjustments. For most of the East-Enders, it then becomes as natural as it would be for a sailor to smell a stormy wind heading for his boat. For the others, well..." I dared not continue.

"What happens to the others?"

"East End simply swallows them. And the recent murders are just an example of how it's carried out."

"The way you describe it doesn't seem to bother you."

"It's just one of the rules. You must not feel bad for what you may see and especially avoid denying the fact it actually happened. Up to a certain extent, this learning process is fascinating. Let me show you."

"Are you serious?"

"Absolutely. Start by observing people's hands without looking at their faces or minding how they are dressed. Then look at the faces. Do you notice something unusual?"

"One of the women's hands looked like hands of an old woman. They were extremely chapped with broken nails. But her face, revealed someone as young as I."

"Excellent observation. She certainly earns her way picking oakum or preparing the caulking for vessels in workhouses. What else?"

"I noticed that almost all the men whether young or

old had terribly dirty hands."

"It's whom they belong to that matters. Anything else?"

"There was this man biting his nails from his right hand as he was entering a shop. He was pushing the door in with his left hand. I was amused to see that the left hand nails were of a normal length."

I smiled and turned towards Elizabeth. "Maybe he was so nervous about how he would repay what he owed the shopkeeper."

"There was also this old lady sitting alone on a bench. Her right hand was horribly crippled with her fingers almost tread into knots. How could she have managed to survive so long with only one hand? Then there were two men whose profession I swore I could figure out."

"Really?"

"Yes. One had big hands with massive fingers, a mason I thought. The other, on the contrary, had very thin fingers, the hands of a tailor."

"I'm amazed. What you just described are the hands of labourers. Their hands are their tools. Without them, they will fall into destituteness in a matter of days."

"I even looked at your hands. They are clean," she said looking at my right hand covering hers. "You have long fingers like those of a pianist, but you don't play piano."

"Maybe one day I shall. Did their faces reveal anything special?"

"Despair."

"Nevertheless, they still go on like a sail ship in the fog with its crew making noise for others to know where they are."

"Is that what you are doing?"

"Not anymore."

"Why? Has something changed in your life?"

"Everything has changed. I thought I had a life all planned out. I left my job; I'm hunting a murderer; I'm helping you re-establish these poor families."

"Any regrets?"

"That word has never been part of my vocabulary. So I can't answer you. What I sense now is as if I had a purpose. However, it's still vague."

A few yards in front of us, just before Flower and Dean Street, a man in his thirties was leaning against the wall, both hands in his pockets. "Now there's someone she won't be able to figure out easily," I said to myself.

A worn felt crusher hat topped his head. His shoes looked as old and filthy as the side-walk he was standing on. What he wore between offered nothing to improve his appearance. The overalls and shirt he wore were stained with grease, making him probably a docker. But what drew my attention even more was the way he looked at those passing by him, the kind of person who would translate your own appearance into pounds, shillings and pence. If you looked worthless like most of the East-Enders, you would be safe, otherwise, you should expect the worst which I did.

We passed by him, without paying any attention. But only a few feet away, I slightly turned my head to the left and noticed he had decided to follow us.

"Do you remember, Elizabeth, what I told you about potential treats?"

"Yes," said.

"There could be one behind us. Stay calm. It will be alright in a matter of minutes." I reached for my switchblade in the right hand pocket of my coat and opened it. We turned right at the corner. Again, I could see he was still following us. On our right, we took the entrance to a courtyard which seemed to offer some protection. "I want you to quickly move behind me."

I barely had time to lean against the corner of the

walkway when his shadow appeared, then him. I grabbed his left shoulder and spun him as fast as I could, bringing my arm around his neck almost choking him.

"Now fool, what shall it be?" said I, pressing my knife against his throat. "We could both learn how sharp my blade is but then, I'd be the only one to talk about it later or we could find a form of mutual understanding."

"Let's talk," he muttered.

"Good. But I warn you. I'm one of you dressed as one of them. So don't even think playing games with us. It would be your last one. Did I make myself clear?"

"Yes."

I slowly released him and brought him to face me, making sure Elizabeth was behind us. A quick glance at her made me aware she was terrified probably more by my own reaction than the man I held.

"Now," I asked him, "What were you trying to do?"

"My family hasn't eaten for two days. For us, it was either a shelter or food."

"You could have asked instead of risking your life, don't you think?"

"I never expected someone so handy with a knife."

"That's because you haven't been here long enough. What's your name?"

"McGrath, Thomas McGrath."

"Any relation with Evelyn McGrath," asked Elizabeth who came by my side still shaken by what had just happened.

"She's my wife," he answered.

Elizabeth and I both looked at each other, then back at him.

"That was really foolish of you. We were on our way to meet both of you. I'm Woodrow Reily, and the lady is Elizabeth Fitzgerald."

"Oh God," said he, bringing down his head. "Oh God, I've destroyed all our chances of freeing us from this misery."

"No you haven't," said Elizabeth. "You have just proven me how desperate you are. Woodrow, we must do something now. Quickly, let's start by getting some food for the family."

We hurried and managed to find what was needed, gave McGrath some money for the coming days and followed him to where he stayed. We learned that the youngest of their three daughters had died days ago. McGrath's wife, so weak, couldn't breastfeed her no more.

"Had we gone to a workhouse, they would have separated all of us. And we couldn't live with such a decision," he told us.

We explained our intentions and proposals which they accepted without any hesitation. The other four visits we had planned took place without any problem. One family preferred staying in England where they were convinced they had better chances of making a living.

"Now that was an exciting day, wasn't it Elizabeth?" I asked her as we were leaving Fashion Street.

"Exciting! Are you serious, you had to use a knife to defend us. I never would have suspected you were at ease with such a weapon."

"Guess what?" I laughed nervously. "Neither did I."

"You..., you..." She couldn't add a word probably unable to decide between anger and relief.

It was a little past three when we reached back the corner of Commercial and Whitechapel where Timothy was waiting as promised.

"I'm exhausted," Elizabeth said once inside the cab. She placed her hands on mine and leaned her head on my shoulder. I believed she slept until we reached her father's house. Fitzgerald greeted us as we arrived.

"I shan't ask how your day went," Fitzgerald said.

"Lizzy looks terrible, which tells me all I need to know for the moment."

"I think I shall rest until dinner, if you don't mind," she said.

"Do so, darling," her father responded as she climbed the hallway stairs. "As for you Woodrow, If you still plan on leaving Monday, you shall stay with us for the night. We could check out Bradshaw's Railway Guide to find an appropriate time of departure for you. But maybe you would like to clean up before we have a look. You can use the same room you had the last time."

"Thank you sir. Give me an hour or so and I'll be back to you."

Fresh clothes were laying on the bed obviously for me to wear: a fine woollen frock coat with satin lapels and matching black trouser, a wine coloured vest, a puff black tie and a linen white shirt. After washing myself and shaving, I tried on the clothes, the reflexion the mirror offering me a view of my appearance I never imagined I would have. I could only smile out of amusement.

Minutes after, I was back in the drawing room. Fitzgerald must have heard me coming down the stairs for on entering I noticed he was pouring glasses of his finer Scotch.

"Now," Fitzgerald started as he offered me one, "How did things work out with the families?" he asked pointing at an armchair for me to sit in.

"Besides a small incident, everything went rather well. Except for one family, all the others accepted our proposal. We still have many other families to visit. It wouldn't be advisable for Elizabeth to meet them alone giving the area where they live."

Fitzgerald frowned at my words. I preferred not giving any details concerning my encounter with McGrath. He would probably have become even more worried by the presence of his daughter in Whitechapel's streets.

"I totally agree and shall make sure she waits till you get back. By the way, whilst I was waiting here, I looked into the guide and found a departure to-morrow at noon from Euston Station. You would arrive around five at Manchester Piccadilly station right in the middle of Manchester. I recommend you enjoy the luncheon car. Oh," he added, picking up a thick book and handing it to me, "the Bradshaw's guide will come in handy if you need to take a different train or plan a new destination. Keep it."

"Thank you sir. As for the meals, I'd rather eat something before leaving to avoid unnecessary expenses as much as possible."

"I believe I am as involved in this operation as you are and feel I should do my share. So let me take care of those expenses."

"You have finally decided to go ask the Fenian for some help in order for you to catch Tumblety." It was Elizabeth who had quietly entered the room. She was lovelier than ever with a green velvet evening gown with a lace collar.

"You look marvelous, if I may say so."

"Thank you Woodrow," she said. "What about you?" She came closer to me, appreciating the way I was dressed by touching the lapels and collar. "A real gentleman."

"What does that make me?" asked Fitzgerald rather amused by seeing both of us admiring each other.

"Father, you are and shall always be the most charming of all men."

"I think we should have dinner, and cover the final details before you leave, Woodrow," pointed out Fitzgerald.

"One thing for sure," said Elizabeth, "I shall

accompany Woodrow to the railway station. Now let's go enjoy another of Madame Padoue's culinary surprises."

And such it was. 'Filet de boeuf en croûte' was the name of the main course. We covered all the aspects deemed necessary for my journey to succeed. I listened carefully to every word said but was even more interested in observing Elizabeth. Whatever aspect Fitzgerald or I examined, she kept showing signs of worry. I tried to convince her that it would be safer than walking the streets of Whitechapel making sure I would not let out any details of what happened earlier in the day. Nevertheless, it seemed clear to me that I had not achieved in changing how she felt.

Fitzgerald left us alone to end the evening before my departure.

"I may understand why you are attempting to catch Tumblety. But I wonder why you are doing this all by yourself. You don't have the resources or even the experience the police have, and still you go ahead. Are you aware your stubbornness might kill you?"

"Must I understand you're worried? Don't be. I am not blinded by what you define as my stubbornness even if all this has turned into something personal."

"I won't say a word more. It would be useless. I think I shall go to bed now."

"Let me help you up."

She offered me her arm as I lead her to the stairway. At her door, I looked at her blue-green eyes, slowly approached my lips against hers and kissed her.

"If I have good reasons to leave, I have an even better one to come back," I told her. "This reason is you, but you already knew that didn't you?"

"Promise me you shall be prudent."

"I shall. Sleep well."

MONDAY, OCTOBER 8, 1888

Timothy was waiting for us outside holding the horse's harness with one hand and caressing its head with the other. Elizabeth hadn't spoken a single word since she came down. She would maintain her silence all the way to Euston's station.

Passing through the station's columns gave me the impression I was entering a Greek temple. Its immense great hall amazed me.

We walked amongst the people either arriving or leaving in a hurry. Porters were trying to find a passage through those standing in their way loudly asking them to move out and to let them pass through with their heavy luggage carts. We could hear the sounds of the steam turning the squeaking train wheels against the rails allowing them to roll out of the station. The high pitch of train whistles would cover your voice. The smell of burning coal filled your nose and impregnated your clothes. If the streets on Whitechapel left you mindless with its crowded mob moving slowly, the railway station brought you a new level, that of absolute chaos. As we came close to the gates leading to the trains, Elizabeth stopped me, stared at me, which rather surprised me.

"Isn't there something you should tell me before leaving?" she asked.

"I do have a couple of things I would like to say, but it seems inappropriate," I said looking around us.

"Why?"

"Because of the place we are in. Even if we were alone here, it would still be inappropriate."

"Again, why?"

"We come from two different realms, and they will never merge together. They can only collide against each other as they have always done destroying everyone believing the contrary or caught in between. So whatever word I would dare speak out would not only be inappropriate but also hopeless."

"Then if you can't or are afraid to say them, I shall tell these words for you because they would also be mine. I don't care about what you've just said. I only care about us." She paused a moment and continued. "You know those families we met and the help we are offering them, well they would have only been an idea in my mind hadn't you allowed me to enter your world. Nobody else could have done it like you have. Since the first day I met you, I felt there was a common reason for us to learn more about each other. This reason is now clearer than it has ever been before. It is to love each other. Yes, I fell in love with you, and I beg you now to tell me if I am wrong or if it is only I who feels this way."

I couldn't do anything else but look at her, forgetting that a world around us even existed and kissed her.

"If there is only one thing I am certain of, it's my love for you, Elizabeth."

I held her in my arms and kissed her again. "It's time for me to leave."

We let go of each other. I hesitated for a moment, wondering if I was doing the right thing in finding who knows what somewhere out there. I picked up my suitcase and directed myself towards the passenger cars.

I waved at her and saw her turn around with her head down to better hide her tears.

I asked one of the conductors for a place to sit in the first-class section showing him my ticket. Once inside, I placed my suitcase on the overboard and sat near the window. As the train started to pull out, I noticed a man running along the deck trying to board the train. "A latecomer," I said to myself and smiled. He was wearing a long grey overcoat, his neck wrapped in a red scarf, and held his black fedora on his head with one of his hands.

I reached in my jacket's inner pocket and pulled out the day's paper for me to read the headlines. To my surprise, the latecomer had not only managed to get on the train, but was in my section of the car walking through the aisle catching his breath. He stopped, glanced around, decided to walk back towards my direction finally sitting right in front of me.

"You almost missed the train," I said.

"What makes you believe I would have missed it?" he asked.

"Well, I saw you running rather quickly to get on."

"Maybe moving fast at the last moment could also be a way for me to avoid curious people knowing what train I'm about to board."

"Oh! Sorry if I seemed to intrude. Perhaps, I should mind my own business."

"Maybe you should, unless your business whatever it may be would matter greatly to me."

"I doubt it would," I said as I continued reading the paper.

My clumsy remarks abruptly ended any conversation either one of us could have wished to hold. I put aside the paper and instead, opened a book I brought and began reading. The monotonous sound of the wheels clicking each rail section combined with the surrounding landscape gave the measure of time passing by. Every now and then, the train blew its whistle warning towns and villages of its approach. Minutes quickly turned into hours. My fellow passenger hadn't budged an inch. He still had his overcoat on, collar up wrapped around with his red scarf. I would have sworn he was sleeping when suddenly he spoke out.

"We're about to arrive to Manchester where you're probably heading for."

"Yes. How did you guess?"

"A hunch, a simple hunch. That's where I'm going as well."

"You live there?"

"No, nevertheless, I've been there so many times for so many reasons that I should have set up a place there to live. And you?"

"It shall be my first visit. Since you know your whereabouts, is there a hotel you might suggest?"

"Manchester has a lot to offer as far as hotels are concerned. My recommendation will depend on what kind of person you are and how you want to spend your time. Let me see."

He looked at me from the top of my head to the sole of my shoes.

"You're dressed in a rather unusual manner for someone traveling in a first-class cabin. Your close shaved face, however, tells me you mind for your appearance. If you intended to disguise yourself as a worker, I suggest you let some hair grow a day or two. Wear an old cap not that almost new fedora. Even if you don't have a strong accent, the tones of your voice suggests your Irish origin. So I would recommend Mitre Hotel right at the foot of Manchester Cathedral."

"And if I wanted to have a pint and throw darts with some of our fellow Irishmen, where should I go?"

"They can become quite rowdy at times. I would start at Sawyers Arms or the old White Lion and then see how things evolve."

He added a few comments about the city wishing me a nice visit.

He stood up, and in a matter of seconds reached the door at the rear of the car. I swear the bloody fool must have jumped off the train before it came to a complete halt for I saw him running on the ramp, his red scarf covering his face. Meeting the man left me with a strange feeling. We never introduced ourselves. Our conversation had ended without having really started. Not that I needed someone to talk to on the train. I pulled my suitcase off the upper shelf and exited the train. In the station's main hall, I looked around hoping I would see my unknown co-passenger. He had vanished.

Only a few footsteps away from the station's main entrance, cab drivers, whip in hand, were waving at me hoping I would choose them. However, I preferred walking after asking my way to a policeman standing on the corner of a street.

"Beware of certain areas," he told me, "as you might suddenly find yourself surrounded by scuttlers using you as an opportunity to prove themselves against their friends and others".

He described who these people were, usually bands of youths, and mentioned the places I should avoid. I tightened my grip on my suitcase, prepared myself with the idea of having to use my knife, and went with my walk. Manchester smelled differently than London. It seemed to me it had a scent, almost a distinctive but constant aroma compared to the succession of street odours the City gave away all day long. Cotton, it was certainly the whiff of cotton coming from mills and warehouses Fitzgerald had told me about with overtones of burning coal.

Heading towards the hotel, I had a feeling that someone was following me. Even with frequent slight turns of the head, I couldn't figure out who it might be.

Crossing over onto the other side-walk, I noticed that the only person doing the same would be a young lad. He couldn't have been more than twelve or thirteen years old. Rather young for a scutler. His toes were coming out from the torn off toe boxes of his shoes. Having grown the habit of never underestimating the behaviour of others, I entered the food store on my left. The large opened door provided an excellent place for me to hide behind and surprise him. He entered, looked around trying to find me ignoring totally that I was now just behind him. I grabbed him by the shoulder and spun him around towards me.

"And what do you think you are doing, young lad," I asked.

He felt more angry for being caught than scared of what may happen to him. People close by laughed. One of the employees behind the counter wearing a walrus moustache smiled.

"Ya got one o' them," said he. "One of whom?" I asked.

"One of those street rascals," answered a woman holding a basket full of potatoes.

"Leh me go, leh me go," the boy cried out. "I ain't doing you wrong".

I dragged him in one of the quieter alleys of the store, looked at him and smiled.

"You should learn to better follow your prey otherwise you'll find yourself in serious trouble," I told him. "Let me see now. That's probably what you're doing aren't you?"

"No I ain't, leh me go," the poor kid cried whilst bashing me with his small hands.

"Now calm down. Learning to follow without being caught. That's what you're doing, and one of yours is watching somewhere near to see how well you are operating. At least your trainer knows how to do it."

There was no sign of him however hard I looked through the store's windows.

"I said calm down. I have something that will most certainly interest you."

I pulled out from one of my pockets a small pouch containing some coins and shook it over his head allowing him to figure out its content. He tried to grab it, but I was quicker, and raised my hand way above his reach.

"I'll give it to you letting your friends clearly know how good you are in picking pockets, but you have to calm down first and help me out. Promise?"

"Promise," he answered.

"I'm serious. So don't try to fool me. Understood?" "Yes. What j'you want?"

"You're Irish and I am too. So you learned how Irishmen have to depend on each other to survive. Do you?"

"Yes."

"Good. I need to find some friends who will also help me. It's a serious matter. I need you to tell me where I can find these friends."

"Who?" he asked.

"The Fenian or the Brotherhood." I answered.

"The Hood! If I spoke they..., they could..., they will..."

"Don't you worry now. They won't hurt you. As a matter of fact, they'll probably thank you for telling me where to meet them."

He looked around, made a sign for me to lower down a little and whispered to my ear, "Sawyers Arms. Maybe there".

"Good boy." I was quite surprised he suggested the same pub my unknown voyage partner did. Such a coincidence in a very short period of time leaves you with a strange feeling.

"What's your name, lad?"

"Willie, sir."

"Here's your reward, Willie. Now you will be able to prove to the others how brave and clever you are. You must remember what you've just learned. Most of the time, your prey shall be wiser than you think so think twice. First as you would yourself and the second time as the other would."

He tossed the pouch from one hand to the other, went to the door, looked outside and then back at me and offered me a proud smile.

Once in my hotel room, I unpacked and within minutes was back on the streets hoping to meet someone at Sawyers Arms who would connect me with the Brotherhood or even better reveal significant details on who Tumblety really is.

Walking down on Deansgate gave me another perspective of Manchester, its cultural side. On my left, yards away from Sawyers Arms, the construction of a impressing red sandstone building was almost completed. It's intended to become a library I hope would eventually contain books on the practice of medicine. I should come back some day and spend so time reading there. The instant I entered the pub I was brought back into the kind of world I was more familiar with. The faces were different but would they be sitting at a table or standing near the bar, almost all of them wearing the same expression of dismay. Here, as in Whitechapel, exchanging words with those surrounding them had no other purpose than offering a short respite.

Similar people always manage to gather in similar places wherever they may find themselves. Even th doors were familiar, the workers, wearing day after day the same sweaty clothes, would open them with their dirty hands darkening the handles. They gave an imposing overtone you would hope the vapours of alcohol would dissipate. The barman looked at me as I approached him. "A pint please," I asked him.

"Yus sir, comin' up," he answered as he picked a glass and pulled down on the handle of one the beer towers to fill it up. "Ain't seen you here before. Movin' in," he asked.

"No, just passing by."

"Mind if I ask ye where ye from?"

"London." I didn't want to give him details on what part if London I lived in, but the expression on his face offered a clear indication he expected more.

"Bad things happenin' there to wimen, real bad," he added. "Any family of yers?"

"No."

"Ye probably live somewhere in London away from these killings," he said still waiting for me to tell him more and wiping an imaginary piece of dirt on the bar with a torn rag.

"As a matter of fact, I live in Whitechapel where it all happened. Soon enough, each man living there shall become another person's suspect."

"Including you," he added grinning at me and bringing himself closer.

"Including me. You know," I went with an obviously arrogant look, "I could actually be the Ripper looking for a new territory." I deliberately paused and slowly asked him: "Have any nice streets I could explore?"

He pulled back strait up in an instant and lost his smile.

It was my turn to offer him a smile.

"Let me reassure you, my friend. Had I been the Ripper, suggestions would be the last things I'd be asking. I, however, need some help. Maybe you could provide me with some information."

"Depends on what ye want."

"I have this person I know in London. He's quite a special character who wants me to work with him.

Before accepting his offer, I need to understand him better. I was told he may have some friends in Manchester, and even comes here from time to time. Maybe they could help me out."

"I recognize most of the faces but can't say I know them all."

"Come closer. I'll whisper just a few words. Trust

me, they will certainly mean something to you."

He bent towards me and turned his head sideways.

"The Fenian." I said.

Again, he pulled back.

"The Fenian?" he replied in a low voice. "Ye want to meet them. Are you mad? Even if I knew them, what makes ye think I would tell ye bout 'em. Ain't gonna snitch. Never did, never will," he said as he moved on to serve another client at the other end of the bar.

My first attempt was failing and left me wondering if I had been so foolish to believe I could get in contact with the Fenian only by asking the first person I met. I took a sip of beer, turned around to better see the kind of people gathering at Sawyers Arms. At the other end of the pub, a group of cheerful men sitting at a table almost set against the wall seemed to be spending a pleasant time. One of the waiters kept going back and forth to the bar bringing them refills.

"Hey," said the waiter taping on my shoulder to get my attention. "I think I can 'elp ye".

"Really!"

"I spoke to a friend and he sez he could give some information. See the door near the stairs, E's outside waiting for ye."

"Can't we meet here inside? It would certainly be safer for both of us."

"I don't set the rules. 'E does."

I could either fall into a trap, try my chance somewhere else or trust the barman. Having traveled this far, and spent so much energy on finding who Tumblety could be, it would have been ridiculous at this point for me to refuse taking any risks. I opted for the latter and walked towards the door, opened it, looked before crossing into a dark open but small yard. I could only see a man about my size. Obviously waiting for me since he waved with his hand for me to come to him. He was alone, which offer some comfort as to my safety. Without saying a word, I approached him.

"You asked to meet with members of the Fenian?"

"Yes," I answered. "Can you help me?"

Suddenly, someone grabbed me by the neck. I tried to release myself from his grip and was about to succeed when a second one helped him bring me down onto the ground laying on my back. The first one held my shoulder to the ground whilst the other knelt over me both preventing me from making any move. It was useless for me to try to free myself. I calmed down trying to regain my strength, but and expected the worst.

"Who are you? What matters of interest brings you here? Patrick, make him understand."

The man kneeling over me threw a quick but hard fist at my face spinning my head to the side. I could feel the blood dripping from my lips and spat it towards one of my adversaries. The pain started to grow all across my head.

"Speak up or you may regret ever coming to Manchester," said the voice at the back of the yard.

"I just came here to learn more about a man who offered me some help in London. His name is Francis Tumblety. I was told somebody in the Fenian here in Manchester could probably help me learn more about him."

"That's not enough," said the voice.

I was about to be served another fist when another voice spoke out.

"It's enough for me. Let him free." Both men holding me pulled away immediately.

This time, I recognized the voice. It was that of the man who sat in front of me in the train. I stood up, wiped the dust off my clothes, and looked at those who held me down, in particular, the man who hit me.

"Follow me," said my co-traveler.

I approached him at a slow pace, still feeling dizzy from the attack against me. The goons were just behind me. I started to walk, came to a stop and reaching deep inside me to bring up all my energy, curled my fingers into a tight fist. I turned around and smashed the closest face I could reach. One of them fell on his back. The two others moved away whilst I looked down on my opponent. I was amused to see it was the same who had hit me seconds earlier.

"Just wanted to introduce myself in case we come across on another day," I said looking at all three men.

"I'm Woodrow Reily, if you or your friends wanted to know."

"May I?" I asked him whilst lending him my hand to help him get up. Obviously full of anger or confused to say the least, he refused it.

"Are you done or does any one of you still want to prove something to each other?" said the traveler.

"Come mister Reily. We need to talk."

He opened the back door leading us into the pub. A small crowd of curious clients probably trying to figure out what had been going on moved away from the door as we walked in.

"I'm Derrick O'Connell. Forget what just happened. I'm usually surrounded by a thick wall of friends and followers who sometimes tend to overreact, and you, I must say, presented them with an excellent opportunity to do exactly that."

"Come, let's sit right there," he said pointing at the same table where a group I noticed earlier was enjoying their drinks. As we sat down, others joined us. It took only seconds for a tight circle of people to form a protective barrier around us.

"What did I tell you?" he added as he laid back on his seat with a proud smile. "Listen friends, him and I need to have a little privacy here. So if you don't mind, show me you're not interested in what we are about to say."

Almost everyone, with the exception of those sitting with us at the same table, moved out and returned to their usual business. No one dared to sit at the tables surrounding ours which was a clear indication of O'Connell's importance.

"When you took the train in London, you knew I was coming here, didn't you. You boarded the train at the last moment not because you were late but to avoid being recognized. That explains the scarf over your face. You probably even had a good idea of what I was looking for. Who gave you this information? Why didn't you let me know?" I asked.

"You're smart enough to understand why I won't tell you how I was informed on your intentions. Let's say us Irishmen are close to each other. Maybe not those like you who chose to isolate themselves, but the rest of us are. Why I stayed silent on the train? To better know what kind of person you were. I must admit I was a little disappointed. I, however, liked the way you handled Willie."

"You know him?"

"Who do you think paid him to follow you, and convince you to come here? Made me laugh when he told me you gave him more money than I did."

"I thought he was one of those street gang apprentices learning his trade."

"Indeed, he is. He could teach you more than you can imagine, believe me."

"Collins, bring us a couple of pints will you. My friend here Woodrow is paying," he said with a sparkling smile. "Now let's get serious if you don't mind.

You must be foolish to think that you can simply ask someone here a question and expect an immediate answer just like that," he said snapping his fingers.

"It was stupid of me, I must admit."

"We learn to depend on each other and build some trust between us. Trust is not a given, but built through the years or generated by special situations. Now you, you've just arrived here, and unless I missed something, nothing special happened yet to make you deserve this trust. If you're serious about what you are looking for, and expect some help you got to prove you are trustworthy. Otherwise, you might find yourself in a delicate position."

"I think I know what you mean," I told him as Collins approached us with two fresh pints. I reached in one of my pockets and grabbed enough coins to pay him.

"Do you? Just to make sure you're aware of what could happen, let me give two examples."

O'Connell placed a hand behind Collins back bringing him closer to us. "Listen here Collins, this concerns you," he added. Collins stopped, looked at both of us wondering what would come out. "Collins' son was killed last year by some radicals because they believed he had given some information to a police inspector concerning the Brotherhood. He was only fourteen years old. They were wrong and were taken care of. Still, a shadow of a doubt remains in some sick minds hovering over all his family. Twice, Collins tried to put an end to his life. Had it not been for members of our group, he would have succeeded."

"He told me he wasn't a snitch, and I believed him," I answered whilst looking at Collins. "I'm sorry for the loss of your child, Collins, and shall never bother you again."

"The other example involves Patrick, the young man who... let's say insisted physically upon you. His father, Kevin O'Donahue, refused to admit he knew anything about the Brotherhood which was the case and was clubbed to death by some mad military. The investigation concluded that it was a sad accident, and the soldier sent away unpunished..."

"So Patrick's mind is set on avenging his father's murder on any occasion he has. I gave him quite a good one, I believe," I added as my hand went over the swollen side of my face. "Am I correct?"

"You sure did," O'Connell said. "Listen, I'm willing to give you a chance at proving yourself. It could become dangerous, and I would understand if you refuse to accept."

"I'm prepared to do anything you ask of me."

"Don't be so hasty, and let me finish before deciding. I have this important document I need to send to Dublin. I thought you could be the one to deliver it to Liverpool where a contact will pick it up and cross it over to its destination. The courier needs to carry this document as if his life depended on it." He turned his head around, searching for someone. "Patrick, come over here a minute. You won't be traveling alone. Someone will accompany you, and serve as your personal guard. You should learn to trust him as much as I do."

As he came closer to the table, everyone moved away to let him pass and quickly understood why. In the darkness of the courtyard, I hadn't paid much attention to the man I sent to the ground. Now in full view of him, I could not believe I had succeeded. He was quite tall with large shoulders. He was probably in his mid twenties. His face was that of a young boy on a grown man's body. He wore a vest much too small to fit him and letting his large and strong thorax show. He frowned at me clearly indicating what he thought of me.

"Patrick, you've met Woodrow here. I'm quite sure both of you would have preferred a more pleasant initial encounter. Since I have a document to be delivered in Liverpool, and asked Woodrow if he would help us, I need you to travel with him to make sure the document won't fall into unwanted hands."

"But sir, is there no one else to do the job?" asked Patrick.

"You're one of my best, and the only one available. Normally, I would have done it myself but have urgent matters to be taken care of. So Woodrow, what's your decision?"

"I blame the poor guy who would try to take the document away from us, and would take pleasure in helping Patrick serve him the same treat he gave me," I answered with a smiling glance at Patrick.

Maybe surprised by my response, he hesitated a second. "...but if you get to him first, there won't be a lot left for me to do."

"I take it as a yes from both of you. Excellent. I have to leave now, and won't be here to-morrow to give you the document. Come back around eight, and Collins will have it ready for you. Woodrow, do you mind walking a few minutes with me? I still have a couple of things I'd like to discuss with you."

"As you wish," said I as I followed him outside.

"Since Patrick's father died, I took care of him as if he were my own son. He's a good boy, and I'm proud of him. He reacts quickly, and realizes, sometimes too late, he has made a mistake. So be careful, and try to make him avoid any confrontation."

"Are you telling me he's unpredictable?"

"Quite the contrary. What I mean is that once he gets into a fight, he'll hit a weak opponent exactly the same way a strong one, hard, very hard."

"I can easily imagine why, now knowing what happened to his father."

"Good. Now, tell me. Have you ever used a gun?"

"Never. Why?"

"Because it might be the only way left to defend yourself. I never had to use it but always wore it on me. Let's turn left here and I shall show you how to use it."

We turned at the street corner, walked down an aisle until we met an end. He pulled out a revolver from his coat and showed me how to arm it, point it and reload it.

"He's some extra cartridges just in case. Now if you have no other choice but to use it, make sure you get rid of it after. Otherwise, if you get caught by the police with a gun you'll be facing a bigger problem than the one you just got out of."

His words seemed fading as if I had been knocked unconscience. I slowly put the handgun in my coat pocket, and I felt I had to follow his instructions and advice without questioning them contrary to what I've always done with others all my life as long as I could remember.

"Are you all right?" he asked.

"Yes. Maybe a bit tired, but I'm fine, thank you."

"Good. To-morrow, Collins shall have the money you and Patrick will need for the train tickets, meals and other expenses. You shall be told to whom the document must be delivered. Once the task is completed, you will be informed on how to get in contact with me again. Do you have any questions or concerns you want to share?"

"None. Everything is quite clear. The journey should be rather easy and without any problem, I believe."

"Then, good luck," he said as we went each of us on our own way.

As I returned to my hotel, everything I been through during the past two months came back to me.

Before meeting Francis Tumblety, I thought I had everything organized. My life was simple and modest. I had a rather good job, enough money for my food and shelter. I even managed to put some savings aside should any misfortune hit me. I lived alone, and needed no one, the Faculty's students and the corpses of the Pathological Institute offering me more company than I desired. Besides Fillmore's unpleasant remarks, no one complained about me. I had no quarrel with those surrounding me and never got caught in a fight with anybody. I obeyed the laws, and respected the rules of the streets of the East End. Indeed, I had quite an easy and peaceful life. Now, I find myself being an armed courier for the Fenian trying to prove himself to them in the hope of gaining some evidence against this Tumblety, the man whom I believe murdered and mutilated some miserable women of Whitechapel. I left a woman I cared for and a protector to try to accomplish alone what the police has the power and means to do. I find no pride in my decisions to pursue this mission nor any explanation to justify it. I am compelled to bring it to an end whatever it may be and damn me if I shan't end it whatever the cost.

TUESDAY, OCTOBER 9, 1888

I woke up early this morning, drank a cup of tea, chewed on a couple of biscuits in the lobby. I felt necessary to warn the front-desk clerk that I may be returning to my room the next day only. I left my room, and headed as fast as I could towards Sawyers Arms On my way, I picked up to-day's edition of the Manchester Guardian hoping time would pass faster on the train if I read it. The headlines showed no indication of another murder in Whitechapel. At seven o'clock, I arrived at the pub. It wasn't open. Was I too early? O'Connell had given us eight but expected to find everyone coming in before the deadline. I knocked on the door as hard as I could, and saw Collins hurrying to open it.

"Come in Woodrow" he said. "Sorry about the door but I didn't want anyone else but you and Patrick."

"Good idea, Collins. Has Patrick arrived?"

"E didn't want to miss ye and slept here. Come, I got some tea, and fresh bread for ye."

"Thank you so much, Collins. I felt a bit chilly this morning, and shan't say no to a warm tea."

I noticed Patrick sitting at a table near the bar gently patting a white cat sleeping on his laps. He had this boyish smile a younger brother would offer you had he not seen you for a long time.

"Good morning Patrick. You seem to be in a better shape than I," I said.

"I always sleep well after a good fight. But we didn't really fight, didn't we?" he asked.

"Not really," I answered.

A smoking tea pot, eggs and sausage were inviting me at the table, and I couldn't refuse.

"If yur hungry, make it fast," said Collins, "cause yur train leaves in an hour." He handed me a packet O'Connell he had given him earlier. "It's for you," he said.

An envelope with my name on it was attached. I opened it, and read the hand-written note. O'Connell was asking me to wear the clothes in the packet, and leave mine to Collins. It ended with an underlined additional request, "Make sure no one sees your face." The packet contained the same clothes O'Connell wore the day before. Without asking myself why he wanted me to wear his clothes and, trusting his good judgement, I changed. I would eventually discover why he had asked such a thing.

"Here's the train tickets, some money and the document case," Patrick said. "It's locked, and the key's already in Liverpool."

We each took our ticket and split the money he had laid on the table. The document case he handled to me was covered with fine leather and had a gilded flop lock with shiny metal corners. It was small enough to fit in my coat's inner pocket without leaving a trace.

"Some'n 'll pick ye up at the Liverpool station, and

drive ye both to yur contact. Patrick knows 'im, so ye won't have to worry."

"His horse has a painted white shamrock on his forehead. Can't miss it," added Patrick with a smile.

The train ride was a short one, but with every new piece of landscape, I noticed how Patrick's eyes would glow each time as if he were opening a birthday gift.

"I always wanted to be a farmer, and raise some cows," he said. "What about you?"

"I'm still asking myself that question."

"Cows are nice and gentle. I'd have some dogs and cats also."

He turned his eyes back at the window admiring what the tracks offered him. Such a strong young person speaking out such simple words made me understand why O'Connell took him under his protection, in many respects he still had the mind of a defenseless boy. Maybe one day I should question myself as to why I never considered myself as someone responsible for others nor did I have any disposition to do so. Not to-day however. What mattered more to me was figuring out is how a seemingly meaningless but safe voyage on a train could prove to the Fenian I was trustworthy, as well as learning more about Tumblety and his possible link with the Whitechapel murders.

I pulled out the Manchester Guardian from one of my pockets and searched for any piece of information related to those crimes. I was relieved to read that no other women had been killed. Fewer women were on the streets of Whitechapel and Spitalfields at night, and had they needed to be there, they would walk in groups of two or three which provided them with a defensive option. On a darker side, Her Majesty refused a petition to review the decision concerning a reward proposal the Whitechapel Vigilance Committee had sent her. Had three Lords or a single Lady been murdered in a short period of time in Whitechapel, I'm quite certain she would have herself issued such a proposal to her government.

Once we arrived at the train station, the boy in Patrick's mind left its place to the protector.

"Keep a certain distance behind me," he said in a low voice. "No one knows you here so you won't be suspected of being one of O'Connell's men. Get on the carriage only when I'm in. It's a red closed one. Remember the horse's white forehead, just in case."

I let him move ahead of me keeping my face covered as instructed by O'Connell. I quickly noticed the Brougham and recognized the horse. Patrick was rather surprised when he approached the driver. I could hear him arguing with him but was to far away to catch a single word. Both arms were extended on his sides fists clinched. Anybody more annoyed than he was would probably start a fight. He glanced at me, and hesitated a moment before climbing inside. I quickly jumped in after him.

"Is something wrong?" I asked.

"It's not Kirk, the driver who always picks us up. This one, his cousin, he says and whom I've never met told me Kirk had an accident this morning."

"Can we trust him?"

"We'll find out soon enough," he frowned.

I couldn't resist reaching for my pistol and arranging it so it would be quick to pull out. Patrick's reaction surprised me. He comfortably set himself against one of the carriage's corner, laid his head down, pulled his cap over his eyes and crossed his arms and legs. He didn't seem to worry at all.

"The best thing to do is rest a little. We still have some road to do you know," he said.

"Where to?" I asked.

He raised his head up at me and muttered, "A

gatehouse lodge somewhere on the way to Oldham."

Heavy rains must have fallen during the night softening the dirt road turning it into a murky soup. We were having a rather bumpy ride, water splashing continuously against the side of the brougham even if our driver had slowed down his horse. Had the top been pulled back opened, we would be soaking wet and covered with mud.

The carriage slowed even more and turned left then right. I could hear the driver whipping his horse and yelling at him to speed up.

"We're not supposed to turn. The lodge is strait ahead," Patrick said. "Bloody hell, where's he taking us." He turned around, lifted himself up a little, and banged on the window behind the driver's seat. "Hey, you're going the wrong way." He pulled hard on one of the window straps expecting it to open which would allow him to take hold of the driver but only succeeded in tearing the strap off its hinges. He tried the other strap. It was caught inside the body, and wouldn't budge. "Go back immediately or I'll have you swallow all your teeth," he yelled.

The driver didn't pay attention, and whipped his horse even more to speed up. Patrick's expression redefined the word fury in its worst sense. His opened lips were thinned out. His jaws were so tightly locked against each other you would expect his own teeth to pop out of his mouth. His cheeks pushed his eyelids up almost hiding his eyes. His eyebrows pulled close together wrinkled his forehead. Never in my life had I seen such anger in a human being not even in my father's face, and he was hard to beat. I could easily imagine any of the Whitechapel victims freezing out of fear had the Ripper revealed only half of what Patrick showed. I myself would never have hit him in the face had I seen him this way.

"We have to stop him or get out," he said banging at the driver's window.

I looked through the side window to see if there was a safe landing space should we decide to jump out of the carriage, but trees almost walled up the roadside. I moved to the other side. It was even worse, large stones lined the edge.

Finally, Patrick broke the window and reached with both hands for the driver's feet. The driver rammed his whip's handle onto Patrick's hand causing him to scream out of pain. At the same moment, the driver pulled hard on the horse's bridle reins forcing him to come to a quick stop brutally sending us to the front of the carriage.

Someone grabbed the door handle from outside and pulled it wide open. "Get out," a voice yelled "or I'll blow off either one of your heads off."

"Let's do as he says," Patrick whispered. "But keep your eyes open and prepare to react quickly."

He went out first, slowly placing a foot on the carriage step, and staring at his adversary. There stood this man holding a gun in his hand dressed up as a hunter, waistcoat, knickerbockers, and strapped ankles.

A second one, on his left, looked more like a farmer wearing a dirty shepherd's smock and torn corduroy trousers. He was tapping the inside of one of his hands with a rusted bayonet almost as long as a sword that could still cut you open, and have yours guts spill out with a single up-twisted stab. And there behind them, was our bloody driver. Two agitated horses were tied to a tree for the thugs to get away quickly.

"I'm sorry," he said. "I'm so sorry. My cousin refused to help them," he added pointing at the two men, "and had both legs broken right in front of me. They told me they'd do the same to me if I refused to replace him."

Patrick slowly moved down stepping aside for me to follow him. The driver had brought us off the road by the side of a marsh in a clearing in the woods. Even if vegetation emerged from its banks, dead tree trunks, some still standing up, others leaning on broken-down branches, gave it an unwelcome appearance. One could get rid of almost any undesired object in this marsh, floating moss would cover it for ever.

Only a few feet separated us from the goons.

"Now if you two gentlemen would hand me over the document in your possession, we will let you go on with your journey," said the hunter-dressed hoodlum.

"What document?" I asked.

"Don't play games with us or else you'll become a permanent guest of the waters behind me. Your only option is to give me the document."

Patrick looked at me and with a barely perceptible movement of his eyes towards his feet spoke out. "He may be right. Our options are limited. Wouldn't you agree Woodrow?"

He looked again in my direction and down on the ground where I noticed a thick piece of branch just waiting to be picked up.

"Quite limited to be honest," I answered. "Now if you let me pull it out I'll give to you," I added just to warn them of my intention.

I slowly reached inside my right-side jacket pocket, hesitated then stopped. "Patrick, to whom should I give it to?" I asked wearing the best whimsical look I could fabricate.

"To the nice man with the gun, of course," he answered with a reassuring smile letting me understand he was ready.

"Of course."

That was the signal. In less time it would take me to wink, Patrick kicked up the branch almost directly in my hands. I held it tight and swung as hard as I could on the hunter's arm knocking his gun out of his hand and into the marsh. I swung it back upwards and hit him under the chin. The cracking noise coming from his jaw and his nasty fall on the ground ended any threat he could bring us.

Patrick threw himself at the motionless farmer clearly surprised by my move, but for an instant only. His bayonet pointing up inches away from Patrick's chest bringing him to an immediate stop.

"Give me the damn document or your friend..."

He never finished his words. I dropped the branch and pulled out my pistol. Without really aiming I took a shot at him. The bullet hit him in the head splashing blood and brains all around.

"Fine shot, Woodrow," said Patrick turning back at me, his face smeared with blood. "What a fine shot!"

I felt my jaw falling. My shaking hand let go of the gun. I had never used a gun before in my life, and suddenly became aware I could have wounded or even killed Patrick instead. I was in shock.

He gave me a friendly pat on the shoulder, wiped his face. "Come now. Let's not waste our time. We'll use their horses to get to our rendez-vous point."

"What about him," I asked pointing at the man I hit with the branch. "He may be still alive."

Patrick picked up my pistol and fired the remaining shots into the laying hunter's body. "Now he's dead."

He threw the pistol in the marsh as far as he could.

"As for you", he told the driver, "dump those bodies with some heavy stones and go take care of your cousin." The poor man was exactly at the same place he stood when all commenced, obviously frozen by what had taken place in front of him in a matter of minutes.

"One last thing," Patrick added. "This never happened, understood?"

He acknowledged by bowing his head, and began rolling the two bodies into the marsh.

Half an hour later, we arrived at the lodge, tied the horses down. I hadn't spoken a word whilst we rode away and was still not in any mood to start a conversation. "Do you mind if I stay outside for a while?" I asked Patrick. "I need some time to think this over. Here's the document."

"Don't worry yourself. It was either them or us."

While walking away from the lodge, I tried to figure out how I ended up killing a man. I'm running after the Whitechapel murderer, and now I, myself, have ended someone's life. Defending our lives may be an acceptable reason, but I somehow fell I could have avoided all this. I took deep breathes of the country road's fresh smell and searched around me hoping to find something appeasing. The autumn winds were spinning fallen leaves in front of me. I noticed a farmer at my right, a real one this time. I stopped and leaned on the fence separating the road from the fields to better observe him. He was on a horse-drawn harrow, its tines pulverizing the clods of the top soil one field length after the other. His life seemed much simpler than mine not that I wished to change. But at least, he could see the direct results of his efforts.

The sound of approaching footsteps brought me quickly back to my reality. It was O'Connell.

"You here! Didn't you have some business to handle elsewhere?" I asked.

He didn't respond, not even smiled, but his eyes could tell he understood what was going on inside me. He stood by my side, looked at the farmer. "I've always been fascinated by what a farmer can achieve with simple tools. He doesn't keep asking himself if he can handle every new day, but just pulls the best he can out of a poor soil. At the end of the day, he becomes more aware of himself being the only one having been able to do it without ever believing he's better than everyone else."

"What does that have to do with me?"

"That's how I think you reacted in front of an unexpected situation. No one else but you could have decided what had to be done. You just did it."

"Killing a man?"

"No, saving the life of someone I consider as my son. You may believe you weren't equipped as much as that farmer over there is," he said pointing at him with a head movement, "but you had it all inside you, and I somehow knew it before you did."

"I didn't expect to go this far to gain your trust."

"You won something worth so much more in my mind than trust. It's my friendship as well as Patrick's and only a few can claim to be known as one of our true friends."

He turned at me and offered his hand to shake. I never had someone who offered me his friendship before in my life nor did I seek one's friendship. Now, as I shook his hand, I felt good knowing that friendship can happen without you even being aware of it, and accepted his. We walked back to the gatehouse. On our way, he told me he had the real document on him. He had figured that someone at the pub might overhear parts of our conversation, and would follow us the next morning instead of him. He had then traveled all night, and made sure his document containing the list of the most important members of the Fenian would arrive safely in Dublin.

"The case. Can I have the leather case that contained the document you entrusted me with?" I asked. "It may seem childish, but it would always remind me of what you've said."

He pulled it from one of his pockets, a set of keys from another and gave it to me. "Always remember that what's inside any container often has a greater value."

On our way back, I noticed Patrick coming out of the gatehouse. Again, he wore his boyish expression on his face. Even if the Ripper's murders had introduced me to a ruthless thug, still I couldn't explain to myself how he could go on with his usual occupations as if nothing had happened only minutes after coldly killing a wounded man.

"Woodrow, can I have a word with you," he asked as he approached us.

"Of course, you can, my friend."

"I'll let you two alone," said O'Connell.

"That won't be necessary, sir," said Patrick. "I don't mind you listening to what I want to say."

"You know Woodrow, those men at the marsh would never have allowed us to stay alive. Had we managed to escape, it would have been only a matter of days or weeks for other members of the Fenian to share the same pernicious fate they intended for us to meet."

"What makes you think they were seeking members of the Fenian?" I asked him.

"We had too many unexpected visitors during the past few days, including you," said O'Connell before Patrick could even put in a word. "They were all asking questions about the Fenian. Something was about to happen, so we got prepared."

In a sense, maybe Patrick was right. It perhaps explained why he didn't thank me for having saved his life. In his mind much more was at stake, and it was obviously my duty to have acted accordingly.

"I think we deserve a bloody pint. Don't you think so Woodrow?" asked Patrick.

"Let's start with one and see how far we can go," said I, with a radiant smile.

"Oh my God. Don't tell me it's going to be one of those terrible evenings again", added O'Connell. "Now if one of you starts singing, I'll club him good night."

We all laughed and made it back to the gatehouse as fast as we could.

The gatehouse was old. The mortar holding most of the stones of its walls was crumbling. The wood window frames were so loosened up, air would come in, and with it the dampness of the surrounding forest. Patrick poured some lamp oil on the wood he had stacked in the pot-belly stove for it to start burning. He pulled out a chicken from a leather bag he had brought with him on the train. In a matter of minutes, he had plucked it, cut its head and legs off, emptied it and placed with some potatoes in a pot full of water on top of the stove.

"We'll have something to eat in an hour or so," he said with a smile of satisfaction which disappeared behind his mug. We had observed him without saying a word, and he just noticed it from the bottom of his glass bottom beer mug. It was one of those peculiar pewter beer mugs with a glass bottom allowing the drinker to see from the bottom whilst refreshing himself.

"What! Did you think I'm only good at fighting?"

"Patrick, you'll make a perfect Irish bride once these problems are all over," I responded bringing all three of us laughing our heads off again.

During the evening, our conversation quickly shifted to the question of the Irish Republican Brotherhood and its American counterpart, the Fenian Brotherhood. O'Connell brought me back some two hundred years before, when Irish Catholics were deprived of almost all rights under the 'Na Péindlíthe', the British Penal Laws.

"They couldn't own a good horse to work on the land, own a piece of land or inherit from their Catholic parents unless converting to the Anglican Church," he said.

Firearms, joining the army or holding any job related to public office and judiciary system were prohibited. For many, Ireland was a conquered country, and should remain as such, religion being only a secondary aspect of the Irish question. Even if an Irish was eventually allowed to own some land, it would never or rarely be enough to feed a family. Then came the great famine which began in 1845 and lasted until 1852. Potato had become the base food of those Irish with lesser means, and practically such was the case of the majority of Irish Catholics. The blight disease covered Ireland's potato fields destroying half if not more of all the crops during the first years. Good seeds were either hard to find or priceless. Government's response was slow and inappropriate, some even saying deliberately intended to be so. O'Connell quoted a famous declaration of a young Irish political leader, John Mitchell, "The Almighty, indeed, sent the potato blight, but the English created the Famine."

"Fighting for Ireland's independence is a question of survival for us Catholics," said O'Connell as he gulped down almost half of his second pint. "Many Irish consider the redistribution of the land and improvement of relations between landlords and tenants to be sufficient. Some even believe that the Government of Ireland Bill introduced two years ago by William Gladstone would solve the problem. Sadly, it was voted out not as much for its content which impacted on Britain's Home Rule, but for having been drafted by people outside the usual political loop."

"But you think differently?"

"It's only a step towards our complete autonomy. That's why we must keep on sending clear signals to the British authorities for them to understand what we want to achieve."

"By that, you mean using violence and terror?"

"Some consider it to be the only way to defend a cause whilst others are strictly using our goals as an opportunity to fight against any British they meet or those closely tied to them. The Irish National Invincibles are just one of the groups thinking this way. By the way, you might not know that they hacked their victims with long bladed surgical knives. It is said that these knives were carried in the skirts of one of the attacker's pregnant wife. Must have made quite a disgusting mess quite similar to what the killings in Whitechapel did."

I stood up, moved away from the table we sat at and came close to one of the gatehouse windows to take a peek outside. I didn't feel comfortable about his way of seeing things but needed to understand O'Connell more.

"Don't you sometimes feel that violence leads nowhere?"

"I usually do. As you personally experienced yesterday, a violent confrontation is not something one seeks, but one should not exclude it when it comes to protecting one's life. I make it a rule to rely upon more discreet methods. They may require more time, more thinking, but the impact is, by far, much greater. Some have taken an intermediate road such as Charles Stewart Parnell who has been trying for more than ten years to bring in changes through the parliamentary system, and now has been falsely accused of having supported, what I hope you remember, the1882 Phoenix Park murders."

O'Connell noticed I didn't quite understand what he meant. "Have you ever played chess?" he asked.

"Yes," I said coming back to the table after opening another bottle of beer. I was a bit surprised to hear for the third time someone coming out with the chess game comparison, Tumblety and Elizabeth having done so recently. We started eating the food Patrick had brought onto the table. He didn't seem interested in our conversation, but listened to every word coming out of O'Connell's mouth.

"Then you must be aware that there's more to the game than simply moving pieces on the board one after the other, and hoping to eventually checkmate the opponent's king."

"I suppose there is," said I, wondering where he was bringing me.

"Strategy," he said without even giving me a chance to finish my answer. "It's all about strategy, yours and your opponent's. It's a game where pawns, simply by the position they occupy on the board in certain situations can outmaneuver an adversary's own surrounding pieces regardless of their specific value."

"It depends how one plays the game."

"That's the point. Patrick, bring the chessboard. Woodrow, you shall learn much easier what I'm saying if I show you what I mean" he added looking at Patrick then back at me. "Learning the game leads you to notice the importance an opponent gives to some of his pieces. In the real world, it's often the same."

He started placing the pieces on the board. "Those considered to be in at the top of the hierarchy of power, queens and kings, for instance, are not always the ones who actually rule. Those who appear to be ordinary pawns may, in fact, be imposing their way of governing to those at the top of the hierarchy of power. Black or white?"

"White," said I.

"I'll let you start. Once you've figured out who these pseudo pawns are and how they operate, you come to the only logical conclusion which is to neutralize them as fast as you can."

"You mean killing them?"

"Patrick," he said, "I think we're getting way too serious. Open me another one of those beers." He took a deep breath, and, in a somewhat disappointed tone, went on. "You don't have to kill someone to render him powerless. A strong incentive is quite sufficient to have them removed from the chessboard.

"In other words, you're blackmailing people into

doing what you want."

"I rather consider it as preventing them from accomplishing what might stop us from achieving our goal. Now if one manages to render all of them useless in a swift simultaneous operation, the result is an uncommon turmoil."

We moved our pieces rapidly. Even if I considered myself to be a good chess player, O'Connell was in a much higher league than I, and quickly gained a serious advantage.

"The sudden absence from the political chessboard of so many opponents and the strategic position held by your own pieces make the difference between a bloody stalemate and... let's say, a peaceful checkmate," O'Connell added with the smile of a chess tournament winner.

"I presume that's what you hope being able to do."

"Trust me, it can be done."

"But the police have been constantly on the lookout since the Jubilee Plot," I said, expressing serious doubts.

"I'm quite aware of that. What you must know is that it was the British Government who planned the plot which, if it had succeeded, would have given the authorities the perfect excuse to seize members of any Irish organization favouring directly or indirectly the Irish Home Rule. However, even if they most likely expect a violent attempt of the sort from you now know who, we're working on a non-violent alternate way."

"It seems you've covered all the angles."

"I'm sure we did. Check, and if you don't pay attention to your game, you'll be checkmate in a couple of moves."

I looked at the board and examined where his attack would come from but couldn't figure it out.

"To show you up to what extent we've prepared our next round," he said, "there's one last part in our strategy." He waited a second, took a deep breath, glanced at me with such an expression of pride, say that of obvious superiority and went on. "If one keeps the Home Office and the Yard occupied elsewhere, the chances of succeeding are greatly increased; wouldn't you think so?"

"I do. However, not having details on how all these elements fall into place; I can't give you a definite opinion."

"I won't give you details of the operation not because I don't trust you. It's just that if I told you, and if you eventually found yourself in the hands of people who, by any means, will attempt to obtain that information, you can easily imagine the outcome. Let me point out one aspect. This is not an Irish Brotherhood or American influenced Fenian plan, I've been working on. It's something me and some very close friends of mine have initiated. So if someone eventually speaks of another Fenian or Brotherhood conspiracy, they would be way far from the reality."

The few pints I had poured behind the collar put my mind to a rest. Hence, I didn't pay much attention to what he had said about drawing off the authorities. I would eventually understand the full meaning of his words, but it would be much too late for me to have done anything.

"Checkmate," O'Connell said contemplating the board. "Now Woodrow, look closely to my pieces and compare them to yours. Tell me what you see."

"Almost all my pawns are gone, and I took only two of yours."

"My pawns were more than pawns. They fought to survive. For them, it shall always be a question of survival whilst the other pieces take for granted they will live on for ever, simply because of their foolish belief in the title they wear. And that's just to show you the attitude we must have to defeat them."

"You mean you would play the game differently than the way you just did?"

"Of course. As in a chess game, one will create a diversion knowingly sacrificing some of his pieces, pawns and higher ones, whilst he sets up his real attack elsewhere on the board. Strategy is the name of the game."

In the following hours of the night, we covered as many subjects as we drank bottles of beer, and I must admit we had quite a few. Learning more about Tumblety was the main reason of my presence in the region. Since I was sure about the relation he may have had with members of the Fenian and the Irish Republican Brotherhood, I preferred listening to whatever O'Connell would say about him, and go in further with specific questions should anything even remotely linked to the Whitechapel murders come out.

He told me that Tumblety was very well-known in the United States and Canada. However, contrary to the impression he gave me and the Hospital's authorities, it wasn't as much as a trained physician with high standards but more as a quack, a charlatan who made a fortune selling what he called 'Indian secret herbs and remedies'. Even if he was frequently arrested or brought to court for various reasons which affected his reputation, he continued his profession moving from one place to another in both countries. He managed to preserve his integrity by always having letters of well-known people he could use to confirm it.

"Overseas, you'll find many who consider themselves to be real physicians because of their relations with universities and hospitals. Others, such as Tumblety, use the term physician but are more into selling products than actually practicing medicine. The physicians refer to the men like Tumblety as snake-oil salesmen and try to do as much as they can to destroy their reputation. I for myself consider him to be a kind and generous person."

"You have to admit he's a bit excessive in a certain way."

"I'd say almost theatrical in many ways. We know he has often given money to help those he felt needed it, mostly amongst the Irish community. On the other side, wherever he is, his preference for young men draws controversy to say the least."

What he just said confirmed the impression Tumblety gave me and the certain distance I maintained in the relation between us.

"The particular kind of young men surrounding him would lead away anyone who might suspect him of aiding the Fenian which he actually did for years and still does," said O'Connell.

"Or committing more serious crimes," I pointed out.

"Are you referring to the Whitechapel murders?" he asked.

"Precisely."

O'Connell was surprised to hear the reasons I had for suspecting Tumblety. I told him about the lost surgical knife, his sudden and unexplained absences when the murders happened, his drastic opinion on how prostitutes should be handled.

"What do you think of all this?" I asked.

"Falsely accused so many times by so many people for so many crimes, I could imagine him developing a grudge that could turn into hatred not as much against women only, but towards society as a whole. Then again," he added, "anyone living in the East End could be suspected of being the killer, including yourself."

I felt he was intentionally evasive in his response and needed to go further in.

"Had he committed those hideous crimes, would you

have done something about it?" I asked.

He stood from his chair, looked away from me, "Of course, but not necessarily the way one would expect."

"Such as?"

"Such as handing the killer over to the police. The problem would be solved with discretion."

I tried to read the expression on his face but the obscurity of the interior of the house prevented it.

"Wouldn't you agree that unless he's been caught, people would still think he's somewhere out there."

"It's sad to say, but in a matter of weeks or months, people usually forget what happens around them or even to them. The same shall happen with the Ripper deaths. It will just become another series of bad days for East-Enders."

"As far as I'm concerned, I'll do everything that needs to be done to catch the murderer."

"It's your choice." He turned back at me and looked straight into my eyes. "All I wish to add is there could be more to this than simply deaths of East End prostitutes. So, my good friend, be careful not to put your own life at risk."

I sensed no threat in the tone of his voice. It came out more as a friendly advice from someone who wouldn't say more. He was probably also signaling me that our conversation for the day should end.

WEDNESDAY, OCTOBER 10, 1888

Waking up the following morning, I realized I drank more than I should have. O'Connell and Patrick already ate.

"Ye might want to chew a bit of this before leaving," said Patrick as he handed me a dish containing pieces of overcooked ham and a couple of slices of bread.

I looked at the dish and smiled at him. "This won't

help you find a job as a cook, I believe."

"Consider yourself lucky," O'Connell said trying hard not to laugh. "He gave you the better part of what he prepared. You should have seen how it came out."

Patrick was embarrassed. "I'll go and prepare the carriage and drive you to the train station."

We stopped at the hotel for me to pick up what I had left in my room. The room was in a mess. My suitcase had been emptied of its content and sprayed around on the floor. Someone had managed to get in hoping to find something. Nothing, however, was missing. I grabbed everything and threw it all in the suitcase and hurried down to complain at the reception desk.

"Someone broke into my room whilst I was absent," I said to the attendant surprised by my words. "Have you any idea who may have asked for me while I was out?"

"No sir but I could ask the other staff when they arrive later this afternoon."

"I'll be gone by then."

"I'm so sorry, sir. Is anything missing?" he asked.

"Nothing." I threw the keys on the desk letting him understand how upset I was.

"I believe everything is complete," was his only response.

I preferred not mentioning a word to O'Connell about what had happened considering the possibility some of his own men had visited my room on his behalf before meeting him. Once at the station, O'Connell and I shook hands. He didn't speak a single word. The expression on both our faces carried the deep meaning of our friendship. Patrick accompanied me inside. He pulled out a piece of paper from his coat pocket and gave it to me.

"He wanted you to have this just in case you need to contact him. Read it, learn it by heart then destroy it." I crumbled it and quickly placed in my pocket.

He gave me a tap on the shoulder. "Take good care, now," he said and turned away.

Although I didn't obtain any precise information leading to Tumblety's involvement in the Whitechapel murders, I was, however, satisfied by discovering one unusual side I ignored of the man and believed my pursuit to be one I should continue.

Once in the train and after spending two days with O'Connell, one thing suddenly struck my mind. Was O'Connell's presence in the train a pure coincidence or had he been informed by someone of my intentions regarding meeting some Fenian in Manchester? Besides me, only four other persons knew I was looking for O'Connell, Fitzgerald, Elizabeth, Abberline and Sergeant Thick. The mere fact that he embarked in the same compartment I was meant he not only knew I would be on the train but also exactly where I was seated. My mind was still struggling on all that had happened in only a few days. This new element was too much for me to solve for the moment, but I promised myself I would look into it as soon as I could.

I had almost forgotten the paper Patrick had given me and pulled it out. It had only three words on it, 'Sawyers Arms - Liberator'. I understood it meant for me to return to the bar where I met O'Connell if I needed to contact him and use 'Liberator' as a password. I opened the window and threw it out.

All the way back to London, the presence of voyagers at the train stations and those riding by my side couldn't remove these unbearable feelings of emptiness and solitude I had. No dismay, no guilt, just this strange sensation of being so different whilst everyone else is trying to be the same as the other. You keep hearing them use words like, "We live on the same street", "We work at the same place" or "We share the same interests". It dawned on me that this insisting need for so many people to be the same as the others serves only to better hide or even deny how different they are one from to the other. These past days appeared to have turned me into someone I didn't expect to become, making me deeply feel alone more than ever.

Even after stopping for a moment at my room, I noticed blood from the rather violent encounters of the previous days had splattered on my clothes. I freshened up, changed clothes and wrapped the stained ones in a newspaper to get rid of them later. When I arrived at Fitzgerald's home during the end of the afternoon, I still felt trapped in the same state of mind I carried all the way back from Manchester. I knocked on the door and within seconds, it opened.

"Woodrow! You're back?" It was Elizabeth. With only a few swift steps, she came into my arms gently placing her head against my shoulder. I held her tight as if I hadn't seen her in years. She pulled back looked at me.

"Your face is swollen. Dear God, what has happened to you?"

"Don't worry. It's just a fellow I met in Manchester who took me for someone else, but now, we are close friends."

"Come in quick." She took my hand and led the way to the drawing room where she invited me to sit by her side.

"I shall not annoy you by asking questions the likes of a worried mother would ask his child. All I wish to know is if your quest was worth the risks you may have taken."

"Yes, indeed, they were, and I sincerely appreciate you not wanting to learn more. I must admit I still wouldn't know how to explain everything. Things went so fast."

She covered my hand with both of hers pressing them

gently against mine. I looked at her. Her eyes were closed; her lips slightly opened. My fingers softly caressed the inside of her hands having me wish I could offer her whole body the same expression of my tender love. The long deep breath she took pushed out her already inviting breasts revealing them even more through the low laced neck line of her velvet dress. My free hand gently moved up her arm and wrapped the back of her long white neck. She turned her head resting her cheek in the palm of my hand before starting to kiss my fingers. The lavender tones of her perfume brought me into a dream-world. I got closer to her staring at her green eyes. She looked back at me, her lips only inches away from mine. She closed her eyes and gently pressed her lips against mine. Suddenly, we heard footsteps coming down the stairway. Elizabeth backed off whilst I managed to change seats before anyone would enter the drawing room.

It was Winston. He stood at the drawing room door and hesitated before slowly entering.

"Mister Fitzgerald heard voices down here and asked me to inform you he would join you in a few minutes."

"Thank you Winston," I said.

"It's good to see you've returned sir," he said. "It's bloody good to be back," I answered.

"Maybe Woodrow would like something to drink, Winston," asked Elizabeth.

"If you have something Elizabeth, I'll shall also but would otherwise wait for your father."

"You won't have to wait. A scotch seems well deserved, I believe."

It was Fitzgerald. We didn't hear him come down.

"I hope you don't mind my dressing up this way," he said.

He wore a velvet smoking jacket. Its shawl collar, cuffs, pocket flaps, and buttons were of black quilted silk. When I noticed his soft sole slippers, I understood why we didn't hear any noise on his way down the stairs. "Am I disrupting an important conversation between both of you?" he added.

"Of course not Father. Woodrow just came back minutes ago, and we just had a few words."

"It feels like I haven't seen you in centuries even if I was only gone a few days," I said as I stood up and

walked towards him. "It's so good to see you."

"It looks like you've been rumbling with new friends," he said as he stared at me.

"In a certain way, I did."

He came closer to me, pulled out a monocle from his jacket, raised it up in front of his right eye to better examine marks my face still had.

"Nothing really serious," he said only inches from my face. "It should return to normal in a less than a week."

"Father, look at yourself. It's as if you were examining a piece of dead meat."

Fitzgerald looked at her but didn't respond to what she said other than offering her a smile.

"Don't worry both of you. It's simply swollen," I said. "I've been through worst things, you know."

"Do you mind telling us how this happened?"

"I prefer not hearing more about this. I shall let both of you together and see instead what can be prepared for dinner," Elizabeth said as she left. Winston followed her.

Fitzgerald watched both of us, served me another Scotch, and sat in front of me. "So, how did things really go?" he asked.

"Of the three names Abberline wrote on his list, a man named O'Connell was the first and only one I met. I couldn't believe it. Without having known him yet, he came aboard the same train I took. Not only that, he sat right in front of me trying to figure out who I might be.

Someone had obviously informed him I'd be heading for Manchester hoping to find him, but he found me first. I can't figure out who got through to him. No more than four or five were aware of my intentions. Have any idea?"

"Not the slightest."

Anyway, I met him later that day in a Manchester pub the name of which he had mentioned to me in the train start with. That's where this happened," I said pointing at my face.

"You got into a fight?"

I took a sip of Scotch, lent forward a little bending my head so he couldn't see how embarrassed I was. "I was probably responsible for what took place. I admit I may have asked too many wrong questions. So I found myself in the back of a yard where they brought me to answer their own questions. Good thing O'Connell stopped them, or else they would have beaten me to a pulp. I, however, managed to slug one of them with whom I later made friends with soon after. His name is Patrick and is very close to O'Connell."

"Did O'Connell give you some information about Tumblety?"

"Not as much as I expected, but I had to prove to him I was trustworthy before obtaining any information. That's when things got real serious." I said, insisting on the word serious. "I was asked to deliver a document at a certain address with Patrick, but we were ambushed near a swamp and had to defend our lives."

I stopped talking, stood up, emptied my drink and walked around in the drawing room.

"If you prefer, we could end this conversation right now."

"No, someone needs to know what actually happened." Without asking, I poured another glass of Scotch which I emptied in a matter of seconds. "I shot a man dead with a handgun O'Connell gave me the day before."

"You must be devastated."

"Devastated? Yes, when it happened. Finding myself hunting for someone who I believe had committed murders and becoming a murderer myself was hard for me to deal with although I didn't hesitate a second doing it. On the other hand, I'm rather troubled by the fact I could easily do it again, and wouldn't feel bad about it."

"But only under similar circumstances, I presume?"

"I can't even guarantee that."

Fitzgerald seemed troubled by my words.

"I presume the police shall be investigating on the disappearance of those two men?"

"If or whenever they are considered missing, perhaps," I said as I slowly sat back in the armchair.

"Anyway, they'll never find either them or the pistol I used."

"I'm surely not in a position to condemn you, given your explanation. May I ask what your plans are?"

"I still need to get my hands on Tumblety. My priority, however, is to continue finding families with Elizabeth who are willing to cross over and start a new life."

"Now that's a wonderful idea," said Elizabeth who was returning from the kitchen. "I mean taking care of families."

Neither Fitzgerald nor I heard her coming back.

"I know what both of you are thinking," she said. "Don't worry I wasn't eavesdropping like mother would have done," she said offering an ironic smile to her father.

"I'm well aware of that and suggest we shouldn't bring your mother's way of seeing things in our conversation," said Fitzgerald in a tight-lipped tone which surprised me.

"I'm sorry father. I just wanted to let you know I won't argue with neither one of you about this foolish adventure both of you seem to enjoy even if it's more than dangerous. Anyway, I came to tell you dinner will be served whenever you feel like eating."

"I won't be staying for dinner with you. I've got to get in contact with some people at the Athenaeum," said Fitzgerald.

"The Athenaeum?" I asked.

"It's my club. I hope to have you with me there soon. I always meet interesting people there. So don't wait for me."

"As you wish father. At what time would you like Tim bringing you back?"

"I really don't know and would prefer not having him stay up late because of me," he answered. "I'll take a cab instead."

"Woodrow," he said as he stood up and directed himself towards the stairs, "Whatever your plans are, let me know. I still can make use of my brain if not of my body as I used to."

"Rest assured, sir. I shall consult you before undertaking anything."

Minutes later, Fitzgerald left, leaving us to ourselves.

Elizabeth sat on the settee looking at me the same way she did when I arrived.

"Come sit with me, Woodrow," she said which I did in a matter of seconds. I maintained my composure and sat by her side as near as decency would command. "You surprised me when you mentioned how your mother would have reacted," I said.

"They argue all the time. Both have different views on everything and never manage to compromise on important issues. I think it goes way back since the beginning of their relation together. I sometimes even wonder if she ever had any affection for him."

"You mean love."

"Not in their case. Their marriage was a matter of convenience. Her family from which she inherited very young was wealthy whilst he had close ties to the Duke of Leinster. When they first met in Dublin, she expected him to introduce her to a family member much closer to the Duke hopefully, I can imagine, one of his sons. He made no effort to fulfil her wishes knowing he could lose her. Hence, father was the closest to the Duke she could get. Now don't let me mislead you. He loves her and she has always been an adorable mother, overprotective maybe but otherwise devoted to her children."

"He never mentioned a word about her besides a remark he made about that tapestry," I said pointing to the unicorn tapestry hanging on the wall.

"Mother's rug, he calls it."

"That's exactly how he presented it to me. He said it infuriated her. Maybe one day, I shall have the opportunity of meeting your mother."

"I don't think that will happen soon at least not in the presence of father. They made it a rule not to find themselves in the presence of each other or to interfere with whatever the other one does."

"It's sad to hear that."

"It's dramatic. Father once explained to me in a very few words how he felt. He said 'I hate loving her, and she loves hating me'."

"If this begins to happen between us, bring back what your father said. I'll understand."

"I don't think that day will come," she whispered to me with an inconspicuous smile leaving me wondering what she meant.

"Are you trying to tell me something?"

"What makes you think we might be seeing each other long enough for something like that or, for that matter, anything else to happen between us?"

I was far from expecting that sort of question, the kind any answer you give traps you deeper and deeper into a bottomless pit. My mind was looking for the appropriate words which seemed an impossible task, but she had already decided to go for the kill.

"Well?" she asked.

"I..euh.,I.." I mumbled.

"Is that all you can come up with?"

"I thought that you and I... Euh... How should I say it...Euh..."

I was struggling between figuring out what   could have made her ask me such a question and trying to find the words, the kind that would have normally been so easy for me to say.

"I'm sorry, maybe I should leave," was the only thing I came out with.

"You.., you fool. Can't you see I was just trying to embarrass you."

She obviously noticed I wasn't at ease with what she had demanded, paused a few seconds, and asked, "When was the last time you had a good night sleep?" "Seems like years."

"Maybe you should go and rest a while in the room we had prepared for you. I'll have some food brought up later. It will prevent you from being empty-headed."

Now I felt really embarrassed. "I'd rather stay here with you, but I'm so exhausted. You don't mind if I accept your offer?"

"Not at all. I've got so many things to do."

"I'll just rest a minute or two."

Climbing the stairs demanded whatever energy I had left. Once in the room, I got rid of my shoes, jacket and vest, and laid on a more than inviting bed without pulling down the sheets. I don't know how long I slept, but a knock on the door woke me up. Someone entered.

The darkness of the room didn't allow me to recognize who it was until a voice spoke out.

"May I come in?" It was Elizabeth.

She entered without waiting for my answer. I noticed she was carrying a tray with covered plates on it.

"I brought you something to eat." She placed it on the small table facing the bed, pulled out a match from its holder, stroke it and lit up the oil lamp. She turned towards me.

Something else gained my attention even more than the food she had brought. She had changed clothes and was now wearing a light-green silky nightgown. A matching lace cape tied with ribbons covered her shoulders. The lace ruffles of her gown swept the floor as she walked almost as if she was floating through the air.

"I could leave this for you to eat by yourself whenever you wish unless you preferred it if I accompanied you."

"I'd love for you to stay," I said as I tried to button up my vest as fast as I could, my eyes fixing her all the time. Who could resist such a beautiful woman? Still, I had to maintain an acceptable degree of composure. I got out of the bed and combed my hair through my fingers.

Watching me obviously amused her. "You missed a couple of buttons, Woodrow."

Hoping to avoid messing up even more, I stopped and glanced at her with a smirk. "You make me look like a fool."

She sat on one of the easy chairs close to the table and bowed her head to hide the smile she wore.

"It's better to look like one than being one." As she pronounced these words, she removed the two hair combs holding her hair back shaking it to let them set down.

"I...uh!"

"Are you still looking for your words?"

"No," I said as I approached her very slowly. "They were always present in my mind. I was simply wondering if I should speak them out or keep them for myself. It's time now for me to say them at the risk of you being uncomfortable with them to a point you may cease to see me from now on."

I stopped waiting for a reaction on her behalf. She appeared somewhat frightened by what I might say next.

"Please go on. I need to know."

"Whatever you do, whatever you say keeps revealing me who you truly are. Everything in you makes me want to become a better person. To this day, what I have learned is that I need to see you again, again and again hopefully as long as I live. Do you know why?"

Her response was a short shake of the head saying no.

"It's rather simple. You give a meaning, a purpose to my life. The problem I had in telling you this is I'm not wealthy or educated like your family is. So the only thing I can offer in exchange is who I am. I hope I've answered this afternoon's question adequately?"

She came into my arms and kissed me. "Does that mean you care for me?"

"I'd say there's a little more to it than that," I said offering a smile.

She gently pushed me back. "Then it means you have feelings for me."

"A little more," I added in a desperate way for me to catch up with her own teasing. "You're almost there."

She again pushed me closer to the bed. "Then do you mean to say you love me?"

"I do."

"Why didn't you say it from the beginning?" This time she pushed me so hard, I fell back onto my bed.

"Because I figured you knew it from the beginning."

"And now can you figure out just what might

happen?"

With an innocent look on my face, I could not avoid responding, "I don't have the faintest idea."

"Then let me offer you a hint."

While she slowly walked around the bed, she untied her cape letting it fall onto the floor. The thin silk of her gown held onto her shoulders with only two lace straps leaving no place for my imagination to wander around about her forms. With the slightest movement of her body, her gown either revealed its contour or clung to her hips, her buttocks and legs as a second skin would. The deep cleavage of her gown framed her pear-shaped breasts and offered her nipples a soft place to rub against making them hard and pointy. She sat on the bedside turned towards me offering me an obvious challenge."You shouldn't have buttoned up your vest." She leaned her head down against the pillows and bolsters of the headboard. "I've always wanted to see your strong shoulders."

"What's this silver medallion you're wearing," she asked, her hands making their way around my neck.

"It was given to my brother and I by our mother. On one side, there's the Celtic cross and on the back my initials, WR. My brother had an identical one with his initials on it, KR for Kevin Reily. It's the only thing reminding me of my past, but let's not talk about that."

Her bright eyes couldn't have given me a clearer expression of what she expected from me. I soon found myself naked holding her in my arms and picking up the aromas of her body. My free hand descended along her legs finding its way up underneath her gown. The higher my fingers went up, the more she arched her back out of pleasure. She felt my hardness and spread her legs open inviting me to pursue my exploration of her body. So it was. Our bodies would carry out what our minds and soul wanted to express, our love.

THURSDAY, OCTOBER 11, 1888

As I woke up hours later, my hands searched through the bed sheets for Elizabeth. The bed was empty. I opened my eyes expecting to see her sitting at the room table. Even if the lamp had burnt all its oil, the coming daylight although weak was enough for me to see she had gone. I went for my watch. It was minutes past six. She probably wanted to avoid the housekeepers or her father discovering where she spent the night. She had taken the tray leaving only a bowl of fresh fruits. I picked up an apple and ate it all in just a few bites.

I freshened up and found some clean clothes in the wardrobe. A black slouch hat attracted my attention. I tried it on, looked in the mirror and found it to fit me well. I would wear it. I took my pocket knife I had left in one of the drawers before leaving for Manchester. It may come in handy for my own protection or simply to peel a fruit. 'Food', I thought. Not having eaten much, I grabbed some grapes, wrapped them in a table cloth before placing the pack in one of my frock's pockets and quietly went my way down the stairs.

"Good morning, sir."

I could not have been more surprised by such an early greeting. It was Winston.

"Good morning, Winston."

"May I offer you something that shall certainly help to wake you up?" Winston said holding a plate with small cup in front of me.

"Tea, in a tiny cup?"

"No sir. It's called Espresso. A strong Italian coffee. I took the initiative of adding a bit of honey and milk. I'm sure you'll enjoy it."

Not wanting to waste time, I simply emptied the cup in a single gulp. It tasted rather good. "Thank you

Winston" were the only words I spoke.

But he insisting in a certain way. "Should I write a note telling where you can be reached?"

"I'm just going out and have some fresh air. I must admit having urgent matters to attend to later on, but not for the moment and should be back soon," I told him as I walked through the front door wondering what urgent business I would eventually have to come up with once back with Elizabeth and her father. I didn't even know where I was heading but finally decided I would walk towards the London Hospital although it would require a couple of hours.

I must have been on the street for no more than five minutes. Only then did I became aware a horse carriage had been moving behind me at a very slow pace for a while. Probably the driver had worked all night and was now letting his horse find its way back home. I pulled the grapes out from my pocket and started eating some of them. The carriage was still behind me. I decided to walk faster and heard the carriage also speed up. I stopped. It stopped. It was following me. I turned around enough to have a discreet look at it but kept eating my grapes to avoid drawing any attention. The driver tapped the horse with his whip making him advance. As it came up to me, I noticed passengers in the back.

"Well, well, well, what a coincidence, Thick. It's our friend Reily." I recognized Inspector Abberline's voice.

"What brings you in this part of London?"

I didn't raise my head paying more attention to the grapes I was choosing. "I wouldn't use the word 'coincidence if I were you', Abberline. I bloody hell know you've been following me. So tell me what you are doing here. You're way out of your usual territory."

"The coincidence is not finding you here. It's that the way you are dressed corresponds to the description given by many who said they encountered on the nights of the

Whitechapel murders, thirty to thirty-five years of age, wore a slouch felt hat. And guess what? You're holding a grape stalk in your hands."

"What do my grapes have to do with the murders," I asked remembering precisely the night I bought some grapes for Elizabeth Stride just before she was killed.

"Did you know one witness, a man named Matthew Packer, told us he had sold grapes to a man dressed as you are and that this man had given them to one of the victims, Liz Stride?"

"So much has been written by so many people in the papers. I may have read it somewhere."

I tried to conceal as much as I could any expression on my face letting him figure out I knew more than what he had just said. "Now if you arrest everyone wearing a slouch hat such as mine and of the same age, you'll also have to arrest Thick there, your assistant. He too is wearing a slouch hat." I tossed Thick my grapes which he easily caught. "Now he's got grapes. What were you saying again?"

"Mister Reily, my dear mister Reily. You're starting to disappoint me. You forget one of the most incriminating pieces of evidence."

"And what would that be, mister Abberline," I asked with a rather condescending smile.

"George Baxter Phillips, divisional-surgeon of police and coroner at Annie Chapman's inquiry clearly concluded to the anatomical knowledge of the murderer as displayed on the body," said Abberline. "In Catherine Eddowes' case, Dr. Frederick Gordon Brown said that a good deal of knowledge as to the position of the abdominal organs, and the way to remove them was required. Don't tell me you do not possess both the knowledge and the skills."

His words almost knocked me out. He was right.

How dumb of me for having completely forgotten

that aspect.

"So if you don't want Thick to club you before arresting you, get in here. I got some other questions for you."

I could have told Abberline I had a witness well able to eliminate any suspicion, but preferred climbing in the Clarence hoping to learn more from him than he from me.

"Let's get back," Abberline told the driver. "Now, to be honest, I don't have any direct evidence showing if you're involved in those murders. So Reily, don't try to outsmart me or add a sarcastic comment to what you already said. You'll only manage to get yourself in more trouble."

"May I ask where we are going?" "You'll soon find out."

"How could you know I was here?"

"We have our ways of finding those we're looking for."

"It still doesn't seem to work with the Ripper tough." "Some people like you aren't hiding, others are. But we're working on that, trust me. Thick, pass me some of those grapes before you eat them all." Abberline looked at me with a smirk while filling his mouth with my grapes, "You're not the only one who like 'em."

"Once you've finished eating my grapes, would you then mind telling me what I'm doing here?"

"Oh! Sorry about this. But then you probably understand now how I felt when you were playing games with me minutes ago. We need to know how it went with the names of the Fenian supporters I gave you. Were you able to contact them?"

"Only one of them."

"Which one?" Thick asked.

"Derrick O'Connell, the same day I arrived in Manchester."

"Thick, write that down on your pad."

Thick pulled out a pad and pencil from an inner vest pocket and started writing. "Now that my friend is quite interesting. Are you sure it was actually him?"

"Positive. Why are you asking me that?"

"We've been looking for him for almost two years now without any success whilst you only needed one day to find him and come back alive. That's why," Abberline said with clear signs of doubts on his face.

"What do you mean 'come back alive'? I thought he was a rather pleasant man, if I may say so."

"Pleasant!" said Abberline quite surprised by what I had said. "Thick, tell Reily here how pleasant O'Connell is."

"We have serious reasons to believe he was involved in the death of five men committed in the past three years. All five of them were found with their head smashed with a crowbar he kindly left close to the bodies as if it was his signature. Now what's unusual is that four of them were closely linked with the Fenian movement."

"And the other one?"

"He was living with O'Connell's ex-lover," said Abberline "Once again. How did you manage to get to him so quickly?"

I didn't want to give Abberline any details regarding O'Connell's presence in the same train I took or how he used the young Willie to lead me where I would find him. "I was simply lucky I suppose."

"Luck. Is that all you can come up with?" asked Abberline.

"He should consider himself lucky to still be alive," added Thick.

"I asked my hotel manager for pubs where I could have a drink with some fellow Irishmen. I was given the name of a couple of places. I met him in one of them after asking questions about him."

"And you managed to talk with him?"

"Yes. I actually spoke with him. However, before meeting him I was greeted in an unexpected and brutal manner by those protecting him. I could have been beaten to a pulp hadn't he stopped them."

"You didn't expect a welcome committee, did you?" asked Thick.

"Not exactly," I said.

"You know what, Reily? I think we should end this conversation for the moment and continue it in a more appropriate place. That will give you time to rethink your story and tell us exactly what took place."

Abberline pulled his head out through the carriage window and yelled at the driver, "Faster."

Minutes later, we arrived at a place I already had been to, Scotland Yard.

"Are you arresting me?" I asked.

"Not at all. Let's say it's more like a preventive measure. Come inside. I'll explain it to you," Abberline said.

The room we went into wasn't the same one I'd been in when I last visited Abberline. It was a much larger room in the midst of which was a table covered by a map I easily recognized as that of the East End section of London. The map had four circles on various streets obviously corresponding to the location of the Whitechapel murders. Small markers representing each one of the officers' routes. On the walls, newspaper articles as well as pictures of men were pinned. In one corner of the room, an officer was seated in front of a telegraph unit sending some message who knows where. Abberline noticed my surprise.

"Some might think we are not doing our best to solve these crimes, but they are wrong. This is our Whitechapel command room. Actually, since my superior Chief Inspector Donald Swanson isn't here quite often, we transformed his office into a working area."

"Well, well Freddy. What did you bring us this time?" spoke out one of the two men.

"Ee's picked this one from a richy's cat cradle," said the other.

"Don't pay attention to what they say. These two monkeys are working with me on the Whitechapel case."

Abberline looked at one of them, "Still practicing your cockney aren't you, Wally? He's Walter Andrews and the other is Henry Moore."

"Our friend here, Woodrow Reily, is about to help us out with some recent Fenian issues possibly linked with Tumblety. I don't want a word spoken about his presence here. It's a matter of utmost security. I shall inform Chief Inspector Swanson of his presence. Now Woodrow, come over here. We need to talk."

He hung his hat and coat on the coat hook behind him and sat at small desk in a corner of the room placing both his feet on it. "Have a seat Reily because this may take more time than you expect."

I pulled a chair out knocking heavily against the desk letting everyone feel my anger. Thick sat at my right.

"First of all, why the Hell did you bring me here? And do you mean by me helping you out with Fenian issues linked with Tumblety?"

"Let me give to you in a few simple words. It's for your own security. Thick, don't forget to write everything down." The sergeant already had his pad in hand and signaled Abberline he was ready.

"I can take care of myself without anybody interfering particularly someone from Scotland Yard."

"It's a matter of opinion. But let me tell you exactly what you're up against since you've begun chasing after the Whitechapel murderer." Abberline pulled his feet off the desk both of his elbows banging it hard as a response to me and sat tight,.

"First of all, if anyone from the Fenian organization learns you've been in contact with us before and after meeting with one of their leaders, there's a very good chance they will believe you've been working for us. I won't give you more than a week before someone finds you floating in the Thames with your brains bashed in like the other four guys Thick told you about. Secondly, we've got these Whitechapel Vigilance Committee members who won't hesitate to offer the East End mob any likely suspect just to have them believe their leader George Lusk is doing a better job than we are. Considering the description of the murderer given by the press, you can't imagine what an angry mob could have done to you had you been walking in Whitechapel dressed up as you are right now."

"How about driving me there and find out for yourself what may happen?" I asked him. "Because that's where I was heading when you picked me up. If things eventually turn wrong, well you would know precisely who to arrest. But you already know damn well nothing will happen so don't try to scare me off. As for the Fenian wanting to kill me, I would be surprised to see them do that to someone the Yard has arrested."

"You seem to forget that you willingly came here once and that you're not being arrested this time. For me, that looks more like collaborating with Scotland Yard. Don't you think so, Thick?"

Thick gave his approval by nodding his head and kept writing down everything.

"I gave you a warning when you last came. You had no idea what you were getting into and probably still don't have a clue. So I want you to think it all over once whilst you're here, and maybe, let me repeat it, maybe I can come up with reason to let you go."

"Do you intend to put me behind bars without proper

cause?"

"You'll be staying here. We've got a rather comfortable room where I often sleep. You'll be fed and even have the chance to read all the papers."

"And if I decide to leave immediately?"

"No problem at all. You're free to go whenever you want. But once outside, I shall have you arrested for obstruction of justice before you even have the time to cross the street. Trust me, young man, the porridge doesn't taste the same behind bars."

"I'm not quite sure it's porridge, Inspector," added Thick with a grin.

"You're really two of a kind aren't you? Whatever I say, you'll find a way to keep me here with you until you get what you want. So stop wasting our time and tell me what you want."

"I want to know everything that's been said between you and O'Connell or any other person close to him."

"I need to tell you I didn't spend as much time with O'Connell as you may think. Hence, there's not a lot to say that might be of any interest for you."

"Let us be the judge of that."

"When I got off the train, I immediately got a cab and checked in at my hotel. I was told I could eventually meet Irish people at Sawyer's Inn."

"Who told you to go there?"

I didn't want to give Abberline any details concerning O'Connell's presence in the train, the young Willie setting me up or any other information which could jeopardize my relation with O'Connell.

"Someone on the train. I just asked him where Irish spent time together at the end of a day's work. Once there, I probably asked the wrong question to the wrong people. They tricked me into following them in the pub's back yard and muscled me a bit. That's when O'Connell arrived and had them stop. I must admit I was a bit naive in expecting them to lead me directly to O'Connell."

"Naive wouldn't be the word I would use," said Abberline. "But go on. You finally met him. What did he talk about?"

"The reason I met O'Connell or any of the two others you wrote down on a paper was to better understand Tumblety. Since you openly admitted whilst we were at his private club he had connections with the Fenian, I hoped they could provide me with some information revealing his involvement in the Whitechapel murders. O'Connell refused to tell me anything related to Tumblety when I first spoke with him, but at the end of the following day he mentioned that in his mind, he was not kind of person who would go on a killing rampage."

"And I suppose you believed him."

"Not really. O'Connell said Tumblety would help others even lending them money. I had this feeling he wouldn't cut any link he may have with someone, like Tumblety, who could eventually help him out financially if he hadn't already done so."

"What else did you talk about?"

"He gave me a history lesson on how the Irish have been suffering for decades. I must admit I learned a lot from him."

"He surely gave you one side of the coin. What else?"

"Whilst we played a game of chess, he explained his understanding of the game when transposed into real life."

"Which was?"

"Pawns are more than pawns in the real world. He believes they are the ones in control and allow the queen to move on the chessboard wherever they decide. Those are the ones deserving the most attention."

"Up to a certain extent, I agree with him," added Thick.

"Did somebody ask for your opinion?" said an irritate Abberline.

Thick dared not respond. "Was there any reference made to whom these pawns might be in his real world, individuals or groups?"

"No. Not a word spoken on who they could be."

"Did he mention any period, any date or special event when pawns would be targeted or set into action?"

"No. As I said, since he didn't consider me trustworthy, he wouldn't give either details nor outlines."

"Anything else?"

"That's about it."

"So you spent two days with him and that's all you manage to obtain from him. You'd never make it in the Yard."

"He wasn't with me all the time. I maybe spent a couple of hours together on the day of my arrival in Manchester, four or five the following day and no more than thirty minutes the morning I came back to London. I don't think O'Connell would have revealed any critical information to me in the presence of other people."

"Others were with you?"

"From time to time, there would be others, yes."

"Can you describe them?"

"I'm sorry but I didn't pay enough attention to them to be able to give you something useful. What O'Connell would say was much more important."

"Let's cover another area. We haven't seen him for a while. What did he look like? Did he wear a beard, a moustache, sideburns?"

"No beard, moustache or sideburns. Always clean shaved."

"What was he wearing?"

Abberline's question made me suddenly realize O'Connell wore different clothes each time I met him and now understood why. It would avoid him from being recognized by the way he dressed. He even had me wear his clothes and the reason now became clear. Those who may have noticed what he wore that day and would try to follow him could easily be confused, even more by the fact that O'Connell asked me to make sure nobody would see my face. They would follow me instead. I deemed it to be wise not giving Abberline these details at the moment, and simply said, "The kind of clothes we all wear in a grayish tone. Nothing distinguishable," I said.

"Clock chain, pin, cane?"

"Nothing of that sort."

"Hmm! The man seems to have learned how to blend in a crowd, and avoid being singled out," added Thick as he licked the tip of his pencil.

"May I ask you something?" I said.

"Yes."

"Can I have some of that porridge you mentioned earlier?"

"We don't have any. Sorry," said Thick.

"Why don't you give him your biscuits?" said one of the two other inspectors working with Abberline.

"Andrews, stay out of this if you don't mind," Abberline said.

"He's only trying to help you with the problem you've been having every day since you've been with Emma."

Abberline frowned.

"Emma is Inspector Abberline's wife," Thick told me as he restrained himself from laughing. "Every day, she bakes him molasses biscuits which he brings to the office in a paper bag and throws in the basket."

"They taste awful," Abberline said.

"Then why don't you tell her," Andrews said.

"He's too afraid of displeasing her," Moore responded. "We pick them up and either eat them or give them to visitors. We all think they taste good. Here, try them."

He opened his desk drawer, pulled out a couple of biscuits and threw them at me. I took a bite.

"They do taste good," I said. "Now by any chance, would you have some fresh tea?" I asked Andrews.

"We always do," said Moore.

"That's enough," said Abberline staring at all four of us with an obvious expression of anger on his face

"Where do you think you are? In a tea house? All of you, get out of here immediately. I need to talk with Reily in private."

They all looked at him and seemed surprised by his reaction.

"I mean it," he added. "Move it."

This time they understood he was serious and quickly left.

"Now I don't want to hear a single word from you till I've finished. Is that clear?"

I nodded in agreement to his request.

"Good. I don't know if what you told us is true or not and, for the moment, have no way to verify it. If I ever find out you misled us, you can't even imagine what's going to happen to you." He paused for a moment hoping I would react, one way or another, to what he had said. I was motionless as the corpses of the Pathology lab would be.

"Since we last met, my people kept a close eye on you. You were quite peculiar, and deserved some attention. I know when you left London and when you arrived in Manchester. I took the initiative of asking...mm!" He hesitated a moment, "Let's call them associates, two actually, to provide you a discreet assistance over there should anything wrong had befallen you and with a little luck, capture O'Connell. They seemed to have lost track of you after you left your hotel. Even worse, it's been days since I've received any news from them."

"Someone went through all I had in my hotel room whilst I was absent and left it in a real mess. Did they tell you they did it?"

"Yes. They did what was needed to find a clue as to where you might have been."

It became clear in my mind that the two men Abberline had just mentioned were the same two men who attacked Patrick and me on our way to the cottage. Confused by my wearing of O'Connell's clothes and having kept my face hidden behind my coat collar, they jumped on what seemed to be an opportunity to eliminate a dangerous Fenian but it rather sealed their fate.

"That was the last time they contacted me. Letting so many days pass without reporting back to me is not in their habits," Abberline said.

He was unaware they had found out, one way or another, about the important documents O'Connell would be carrying and managed to set up a trap for Patrick and I to fall into.

"Let's hope O'Connell didn't get his hands on them and apply the same treatment he used with the others. There's much more to this series of sad events than what you may have heard or read. I'm telling you this for you to understand once and for all what you're up against. So I'm giving you one last warning, stay away. My men are out there all the time. You'll never know if the person in front of you, just beside you or behind you is one of them so don't try to fool me. If you pursue this ridiculous chase after Tumblety, I won't hesitate to have you arrested for hindering our investigation. Is that clear?"

"Even if I prove Tumblety is behind this?"

"Can you?"

"Not now, but..."

"'But', that's what they all say. However, they never

come out with some solid evidence and keep wasting my time like you've been doing. Now leave before I change my mind and put you immediately behind bars."

I left his office and, as I made my way down the stairs, officers and members of the staff brought a smile to my face. They were like bees in a hive, each one minding his own business to such a point they ignored my presence. Once on the streets, some of O'Connell's and Abberline's words began coming back to me. Both had a disturbing similar ring. The first one told me, "there could be more to this than simply deaths of East End prostitutes" whilst the other said just minutes ago, "there's much more to this series of sad events than what you may have heard or read." Each one of them tried to prevent me from pursuing my own search for the murderer. Both also seemed to avoid bringing out any new information about Tumblety. O'Connell speaking more of his strategy, how he was about to set it in motion and Abberline, almost exclusively asking me questions about O'Connell. Neither one of them denied Tumblety's direct nor distant involvement in the murders. During the past months, the papers described Abberline as being the inspector in command of the Whitechapel investigative operations, but the conversation I had with him to-day gave me the impression O'Connell's capture now mattered more to him.

I kept on walking trying to figure out the reason why they would provide me with such privileged information. The more I juggled with their words, the more they led me to the only explanation I could come up with, the existence of a link between the Whitechapel murders, the Fenian and Tumblety. However, the nature and the extent of such a link remained unknown to me. From the moment I began suspecting Tumblety, it was like picking up breadcrumbs in a forest knowing in advance where they would bring me. With the warnings O'Connell and Abberline gave me against going further into the search for a culprit, I now felt as if all the breadcrumbs had suddenly disappeared. They were attempting to warn me against risks that could threaten my life. Given the circumstances, abandoning the idea of finding Jack the Ripper would seem a reasonable decision for anyone. Nevertheless, for me, it was like asking someone who jumped off a tree branch to stop in the midst of the air. As serious as their demand may have appeared for them, it remained a silly option for me. I couldn't risk taking advice from Fitzgerald neither as I would normally have done for he may have been the one who informed O'Connell of the date and time of my train to Manchester. At this point, I realized I was now on my own. My only options were to keep everything related to my interest in the Whitechapel murders for myself and make sure every one of my moves count.

The most important thing for me to do was to avoid falling into the hands of Abberline once more only to be served to George Lusk's Vigilante committee as he led me to understand rather clearly. What would the Ripper do if began feeling the heat of suspicion around him? Run away? I don't think so. With his 4-0 card against the police, he would obviously attempt to outplay them by jumping right in the midst of the fire as in the myth of the fire salamander. So shall I. If the committee agrees to hire me, my presence in Whitechapel at all times would be easy to explain to the police. During my vigils, I could engage in friendly conversations with constables walking their beat, asking them how I could assist as a Vigilance committee member and informing them of anything deserving their attention. Now all which remains for me to do is getting things done as soon as possible.

I remember having read from the papers that the

Committee holds its daily meetings at the Crown pub. It would be on my agenda for to-day, but before I felt I had to get in contact with O'Connell. I owed him more than I did Abberline and in my mind, keeping him updated was the right thing to do. I expected, as a favour in return, his help in resolving one security issue of mine: the need of a handgun. A telegram deemed to be the quickest way for me to inform him. Luckily, one of the telegraph offices, the Eastern, was only minutes away from where I stood. I hailed the first cab I saw .

"7 Charing Cross," I told him as I jumped in. "Make it fast."

"Yup," he answered as he whipped his horse.

Even if the streets were already full of vehicles and people, the driver managed to rapidly bring me to my destination. Sending a wire would have taken seconds under normal circumstances. However, if Abberline had someone following me, his man would certainly want to know who the recipient of the message might be and of course its content. I had to make my message readable only by O'Connell. The Caesar cipher, an alphabet encoding method used by Julius Caesar himself, immediately came to my mind. It simply consisted of changing each letter of the alphabet by the third letter following it. There was another problem; if by chance Abberline or any of his helpers at Scotland Yard knew something about encoding and got their hand on my wire, they could learn whatever I wrote. I had to modify the cipher in such a way only O'Connell could decode it and give him clues as to the key he had to use.

The first element necessarily I needed had to refer to the creator of the code, Caesar. The next one would give O'Connell the shift factor. "Let's see," said I as I walked in circles in front of the office. "Hmm! Of course, Patrick's age." I was ready. 'Ave Caesar', would let him know, I hope, the encrypted text referred to the Roman's cipher. 'PatAge' would demand of him to use the 23rd letter the starting point of the shifted alphabet, 'W' becoming 'A'. I went inside, asked for some paper and wrote down the normal alphabet on a line, placing the appropriate replacement letter under it and began writing my message which I encoded. I kept the title uncoded for obvious reasons, 'Ave Caesar, Patage'. The uncoded text read 'Beware, Abberline desperately attempting to find you. Need hard metal defense. Urgent, Woodrow at LH'. I had it sent to Collins, Sayers Arms' bartender with a final clue 'Liberator' for him to understand the wire should be given to O'Connell as agreed upon. The letters LH stood for the London Hospital where he could get in contact with me.

Now all I could do was to hope the message would reach its destination and be decoded by O'Connell. I decided I would stop by at the hospital and try to meet Fillmore this afternoon before attempting to enroll with the Vigilante Committee. A three mile walk wouldn't do me any harm quite to the contrary, given the peculiar events I've been through in the past hours. First, the passionate moments I shared with Elizabeth during the night still fancying those I would again spend with her. Then there were these intense efforts not to lose my composure with Abberline this morning.

The streets of Whitechapel offered me their usual images of fear facing temerity, hope opposing despair, passivity against uncontrollable agitation with all the variations and nuances one can imagine. An outsider wouldn't suspect that any of those horrific murders had been committed nearby. But then, daylight offered East-Enders the safety nights had refused them for weeks now.

Once inside the walls of the hospital, I felt as if I was coming back to a place I considered to be my home.

Meeting Fillmore as fast as I could was the sole

purpose of my presence here hence I preferred to avoid any contact with those I worked with.

"Reily, Reily." A loud and familiar voice behind me made me quickly understand he had found me first.

"Woodrow, it's me." Indeed, it was him. I stopped turned around, glanced at him and smiled. "I'm so glad to see you," said he.

I had become used to his rude criticism whenever we met, but this time it was different. The tone of his voice was such as if he was actually pleased to see me.

"Doctor Fillmore. How are you?

He offered his hand tapping my shoulder with the other as an old friend would do. "I'm fine," he said.

"What brings you here? Have you made some progress in your search for the Ripper?"

He was agitated to such a point I couldn't even place a word. He went on, "You must tell me everything that happened since you left. Come, let's have some tea."

"I accept with pleasure. I actually came here to see you. Any news from Tumblety?"

He led me to the senior staff's private room, a place I've never been to all the years I worked at the hospital. It had everything a men's club reading room offered if only smaller. "Bring us some tea," he asked the servant as we entered. "Earl grey," he added.

"Now, tell me. Did you find anything?"

"To be honest, not much," I answered leading him through some of the situations I found myself in since we last met, but leaving out any detail that could compromise my already fragile situation. Fillmore was like a young boy with his eyes wide opened listening to one of those adventure stories a father would read to his son at bed time.

"Fascinating," he said. "I wouldn't have the courage to do such things."

"I never thought I had it either, but should you

suddenly find yourself in a pond with water over your head, trust me, you try to figure a way out as fast you could." These words I had just spoken out surprised me probably more than they did Fillmore for they expressed precisely what I have been going through for the past three months. I decided to bring the conversation elsewhere.

"How are things going here?"

"I must admit I haven't benefited from the help of someone as good as you were. Even if your replacement is trying hard to meet my requirements, which is quite a difficult task I must say, he's no match yet for what you have accomplished. I've only begun to fully realise all you have done here. If you decide to come back, it will be an immense pleasure for me to have you work closer to me."

"Thank you sir. I really appreciate it. If you don't mind me changing the subject, sir. I'd like to ask you a favour."

"I'm listening."

"I've not been at my room lately and don't expect to lodge there quite often in the coming weeks. Some friends of mine will try to contact me in a day or so and might wish to leave a note here for me at the hospital. Should they decide to do so, would that create a problem for you to take care of it for me?"

"Good. I would enjoy exchanging more words with you, sir, but I have some urgent matters to attend to. If you don't mind, I must leave."

"I understand off course. One last question, if I may. I presume you have spoken to mister Fitzgerald recently. Tell me, how is he?"

"As a matter of fact, we met yesterday. He is doing fine."

"Give him my best regards next time you see him."

"I certainly shall," said I.

"Now do take care young man." he said.

Fillmore's friendly attitude towards me surprised me initially, but the moment he asked me about Fitzgerald's condition, it became clear to me that he was looking for a way that would eventually make me speak of him in a positive manner.

I drank one last sip of tea and left the hospital after telling Fillmore that the Crown pub would be my next stop, the utmost important matters required of me to be quick.

A hasty look at my pocket watch showed minutes past two o'clock. Mile-End road was now crowded at its fullest with men, women and children, either on the street, on the sidewalks, trams, buses, carriages or carts. Many looking tired, hungry or desperate were leaning against the walls watching their lives pass by at the quick pace of those walking in front of them. Others kept moving probably having something to do, someone to meet or run from, and ignored all those surrounding them. And then there were those who hesitated, whose faces and bleary eyes expressed their fear of what the coming night would impose upon them should they not earn the few pennies they would need to pay for a place to sleep. Such was the human tide flowing in and out of Whitechapel day after day. Should you be trapped for a while in this human sea, you would eventually recognize each block's own noises and odours at such a point you could find your way with your eyes closed only by breathing through your nostrils or hearing the sounds bouncing off the walls.

In a certain manner, that's how I knew I was approaching the Crown pub.

For every day near Mile End Road and Jubilee Street where it's located, two young girls no more than nine or ten years old would stand there. One would hold a bouquet of fresh flowers in her hands while the other offered small lavender pot-pourri sachets. The younger one, always wearing a smile, would present her flowers to you by lifting her arms way up as much as she could. "Fresh flowers," "Sir or Mam," she would say. The other one had this deep sadness of a lost puppy written all over her face and never dared to speak out a word. The appealing odour of lavender was suffice to stop passer-bys and have them notice it came from her. I was one of those who would do so every time I saw them at the street corner of the Crown pub. The odour of lavender beginning to fill my nose, I knew I had arrived at the pub. Its facade didn't offer anything quite peculiar that would attract new clients. Large windows, however, had the advantage of letting everyone see if they would find themselves in good company should they decide to enter. Just before entering, I made sure I could easily grab my pocket knife if needed.

I pulled the heavy brass door handle and ventured inside what I knew to be another pub filled with undesirable odours and smoke worse than at my usual pub, the Crown pub. Almost all the tables were occupied by East-Enders, some of which had already drunk their day's worth of cheap gin whilst many others were trying to forget this part of London where they lived. Here and there, I noticed men standing posted between the tables looking around, ready to fall on anyone who dared to create problems or annoyi others. Obviously, private guards.

I directed myself to the bar.

"What will it be for you?" asked the barman.

"A pint of ale," I said.

"Coming up," he responded pulling on one of the taps of the beer tower.

"May I ask you if mister George Lusk or mister Joseph Aarons is here?" said I.

"And what business brings you to them?"

"The Whitechapel Vigilance Committee. I'd like to enroll, if it's not imposing myself upon you?"

"George should be here any minute now. As for mister Aarons, you're speaking to him. See that table there in the corner," he said as he pointed towards one of the pub's corner.

"I do."

"Why don't we go sit there. James," he yelled out. "Come here and replace me."

One of the standing men took his place without saying a word.

Aarons sat in the corner and I in front of him. From the large wall mirror behind Aarons, I could see all that was going on in the pub. I had hardly taken a sip of my ale when voices of some clients suddenly rose. I looked up to see what all the commotion was about. The standing guards cleared the way letting a well-dressed man pass by. Aarons also stood up.

"It's George Lusk, the man you wanted to see," he said.

Lusk came to our table and tipped his bowler hat to wave at Aarons. He kept it on making him appear taller than those surrounding him. A well-groomed black moustache gave him a dignified look. Just behind him, a man wearing a shabby old overcoat followed. He looked more like someone you would avoid meeting alone on the streets, a mad thief to say the least. One would swear he was chewing a rusty nail through his tight lips so bad were his teeth.

Lusk sat down by Aarons side. "And who do we have here, Joseph?" he asked.

"My name is Woodrow Reily. I work at the London Hospital."

"And what is the purpose of your visit?"

"I strongly believe it has become the responsibility of men who, like me, have the time and the capacity to protect East-Enders against the Ripper and hopefully to catch him," said I. "And, with all due respect to the police force, the Vigilance Committee by all means offers the best alternative."

"Well now," said Lusk, "How reassuring it is to hear words so skillfully spoken. Don't you agree Joseph?"

"Entirely, George. Salisbury could not have said it better," Aarons responded with an amusing smile.

"Now Mister Reily", Lusk said. "Before making an even greater fool of yourself, tell us precisely why you want to join the Committee or my friend here behind me, Mister Le Grand, will help you formulate your answer."

In a fleeting glimpse in the mirror, I noticed the image of the mugger unhurriedly approaching behind me. As if nothing out of the normal was happening, I slowly pulled out my knife from my pocket, switched it open and began cleaning my finger nails with the point of the blade. "If your friend advances one more step, I'll clean each one of his teeth with my tool and carve him a smile," said I to Aarons and Lusk.

The man stopped immediately, waiting for a signal from either Aarons or Lusk. First astonished, they then burst into laughter.

"Now that's the kind of man we're looking for," said Aarons.

"Gutsy, I must say," added Lusk. "What's your name again?"

"Woodrow Reily," I answered.

"Well Reily, welcome to the Whtechapel Vigilance Committee," said Lusk. "Le Grand, come over here and meet Woodrow Reily, our new member."

Lusk's thug had a name, Le Grand, and wore it well. He was tall, and his dirty silk top hat added almost a foot to his already randy look. As he came close to us, his overcoat and coat spread open revealing a fully-fledged weapon owner. Hanging on each of his hips was an assortment of knives and truncheons, some amongst them made Police officers' billy club look like matches. I expected him to welcome me into the Committee with a shake of hands, but it would have demanded of him to remove the brass knuckle from his right hand.

"Come," he mumbled.

"Le Grand is a private detective and helps us organize our patrols," said Aarons. "He'll give you all the details as to how we work it out."

"When can I start?" I asked.

"Not to-night," Le Grand answered. "I already picked my men, but maybe to-morrow."

"Excellent. Is there a document the Committee gives us just in case the police wonders what we are doing so late in the night?"

"Yes," Lusk said. "It will be given to you to-night. I expect, of course, you will attend this evening's meeting."

"Of course," I said.

"Good. I'll introduce you the other members," he added.

During the following hours, we covered every imaginable aspect of the Whitechapel murders and their impact on every East-Ender's daily life. After a couple of pints of ale and some rather good ploughman's lunch, we all headed to the second floor where the Committee held its meeting. The reunion was a bit disappointing. Members reviewed the updated patrol results which, obviously, didn't reveal anything new. Most of the present members were either owners of commerce or their managers and strictly mentioned how much they were still losing money. I was introduced to all as their new member, Lusk, to my surprise, insisting on the unexpected whimsical but aggressive manner, I could react to unexpected situations. A document signed by him and Aarons attested my belonging to the committee.

On our way down, Le Grand tapped on my shoulder.

"Wait. I need to speak a few words to you before you leave."

"Please do, your advice on the way to handle the patrols will be very much welcomed."

"It's not some sort of advice. It's a warning," he bluntly said stopping me midway. "I have the complete control of the Whitechapel operations here, and if you even think for a minute tryi to take it away from me, you will soon find out that these poor women had a rather pleasant end compared to what I have in mind for you. Do you understand?"

"Quite clear, my dear... what should I call you, let's say 'fellow'. I have no intentions regarding your... mm … position. For all I know, the Ripper could have been a member of your damn committee since its beginning, and well aware of every move you intend to set up. However, if you are half determined as I am in catching him, and I have my eyes precisely set on someone, I must say we shall form a great team together. Is that clear enough? Now how would a last pint of ale fit you?"

"Damn Irish," he said with an ugly smile. "You always figure out a way to have the last word. A pint it shall be, but you're paying."

We went to the bar and gulped our ale in a matter of minutes.

I looked at my watch. It was minutes past midnight. "It's time for me to leave. Is to-morrow still an option?"

"Be here to-morrow night at ten. We'll patrol together."

"Good, I'll see you to-morrow."

As I directed myself outside through the now over-crowded pub, a friendly acquaintance of mine was waiting at the door on the side-walk. Arms crossed and wearing his usual boyish smile, it was Patrick.

"Good heavens. What are you doing here?" I asked.

"O'Connell got your message, decoded it in a matter of minutes and felt we had to get in touch with you as quickly as possible. Manchester isn't that far away you know."

"How did you find me?"

"Your friend Fillmore gave me all I needed, including your visit at the Crown pub," he said.

"Let's move away from here. I suspect Inspector Abberline may have someone following me."

"There's this Irish private beer-house only streets away I go to when I'm in London."

We took many narrow back streets I rarely use, Patrick obviously wanting to avoid Est-End nightly crowds.

"Listen," said I. "Did you hear that?"

"What?" asked Patrick.

"Footsteps."

We both stopped and tried to distinguish the sounds.

"You're right," Patrick whispered. "Someone's coming this way. Let's go in here." He opened a courtyard door and went in. I followed him turning my head back to see who it could be. Moving light rays made me understand it was a police on his beat. We waited for him to pass before moving on. I could have used my Vigilance Committee authorization but had completely forgotten I had it.

"We might as well take a minute more. I've brought what you asked for," he said. "Take your overcoat and jacket off. Make it fast."

From his shoulder bag, Patrick pulled out a holster with straps attached to it and handed it to me.

"It's a shoulder-strap holster," he said. "It gives you quick access to your gun and conceals it under your left arm. There's a cartridge case on the right side. Unless the

British army attacks you, you'll find it contains more ammunition than you may ever need."

As I put it on, he pulled out a hand gun.

"This is a six round Webly Mark I double action revolver with a break-top using .455 cartridges. To load it, all you have to do is push this latch forward to break it in two. The used cartridges will pop out letting you quickly put in the new cartridges," he said showing me how to proceed.

"Is it legal for me to wear it?"

"You need these papers. Here, take them and always have them with you."

"How did you manage to get all this so fast?" I asked.

"Don't ask. We simply know the right people in the right places."

After zigzagging for a while, we finally arrived to Patrick's beer-house which turned out to be the back-room section of a furniture store still open late in the night. A sliding panel wall separated the two parts of the building. Patrick only needed to wave at an employee who let both of us enter. Four beer barrels with wooden spigots were placed on top of a counter. Those inside would serve themselves without any limitation leading them all into a joyful atmosphere. Almost everyone seemed to know Patrick, calling him either "Pat, Patty or Patrick." He smiled back at them as we moved to a free table.

A man suddenly knocked two pints of stout on our table. "Hi there Paddy, two Beamish for you and your friend."

"Hey there Georgy!," Patrick said. "How's life been since we last met."

"Got harpooned like a big fat whale by the woman of my life and don't regret it at all," he said with a loud laugh.

"Good. That's what you deserved you bloody fool.

Meet my friend Woodrow. He saved my life and I owe him."

"Welcome Woodrow. A friend of Patrick, and he only has a few, becomes one of ours. I hope you'll come to see us often."

"Surely will. I promise."

"You must have better things to do than listen to what I may say so I'll leave you with your friend."

"Take care Georgy boy," said Patrick as Georgy left us. "We're safe here so tell me, what the bloody hell is this Abberline thing?"

"Early this morning, while I was walking, he brought me to Scotland Yard and threatened to arrest me obviously under false pretences. I thought he would question me about Tumblety since he knew I was in Manchester to learn more about him."

"So."

"He spent more time asking me about O'Connell and paid no attention whatsoever to any piece of information I could have obtained concerning Tumblety."

"That's not something I like hearing."

"There's something even worst. It's about the two men who attacked us near the marsh." I paused a moment hesitating on the appropriate manner to tell Patrick what I had learned.

"What about them?"

"Abberline told me he had hired them to catch O'Connell. That's why I sent O'Connell a message."

"Well, we took good care of that, didn't we?"

"We couldn't do otherwise. Now that they're missing, Abberline must be more careful than before, trust me."

"Should we dispose of Abberline also? I could arrange that."

"I don't think it would be a good idea. It would attract even more attention from Scotland Yard. It's better for us to maintain a close link with him, something I managed to do without wanting it. I would learn more and keep you informed."

"Good. Are you still in pursuit of Tumblety?"

"Yes. I'm convinced he's the Ripper. However, the more information I gather, the more I believe that the Whitechapel murders and Tumblety are only two pieces of a macabre puzzle. Too many coincidences have been occurring since I unwillingly became involved in these horrid events. I'm quite sure they're also part of that puzzle, but I can't figure out how they fit in."

"I trust you'll uncover whatever links there may be. That being said, since I'll be leaving early to-morrow morning, I need some rest."

"But you've just arrived."

"I know but O'Connell has something for me to do in the afternoon that can't wait. A matter of personal safety. Talking about safety, O'Connell really appreciated how much you care for his own."

"I learned from you. Both of you are the closest thing I have to a family and I'll do everything I can to protect you."

"He will surely need all the help we can provide him with since he set into motion the plan he's been working on for so long."

"Listen, why don't you come to my room. It's only minutes from here."

"Good idea. I gladly accept."

FRIDAY, OCTOBER 12, 1888

I woke up around eight in the morning completely exhausted by the events of the day before. To my great surprise, Patrick was gone. However, he left me a short note.

It was great seeing you again. Should you need any additional assistance, do contact us. Bought you

to day's paper.
Patrick.

The only article which concerned the Ripper case in to-day's Daily News was rather amusing. It referred to Sir Charles Warren, Chief Commissioner, who had witnessed a private trial of two bloodhounds, Barnaby and Burgho, at Regent's Park and Hyde Park Police during the two past days the first deemed to be successful, but not the second. I could imagine the average constable walking with a bloodhound almost his size and trying to hold on to him with the leash.

Still dizzy from last night's abuse, I, nevertheless, needed to figure out how the bits and pieces of information I had gathered might be linked together.

Fitzgerald would be the best person who could help me. I, however, felt reluctant at the idea of asking him for he may have had something to do with my first encounter with O'Connell. Having a conversation with him was my sole option and would hence require from me a high level of alertness.

I took a cab and headed for Fitzgerald's home, hoping of course to see Elizabeth. I expected Winston would be opening the door as usual, but it was Elizabeth. I offered her a tender smile but didn't anticipate her having such an upset expression on her face.

"You?" she said with her Irish eyes firing more flames than Lucifer would have. "Where have you been this time?"

"I... I simply went for a walk."

"A twenty-four-hour walk! You didn't leave us a note even if Winston suggested it to you."

"Neither did you, if I may add something."

"I was in the kitchen preparing something for us to eat. When I found out you had left, I was so... so."

"Angry?"

"Angry," she growled. "You don't want to see me when I'm angry, but if you ever do this again, you'll experience my definition of anger."

"Maybe I should come back another day."

"Maybe you should say you're sorry."

"I am truly sorry. At least let me give you an explanation."

"It better be a good one," she said stepping aside and opening wide the door. I removed my overcoat and hat and both went to the drawing room.

"As I said I went for a walk which I thought would only take a short while. A block or two away from here, inspector Abberline picked me up in a cab, brought me to Scotland Yard and threatened to arrest me."

"Now that, my friend," said a voice coming from the corridor, "is quite an unpleasant way to begin a day."

It was Fitzgerald who entered followed by Winston holding a tray with a teapot and cups.

"Good afternoon sir," I said as I stood up to greet him.

"On what grounds would he have arrested you?" he asked.

"Ripper suspect," I answered.

"Ridiculous," he added. "It should be appeasing for Elizabeth to hear that after those admonishing words she threw at you."

Elizabeth's face turned red as a ripe strawberry.

"I was worried," she said. "Every time you've been on your own lately, something went wrong."

"You shouldn't worry about me so much. I'm in a rather good position to defend myself," I said, opening my coat to let her see my pistol. "A friend managed to obtain it legally for me."

"Oh," said Fitzgerald. "Quite impressive. May I have a look at it?"

"Of course," I said as I pulled it out of its holster and

handed it to him.

"Some tea, mister Reily?" asked Winston whose reassuring facial expression revealed to me he had not only noticed my handgun, but also approved my owning it.

"Yes, please," I answered.

"Will that be all, sir?" he asked after serving some tea to all of us.

"Yes," said Fitzgerald.

"A Webly Mark I," said Fitzgerald once Winston had left. "A remarkable man-stopper, if I may say so."

"Father, don't tell me you approve of him wearing a gun?"

"One must find a way to protect his life when it keeps getting jeopardized as Woodrow's has," he answered. "It stops being a matter of choice and turns into one of survival."

"I can't believe this. I prefer not hearing a word more of this irresponsible conversation," she added obviously furious if I trusted her face turning red. "I'll be minding something else in my room." She paused, stared at me and went on, "But before that, mister Reily, I would like to have some words with you in private."

"Oh!" said Fitzgerald with a sarcastic look on his face. "Woodrow, you better mind yourself. She's using the 'Mister' word."

"Meaning."

"She's serious."

"Father, please don't try to turn this into a laughable issue."

"May I reassure both of you before this conversation gets out of control," I said.

I gave them a brief resume of my encounter with Abberline, letting them know he was more interested in everything pertaining to O'Connell more than whatever I had to say about Tumblety which drew Fitzgerald's attention if I correctly interpreted his eyes suddenly opening wide.

"I also went at the London hospital and asked Fillmore to help those who would try to contact me which he did. Now comes the important aspects. I met with George Lusk and Thomas Aarons of the Whitechapel Vigilance Committee and enrolled."

"You've what?" asked Elizabeth in a tone which expressed more anger than surprise.

"I've been imposing myself on your household far too much since I began searching for the Ripper", I said.

"For now on, I deem it would be rather better for all of us if I continued on my own. The Vigilance committee patrols are always done with someone else. So you need not worry about my safety. As a matter of fact, I shall begin patrolling to night."

"Why are you doing all this?" asked Elizabeth. "You said yourself that Abberline was more interested in a man named O'Connell than Tumblety. So why pursuing this Tumblety."

I hesitated in giving an answer. I looked at Fitzgerald, at Elizabeth and again at Fitzgerald and decided to give an explanation. "At the beginning, all the clues led me to believe Tumblety was the killer. But now, the more I look into this case, the more I'm convinced that the Whitechapel murders are only a portion of a larger picture. However, I still cannot figure out how Tumblety, the Ripper and O'Connell could be linked together. Every piece of information or evidence I can lay my hands on may turn into another piece of the puzzle."

"You haven't answered my question. Why?"

"It's something I need to do and at this moment. I have a strong feeling I've been lied to by someone I trusted and who I suspect of being Jack The Ripper."

"Tumblety?" she asked.

"Yes. I need to find him more than ever."

"And meanwhile what I'm I to do with the families we plan to re-establish in Canada? Wait for you to deem it equally important?" she asked with an exasperated look on her face.

"I will continue working with you whenever you need me to. Nothing has changed."

"Maybe nothing has changed yet," Elizabeth responded, "but in a matter of minutes, you could lose everything you have and, must I add, that includes your own life. It will all depend on the choices you're about to make. I dearly hope you understand me."

"Is that what you wanted to tell me in private?" I asked.

"It's just a part of what I had to say. Now if you don't mind, I prefer waiting for you to be in a better disposition to tell you the remaining. Since you will be out all night, I imagine, maybe you would want to rest a while and have a good meal."

She stood up and without saying a word or looking at us, headed slowly towards the dining room door.

"Now you're becoming cynical," I said as I walked towards her. "I find it quite unfair, although I can easily understand that all this may be upsetting you, but you have to trust me."

She turned around, gently leaned against the door. "Is that all you have to say for yourself?" she asked.

"I will surely have more to say."

Fitzgerald could feel the tension growing between Elizabeth and I. "Will you be patrolling all night?" he asked, trying to bring the conversation elsewhere.

"At least three or four hours, I believe," I answered, looking at Elizabeth.

"Nothing else after?" he said. Without waiting for my answer, he added. "Because I could ask Timothy to pick you up and bring you back here once you've finished,"

Fitzgerald said. "This way, we would all be sure everything would turn out for the best. Does that seem reasonable, Elizabeth?"

"Sir, I would still be imposing myself on your household," said I. "But if Elizabeth agrees, I would accept your offer."

We both looked at her, waiting nervously for her to speak out. She seemed hesitant moving from one side to another. The anger she expressed disappeared, a deep sadness replacing it. "Since I can't have you change your mind, at least I know someone I trust will be taking care of you. I have no other choice than agreeing."

She suddenly left the room. We could hear her crying as she quickly climbed the stairs.

Fitzgerald and I looked at each other. "Quick. Go and talk to her," he said.

I ran and caught up with her as she had reached the top of the stairs. "I don't want you to die," she uttered with sobs. I held her in my arms, my fingers softly wiping the tears from her cheeks.

"My brother died in a stupid accident trying to prove to all of us, particularly father, that he had become a man. You're doing the same," she said, slowly pulling back from me.

"I'm not trying to prove anything whatsoever to anybody," said I, holding her hands. "Let me tell you a story and after, you decide if I should abandon what I'm doing."

Again, not a word from her.

"There was this ten-year-old boy who lived in Derry close to the Foyle river. He was the youngest of the two children his parents had. His father was a drunk, a brutal drunk who would beat his wife and boys every day after spending almost every penny he had earned. The mother, hopelessly attempting to survive, I believe, preferred taking sides with her husband instead of protecting her children against him."

I paused a second.

"The older brother, twelve, would always stand in front of the younger one, and cover him as much as he could for him to avoid the father's fists. One day, the older brother got struck so hard he fell unconscious to the ground hitting his head against a wall corner. The mother simply pulled him up a bit, leaning him against a chair and left him there, the drunk man yelling at her, "If you touch him again or say a word to anyone about this, I'll slice your throat." The man went on beating his wife and the younger child yelling at them as if nothing bad had happened to the other one. Hours latter, the older brother died. He took the silver medallion the boy wore around his neck, put it in his pocket and left."

"How terrible," said Elizabeth.

"The story isn't over. The next day, the younger one ran away, moving from one town to another, and after two months managed to make it to London where he still lives. Years later, he learned his mother had been found dead, her throat sliced to the bone as his father had sworn he would do."

"The boy, it was you," said Elizabeth.

I didn't respond and went on.

"He believed that the best way for him to overcome what had he went through was to forget his past and decided to do so. He even tried to forget who he really was. Selling trinkets, newspapers, he found it in him through the years to better his situation, although refusing to consider whatever gifts life could offer him until recently. A few months ago, he met a man who was the first one to show some real interest in him, to give him some importance and to ask him to help him conduct a study. He accepted. Things seemed to go well between both of them, at least at the beginning. But then, he soon had reasons to believe this man kept lying to him and that he could actually be the Ripper, the man who slices throats of unfortunate women in the same manner the young boy's mother had been killed. By fleeing his home, this boy who thought only of himself instead of staying and try to save his mother is now a man and will do anything he can to prevent the Ripper from murdering again."

I pulled back a little, letting go of her hands and asked her, "What would you say to this boy?"

Elizabeth looked up at me, still in tears, "Find him, my love," she said bringing me in her arms as a mother comforting her child would have done.

"I will. But you must not worry; I shan't compromise my safety."

It was now I who held her closer to me. I could feel her firm breasts against my chest and remembered how soft her skin was. Had I more time, I would have led her to her room and share the same closeness we had days ago. I, however, had this self-imposed mission to complete, finding Tumblety, which prevented me from doing so. Nevertheless, I couldn't avoid kissing her before gently moving away.

"I must ask your father for some piece of advice if I want to safely succeed in catching the Ripper."

"I already warned you about my father. Remember?

So beware. He often underestimates certain aspects of a situation others may consider to be of the utmost importance."

"Then I shall keep you informed of any suggestion he may offer me."

We both began going down the stairs, but after a few steps, Elizabeth stopped.

"I think it would be better for you two to converse together alone," she said. "I shall rest for a while in my room."

"After putting you through all these emotions without

caring enough for you, I can understand your need for a rest."

As I entered the cigar room, Fitzgerald stood up from his leather armchair sipping what seemed to be the last drops of his tea and came up to me.

"Did things work out fine?" he asked.

"Better than I expected," I answered. "I must admit I could have prevented all this turmoil had I paid more attention to her feelings."

Fitzgerald smiled letting me understand he was pleased by the outcome of the conversation I had with her.

"May I ask you a few questions before I return to Whitechapel?"

"Why of course," he said. "Have a seat," he added pointing to an armchair in front of his.

At the exact moment I sat, Winston appeared. "Some tea, sir," he asked me.

"Yes, please."

He poured hot tea in a cup, served it to me, turned towards Fitzgerald obviously waiting for any instructions he would have received.

"That will be all, Winston. Unless you wish for something, Woodrow."

"No thank you," I said. I watched Winston leave and followed behind him to close the door. I wanted to make sure nobody else would hear what I was about to say.

"Now, what seems to be the problem?"

"The events of these past days left me puzzled."

"How so?"

"Remember when I mentioned that O'Connell had not only took the same train to Manchester I did but also rode in the same compartment I was in?"

"Yes, I remember."

"The more I think about it, the less I believe it was a coincidence."

"And what brings you to such a conclusion?"

"Only a few people were aware that I was trying to get in contact with a Fenian in Manchester who could provide me with some information concerning Tumblety," I said looking down into my cup of tea as if it's content was as important as my words were. "Someone must have told O'Connell he was one of the Fenian I was hoping to meet."

Fitzgerald being one of those few well informed of my intentions concerning the Fenian, I glanced at him hoping his reaction would indicate if he was aware of something I myself ignored. Nevertheless, he maintained his composure. He placed his cup on the table at his side, crossed his legs, sunk further back in his chair and pulling up his left arm, he slowly rested his head between his fingers, all this without any slight change of his expression.

"Is that it?" he asked.

"There's much more. He must have been tipped off way before I left for Manchester which gave him sufficient time to plan all his moves. He probably figured out I wouldn't represent a threat, giving him the opportunity to observe me and learn more about me without having to reveal his identity."

"A bit speculative, don't you think?"

"Maybe, but he was cocky enough to make sure I would remember the name of the pub where I could possibly meet the man I was looking for and have a young boy named Willie follow me from the moment I left the hotel."

"I'm beginning to understand what's going through your mind."

"Good. Now let's have a closer look at Inspector Abberline. He gave me the names of those three Fenian only to use me as a bait, probably thinking it would be easier for me to contact them. He hired two privates to follow me and hopefully catch either one of them. Patrick, O'Connell's 'protégé', and I disposed of them as they would have done with us."

"You couldn't have done otherwise," noted Fitzgerald. "It was simply a matter of survival."

"Yes, survival! No other word could better define what us East-Enders face every day. But in this case, it seemed to me more than survival."

It was I who began feeling nervous and at such a point I stood from my chair and walked in silence around the room ignoring Fitzgerald as much as I could.

"Is everything alright?" Fitzgerald asked.

"Yes, I'm fine." I paused a moment and returned to my armchair. "You know, what really surprised me was when I came back to London. Abberline showed much more interest in everything I could have learned about O'Connell but nothing concerning Tumblety."

"It obviously brought questions to your mind?"

"Precisely. Why would two opposing forces, the Fenian and Scotland Yard, wonder more about the way I'm looking into these murders instead of seriously considering Tumblety being the Ripper?"

I looked up at the ceiling, trying myself to understand the predicament I was in.

"The only answer I can stir up, sir, is that maybe, without knowing it, I placed myself in the middle of something more important than the death of those ill-fated women in Whitechapel. Something that has a certain external connection with these murders. What do you think of all this?"

Fitzgerald stood up, walked towards the fireplace and leaned against the mantle. "I think we should move on."

"And forget everything?"

"That's not what I meant. Winston," Fitzgerald bellowed, "bring us some scotch."

To my astonishment, Winston appeared in a matter of

seconds and served both of us a glass of Glenlivet. I would have sworn he was waiting behind the door and heard every word we spoke. I emptied my glass in a gulp looking at both of them.

"Serve him another one," Fitzgerald demanded. "It will help him straighten out his thoughts."

As Winston refilled my glass, he experienced some difficulty in controlling his hands. They were shaking so much he had to use both of them to pour more scotch showing obvious signs of nervousness.

"You may go now, Winston, but leave us the bottle," said Fitzgerald who remained calm.

He stood from his armchair, directed himself towards the fireplace and leaned against its wooden mantle. He took a wood poker, stirred the few remaining bits of unburned wood and replaced it against the fireplace.

"Oh yes, I almost forgot," Fitzgerald said looking down into the fireplace. "You wanted to know what I think."

"I would appreciate it, sir."

As he returned slowly to his armchair, I had a strange feeling he knew more than he was willing to share, something that suddenly made Winston nervous something that alerted me and had me prepare myself consequently.

"Have you ever looked up in the sky and saw a cloud that had a human figure, the head of a dog or some known object?" he asked. "Of course you did," he answered even before I opened my mouth to respond. "It happens to everyone because people have this tendency to see what they want to see and hear what they want to hear."

"In your opinion, I'm imagining all this."

"Let me explain it better. It's just that our mind plays games on us. It often turns unusual objects, sounds, situations into something more familiar, something we can handle much easier."

"Maybe it can happen from time to time to all of us but not all the time. What if it wasn't happening to me this time and if all I said actually occurred?"

"In that case, it seems to me your ship, to use a metaphor, is navigating full speed ahead towards the tip of an iceberg. I presume you can easily imagine the consequences you shall face if you don't change your course and keep clear of it."

I was a bit surprised to hear him serving me a friendly and discreet warning and considered it would be better for me to repress myself from making him aware of it.

"Perhaps you're right, but in the meantime, I made a commitment to the Vigilance committee and even agreed to patrol to-night. Does that present a problem?"

"It shouldn't be. The problem will rather occur if you get yourself involved with those who may have an agenda other than yours and could use you without you being totally aware of it."

"Are you referring to O'Connell and Abberline?"

"It's a more general opinion than something related to individuals in particular."

I understood by these words that nothing more that could help me would come out of him. Hence, continuing to find Tumblety meant if something went wrong, I would have to rely on myself only. I decided I would pursue my quest without letting him or anyone else for that matter know what move I would make. Deception should become my motto and I would begin immediately.

"I'm grateful for your advice," I said clearly aware I would have to be careful from now on with every word I exchange with him. "With your permission, sir, I would like to have a few words with Elizabeth before returning to Whitechapel," I added.

He nodded with a smile indicating he had convinced me to forget looking further into the links I made between Abberline's interest in O'Connell, the murders and Tumblety.

I ran upstairs, knocked on Elizabeth's door. She opened it and offered me a refreshing look.

"How did things go with father?" she asked.

"Rather well I should say. It may even please you to know that he didn't suggest any rainbow chasing."

"So that means everyone has come to the conclusion that you should abandon this pursuit."

"I might even decide to do so," I said feeling it would be better for me to let everyone think I was following their advice. My response seemed to have satisfied her.

"However, I can't stay longer," I said. "I need to make arrangements for the night patrol I promised the head of the Vigilance committee I would do it with a man named Le Grand. Now if you are to tired to-night, you don't have to pick me up as you proposed."

"I'll be waiting for you at two in the morning at the Crown pub."

"Then two it shall be," I said as I left.

It was the middle of the day. The sky was cloudy and London's autumn cold rain was expected to fall upon us soon. All around me, people in a hurry to avoid getting wet were as nervous as bees returning to the hive. Still, I decided to walk back to Whitechapel.

An uneasy feeling grew in my mind as my soles beat the side-walk. Only two months ago, my life consisted of becoming accustomed to a world surrounded mostly by silent decaying corps laying in the pathology lab and by an abusive superior, Fillmore. I was well aware I couldn't trust anyone and accepted the fact I would be on my own for God knows how long. What's about to become exasperating, since then, is that I met people seemingly honest and trustworthy at the beginning, turning away from the moment I need them the most. No matter how many now surround me and wish to help me, I feel I can only depend on myself. What seems to make things even worst is the more I move on, the deeper the trouble they say I'm getting into. All the bits and pieces of information I gathered don't add up. None of this makes any sense at all, at least for the moment.

When O'Connell and I played chess, I remember him telling me he insisted on the importance of strategy. But if one can only observe pieces spread across a chess board without having followed his opponent's sequence of moves, how can he infer any plausible strategy and knowingly respond? Hell I can't even figure out who the real opponent may be, Tumblety, O'Connell, Abberline? What may be going on in Tumblety's mind still escapes me. O'Connell for whom I have the greatest respect is an idealistic and unpredictable romantic As for Abberline, I learned the hard way he had used me as a pawn, but is he an opponent?

Dismayed I was, to say the least. I looked around hoping it would bring me back to my senses. But the only thing apparent to me were the faces of the people on the street. Some looking more like ghosts wandering in the night, the human being side of them having vanished, others having nowhere else to look but down on the ground probably expecting to find a dropped penny. None of them expressed a glimmer of hope for it was still too early in the day for them to even smile. They were hungry not only for food but, above all, for a life. Most appeared as if their destiny depended on something beyond them, on someone else and would have accepted turning into anybody else's pawn provided they could benefit from it one way or another. They were all sending me back the image I had of myself until these past days, someone slowly disappearing into a deep and unforgiving abyss. It wouldn't turn out to be the case for me no more. If there's an opponent pulling strings behind this morbid series of deaths, I swear I'll find whoever he might be if it's the last thing I ever do in my life.

SATURDAY, OCTOBER 13, 1888

As promised, I was at Crown pub around ten. The tobacco smoke, thicker than the clouds covering the sky earlier in the day, filled the air almost hiding the men and women standing. It was only when I made my way inside the pub that I noticed it was more crowded than usual as if there would be a good reason for them to gather and celebrate. I must admit that the Ripper didn't strike during the past two weeks. Despite this period of relief, the wrinkles on the faces of almost all the women in the pub still spelled the word fear. Those other poor women who were laughing or talking out loud had found a way to hide their own fear the good old way, behind glasses of cheap gin they managed to pay by selling themselves on the street. Le Grand was leaning back against the bar, both elbows resting heavily on its counter. A half-filled pint in one hand, he firmly held his cane in the other. The brim of his hat was folded down hiding the top of the eyes letting him, however, able to watch whatever was going on.

"You seem ready to stop any fight," I said.

"Or trying to provoke one," he responded with a smile.

"We can begin our patrol whenever you want," I said glancing around to find who would want to start a fight with him.

"Still have some beer to finish. Ye might as well have one too instead of looking like a talking lamp post."

I signaled a pint to the barman who quickly brought me one.

"That'll give me time to assign the routes to the others," said Le Grand.

"Others?" I asked.

"Did you think we would be the only ones to walk the streets in the East End? To-night, ten other men will do the same as us, and I have to give them their beats," he said as he left me with my beer to drink and joined a group of men gathered in a corner of the pub.

Minutes later, he came back. "Finish that beer, we got a job to do."

He didn't wait for me and quickly left the pub. I emptied my glass in a single gulp and ran after him.

"Now this is how we work," he said hearing me catching up with him. "We share the same beats the bobbies have but maintain a distance half way from them. We walk at the same pace they do, that's three feet per second or some two and a half miles per hour. A bobby normally covers his territory in no more   than fifteen minutes. With our help, his patrol route is covered every seven minutes. Every two hours, we change beats but inform our bobby of anything unusual we could have noticed before going for another one.

Understood?"

"Completely."

"Good. You and I will only be doing two beats to night cause it's your first night. Now one last thing. Your shoes have hard leather soles and heels. Anybody on the street with unlawful intentions will hear you coming from a distance and wait till you pass before doing whatever he wants. So the next time, if ever there's a next time, you'd better wear something less noisy. Is that clear?"

"Quite clear," I answered almost adding 'Constable' impressed I was by the care the Vigilance committee took in setting up their patrols in the same manner the Metropolitan police did.

"Good. We'll begin with the Berner Street beat. Constable Smith has probably done half his route, so we'll begin right here on Commercial. Let's go."

The beat had us walk six streets: Commercial Road, Berner Street, Fairclough Street, Batty Street, Christian Street and Grove Street.

Le Grand didn't say a word during the first round limiting himself in observing any activity possibly going on in alleys and courts and maintaining a steady but fast pace. I kept silent also, believing that doing so was how the Committee's patrols were carried out. But on the second one, he began talking.

"You must find this boring. Don't ya?"

"No. As a matter of fact, I did my own night patrols weeks ago and found it rather exciting."

"But it could turn out to be dangerous for someone like you."

"What do you mean by 'someone like me'?"

"Have you ever been in a fight?"

I exploded into laughter. "I'm Irish. That means we're born, raised, work and will die in the middle of a fight."

"Ever used weapons?"

"Yes I did," I answered pulling out my knife and snap-opening it's blade to show him.

"If the Ripper is using an amputation knife like some say, he'll have a longer reach than what yours can provide you with. You might as well let me handle the situation if anything goes bad," he said. He stopped, spread out both sides of his overcoat revealing many inner pockets containing billy clubs and long blade knives. He closed his coat and continued walking leaving me behind, amazed a second time by his personal weaponry.

"I'll be able to cope with more than you think," I said as I ran up to him.

"We'll see, won't we?"

A couple of hours later, he suddenly stopped.

"We'll wait for Constable Smith whose beat we're walking on. After, we'll go for another one close by."

Minutes later, the constable showed up, looked at me then at Le Grand.

"Where d'ye pull this one out from, Le Grand?" he asked laughing out loud. "Does 'is mum know 'ees out this late?"

Both began laughing even louder, which infuriated me. "Is that the only thing you're both good at, making jokes about those helping you out?" I asked.

"Calm down young pup," Smith said with a chuckle. "Ya don't need to take it personally. It's only a way for us to relieve the tension. Now let's get serious. Anything special?"

"Nothing unusual during the past two hours," Le Grand said. "We're heading for Watkins' beat now."

"Good. Be careful," Smith said.

"You too. Ready for another beat Reily?"

"Definitely ready."

A few blocks away, Le Grand stopped, turned at me his face wearing a clear sign of discomfort.

"Did you know that constable William Smith was on patrol the night Elizabeth Stride was murdered two weeks ago?" he asked.

"No I didn't."

"He took it hard cause only minutes before she was killed, he saw her on Berner Street with a man who probably was the Ripper," he said looking straight ahead. "Making jokes with those Smith knows well is his only remedy. So don't you ever, ever make that kind of face again when you don't have a single clue of what's going on. Do You understand?"

I could feel his anger.

"I do. I apologize for having made a fool of myself." And a fool, I really had been. Smith could have possibly recognized me as the man who spoke to her before being murdered.

"Apologies accepted."

Our next beat turned out to be the Mitre Court area where Catherine Eddowes was killed. I found it rather peculiar that we would be patrolling in two perimeters where the Ripper had committed a murder. Why would he strike a second time in the same locations since Chapman and Stride already provided him the encores his sick mind may have needed? But then, maybe Le Grand simply wanted to initiate me with well controlled beats. The beat covered Duke Street, Heneage Lane, Bury Street, Cree Church Lane, Leadenhall Street, Mitre Street, Mitre Square, King Street and St James's Place.

"Is there anything special I should know about this route besides the fact that Catherine Eddowes was murdered in this area?" I asked Le Grand.

"Yes. The constable who's patrolling this zone is Edward Watkins. He's the one who found her body.

Even if it wasn't the first time he dealt with a murder case, he had never seen a body so mutilated."

"I remember the description Dr. Brown, the London police surgeon, gave."

"He and constable Harvey had a common section in their beats, Mitre Square. Neither one of them noticed anything wrong there before the murder even if they were separated from each other for only a few minutes. Some say, and I'm one of them, they wasted their time during their patrol. Oh, one other thing. He's not in good terms with me because of that."

"Can't understand why. You're such a pleasant person," I said with a smiled.

"Talk of the devil, there he is."

"Well, well, well! If it ain't Le Grand himself. Still trying to make us all believe you're a good and honest Londoner aren't ya?"

Le Grand looked at me.

"You see what I mean!"

I nodded.

"We'll be helping you out on your beat for couple of hours. Here's Woodrow Reily, one of our new members."

"I don't need help from anyone."

"Glad to meet you anyway, sir," I said. "We'll go on our way and let you know if something happens."

"This way Reily," Le Grand said as he went in the direction Watkins was coming from. "I'll explain it later."

On Duke Street, Le Grand told me that by walking in the opposite direction, we would normally meat Watkins exactly at the middle of the route and again at the beginning if all three of us maintained the same pace. If we kept arriving before him, it would probably mean Watkins was dragging his feet which Le Grand believed he did the night Catherine Eddowes's throat was sliced opened.

"Let me go, you bastard."

Le Grand and I both came to a halt. Without waiting for him to decide what to do, I ran in the direction of Church passage where a women's voice seemed to be coming from.

"I said 'let me go'," the voice said much louder this time indicating I was getting close.

I ran as fast as I could and reached a passage leading to a courtyard. It was narrow and wretchedly lighted, but the pale gleam of a lantern lamp hanging on the wall revealed the shapes of two persons, a tall and broad-shouldered man with both hands around a women's neck.

I slowed down as I approached them.

"Leave her alone," I said.

The unshaven and dirty-face man looked down on me and laughed.

"Or what?" he said. "Beat me up?"

I came closer to him, pulled out my revolver, cocked the hammer and pressed it against his head.

"No," I smirked calmly. "I'll simply blast your head off in three seconds if you don't let her go. Three, two..."

"Damn you," said the man releasing his grip around the women's throat.

"What's going on," asked Le Grand who caught up with me.

"She refuses to pay her dues," said the man.

"And strangling her was your way of asking her politely to pay you," I said keeping my revolver pointed at his head.

He let go of her.

"I don't owe him a penny," the women said. Even after being released, her body was still shaking out of terror.

"She's stealing the men from my girls and won't pay me the share they pay," said the man. "Ask him," he added staring at Le Grand, "he knows how it works."

"You know this man?" I asked Le Grand.

"Not really," he said rather embarrassed that the seemed to know him, "but I've seen him around many times. He often hangs near the pub. I think he minds whores."

"Are you doing business with this man?" I asked the women.

"Never did and never will," she said.

"This settles everything. She doesn't owe you anything. Now let me make it as clear as possible, you bastard. If you ever touch this woman again or threaten her or any other women in the East End, I'll find you and blow your head off. You'll find yourself in hell before your brain splatters the walls of Whitechapel. Am I making myself understood?"

He nodded.

"Good. What's your bloody name?"

"Don't waste your time with these details," said Le Grand. "His lives somewhere on Buck's Row."

"Now listen you half-bred worthless scum, disappear from my view before I change my mind and end your life right here."

As soon as I let him go, he ran away.

Le Grand's eyes were wide open. He stood there wordless.

I put my revolver back in its holster and placed the women's hands in mine. "Don't worry mam, everything will be all right. What's your name?" I hadn't paid attention to her until this moment. She must have been close to fifty years old. The clothes she wore were old but clean. Her salt and pepper hair was messy with a quickly made top knot. Oddly enough, her fair skin and her beautiful smile revealed a once lovely woman had she not been condemned to live in the East End.

"Jane Jackson," she said.

"Do you have a place to sleep, Jane?"

"Yes."

I dipped my hand in my pocket and pulled out the few coins I had and gave them to her.

"Here, take this and go back to your home."

"Thank you," she said, adding, "You're a kind man, ya know, even if ya scared me a bit."

I offered her a comforting smile. She looked at both Le Grand and I and left.

"Let's move on. We still have some patrolling to do," I told Le Grand.

"Are ye all right?" he asked as we continued our patrol.

"What a silly question. Why shouldn't I?"

"I didn't expect you would react this way."

"I know. You never believed a laboratory assistant would fit in with the Vigilance Committee. Didn't you?"

"I..."

I was amused to see I had intrigued him a bit. "Who are you really?"

"Good question. I'll let you know as soon as I find the answer myself. For the moment, let's say I'm just another Ripper hunter."

"If you don't mind me saying so, I'd rather be on your side than in anyone else's boots."

"Then let's try to get hold of the Ripper."

We patrolled uneventfully until two in the morning, Le Grand, nevertheless, noticing that constable Watkins having suspected being watched, maintained a steady pace.

"Oh," I said as the Crown pub came into sight.

"What?" said Le Grand noticing a cab driver waving at us.

The carriage was waiting by the pub's entrance. It was Fitzgerald's carriage. "It's just someone I know," I said.

The driver turned his head around and smiled at me.

"Good morning, sir."

"Good morning Tim," I answered.

"What the bloody hell is this?" asked Le Grand taking his hat off and hitting his overcoat with it. "A rich man's carriage and driver waiting for a lab assistant."

"It's a long story," I said.

The carriage door opened. Elizabeth's head appeared offering both of us a radiant smile. "We must do this again soon, Le Grand," I said as I entered the carriage which immediately left.

"Do you mind telling me what was all that about?" asked Elizabeth who obviously had heard us talking.

"Not now," I said. "Being with you is much more important." I softly held her hands, lifted the lace veil covering her face and pressed my lips against hers.

SUNDAY, OCTOBER 14, 1888

When I woke up this morning, I expected Elizabeth would have left the room as she had done before.

I was wrong. She was sitting by the foot of the bed observing me.

"Good morning," she said.

"Morning," I answered. "What time is it. I must have overslept."

"It's close to 10. You obviously needed to rest. You must be hungry. I'll let you get up and will be in the kitchen to have something prepared for you."

She kissed me and left the room. Minutes later, I joined Elizabeth and Madame Padoue who were sitting at the staff's dinning table talking with each other.

"I love the smell of fresh coffee," I said to attract their attention. "May I have some."

"Of course," said Madame Padoue smiling at me for reasons I suspected. She went to the stove, picked up the coffee pot, poured some in a large cup and served it to me.

"Thank you," I said. "You both seem to have a serious conversation. I won't disturb you."

"You're not disturbing us at all," said Elizabeth.

"Madame Padoue was informing me of something that will most certainly interest you. Tell him what you've heard this morning."

"When Gregory, the gardener, came in this morning," Madame Padoue said, "he mentioned that something special happened during the night in Whitechapel."

"Don't tell me another woman was murdered," I said pretending as much as possible to ignore what I was well aware of.

"No. Quite to the contrary. A man rescued a woman who would probably have been killed."

"Really, is it mentioned in this morning's papers or is

it another one of those clothesline conversations?" I asked.

"Keep quiet and listen," she added. "Oh! Sorry monsieur Reily. They say he almost shot the attacker with his handgun."

"Weren't you patrolling in that area?" asked Elizabeth, "and you had your revolver didn't you?" she added turning towards me with a teasing expression on her face.

"At a certain moment, yes I was in that area, and yes, I had my gun on me."

"No one seems to know who he is," said Madame Padoue.

"Does it matter?" I said as I went to refill my cup."Oh God, this coffee is so tasteful," I added hoping I could avoid revealing the real cause of my excitement.

"It does to me as it would to many Londoners," said Elizabeth. "Can't you see it gives a meaning to what some people try to accomplish in their lives."

"And what would that be?" I asked knowing she had figured out by now I was actually the person they were talking about.

"Caring more for others than for themselves at the risk of their lives."

Madame Padoue kept turning her head in my direction then in Elizabeth's watching us throwing the ball back at each other.

"And what if that man like the one you're talking about had to choose between what he's doing, and he appears to be quite able in doing it, and helping someone else improve the lives of others without any risk."

"He doesn't have to choose. It's who he is and his purpose in life is to always help others regardless of the risks. Sadly, I believe he still cannot admit it."

"You both know him," said Madame Padoue. "Tell me who he is? Tell me?"

"He's just an imaginary person," I said.

"Only if he chooses too," said Elizabeth.

"Didn't we agree that our priority to-day would be to find more families interested in new opportunities overseas?" I asked her.

"Yes," Elizabeth answered.

"Then, perhaps, we should work on it now."

And so we did.

We already had a group of families, almost twenty, who could cross over quite soon. We managed to find trustworthy people who would assist them once they would arrive in Quebec City where an important Irish community had close ties with the local French Canadians. A job related to their skills was waiting for each head of the family. Elizabeth had set up an account with sufficient funds in case something unexpected happened. We, however, deemed necessary to relocate them into more convenient places if only to avoid any health hazard before they left.

The remaining task for us was choosing the departure date and buying the tickets which we did during the afternoon making sure the families would leave together. We quickly decided to avoid the steerage cabin category having heard so many horror tales of the conditions they would have to endure. Had we decided otherwise, our families would have met worse conditions than those they lived in the East End. Regardless of the number of members in a family, a steerage ticket considered them as one single adult unit hence they would have to share between all of them the food supplies for an adult. They would also have to provide their own utensils, pans, cans and basins as well as bedding which they obviously didn't own. We opted for main deck cabins where at least four beds were available per room. Passengers would be able to access the main deck at any time which wasn't possible for the lesser classes. Two mail packet steamers were scheduled to leave in the beginning of November, the Oregon and the Circassian, both leaving on November first from Liverpool. It would take them less than a week and a half to reach Quebec City.

TUESDAY, OCTOBER 23, 1888

To-day was the last day of the inquest of Elizabeth Stride's death. I was surprised to see that the merchant who sold me the grapes I offered her before she was killed wasn't asked to give his testimony. I had no idca why his testimony wasn't offered. At least, the important discrepancies in the description of the man witnesses admitted seeing with her would eliminate me as a potential suspect. The jury came out with the usual verdict of 'wilful murder against some person or persons unknown'.

BERNARD BOLEY

5 THE EVENTS OF NOVEMBER 1888

THURSDAY, NOVEMBER 1, 1888

For the past weeks, I've combined Irish family searching with Elizabeth and Ripper hunting, most of the time with Le Grand.

Our first group of families had left the day before for Liverpool where they would embark on this day for a ten-day journey across the ocean and arrive in their new home, the city of Quebec. We would hear from them once they hadarrived.

Hunting the Ripper provided me with unsuccessful results. However, it gave me the opportunity to build the personal relations I needed with most of the East End constables. Once Abberline learns about it, he shall be infuriated but would have to accept my presence on the streets from this day on as a well-known member of the Vigilance Committee.

I collected as much information as I could regarding all the victims and wrote it down in my pad, the kind of notes constables, detectives and inspectors would keep on them. It contained their daily schedule, places they would go to, people they knew, what they ate and drank, whether they would spend their nights with friends and family, in a workhouse, sleeping over a rope in a two penny lodging house, in a doss-house or walking all night on the streets possibly picking up a client.

I transferred everything pertaining to each victim's situation onto a matrix sheet seeking any similarity among them, any pattern the Ripper could have used to choose them instead of another. For in my mind, he didn't select his victims randomly, but I hadn't yet figured out his mindset and methods. I looked at the notes I had written about Tumblety a month ago hoping they would now reveal more to me than they did before. His intelligence and his charms are only two of his distinctive traits the Ripper must also have used to attract women.

For the moment, this man has proven to himself and to Londoners he could do whatever he wanted with his victims hence I was convinced there would be more murders. He may also decide to enlarge his turf. Could he be more brutal? Perhaps. Walking the same streets and prowling in the same pubs, the victims were probably aware of each other's existence if not knowing each other but to what extent, I still ignored it. My gut feeling was that this killer would not choose a prey who would have been recently in presence of others, fearing they would provide the police with a description of the last persons the victim had met. He would also prefer asking his prey to meet him at the eventual murder location or follow her from a certain distance and not being seen walking with her.

One thing was clear to me; he now feels safe in doing what he has done, maybe too safe, and that's why he will begin committing errors revealing who he might be.

All were women and considered of ill repute for having sold their body as many East End women would also do to feed themselves or their children, to pay for a shelter or simply to buy some cheap gin. They would know their territory and would engage not far from where they were picked up but how far? All died within a square mile range from each other. Distances appeared to be a significant aspect the Riper may have considered. Did he live close to his prey or was it more convenient given their abundance in Whitechapel and Spitalfields? I needed to explore more deeply this question of distances. They were neither young nor old, all being between thirty-five and forty-seven, and had distant, if any, relations with their family and spouses. None of them were Jews. They came from different regions, none however appeared to originate from my homeland, Ireland.

I carried my notes on me wherever I went adding everything that could relate Tumblety to the Whitechapel murders.

Visiting Irish families with Elizabeth gave me well needed moments of relief, although it presented a certain risk if she had decided to visit each and everyone of them where they currently lived.

"Why can't I meet all of them?" she asked me one day.

"Unless you don common wear, you will cause quite a commotion in certain areas of Whitechapel and Spitalfields where slumming is unwanted."

"And what does slumming mean?"

"It's what some upper-class people do out of curiosity or simply hoping to experience unknown sensations. They disguise themselves as ordinary East-Enders and walk around as they would in a zoo, the only difference being the absence of cages. As soon as one of them begins to speak, they are recognized, which sometimes provokes unexpected reactions. Remember when we were followed by that man the first time you went in

Whitechapel?"

"I do."

"It was almost slumming. Now if you don't mind, I could go out first and select some more families you could then meet and decide whether or not to include them."

"It's an excellent idea."

The word quickly spread out that we would be helping families establish themselves overseas. On many occasions, as we walked on Commercial Avenue, some people Elizabeth and I had met pointed their fingers at us causing those around them to ask us if we could help them as well. "Why them and not us?" someone demanded as we tried to explain how we managed our selection. Seeing so many feeling either unhappy, frustrated or even angry for not being part of her project was painful for Elizabeth. I often had to make them understand I was one of them and wouldn't tolerate any misbehaving on their part.

When we met those who were selected, I could easily relate to those we refused, hearing Elizabeth explaining how they could start a new life overseas with the help of Fitzgerald's wealth made me wonder about all the opportunities I could also benefit from if I went overseas.

Those thoughts were still in my mind as we were returning to her father's home by the end of the afternoon.

"Is something worrying you?" asked Elizabeth. "You haven't spoken a word since Timothy came to pick us up."

"Maybe I should accompany them," I said.

"Who?" she asked.

"The families who will be crossing over."

"And why would you want to do that?"

"Well, they wouldn't feel abandoned by themselves

once they arrive. I could help them out."

"But you know nothing about where they're going or what they will be doing."

"I thought my presence would suffice."

"What do you mean by your presence? Are you saying you would be going without me?"

"It could be an option given all the help you have already provided to those families."

"This is completely absurd. If there's something behind this idea of yours, we should talk about it on another day."

"Are you trying to avoid discussing this matter? Why not now?"

"Because we've arrived home and got more important matters to attend to."

"And what would that be?"

"You'll find out soon, silly."

Once inside, I heard conversations going on in the library and went on to see who might be there. Elizabeth grabbed me by the sleeve, preventing me from entering.

"We must change before."

We went upstairs and hastily entered what I considered to now be my room.

"Let me see," Elizabeth said as she opened the large wardrobe. "Where did he put his evening clothes? Ah! Here they are," she added puling out trousers, jackets, shirts and other apparels and throwing them on the bed.

"What are you doing?"

"Gentlemen always dress up during the evening when they meet together. Even if men's dress code is limited, my brother had so much evening wear, some he never wore. You might as well use some."

She brought more onto the bed, looked at it. "This, this and this will do," she said picking a jacket, a waistcoat and trousers. "Now for the shirt, collar and tie."

"Don't I have a word to say about what I would like to wear?" I asked. "You're like a mother dressing up his child."

She immediately stopped, came up to me and kissed me, almost devouring my lips then pulled back.

"Would a mother kiss this way?"

I couldn't find a word to say.

"Now freshen up. I want you clean-shaven when I come back," she said before leaving the room.

I looked at the jackets, held them up and preferred the shawl-collared jacket to the peaked lapel one. Once soaped up, shaven and dressed, I sat upon the bed waiting for Elizabeth, who came back minutes later.

"No collar nor tie," were the first words she said. "It's too tight."

"Well until I get you a larger one, instead you'll have to tighten the bow more," which she helped me to do. "All you need now is a pair of cuff-links."

She went to the cabinet, and in a drawer, she managed to find cuff-links. They were made of gold and wore the letter 'W' on them.

"They belonged to William. How amusing? He and you have the same initial."

"Now we're ready. Come."

It was only then, did I noticed her dress. It was a long blue satin dress with a matching colour laced collar and long sleeves. She wore a long pearl necklace. Her hair were set in waves and curls tied with a matching blue ribbon on top of her head.

"You are absolutely gorgeous," I told her.

"Thank you. I thought you hadn't noticed the change."

She placed her fingers on my forehand as we descended the stairs. Entering the library, I was surprised to see so many people. Maybe ten or fifteen gathered in small groups and engaged in what seemed serious discussions.

"Ah! There you are."

It was Fitzgerald greeting us.

"Come. Let me introduce you to some friends."

"I'll catch up with you in a minute," Elizabeth said as she moved away leaving me with Fitzgerald.

"Henry," he said while tapping on a man's shoulder forming a small circle with others. The man turned around.

"Finally, Gordon we can talk together about this project of yours."

"We shall. But before let me introduce you to our guest, mister Woodrow Reily. Henry, Henry Winkler, to be precise, is one of my business partners."

"Pleased to meet you mister Reily," said the man smoking a nasty cigar.

"And this man here on my left, is Thomas Redwood, my banker. To his left is my old friend Lieutenant-Colonel Richard Armstrong."

"Retired Lieutenant-Colonel, Gordon," said Armstrong.

"Now if you don't mind, I shall let you mingle while I greet those who have just arrived. I must warn you, mister Reily takes notice of every word one may pronounce," said Fitzgerald with a curious smile at me.

"And what's your business here in London?" asked Redwood.

"I... I'm at the London Hospital but on leave," said I.

"Oh!" said Armstrong. "A physician."

"No. I'm a..."

"He collaborated in one of the most known physician of United States' research project," said a voice I immediately recognized.

"Doctor Fillmore!" I said as he squeezed himself to my right.

"Mister Reily is currently searching for something

much more important the nature of which would be inappropriate to divulge. Am I right?"

"Uh! Yes, doctor. It surely would," said I. I moved closer to him. "I don't know how to thank you getting me off the hook," I whispered to his ear. "How can I repay you for your kindness?"

"Ha! Ha!" Fillmore bellied out to my astonishment but quickly responded to me in a very low voice, "You owe me nothing, dear Woodrow, absolutely nothing."

"What did he say?" asked Winkler.

"Yes, what?" added Armstrong.

"Woodrow, you don't mind if I call you Woodrow, don't you?" asked Fillmore. "Woodrow just remembered me of the bet I won with him, a dinner at Benekey's."

He managed to give himself the upper-hand as he always did at the Hospital, but this time, I had to admire the way he decided to have me pay him back, and smiled even without knowing what it entailed.

"Benekey's!" said Redwood. "Their wine cave is one of the best in London."

"I particularly appreciate their privacy booths," Winkler added.

I never enjoyed participating in mundane conversations, and this one was probably the worst one I ever endured. I could feel my patience plumeting faster than the hundreds and hundreds of dull words pouring out of the mouths of those I stood with. Fillmore felt it. "Let me handle them. Walk around a bit. There must certainly be others here discussing matters much more interesting than wine."

So I did but only a few feet away, I was stopped by someone.

"Ah! That must be him," he said. "Our throats are all dried up. Replenish our drinks and make it fast" he added handing me his empty glass.

"What?" I said. "I'm not part of the staff."

Trying to hold down my anger, I, however, needed to serve him with an equally disrespectful choice of words. "If you're that thirsty, my dear sir, there's a table just behind you. I presume you are still capable of walking and know how to pour yourself a drink."

Satisfied with my response, I moved away and saw Winston serving drinks to the guests with his usual tray.

As soon as he noticed me, he came to my rescue.

"Mister Reily, I'm quite sure you will appreciate a Glenn. I know I would if I were you," he said with a wink.

I poured the content of two glasses in a third one and picked it from the tray.

"That should do it," I told Winston.

"Mind me saying this, mister Reily," said Winston. "Do stay calm."

"I shall try my best."

As I moved across the library, I suddenly caught a glimpse of Elizabeth helping Madame Padoue place appetizers on a table. I went in their direction but was again halted by another guest.

"Good afternoon, sir," he said. "Since I know all those present here, you must be the special guest Fitzgerald mentioned to us earlier. Am I wrong? By the way, my name is Kenneth Stuart, one of Fitzgerald's legal advisers."

"I totally ignore if I'm that person, sir. Fitzgerald never said a word to me about it. I was even unaware of this meeting of friends of his. My name is Woodrow Reily if that rings a bell with you."

"Sorry, it doesn't. Glad to meet you, mister Reily. Where are you from, if I may ask?"

"To be honest, I feel as if I just fell down from the moon. Now if you don't mind, I need to speak with someone and will be back in a moment."

Gulping almost all my scotch, I threaded my way

between those in front of me and managed to catch up with Elizabeth.

"Come," I said. "We need to talk. Now," I added trying not to raise my voice.

"But Madame Padoue needs some help."

"She can survive a moment without you," I said, now becoming exasperated.

Pulling her arm, I dragged her through the library door leading to the hall.

"Let's go to the kitchen. No one will disturb us there."

"You better have a good reason for this."

"Trust me. I do."

I stepped ahead into the kitchen to make sure we would be alone. Elizabeth followed.

I leaned against the meat table and emptied my glass.

"What in the name of God is this all about?" I asked feeling completely aggravated. "Had it not been for Fillmore, I would have been cornered by the questions some were asking me. And by the way, what is he doing here? Then there was this man asking me to serve him a drink. To add to the insult, another one informed me I was some sort of special guest. Guest? With the clothes you made me wear, it's as if you've turned me into your father's latest dressed-up barrel organ monkey he wants to show to his friends."

"Stop it," she said. "You don't know what you're saying."

"Don't I? Once the families we worked with will have crossed over and when the Ripper is caught, what do you think will happen? Those men made me realize even more how far apart our backgrounds may be. You come from a wealthy family; you're educated. As for me, almost everything I own could easily fit in one of these pockets," I said pulling out the pocket linings from my trousers.

"Have you finished? Will you let me say something or is it all about you and only you? Does the way we feel for each other still mean something to you? And how dare you say such words of my father? Everything he has done for you from the beginning, does it not deserve some respect?" she said walking back and forth in the kitchen obviously irritated by my words. She came back to me, looked strait up at me. "As for Doctor Fillmore, he and father have known each other for years. Before entering at the London Hospital, he was father's personal physician. That's why he is amongst us. As for those men you seem to despise, they are father's close friends and partners as well. Father is so proud of you; he wanted to surprise you and introduce them to you."

"Why? Why on earth would he do that?"

"Because you care more for others than you care about yourself regardless of the risks it may entail."

I suddenly froze. It was Fitzgerald's voice and it spoke out almost word for word those that Elizabeth had said to me earlier to-day. How long has he been listening to us? I couldn't say and felt totally embarrassed.

Fitzgerald slowly walked towards us. "And now you deserve to have more of us caring for you"

"I was looking for both of you and finally found you," he said. "I never expected you would be quarreling. If you feel deeply uncomfortable being with my friends and would prefer leaving, I would understand. But before, let me say a few words. Besides Fillmore, those men in the library as well as I, all started with nothing in our pockets. Armstrong's father was a carpenter, Winkler, a miller, Redwood, a mason, Stuart, well Stuart's father was murdered because of his Irish beliefs in the idea of freedom for his countrymen. We struggled as you have and became who we are, each of us with our own personalities. I wanted them to remember who they once were and have them help you from this day on as they did with others. That's what this is all about."

He had heard every word spoken, obviously, I said to myself. If I felt embarrassed by what his friends had said and how they behaved, it was nothing compared to how I felt utterly ashamed of myself.

"I made a complete fool of myself and owe both of you an apology," I said. "You didn't deserve this at all. It would be better for me to leave before getting obnoxious."

"Remember Elizabeth when I told you he could behave like me and William did," laughed out Fitzgerald, "and you refused to believe me."

"Yes, you did indeed warn me."

Their reaction surprised me to such a point it left me at a loss for words.

"I accept your apology, Woodrow, and refuse to see you leave us. There's one last thing you need to hear from me but my friends also need to hear what I have to say. So let's all go and join them."

"We haven't finished with you yet," added Elizabeth smiling at me and at her father.

Once back at the library, Fitzgerald picked up an empty glass and stroke it with his pocket watch to draw everyone's attention.

"May I have a moment, please," he said. "This will only take a few minutes."

Everyone quickly turned in his direction and toned down whatever conversation they held.

"Earlier, some of you may have met my guest, mister Woodrow Reily, here at my side with my lovely daughter, Elizabeth, you already know," he said.

All his friends and partners looked at us as if they expected an important announcement.

"For the past months, Woodrow has been endeavouring in two fascinating activities. The first one is helping my daughter find families to send overseas where a new life awaits them. In so many cases, the words these families shared between themselves, with their friends and neighbours had ceased to include one we use almost every day" He paused for a second and looked at all those in the room. "The word is hope. Selecting one East End family rather than another one is like deciding between who will survive and who may not. Richard Armstrong and I know exactly what that means, don't we Rick?" The colonel nodded his head. "But back then, decisions involved soldiers, not husbands, wives and children. Still, selecting families creates turmoil among them turning Woodrow into a target upon which they can cast their deception, frustration or anger. He was aware of this and offered my daughter his protection. We both thank him very much."

Again, he paused and looked strait in my eyes. "In a certain way, his second activity also involves protecting others, but at a much higher level with much higher risks, of course. He's been asking me for my advice since I met him, and consequently, we shared privileged information, it would be inappropriate for me to give any details. If he desires, he will let you in on certain details. London should thank him for doing that."

I noticed Fillmore offering me a friendly wink and winked back at him.

"Let me say to all of you how much I admire him for who he is and what he is doing. This being said, I have an important announcement to make. As you may notice, I'm not getting younger neither does my dear friend Liam Gallagher who is second in charge of my estate."

Everyone in front of us turned around and looked at the back of the library where an old man was sitting with both hands on a silver handle cane smoking an ivory and briar pipe.

"He recently informed me that he wishes to spend more time smoking his pipe than on a smoking hot deal."

They all laughed and even more when Gallagher puffed harder on his pipe filling the surrounding air with smoke.

"I granted him his wish and would like to thank him for everything he has done for me, including teaching me how to appreciate a Glenn," he added raising his glass in his direction. "Hence starting immediately, and if he accepts, Woodrow Reily will become in charge of my estate. He will be given the power of attorney over everything I own, and I shall require of my daughter to guide him as she has done with me."

He paused, looked amusingly at me my jaw dropping of astonishment. A glance towards Elizabeth wearing the smile of an accomplice led me to understand she must have been behind all this.

"Gentlemen, I am proud to introduce to you mister Woodrow Reily."

They all applauded and came closer to the three of us.

"Would you like to say a few words?" asked Elizabeth.

"I don't know what to say, I... honestly," I answered. "Just start with those words and trust yourself with the rest," added Fitzgerald.

I looked at all those in front of me and took a deep breath.

"I feel at the same time deeply humbled and honoured by your offer, sir," I said to begin. "Honestly, I believe I should be the last man to be given such a responsibility. I never saw myself as a protector as you just described. I simply do what seems to me must be done and will continue being who I am in protecting your estate as long as Elizabeth keeps challenging me whenever I'm in doubt as she has done to this day. I am new at this and will appreciate every word, every piece of advice from all of you. God bless you all."

Elizabeth came to me, tears in her eyes. "I love you, Woodrow," she said gently kissing me on my lips.

"One last thing, my friends," Fitzgerald said. "I would like to invite all of you at my club where I made some arrangements for all of us."

"Now to make things clear," Fitzgerald said. "You must not change your Ripper hunting plans but be careful." He shook my hand, bringing me close to him. "Maybe I should call you son from now on."

"I don't know what to say, sir," said I.

"You were supposed to begin with those words, silly," said Elizabeth. All three of us laughed.

"Feel free to join us, Woodrow. I'm quite sure I'll be spending the night there, but Winston could bring you back whenever you wish."

Elizabeth read my hesitation on my face. "You should go with them. You'll have the opportunity to meet each and everyone of father's friends."

"Are you sure?" I asked her.

"Absolutely. Now go and enjoy yourself."

I must admit, I did, indeed enjoy exchanging with Fitzgerald's guests none of them ever asking questions about my Ripper hunting activities. All would be directly or indirectly involved in my future duties regarding the estate and promised to help me in any manner they could. However, when the clock marked eleven, I left. Winston had been waiting outside the club and drove me back to Fitzgerald's home.

Elizabeth was in the living room, her head leaning against the back of the sofa. She had fallen asleep while reading a book she still held in one hand. I gently removed the book from her, picked her up in my arms and headed for the stairway to bring her to her room. She opened her eyes, smiled at me.

"Hey, where are you taking me mister Reily?"

"I'm bringing you to your room where I shall spank you for not having told me something like this was coming?"

"You know what will happen to you after, if you do so."

Such was the manner we began the night together. As the hours went by, it would, however, turn into more passionate and intimate moments.

WEDNESDAY, NOVEMBER 7, 1888

All day long, some words Fitzgerald had said kept coming back to me, "You must not change your Ripper hunting plans but be careful." It was as if he now insisted on me going on with my Ripper pursuit. I had no idea whatsoever what could have made him change his mind but since then I was intrigued by his new position.

Again to-night, I would walk the streets with Le Grand, unenthusiastically I must say. Both hands in my side pockets added to low pace must have given him some indication of my mood.

"Is something on your mind?" he asked. "You seem different to-day."

"Really?" I said turning my head in his direction. I didn't expect him to notice what was troubling me.

"We've been walking for more than an hour, and you haven't spoken a word yet, which is unusual."

Le Grand seemed bothered by my silence and suddenly stopped. "Have you seen yourself? Your face looks like a giant question mark."

"I'm not in the habit of discussing personal matters," I said barely slowing down.

"Damn Brit."

"Irish, not British."

"For me, it's the same. Either you tell me what's

going on or you focus on what we're doing. Otherwise, you're useless and I might as well patrol by myself."

I hesitated for a moment not knowing how to begin. "It's just that in the past few months, everything in my life seems to have changed. I used to work in a pathology lab. You know, a sort of hospital mortuary where I prepared corpses and body parts for students and teachers to dissect."

"Something everyone in this world would love to do" he said with a smirk on his face. "I understand how you may now feel."

I stared at him.

"Sorry. I couldn't resist."

"I never was the kind of person engaging into conversations with people around me. Never needed to, never wanted to. That's what I appreciated with the dead bodies I handled. They never talked back whenever I said something. I did what my superiors asked me to do and performed quite well. I managed to spare enough time to learn more than many others. My life was well organised. A pint a week, always in the same pub and a visit every other week at Kew Gardens. Almost everything was under my control. Now I don't have the slightest idea how to-morrow will turn out to be."

"Hard for me to imagine you that way. Since we met, you've been everything but someone who lost control."

"It's more complicated than that. I can't imagine turning back. During the day, I now administer a large estate belonging to an Irish. During the night, I turn into a relentless although still unsuccessful Ripper hunter.

The only link I have with my past is my flat near the London Hospital. I often wonder if this is the kind of life

I want to have. I must admit that the estate's owner is quite a remarkable man, and that I fell in love with his lovely daughter whom you met."

"So why are you complaining? You have a fine job

during the day and spend your nights in good company either with me or your... remind me of her name again?"

"Elizabeth. The point is that my life was much simpler, much easier."

"You fool. You didn't even have a life. Spending so many years with corpses, you turned yourself into a living corpse. Now you're alive and no one ever said it would be easy. So you'd better get over with it."

I had to admit he was right even if doubts were still running in my mind.

We approached the Berner Street beat and noticed P.C. William Smith, who covered it. As we had done every time we switched territories, we exchanged information with the constable on duty. Smith told us that the area was rather calm, and that we shouldn't expect any serious trouble.

We had only walked a few steps away when we heard him coming back to us.

"I forgot to mention something, which might interest you," he said. "Could be related to the murders if what I heard is true. Anyway, it's the only thing that's happened this evening that's worth telling." He paused, wondering if he could go on.

"Speak up, man," Le Grand said. "What was it?"

"Earlier this evening, a tall American was arrested behind the Molly house we closed down last spring on Commercial road. They were arguing at the station about the charges to set against him possibly gross indecency."

"What?" I cried out. "Was this man tall, in his sixties wearing rings on both hands with a brass knob walking stick?"

"That's him. You know the man?" Smith asked.

"I've been looking for him for the past month. Where did they bring him?"

"At the H Division Police station," he answered. "But if they charge him, they'll probably transfer him to the

Marlborough Street Police Court."

"It's only minutes away from here," Le Grand said. "This time, I've got you Tumblety. Let's go Le Grand," I said as I eagerly picked up my pace. "We're about to have a serious conversation with this man."

"With the kind of face you're wearing, something tells me this conversation might turn sour."

"I've only got a few questions I need to ask Tumblety," I said distancing Le Grand. "Bailing him out shall make it easier for both of us" I said eager to meet the man I suspect of being the Ripper.

He quickly caught up with me. "You don't want unnecessary witnesses to a private and friendly conversation, don't you," Le Grand said with a wide smirk on his face.

I preferred not adding a word, simply shooting a castigating glance at Le Grand as I kept walking sufficed for him to understand I was not in for humour.

We both stopped in front of the station's limestone entryway.

"Ready?" asked Le Grand.

"Ready."

In the station's lobby, we noticed constables moving those they arrested back toward the charge room which was crowded with men, women and young children. Most would be released the nex What did you sayt morning having caused less than minor offences. They all past in front of the desk of a constable who would sort those coming in.

Obviously, he was the duty officer I needed to talk to.

"Officer, if I may," I said as I extended my arm through the crowded place to grab the corner of his raised desk.

"I'm quite busy as you may have noticed, and it's sergeant," he answered as he went on writing in a ledger.

"I was informed by constable Smith that a man

named Tumblety was arrested and brought here. "What did you say?"

"I have all the credentials you would require for me to bail him out," I said searching in my pockets for my wallet and other papers he could eventually ask for.

"That shall not be necessary, sir."

"And why may I ask?"

"Because I had to let him go just minutes ago," a voice behind me said, which was one I easily recognized. It was Abberline's. I turned around. He carried a large smile on his face as if he knew his decision would not please me.

"What have you done?" I asked in a low voice as I came closer to his face to avoid anyone from hearing what I would say. "Are you aware you've just released the Ripper regardless of all the evidence I had given you?" I whispered.

"It's a matter of opinion, mister Reily, and as you said, 'if I may', what the bloody hell are you doing here? Didn't I warn you to stay away from this case?"

"I'm an approved member of the Vigilance Committee. These are my papers if you need to verify my credentials" I added pulling out from my pocket the signed document Lusk had given me.

He looked at them and gave them back to me.

"Again, I ask you why did you release him?"

"Follow me, you young idiot"

He directed himself towards a windowless office in the reserve room, opened the door and entered. "Sit down right now," he told me pointing his finger at one of the chairs in front of a desk. "I don't have time to spend with amateurs," he said holding the door knob. "So I shall make sure one last time you understand clearly what I already told you."

Once I was in, he slammed the door close.

The office had a couple of chairs and a desk covered

with files. Newspaper headlines and pictures of wanted criminals hung from the walls. He sat at the desk, pulled out a bottle and two glasses from one of the drawers and poured a drop in each glass pushing one towards me.

"Take it. It will clear your mind for a moment."

We both emptied our glasses in a single gulp. The taste was awful.

"What is this stuff?" I asked grimacing as I looked at the strange colour it gave through the glass bottle.

"They say it's used on steamers to clean rusty pipes," he said smiling at the way I reacted to his drink. "Now listen carefully. If you reveal to anyone a single word of what I'm about to say, trust me, you have no idea of what will happen to you. I shall not provide you with all the details explaining why I authorized his release. It's none of your business, never was and never will. However, for the record, let it be known Tumblety was seen in a rather embarrassing situation with someone well known from us and was simply asked to come to the station to answer some questions. Here, we found he had in his pockets some incriminating items the nature of which I will not reveal as you might suspect. The Marlborough Street Magistrates Court granted him bail after he gave the required sureties. As for any criminal charges related with the Ripper case, the evidence we had against him was deemed insufficient, but we did not let him know of it. That is why I had to let him go, letting him clearly understand we had motives for further charges. Suffice for me to tell you that as part of the deal between him and I, I gave him time to think about certain matters and provide me with the information I need. Anyway, his committal hearing on the gross indecency charges is set for 14 November giving us a week to gather more evidence and better present our case."

"In other words, what you're saying is that you framed him."

He stood up, crossed over to my side and place one hand on my shoulder. "You seem to be an honest young man with good intentions. However, you don't have the slightest idea of what has been actually going on in the past months and the mess you now got yourself into." He paused for a moment. "As far as I'm concerned, there's a price one must accept to pay in order to preserve some minimal level of order in our society, and I'm willing to contribute to it regardless of the price I shall have to pay. As for you, I still wonder what you're hoping to achieve. You must, however, be aware your life is in danger. Believe me. Every move you make, every word you pronounce regarding your Ripper quest has a damn good chance of being fed to the wrong people. You know, the kind of people who hate leaving traces of their sources, and you've become one of these sources."

"I've recently become quite aware of what you're saying."

"And you are keeping at it anyway?"

"Yes. That's not all. I have this strange feeling that something bigger maybe going on, the Whitechapel murders being only a part of that larger portrait."

Abberline's eyes suddenly opened wide.

"Really?"

"Yes. You were the first one, by the way, who led me to think this way when you asked me so many questions about O'Connell, and showing no interest for whatever I had to say about Tumblety. Remember?"

"I do. Regardless of what I may have asked you, has anyone ever told you had a fantastic imagination? If not, let me say such is the case, and it's not helping you at all."

"Let me quote you, 'It's a matter of opinion'."

"I don't know what to add that will convince you to stay away from this case. I'll simply repeat that your life is in danger. Now get the hell out of here."

I walked out of the office and grabbed Le Grand by his sleeve. "Let's go. We're done for to-night."

"I found something that will surely interest you," Le Grand said with a smile of satisfaction.

"Not here, outside."

We hurried away from the station.

"What was it you wanted to tell me?"

"First tell me how it went with Abberline."

"Rather well, even if he didn't explain why he really released Tumblety," I said preferring not giving any details.

"You'll never guess what I've found out. While you were with the inspector, the officer you talked to was distracted by a group of noisy drunks who were brought in. I managed to look at his ledger and fell on the lines concerning Tumblety. It showed his address."

"Great job. Let's get there quickly and have a word with him if you know what I mean."

Excited as I was, I didn't notice that Le Grand had stopped.

"What?"

"No use wasting our time. I know exactly where that house is or, to be more precise, was."

"What do you mean 'was'?"

"It was demolished a few days ago. I was sent there to evict the scavengers just before it was torn down. No one will know where he is now."

"Trust me. Abberline surely has plain clothesmen following him constantly."

"Wish you were Abberline. Would make things easier."

"I'm trying to imagine you patrolling the streets with Abberline."

Both of us laughed it out.

"Still it's not over as far as I'm concerned," said I.

"For me neither, but for to-night it is."

As usual, Tim was waiting for me in Fitzgerald's coach. I was exhausted and made efforts to pull myself in. On our way back, I kept wondering why Abberline let Tumblety go. He knew about the hospital's stolen amputation knife, the organs Tumblety had brought me, Chapman's missing brass rings and those in his wallet. Perhaps he considered these facts to be pure coincidences, which a court would not retain against Tumblety, no direct witness having seen him in the presence of the victims. Abberline mentioned having given him 'time to think about certain matters and provide him with the information he needs'. Those wouldn't be the words I'd say to someone I suspected of having committed a murder, but they were spoken by a man who must have had good reasons to risk losing a murderer. What could be those matters? What information is he seeking? I can't imagine Abberline would trade in information Tumblety's could bring him regarding others like him who have an unusual interest in young men against his own involvement and possible charges he would face. There must be someone else who could provide Tumblety with important information? O'Connell. Of course.

I opened the cab's trap door. "Bring me to the closest telegraph office as fast as you can," I yelled at Tim.

He whipped the horses and made it turn so tight to his left that the cab almost rolled over. In a matter of minutes, we came to a station. As I did before, I used the Caesar cipher to send my message to O'Connell this time using to-day's day name as a shifting factor. I warned him to avoid any Contact with Tumblety, who most certainly intended to obtain from him or Patrick information he could then give to Abberline preventing him from being charged with gross indecency, the misdemeanour for which he had been arrested to-day.

We returned to Fitzgerald's home where I quietly went to my room.

SATURDAY, NOVEMBER 10, 1888

Yesterday, at about ten o'clock in the morning, I was in Fitzgerald's study room looking over documents Thomas Redwood, his banker, had sent me. Winston suddenly appeared trembling, which interrupted me. His face was as pale as a corps would have been.

"Anything wrong, Winston?"

"He did it again."

"Who did what again?" I calmly asked expecting him to tell me about the latest prank one of the staff would have pulled on him.

"The Ripper. He killed another woman."

I jumped up from my chair. "What?"

"Yes he did, sir. However, this time, it's worse than with the others. He cut her to pieces as a butcher would have done in a slaughter house with a piece of beef carcass. The only thing he didn't do was hang her by the feet from a rope hooked up in the ceiling."

Winston had placed to-day's newspapers on the dining room table, but I hadn't read them yet.

I picked up the Daily News. It gave us the name of the victim, Mary Jane Kelly, a young woman aged 26. The paper mentioned that it had taken place inside a room she had been renting on Dorset Street. The Ripper had obviously decided to up-scale his methods by barbarously cutting his victims to pieces without having to worry about being disturbed.

I read the detailed description the Daily News gave of the slaughtering of the victim, and almost threw up my meal.

'The spectacle that was presented on the door

being thrown open was ghastly in the extreme. The body was so horribly hacked and gashed that, but for the long hair, it was scarcely possible to say with any certainty that it was the body of a woman lying entirely naked on the wretched bed, with legs outspread and drawn up to the trunk. The ears and nose had been slashed off, the flesh cut from one cheek, and the throat cut through to the bone. In addition to this, one breast had been removed, the flesh roughly torn from the thigh, and the abdomen ripped as in previous cases, several of the organs having been removed from the trunk and laid on the table beside the bed. It was stated in some of the evening papers that the particular organ missing in two previous murders was also found to have been abstracted in this case also. That, however, is not the case. Small portions of the body are missing, but that, it is somewhat enigmatically stated, can be accounted for. In addition to the various mutilations this described there were miscellaneous cuts and slashes about the person of the unfortunate young woman, as though her fiendish assailant, having exhausted his ingenuity in systematic destruction, has given a few random parting strokes before pocketing his weapon and going out into the night.'

Elizabeth would have fainted had she read any of descriptions the papers gave. So I quickly gathered all the newspapers and hid them on a chair.

"I presume you will be patrolling to-night in another attempt to drive him out," asked Fitzgerald.

"I really don't know. To this day, he never killed on two consecutive nights."

"I thought the Ripper had stopped," said Elizabeth suddenly joining us. "Everything seemed to have turned back to normal during the past weeks even if our dear

Reily here kept searching for him," she added with a smirk.

"He probably figured out that too many people were looking for him and gave himself time to devise a different tactic," I said. "We must admit that if he decides to continue killing women, he has now come up with a new scheme to do it without having to worry being caught."

"What do you mean?" asked Elizabeth.

"Haven't you noticed that, with every death, the Ripper introduced a new element, either more mutilations or more organs removed?"

"Not really," Fitzgerald said. "But go on."

"I believe the women he murdered were easy targets for him to begin with. No one having caught him yet, he obviously developed an extremely high level of confidence allowing him from then on to think he can kill any women he considers as an interesting prey regardless of where they live."

"And what would be his next move?" Fitzgerald asked.

"It all depends on how he defines himself. If he's the Alexander the Great type, he would take the risk of expanding into a new territory and destroying whatever he desires. But if he sees himself as wise and strategic as Caesar, he would occupy, consolidate and then destroy as he has done till this day before expanding elsewhere."

"You mean he could decide to go anywhere it suits him and butcher whoever he wants?"

"Exactly. He could opt for a different territory or kill during the day in the same area, in both cases beginning with easy female targets and then scale up to a higher class."

"A sadist he is," Elizabeth said.

"It's not that I wish to contradict you, but a sadist would have inflicted pain to his victims, tortured them, and eventually killing them. What the inquests revealed is that he cut their throat almost decapitating them, which ended their lives in a matter of seconds then mutilated them."

"If what you assume is right, then there's no point having more constables patrolling the streets or vigilance committees helping them," said Fitzgerald.

"And you won't need to risk your life anymore if I may add," said Elizabeth.

"If the police forces aren't aware of whom he has now turned into and maintain the same tactics, both of you are correct. I must inform Lusk of my conclusions as soon as possible and hear what he might recommend." I had a telegram sent to Lusk letting him understand the need I had to meet him hastily during the day. His response came quickly inviting me to join him and some members of the Vigilance Committee during the evening at the Crown pub.

The evening was unusually warm for this time of the year, hence I only had to wear a jersey and a light shabby waist coat as it became my nightly habit of putting on the type of clothes allowing me to easily blend amongst the mob. As for the hat, which no Englishman would not cover himself with regardless of his provenance or status, I opted for a dark pinch-front teardrop-shaped crown soft one with a snapped down brim. I believe Elizabeth said it was a fedora. Around eight o'clock, I left Fitzgerald's house for the Crown pub, Tim and I both sitting together on the driver's seat of Fitzgerald's hansom.

"Aren't you tired of pursuing the Ripper?" he asked me.

"I sometimes do wonder about all this stubbornness of mine. It's either my Irish side or everything will perhaps become clear once I've found him. Until then, I feel obliged to continue doing what I've been doing."

"Until it kills you," he muttered.

"I heard that," I responded with a smile. "But it shan't happen to-day."

On our arrival, I told Timothy I didn't know how long my meeting with the Vigilance Committee would last, and hence, I would get back by myself.

The pub was rather crowded. As usual, members of the Committee were tabled on the second floor, Aarons and Lusk sitting at the rear end.

"There's our young lad," Aarons said. "Move over so he can sit, and bring him a pint of ale," he added pointing both at those in front of him and one of the waiters.

"Good evening," said I.

"You wanted to discuss certain issues, didn't you," Lusk asked me.

"Indeed, I did. It's related to the Ripper's last victim."

"A terrible death it was," said Aarons.

"As we all know," I said, "the Ripper's last victim was murdered inside her home. If we or the police do not succeed in catching him, he shall most likely repeat his new modus operandi, for it offers him a major advantage. From this moment onwards, no one can prevent him from ripping his prey as he has shown capable of doing. The question I've been asking myself since it happened is if we should continue patrolling the same way we have till this day, bring an end to our street patrols or begin entering as many dwellings as we can to see if any ill-advised activity may be occurring."

"Good question," Lusk said. "One thing for sure is that regardless of what the Ripper may decide, in a sense, our nightly activities have restored a feeling of safety to East-Enders, which positively impacted on commercial businesses."

After a lengthy discussion covering all practical aspects regarding entering privately owned premises, disturbing lodgers as well as the appropriate manner to act upon screams so often heard in the East End, it was decided Lusk would ask for some advice from the police officials, but in the meantime we shall maintain our course.

I left the pub somewhat disappointed. Until the Ripper butchered his latest victim, Mary Jane Kelly, he never reached the full extent of what his sick mind obviously demanded of him. As he progressed in his killing spree, more mutilations were observed. I was convinced that the presence of additional police in uniform or in plain clothes and the help of committee members in the streets during the past month had given him enough time to figure out an efficient alternative: killing inside.

Walking East on Mile End Road quickly brought me back to the brutal reality of the Ripper's hunting ground.

Although alone and unarmed, I felt I could handle the Ripper if I saw him attacking a woman. However, the evening was rather calm.

Everywhere I looked, people began fighting for a place to spend the night. Shelters, workhouses were lined up with men and women. Benches by the streets were full. One old man, mouth opened showing the one or two teeth he had left, picked a clean bench leaning his head against a tree as if it were a pillow. Many, maybe drunk, were laying in the grass in front of London Hospital. It was rather easy for someone who had lived in the East End for a while to figure out how often any given man slept outside, and there were much to many of them. His overcoat was his blanket and carried the marks of filth from the streets. An old woman, supported by a younger one, had her arm extended in front of her begging for coins. Her face was scared with more wrinkles than any one of Napoleon's hussar could have worn on his body. I pulled out some coins and carefully gave them to her making sure it would not attract others who, like pigeons, would battle over a crumb of bread.

Even though the season was well over, one could still smell the odour of hops coming from the clothes of those who had worked in the fields. It made quite a difference with the usual awful smell most streets of the East End carried.

I decided to walk up Commercial Street and locate Kelly's house in Miller's Court on Dorset Street. I had just passed Wentworth Street when I noticed a group of people in the middle of the street. One of them, a woman, turned in my direction.

"E's the one," she began yelling. "It's im, it's im."

I turned around trying to find the person she might be interested in, only to notice I was the sole person nearby.

Others further away also began yelling words I prefer not putting down. It took only seconds for me to become aware I was the one creating all this commotion.

"E's wearing a slouch hat," a man screamed.

In a matter of seconds, I was surrounded by angry faced men and women whose intentions did not appear to be the friendliest.

"What is the problem?" I asked. "I'm just walking here as I do almost every day. I'm one of you and even a member of the Vigilance Committee."

"You're the Ripper," another voice shouted out.

"E's even got the mustache and the size of the Ripper."

"It's him, get him before he runs away."

More and more people gathered around making me quite nervous. Defending myself against one or two drunk was never a problem, but against a mad crowd! I suddenly felt someone grabbing my shoulders in an attempt to hold me. In a quick move, I slipped out of my overcoat and tried to step away as fast as I could, but I glanced at a woman picking up a bucket of coal dust and smashing it against my head sending my hat up in the air. I fell on my knees and tried clearing the dust from my face with both hands only to feel blood dripping.

"Lynch him" cried out a voice which I barely heard still dizzy from the stroke of metal.

"Yeah! Lynch him."

"I got a rope. Let's do it here," one said.

"Lynch, lynch," emanated loudly from the now delirious crowd holding me on the ground.

I heard the sound of rattles coming close to us. It must be the police, I thought. Then a different set of voices and words confirmed what I had heard.

"Clear the way. Set him free," someone said. "Stop it immediately," said another. More rattle sounds. I could see three or four constables spreading out the mob with their truncheons, hitting anyone and preventing them from approaching me. I was safe, but one last demon kicked me in the ribs taking the wind out of me. I could only lay down on the street trying to catch my breath.

A constable knelt down by me and helped me stand up.

"Bring him to this bench," said another one moving away those who sat on it. I began to breathe normally but kept my arms closed still feeling the pain in my side.

"Now, what the bloody hell is going on? Talk to me," said the officer who had helped me.

"They...," I tried to voice out. "They think I'm the Ripper," I added breathing in more fresh air.

"And you are?" he asked.

"My name is Woodrow Reily," I said trying to contain the pain coming from my ribs. "I'm a member of the Vigilance Committee and just came out from a meeting we had earlier."

The crowd had now gathered and surrounded me and the constables.

"Don't let him run away," one yelled. "He's the Ripper."

"We'd better bring him to the station," said one constable. "These fools have lost all control, and it could turn out bad for all of us."

"I am quite well now," I said although the pain was excruciating, but I didn't share their idea of going to any police station, and risk meeting Abberline again. "You may let me go by myself," I told them. "I can show you my papers if you have any doubt."

"And let them come back at you for the kill like hounds after a fox," said one of the officers.

"No. You shall be better off at the station until they all calm down."

A police cab with reinforcements arrived. Six constables came out to help clear up the street.

Again, I tried to persuade them to let me go, but not only did they refuse, four of them hastily brought me to the cab, one of them throwing me my hat and overcoat he had found.

"Did you lose a medallion?" one constable asked holding something in his hand.

I ran my hand round my neck and noticed it was missing. "Yes, I did. One of those fools must have pulled it off. It's a medallion attached with a leather string with a cross on one side and my initials, WR, on the other."

He opened his hand, checked both sides of the piece and found it to be mine.

"I noticed a woman picking it up and assumed it belonged to you," he said, handing me the medallion. "I've had it since I was a child. How can I thank you, sir?"

"You already did."

We immediately headed for the Leman Street Police Station where Abberline had his command post.

As soon as we entered, the duty sergeant looked at us coming up to his raised desk.

"Haven't I seen you before?" he asked.

"Yes you did," I answered with a laconic smile. "Obviously, under better circumstances."

"What has he done?" he asked the officers by my side.

"We don't know for sure," one said. "Some people seem to have said he was the Ripper and were about to lynch him."

"You won't mind if we check your pockets just in case you'd be carrying some undesirable instruments."

"Do as you please. All I have is my papers and money in my wallet."

"Your name and residence, may I ask?" said the sergeant.

"Woodrow Reily, from Campden Square."

"You couldn't avoid slumming in Whitechapel like the others of your kind do, didn't you?"

"My kind!" I answered him a bit irritated by the tone of his remarks. "I've been living here for years, worked at the London Hospital and now in Kensington. I'm also a member of the Vigilance Committee and had just ended a meeting with the other members. You can easily verify that what I'm saying is the truth."

"We shall, but for the moment, go sit and wait over there."

"May I have someone send a wire at my home simply to let them know where I am."

"I think we can arrange that. Write it, and we'll have someone deliver it at the telegram office."

I pulled out my wallet, gave him the money I deemed sufficient and went for a seat against the wall. Three hours later, the sergeant called me back informing me that everything I said had been substantiated. I was free to go. I walked out the station hesitating for a moment, but heard a familiar voice.

"Over here, Woodrow."

It was Timmy waiting on Fitzgerald's cab. I jumped in and saw Elizabeth smiling at me.

"What happened this time?" she asked visibly not surprised by my condition.

I told her I met the Committee hoping to find a way out from the patrolling beats I've been doing, and on my way back, I was literately attacked by an over-excited group of men and women who believed I was the Ripper.

"The constables brought me to the station, questioned me, and here I am," I said concealing the pain I still had.

"I don't know if should feel angry at you, sorry for what happened or sad. They could have killed you."

"That was their intention," said I, offering her a boyish smile.

"You Irish fool. I should..."

The tender kiss I placed on her mouth prevented her from finishing.

Once we arrived at Fitzgerald's place, we could easily see a shade behind the front door. As we climbed the steps, the door opened. Fitzgerald had been waiting for us.

"Are you alright?" he asked.

"Let's say I had worse moments in my life, and this one unsuccessfully tried to find its place amongst them."

"That's my boy. Bloody good spirit. I know exactly what we now need to do."

"A Glenn, I believe, would seem appropriate."

"Excellent. Winston, prepare us some Glenn."

MONDAY, NOVEMBER 12, 1888

Well in the afternoon while I was discussing with Fitzgerald in his office, we both heard some noise coming from the front door. We didn't pay attention, but seconds after, Elizabeth came to us.

"There is someone at the door who demanded to see you, Woodrow. He says he's a police inspector from Scotland Yard. Should I let him in?" she asked.

I looked at Fitzgerald and Elizabeth rather amused by a visitor I somehow expected sooner than this afternoon. "I think I know who that might be," I replied offering both of them a smile.

"Abberline?" I asked

"It's the name he gave me," said Elizabeth.

"Any objection, sir?" I asked Fitzgerald.

"None. But maybe we should we leave and let both of you together."

"Please stay. I'm quite sure we will all enjoy hearing what he has to say this time. Have Winston bring him here to join us."

A few seconds later, Abberline entered, rolling the brim of his weathered hat with both hands, obviously nervous. He stopped for a moment noticing all three of us facing him then approached us.

"Mister Gordon Fitzgerald, I presume and your lovely daughter Elizabeth. I'm sorry for disturbing you."

"What brings you here, Inspector?" I politely asked.

"I was informed of what happened Saturday and came to see you Woodrow," he said looking straight to my face. "Good Lord!" He leaned his head forward in an attempt to get a better view of my swollen face. "They really messed you up." He paused and pulled out the London Daily News from his side pocket showing it to us. "Have you read the news? There's this article on an attempt to lynch an amateur detective you might want to read out for us. You've gained a kind of fame no one normally desires."

"Have you come to lecture me?"

"Not at all. I'm really sorry for what happened to you.

You didn't deserve it. We have reached a point where adding constables and having civilians give us a hand such as those of the Vigilance Committee becomes insufficient to provide a basic social order in the East End. The mob has begun acting upon its fear, and sadly you were one of the first in its line of attack. Should this continue, the administration will obviously have to consider a different kind of reinforcement."

"The army?" Fitzgerald asked.

"I doubt it but who knows what our political masters will have in mind should the situation worsen," Abberline replied.

"We are obviously not in the presence of a rebellion, if I may give you my humble opinion, but a sick murderer who has been offering victims to whatever god he adores including himself," I added.

"I support your way of thinking," Abberline said. "But you must admit that with these murders, death has become a dangerous social issue we cannot escape. And, if I may say so, that's what you seem to have been ignoring."

"I'm quite aware of what you mean, for death has been around me for decades." I paused emptied my cold cup of coffee, "An unwanted companion, if I may add. But for me there's only two ways of escaping death. The first one is never having been born, and the other one is what I've been doing for too many years, finding a way to ignore I was alive. Whatever may now happen shall bring back my life to me and have me fight every instant to preserve and reaffirm it."

Abberline, Fitzgerald and Elizabeth were speechless, obviously surprised by my words.

"I believe I shall let you respectfully hope what you say is true and leave you," Abberline said breaking the silence.

"I appreciate your visit Inspector and believe we have

more things in common than you suspect."

"You would have made a fine detective, under my supervision, of course. By the way, about that medallion of yours private Irving recuperated, a reward would be quite advisable if it meant that much to you."

"Let me show it. It may not be a valuable piece, but it reminds me of the most important moments of my past with my brother and mother."

I pulled off the medallion from my neck and handed it to Firtzgerald who examined it and gave it back to me.

"I should leave now," said Abberline.

I accompanied him to the door, shook his hand, dropping a half crown. "For constable Irving." We offered each other one of those uncommon looks, that of the beginning of a possible friendship.

TUESDAY, NOVEMBER 13, 1888

Early in the morning, Elizabeth and I received a telegram from Canada informing us that all our families had arrived safely in Quebec City. A second one came in later from Desmond Skeet, one of the first families Elizabeth and I had met. He told us how amazed he was with his first contact with the city, and that the people were more welcoming than expected. We were both terribly excited by the news.

Later on during the afternoon, Fitzgerald encouraged us into going for a walk around Campden Hill Square which we agreed upon. It was a bit cold, but at least we didn't have rain and the midday sun would warm us. A few others like us enjoyed maybe one of the last nice days before the winter frost would set in. I noticed some thirty or forty feet ahead of us a tall well-dressed man walking in our direction at a quick pace. The more he approached, the more I could recognize the smiling face of Patrick, O'Connell's protégé.

"Elizabeth, have you noticed that man over there," I said pointing my finger at him. "It's my good friend Patrick," I let go of her arm and hastily advanced towards him giving Elizabeth a quick look. "Come join us," I told her.

"Patrick, what the bloody hell are you doing here?" I said shaking his hand and tapping on his shoulder.

"We came to take care of some delicate matters involving one of O'Connell's friend and pay you a visit by the same token."

"How did you know we'd be out here?"

"Don't ask. It would take to long."

"So O'Connell is with you. Where is he?"

"Yes, over there in the garden," he said pointing inside Campden Square's park.

"But you needed a key to enter."

"Really!"

Elizabeth caught up with us.

"Elizabeth, may I present you Patrick O'Donahue. One of the two men I became friends with in Manchester. Patrick, let me introduce you to Elizabeth Fitzgerald."

"Very pleased to meet you, miss."

"Likewise," she said.

"Let's all go and join O'Connell in the garden," I said.

"It would be better for me to stay here just in case," said Patrick.

"Of course, we shall meet later," I said totally aware Patrick had to keep an eye on O'Connell from a distance.

The garden door was wide open. On a bench, both hands topping a cane between his legs sat O'Connell, the only person besides us in the garden. Dressed as an English Lord would have been on a national holiday with a beard well groomed, his Homburg hat, an overcoat with an Astrakhan collar, had I not met Patrick, I never would have recognized him. Nobody would have challenged his presence in the garden.

"Good afternoon, Sir," I said.

"Woodrow, it's great to see you again. What happened to you?" he asked, staring at my face still swollen.

"Just a stupid accident."

"A stupid accident, a stupid accident!" Elizabeth said. "A group of mad East-Enders believed you were the Ripper and wanted to hang you. Is that what you call an accident?"

"And who is this lovely young lady giving me an honest answer I expected you would have provided me with?" he asked offering her a charming smile.

"May I introduce to you Elizabeth Fitzgerald".

"Delighted to meet you miss Fitzgerald," he said picking her hand and kissing it. "My name is Derrick O'Connell. Woodrow and I met in Manchester not too long ago and have become good friends,"

"He often spoke of you, in good terms of course," Elizabeth said. "So I'm quite happy to meet you finally."

"Did you get my message?" I asked.

"I did indeed and am very grateful for you having sent it. I arranged to have someone talk to Tumblety and clear things up. What I understood was that Inspector Abberline had set him up and unsuccessfully tried to get a hold on me through him."

"You've taken great risks in coming over here," I said.

"You shouldn't fear for my safety. I have my men watching over every street corner two blocks around."

"Good. Tumblety slipped away through my fingers the night he was brought in at the police station for questioning less than two weeks ago. Had I been there only minutes before he was released, I would have found a way to make him talk. You also allowed for him to go free, even if there was a good chance of him being the

Ripper."

"Maybe you should have asked me to detain him, but I was under the impression from the conversations we had that it had become less obvious that he would be the Ripper."

"There's still a chance for me to get a hold on him soon. This time, he won't slip away."

"I wish you luck." He paused a second. "Although I doubt he would turn out to be the Ripper. I'm facing a similar situation and need to end it promptly."

"Do you? Mind telling me more?"

"Remember when we talked about life being almost game of chess?" he asked as we began to walk in the park.

"I certainly do."

"Well the worst thing that can occur when setting up a live game is having one of your pieces suddenly decide to play his own game with his own set of rules within yours. When it happens, and even if it's a simple pawn, the moves he may choose to make could create an uncontrollable chaos with impacts beyond anything you would have imagined."

"I see."

"A pawn of mine decided to do exactly that, and you can easily understand that everything he does could eventually be linked to the person who set up the game which in this case would be me."

"So you had to abandon the game before it was too late," said Elizabeth who couldn't keep her eyes off O'Connell.

"Precisely. What aggravates me is whatever resources I call upon, none of them are able to find this pawn. He is ghostly moving all over the chessboard."

"It's almost as if your pawn is doing the same thing Londoners have been witnessing in the East End with the Ripper. He'd probably make a fine Ripper."

O'Connell suddenly stiffened obviously shaken by my words but quickly burst out laughing.

I pretended not having paid attention to his reaction and asked, "Tell me, is Tumblety one of the pieces on your chessboard?"

"That, my friend, is a pure chess player's question. You could have asked me directly if Tumblety was my rogue pawn but instead you went for two side moves, associating the pawn with the Ripper and then, the Ripper with Tumblety. I know Tumblety well enough to say he's the kind of person who would rather have you or I on his chessboard. And mind me saying it would not really be a chessboard".

He laughed even louder.

"Please forgive my spoken words, my dear Elizabeth, but I believe Woodrow knows exactly what I ment."

"That he prefers men over women?" Elizabeth asked. "I was quite aware of that possibility."

"Sorry if I interrupt you, but you haven't answered my question", I said as I noticed Elizabeth trying to figure out O'Connell.

"Oh yes, I forgot. Tumblety wasn't on the chessboard. And if it may appease your mind, neither were you which brings me to offer you maybe one last rule which I abide by. Never set a friend or family on any kind of live game even if they are willing to do so. You know quite well that when you play chess, the premise all players accept is that they will lose pieces, many pieces, and I refuse to lose my friends."

"Tell me, when will you be returning to Manchester?"

"In a day or so. An acquaintance of mine was in an urgent need of money. We will meet to-morrow to see if we can help him out and then return to Manchester."

"As I said, I also have someone I shall meet again, but can't say he's an acquaintance. He probably doesn't even expect me nor will he enjoy seeing me."

"Now that would be intrusive."

"I sure hope so. It's Tumblety. His committal hearing is to-morrow and I hope to be able to confront him before he appears in court."

"Don't you think Abberline will be around just to see who shows up? I know I would if I were him."

"I have to admit he knows I'm looking for him, but I'm quite sure I'll find a way around."

"Good luck," he said expressing more doubt than hope in seeing me catching Tumblety. "I shouldn't be challenging the Gods, so I'll be leaving you. But one last question. If evidence would be brought out showing Tumblety is not the Ripper, what would you do about it? Continue chasing the real Ripper? I'm asking you this because I wonder if you're really hunting for Jack the Ripper or rather trying to get back at Tumblety for the disappointments he may have brought upon you."

"I'm beginning to like this man," Elizabeth said, offering O'Connell a smile of complicity.

I was about to respond, but he quickly went on.

He placed his hand on my shoulder. "You don't need to answer me, but you should certainly think about it."

We made our way back to the park's entrance where Patrick was waiting. As we were about to part, O'Connell and I looked at each other and shared a disturbing moment of silence. The only thing we managed to do was to shake hands, holding them tight to better feel the value of our friendship.

I felt the need to wander away from the route we would have normally taken to get back at Elizabeth's house and kept silent all along, head down with both hands joined together in my back.

Having walked two three street blocks, she suddenly stopped, stared at me forcing me to halt. "You either tell me what's going in that mind of yours or I'll return home without you. Is it the question he asked you?"

"No. I'm still convinced Tumblety has something to do with the murders and need to find out what exactly is behind all this."

"What do you mean, all this?"

"I would bet my life that O'Connell is not telling me everything he knows. When we left, I felt he wanted to add something more to what he had just said, but refused to do so, fearing his words might upset me."

"You almost lost your life and now you want to..."

Elizabeth's words slowly disappeared into my foggy mind, which kept playing games with me while I was desperately attempting to figure out what was hidden behind O'Connell's silence. Meeting him could not have been a pure coincidence for Fitzgerald had suggested Elizabeth and I to take a walk to the park. He must have was in the areaknown O'Connell would be waiting there for me. Logically, it meant that Fitzgerald and O'Connell knew each other. Since when were they acquainted? What was the nature of the relation between both of them? O'Connell having mentioned knowing Tumblety, and Fitzgerald being quite aware I would meet O'Connell in the park, hence I can assume a connexion between the three of them exists. Then there's Abberline who seemed to be more interested in having Tumblety betray O'Connell than investigating the possibility of him being the Ripper preferring indecency charges to be set against him.

I must have spent too many years with dead bodies and medical books. Even if they provided me with a realm of knowledge on how the human body functions, they, however, kept quiet when it came to teaching me how humans behave, how they think. Fillmore was my yes I was in the areaonly reference and quite a limited one I might say. It's only now I realize that what I neglected during many years would come in handy.

"I've had enough of this," I yelled.

"What did you just say?" asked Elizabeth as she grabbed my sleeve spinning me to her side forcing me to halt.

"Just thinking out loud. It had nothing to do with what you might have said."

"Might have?" said Elizabeth. "You haven't paid attention to a single word I said?"

"I'm so sorry, my love. O'Connell's words troubled me deeply. They carried me away."

"It seemed quite simple. Firstly, Tumblety may not be the Ripper and secondly, should that be the case, O'Connell wondered if you would still look for the murderer."

"What worries me is that it appears to be a little more complicated than that. Too many pieces of this horrible puzzle are missing and O'Connell just added a couple of unexpected ones. Whatever I might attempt shall remain pure speculation. That's why I had enough. Again forgive me."

"Don't you think O'Connell knew you would be coming?" she asked.

"It wouldn't have been the first time O'Connell had taken a step ahead of me," I said. "But as long as I benefit from his presence, the rest doesn't really matter." It would have been inadvisable for me to share my thoughts regarding O'Connell more than I just did with Elzabeth. I expected my answer would put her mind to rest and succeeded in doing so. Some of my words could have turned out to be significant to him only, he would have then become aware of my concerns and my understanding of his possible involvement.

Once back home, I could not avoid wearing a smile of satisfaction when Winston told us that Fitzgerald had left for his club where he said he would spend the night. I would not have to talk about our unexpected encounter with O'Connell. I gave Winston a short note to Le Grand asking him to meet me early to-morrow morning at Great Marlborough Street Magistrates Court where Tumblety should appear.

"I shall have it telegraphed as soon as Tim is back," said Winston.

"Good," I said.

"You must have had a tiring day, Woodrow," Elizabeth said. "Maybe you should go and rest a while. I'll see what Madame Padoue and I could prepare for diner. I'm quite sure you will appreciate thinking about something else than the Ripper," she said as she went to the kitchen offering a smile which made Winston discreetly turn away.

An hour later, she arrived to my room with a plate of food which we ate. As for the conversation we had, it had nothing to do with the Ripper and began by covering matters a gentleman should not reveal openly. I may, however, reveal they were more sounds than actually words.

WEDNESDAY, NOVEMBER 14, 1888

Although the Marlborough court hearings would begin around 10 in the morning, I arrived earlier, Timmy having driven me directly at the corner of Argyll and Great Marlborough Street.

"Should I wait for you, mister Woodrow?"

"Woodrow, not mister Woodrow. Hadn't we agreed on that? Otherwise, I will have to respond with 'mister Timothy'."

"Shall I, Woodrow?" he said with a smile,

"No, Timmy. I don't know how long this will take so I'll find my way back by myself." I said getting down from the coach. I looked around and noticed Le Grand waving at me.

"Over here, quick," he said.

"Anything special?"

"Yes. Take a quick look over there near the court entrance."

"Hell! It's Abberline."

"And he's not alone."

"We should go around the block and see if more coppers are watching."

"Agreed."

We walked back on Oxford Street and slowly down in Hill Place leading us to the rear of the court building on Marlborough Mews. Besides people moving in and out of the police station including cops, nothing out of the ordinary was going on. We continued onto Ramilies Street until it met Marlborough Street. Still, no constables.

"What do we do now?" asked Le Grand.

"Why not take the bull by the horns," I said offering my companion a sarcastic smile. "After all, there's nothing wrong in attending court hearings out of curiosity."

"Why not? I've been interested in Law almost all my life."

"You meant to say the Law was interested in you, didn't you?"

We both burst out laughing and went for the court's main entrance.

Abberline didn't seem to be surprised when he saw us coming.

"What a pleasure it is to meet you again, mister Reily. You even brought your unleashed watch dog."

Le Grand's fists tightened and the remaining of his jolly smile disappeared instantly.

"If you don't mind, Le Grand is my friend, so I would appreciate seeing you use a more appropriate language."

"I shall do my best but can not guaranty it. What

brings you here mister Reily?"

"I've never attended a court hearing, so I simply
   wanted to see how things work," I answered. "And
not to grab Tumblety, of course."

"Never came to my mind, Inspector. I didn't even
expect him to be here," I said looking at Le Grand quite
amused by my smirk unnoticed by Abberline. "Let's find
a good seat," I said.

"Oh! I should mention that you may enter the
building, but the courtroom where Tumblety will appear
is temporarily closed," said Abberline sneering at me.
"Closed! The hearings are public. Anyone can attend
them," I said

"I know. But the room is full, and the clerks will
prevent anyone trying to enter. Obviously for security
reasons. You know, in case of fire," said Abberline.

"We'll wait here then."

"As you wish. May I foretell that the judge might not
release Tumblety on bail? Who knows? Let's wait
together and see."

Three, maybe four constables surrounded Le Grand
and I letting us clearly understand we had to follow them
outside.

After an hour later during which no word was
spoken, a man waved at Abberline whom he signaled to
join us. I was quite sure he was a detective who attended

Tumblety's hearing and came out to report back to
Abberline.

"What's the decision?" asked Abberline.

"Bail on remand and a committal warrant issued for
November 20 at Old Bailey," said the officer. "You
should have seen Tumblety's face when judge Hannay
explained to him that only money was accepted. Red as
a fresh tomato so much he was angry. He's been
committed to Holloway Prison. He read the notes he had
written down: 'Sir, you wish to provide the court with

diamonds. As far as I'm concerned, not having a certificate establishing their value, they're no better than pieces of glass. Now if someone on your behalf comes up with what the court demands within 48 hours, I'll gladly review my decision. Next case.'"

"And how much was the bail?" I asked.

"Let me guess," said Abberline, "two independent sureties totaling £300."

"Exactly," said the officer.

"You knew about it, didn't you Abberline? You probably set up the whole thing, having the courtroom filled with friends and plain clothed constables like this one, encouraging the clerks to have the doors blocked, making arrangements with the judge."

"You better be careful with what you say, my dear friend. I could have you arrested, and serious charges could be set against you," said Abberline. He was enjoying every moment in attempting to prove himself superior.

"Our good friend Tumblety will have no other choice but finding bondsmen or friends to bail him out."

Abberline's plan suddenly became clear to me.

"So that's what you've been up to since we last met. You're using Tumblety as a bait for O'Connell to jump on, aren't you. You don't care about women being murdered. The hell if Tumblety is the Ripper or not. It's O'Connell you're after."

"I won't comment. Now leave or I might just put an end to our relation in a manner you wouldn't appreciate."

"Let's leave, Le Grand," I said, "We have better things to do than listening to him. I need something to calm me down."

"There's a pub across the street."

"Too close. We'll find another one, follow me."

Minutes later, we were sitting at a pub ordering the strongest drink they had.

"Scotch?" suggested the waiter.

"Yes. Fill us both a glass."

"Who the bloody hell is O'Connell?" asked Le Grand.

"He's a very good friend of mine. Abberline wrongly believes he is one of the radical leaders of the Irish Brotherhood and has been trying to get a hold on him for quite a while."

"Shall you warn him?"

"It's the least I should do. However, there is a problem. I know he's in London, but I ignore his whereabouts. I shall have to get in contact with him indirectly and hope the message gets through."

"In case Tumblety manages to obtain sureties and reappears in court Friday, Abberline and his men will still be there waiting for him."

"I'm quite sure he will, but I may have an idea that will give us the upper hand." I picked my glass, brought it in front of my eyes. "You see how cloudy this whisky is?"

"We can't see through the glass."

"Precisely. All we have to do is cloud Abberline and each group of officers. We'll need some help to achieve that. Can I count on you?"

"Of course."

I gave Le Grand details of the plan I had in mind. It was essentially a matter of pre-arranging pieces of a chessboard in such a way I would win, cheating a bit like Abberline did with me. I gave him sufficiently enough money to cover any expense the plan might entail.

"Friday, I shall bring something better to drink than this military button polisher," I said clinking our glasses with a smile that quickly disappeared once we both emptied them and left the pub.

On my way back, I managed to send a telegram to Collins at Sawyers Arms pub asking him to urgently warn O'Connell of the trap Abberline was setting up.

FRIDAY, NOVEMBER 16, 1888

At 6 o'clock in the morning, I kissed Elizabeth assuring her I was about to have an enjoying day.

"I'm out to play a game of chess with Abberline. You know how I love that game," I said.

The look on her face didn't seem to indicate I had convinced her.

"You and Abberline, a game of chess! That needs to be seen."

Le Grand was waiting for me outside Fitzgerald's house chatting by the carriage with Timmy who was brushing the horse's dark coat. I barely recognized him for he was clean-shaved, dressed up like I never saw him before.

"I know we are going at Marlborough's courthouse, but what made you change your appearance?" I asked him.

"Everybody is used to see how I'm dressed, but I prefer not having Abberline know it's me once we get close. Otherwise, he'll conclude both you and I orchestrated the whole thing which would not be a good idea. Keep a short distance from me and do what you deem necessary. I'll take care of the rest. Understood?"

"Yes Sergeant. If I may open the door of your coach, Sir," I said to him. Timmy, Le Grand and I laughed out loud as we headed for the courthouse.

I was rubbing my hands out of joy to see that we had arrived at Marlborough Street's Courthouse before Abberline and his 'hounds'. Le Grand and I toured the adjoining streets to make sure my chessboard pieces would be well set. We found a place for the coach close enough for us to see those entering the courthouse without Abberline suspecting our presence. All that was left for us to do was comfortably wait for the game to begin upon Abberline's arrival, which occurred at seven precisely. We observed him as he placed detectives and officers almost exactly where they stood on Wednesday. A couple of constables passed by our coach without paying much attention to whom it might have been carrying. Le Grand and I were too young to correspond to any description he probably gave of O'Connell, a man in his fifties.

"Chilly morning," said one of them to Timmy. "So it is, but it'll warm up," he responded.

As time past, Le Grand and I noticed men and women slowly appearing in small groups walking all over the area conducting what seemed to be their usual daily business.

"Is it just me or are there more people to-day than Wednesday?" I asked Le Grand as I spun around almost stupefied by what was happening.

"You wanted me to do something, didn't you?"

"Yes."

"Then wait and watch."

More kept arriving and spreading out all around.

"Woodrow, look," Le Grand said pointing to the courthouse entrance.

Three men were coming close to the doors.

"My God! It's O'Connell, Patrick and obviously Tumblety's lawyer. They didn't get my message. We have to move quick before Abberline gets to them."

We jumped out of the coach and headed towards the entrance.

"Now don't you worry, Woodrow. Let me handle everything. Just walk through as if nothing out of the ordinary was happening. Remember to keep a distance."

We couldn't avoid passing in front of Abberline who was accompanied by sergeant Thick. They both noticed us and began walking towards us.

"Smile," said Le Grand with an insisting expression on his face which I did.

He moved away from me, pulled a whistle out of his pocket, and out came a single loud note. Some fifteen, twenty men who appeared to be journalists with pencils and pads in hand surrounded Abberline, Thick and the three constables with them. They began asking them all sorts of questions obviously preventing them from moving.

I waved at Abberline offering him a kind smile and I could see his face turning red out of anger as Le Grand and I passed him.

Le Grand blew twice in his whistle. Another group of men seemingly drunk marched in front of other constables and began quarreling between themselves. The constables couldn't ignore them and intervened, unsuccessfully though as more observers gathered around encouraging the noisy fighters.

"Who are those men?" I shouted out.

"Some of my good Irish friends," Le Grand said.

O'Connell, Patrick and the lawyer turned their heads in our direction just before entering the court. O'Connell noticed me, smiled, waved and went on.

I heard the cracking sound of a rattle, probably coming from one of Abberline's constables. It was a call for help sent to any available police constables the inspector had brought with him. The response was unexpectedly quick as a dozen constables hurried on Marlborough Street.

Again, Le Grand took his whistle and blew in it three times. Almost everyone on the street looked   towards him. He drew a large circle above his head with his hand and blew again. Those who understood his signal acted upon it and took care of the constables. One small group of men and women surrounded some constables. One of the women started yelling at a man. "Ain't ya gonna take care of me now that you bellied me up with child," she screamed. The crowd encouraged her, pushing the man she was addressing. He came close to her pretending to hit her, which forced the constables to grab him. Trying to liberate himself and yelling words I dare not repeat, the mob grew angrier forcing more constables to come and help their colleagues.

I glanced at Le Grand and laughed out.

"I can't believe what I'm seeing," I said. "This is probably the most amusing public show I have ever attended to in my life. I'm simply amazed."

"Almost front row seats," he said.

"And free drinks included," I added pulling out a flask from my coat and offering it to him. "Best Glenn, you'll ever taste."

Abberline had completely lost control of the situation. I admit enjoying it and cheerfully waved at him as an old friend would have done. He obviously wasn't sharing the same feeling and responded by holding up his fist. At that moment, O'Connell, Patrick, Tumblety and his lawyer came out of the courthouse meaning his bail and sureties had been accepted by the magistrate. Patrick and the lawyer took the north direction on Argyllis Street while O'Connell and Tumblety went south on Carnaby Street.

Abberline again tried to break loose from those surrounding him, but the fake journalists kept moving with him.

"Are you ready to release those poor bastards?" asked Le Grand amused by what he had accomplished.

"Let's wait a minute more and make sure O'Connell has a good head start", I said. "We should keep a distance from Abberline who surely will threaten us with a police obstruction charge, but not too far from him, which will allow us to see the cat chasing his mouses." Timmy drove the coach by our side.

"Is everything going as you wish?" he asked.

"It could not have gone better than this," I said. "Stay

behind us, just in case we need to move away fast. Le Grand, we can let them free now."

He pulled out his whistle and blew two short notes followed by a long one. Everyone involved in his scheme disappeared as fast as they came leaving Abberline mindless. He and Thick decided to go south while the other constables went north. We could see O'Connell and Tumblety far away in front of all of us. We entered a store to hide away from Abberline and better follow both of them. They soon passed by.

O'Connell and Tumblety turned left onto Beak Street and began zigzagging between streets to lose any eventual followers. What surprised me was they were walking at a normal pace, O'Connell looking behind from time to time. Was it done on purpose or did one of them had difficulties in moving fast? Something was going on, but I had no idea what it could be.

Abberline made efforts to catch up, maintaining some fifty yards or so away presumably to find where they would hide with other members of O'Connell's group.

"Pay attention, Woodrow," said Le Grand, "Your friends are slowly entering a shop. They are looking in our direction as if they wanted any follower to be aware of it."

"We need to be careful. If some of his friends are close by, the kind I met in Manchester, they'll think we are with Abberline and can get us into serious trouble."

Ahead of us, Abberline and Thick had noticed the same thing and stopped to better see from a safe distance what the two might be up to. A couple of minutes later heads down, O'Connell and Tumblety came out and pursued their route until they met the end of the street and had to turn either left or right. After hesitating a few seconds, they turned right. Abberline and Thick advanced at a faster pace fearing losing sight of them.

I found myself dragging my feet, which did not

please Le Grand at all.

"What are you doing? We're about to lose them all. Move, move. What's the problem?"

"This may seem ridiculous to you," I said, "But I may be facing a serious one in a few minutes."

Le Grand came to a halt, looked at me, surprised by my words. "A problem? You? What the bloody hell are you talking about."

"Let's keep walking. I don't want to lose them either, but I shall probably have to choose between protecting O'Connell before Abberline gets a hold on him or ignore what may happen to him and capture Tumblety instead."

"No problem there, my friend. Just pick one, and I'll go for the other."

O'Connell and Tumblety went down on Warwick Street. They were moving faster as they crossed from one side then back to the other between carts, trolleys and coaches. They turned left on Brewer Street, again, moving from side to side. They went on turning left until they reached Golden Square where they simply stopped and waited sitting on one of the benches.

Abberline and Thick slowly caught up with them.

"Make it fast, Woodrow. I'll stay here just in case," Le Grand said.

I ran as fast as I could. The minute I arrived the two men sitting raised their head, took their hats off and saluted us. It wasn't either O'Connell or Tumblety, but two men dressed exactly like them.

"Good day, gentlemen," said one of them. "May we be of some help to you?"

We looked at each other and could not believe it.

"I just feel like arresting you for what you did back there, you damn fool" Abberline said pointing towards the courthouse.

"I have nothing to do with it. I was surprised as you may have been and could only watch the live theater where you were caught in. They should call that superb performance 'The trapped Trapper'"

"O'Connell tricked us when he and Tumblety walked in the store and had these two men sitting in front of us come out in their place, dressed exactly as they were," Thick said.

"You should have let me get Tumblety this past Wednesday. Now, I lost him and you lost O'Connell. We're both even."

"I'm not worried about Tumblety. He has to come back for his trial," said Abberline.

"If you want my opinion, he shall abscond, and you will never see neither him nor O'Connell ever again."

"If he even tries to leave the country," Thick said, "we have ways to prevent that. He shall have to swim to evade us."

I looked at both of them and couldn't imagine how naïve they were especially if O'Connell lends Tumblety a hand. "All I can say is 'good luck'. I'll try my own way and should I find Tumblety, trust me, he shall not flee. In any case, I will let you know."

Timmy and Le Grand were waiting for me, both heavily engaged in a conversation and emptying the flask I had left in Le Grand's hands earlier.

"Empty handed, aren't you?" Le Grand said. I didn't respond. He went on,"The good thing about it is that you didn't have to choose as you thought you would."

"Any of that liquid left?" I asked.

"Of course," Timmy said, offering me the flask with a smile matching his half-closed eyes.

"Drive us home, Timmy," I said as Le Grand and I climbed into the coach. I took a couple of gulps and gave it to Le Grand who emptied it. "Sorry," he said, "no more 'Holy water left'. Too bad."

"Now that Tumblety got away, we are facing a new problem," I told Le Grand.

"I'm beginning to like the problems you come up with, Woodrow. What's this one all about?"

"I'll bet everything I own that Tumblety will not appear in court when comes time for him to do so. He knows Abberline framed him and tried to use him to catch O'Connell. He still has the Ripper murders charges up his sleeve just in case Tumblety manages to have the indecency charges dismissed. So the only logical option he has is to leave the country as soon as he can. Abberline let me understood he could control the ships leaving for Canada or the United States in all the ports. We need to outsmart him again, but I'm not too sure I know how."

"If you put yourself a little deeper in your friend O'Connell's mind you'll probably find a way he would have eluded Abberline."

"You are dead right. In a game of chess, and it's O'Connell's favorite game, a good player will fool his opponent by letting him believe he is setting up his pieces in a given way and hides his real plan."

"So if Abberline thinks Tumblety will attempt to go to Canada or the States..."

"...and if I were wearing O'Connell's shoes," I said, "I would know it would be the logical way to proceed. Hence, I would instead suggest Tumblety to head firstly for France, Portugal or Spain and from thereupon, go wherever he wished without no one knowing it."

"Precisely. It means we would have fewer ports to control."

"We must find a way to cover the ports leading to these countries. By the way, what would be the shortest way out of the country from London?"

"From London to Newhaven, then over to Dieppe, more or less one hundred and fifty miles. But I doubt he will take a ship at Dieppe." Le Grand noticed my disappointment. "Dieppe is a more commercial port than a place for cruise ships, and I don't think Tumblety will consider himself as a piece of cargo. He'll have a better choice of passenger ships in Le Havre."

"So we'll focus on Le Havre."

"Let me see what I can do about that."

"Excellent."

I asked Timmy if he wouldn't mind dropping me close to Fitzgerald's home and continue with Le Grand back to the East End.

"Shall do," said. Timmy.

I had him stop by a post office allowing me to send a telegram to O'Connell asking him if he had received the warning I gave him days ago, demanding he explained to me the relation he had told me he didn't have with Tumblety but proved to be quite the contrary by helping him with his bail. I concluded by telling him that, in my opinion, had I not made the arrangements to capture Tumblety once his bail had been granted, he would most probably would never had been able to escape Abberline. Hence, I honestly believed I deserved some form of explanation.

TUESDAY, NOVEMBER 20, 1888

For me and Le Grand, yesterday was a special day. Tumblety had been scheduled to appear at the Old Bailey. I was never convinced he would be present, but we both had to be there just to make sure and what happened simply confirmed my prediction. Instead of having him at court, we saw his lawyer, Archibald Bodkin, submit a request for a postponement which was granted without the need to offer any plea of being guilty or not-guilty. The decision made read something like this: "Upon application of Mr. Bodkin for defense and after hearing Mr. Muir for prosecution the case is adjourned till next session all recognizances being respited."

Le Grand and I tried to estimate the time it would require him to get to Le Havre, the most obvious route he would take in our minds. It would at least require two, maybe three days. Now if I were he, I would arrive there well in advance to provide me with the most options possible, which meant I would have left London the moment I had received the court's decision or even before, the court not having reasonable motives to suspect I would abscond. I decided to double the surveillance, I had planned in the port of Le Havre.

What, however, remains of the utmost importance is that I shouldn't put all my eggs in a single basket. Moreover, I still had this disturbing question I kept asking myself in the past days. Giving the fact that O'Connell helped Tumblety, doesn't one have to assume he wouldn't have done it had Tumblety been the Ripper? Perhaps, unless he was an accomplice which seemed unlikely considering what I knew of O'Connell?

Nevertheless, until Tumblety explains to me a few damaging pieces of evidence against him, he remains a serious suspect in my mind and worth having me continue to look for him. I needed to know where he got his two brass rings, seemingly the same Chapman wore the day of her death and were said to be missing. I also had to elucidate what may simply be a coincidence when Tumblety would tell me to expect female organs exactly on the following morning of every murder. And not to mention one of the hospital's pieces of its medical instrument collection, the amputation knife, disappearing from our lab when he came to visit us. However, given the current uncertainty of the evidence I may have against him and this need I have to capture the Ripper, I had to continue with the night patrols with the Vigilance Committee.

Later during the evening, Timmy, as he would often

do, brought me close to the junction of Whitechapel and Commercial where I would meet Le Grand leaving him wait until my patrol ended. Le Grand and I were again wearing out the soles of our shoes on one of the East End beats near Aldgate and Duke Streets.

"Do you sometimes wonder if what we're doing is still worth it?" Le Grand asked.

"Are you asking me this because I can't figure out why O'Connell prevented us from capturing, Tumblety, the man I believe is the Ripper and who has left England?"

"In part, yes. It's also because the Ripper seems to be methodical and well organised. I think he killed those women knowing he wouldn't get caught."

"Even on the double event night, when he quickly left one victim dead to better cut out another one?"

"Yes. The East End is his territory and like any good predator, he probably knows every square inch of his hunting ground."

"On the other hand, the more daring he becomes, the greater the chances are of having him commit careless errors that may reveal his whereabouts. We now know what he does to his victims. We must learn how his human predator seeks its victims. If the Ripper is organised as you said, he is not waiting for his preys to approach him, he seeks them. Walking these streets and observing how many behave provides us with an opportunity to do so."

"Then let's walk."

The night was cold and damp, but it didn't seem to bother the people of East End. They would keep coming out even if no apparent reason justified their presence.

The uneventful patrols Le Grand and I had been experiencing lately have convinced me to leave my heavy pistol at home.

"Have you ever noticed that so many of these poor

people appear at the same place and at the same time every day?" I asked Le Grand as my eyes were discreetly surveying the streets and courtyard entrances.

"It's simply their way of defining and protecting their territory. Much too often, it's the only way they have to show they exist, which makes it easier for all the human predators including the Ripper."

Hours ago, the chaotic sounds of the daytime activity had left their place to the waves of turbulence of the night. Here, the whinnying of exhausted horses pulling carriages, there, the mumbling between arguing drunks stumbling over every stone or grabbing the closest person standing by them. But what made both of us come to a halt, was the loud cry of a woman. Hearing a woman yelling at her man or screaming out of pain was frequent at nighttime in the East End. This time, the sound was different, a mixture of moans, fear and helplessness. It could simply be a wounded woman who fell or was pushed down. In any case, we decided to go see. We both had bullseye lanterns, one lit and the other kept as a reserve.

We managed to zero in on origin of the sound of the woman's voice. It led us to a narrow and rather long courtyard entrance offering us only the dim shapes of its structure. I lit the second lantern as we both proceeded through the passageway.

Held by a man against the left side wall of the yard with his arm crossing her throat was the terrified woman. I hastily moved towards them smashing my lantern on the man's back of the head splashing the inflamed kerosene over the cobblestones. The man fell to the ground. His hands wrapped his head feeling the blood dripping down his neck. But his attention shifted to the fire catching up on his coat which he began to sweep off. Le Grand lent a hand to the woman moving her away from her assailant.

"I'll be back as fast as I can," Le Grand said, "Don't do anything stupid."

I was left with alone, no lantern, the moon barely offering me its partially full light. Still dizzy, the man managed to get up and turned towards me. I couldn't believe it. It was the same man we saw on Duke Street more than a month ago and whose head I threatened to blow off.

"Damn bastard. Didn't I warn you what would happen if I caught you again attacking a woman?"

His nasty smile meant he had come to the same conclusion. He drew a knife from inside his vest. Its long sharp blade, obviously a butcher's knife, forced me to pull back sideway to avoid the first strike as he came strait on me. I took a swing at him hitting him hard on the side of his face sending him off a few feet which allowed me to remove my overcoat and use it as a shield.

He kept coming back at me striking without success as I kept dodging as fast as I could. He aimed at my chest, my face, my hips and legs, growling like a mad dog. No one was looking through the windows above us to see what was going on as if a murderous Street fight was simply one among any other boring daily activities East Enders observed. For me, it was a matter of survival.

I suddenly got caught off guard as he feigned a movement towards my left side but shifted with all his body weight to my right. He grabbed my neck and pierced my overcoat and vest with his knife. I felt the blade sliding against my flesh. I was cut.

I dropped my overcoat, seized his shoulders with both hands bringing him closer to me and kicked his groin with my knee. He bent back tearing the collar of my shirt, snapping off the chain holding my family medallion. He straitened up, looked at it and seemed surprised. It was the error I was waiting for. I grasped the hand he held his knife with both of mine and pushed it way up his stomach turning it from side to side to create as much damage as I could.

He let go of the knife, looked strait into my eyes and again at the medallion and said, "You're my..."

I didn't let him finish and struck him again and again.

He slowly dropped down, murmuring to me, "My..., my..."

Those were his last words. I took back my medallion and chain slipping them in one of my pockets.

I heard someone running through the courtyard's entrance. I took the knife and prepared myself for another attack. It was Le Grand.

"What happened? You knocked him out?"

"No, I think I killed him," I said holding my side with my hand.

"Good Lord!" Le Grand said. He kneeled down and checked the man's pulse. "He's dead." He quickly came to me. "What about you? Are you all right?" he asked.

"He cut me." I opened my vest and saw my blood soaking shirt. The cut was long, but not deep.

"Take your shirt off. I'll use it to cover the wound and stop it from bleeding. We got to make it fast before someone comes here."

It took only a couple of minutes for him to tear off the sleeves, tie them together and wrap them tight around my waist. I moaned out of pain, and put my vest and overcoat back on.

"We got to do something with the body," Le Grand said. "We can't leave it here. Go get Timmy while I move it away."

I didn't dare running to avoid worsening my wound, but managed to find him after endless minutes of painful walking holding my bleeding side.

"Help me in," I asked him with a grimace. I gave him the direction where Le Grand was, begging him to make it fast and arrived only minutes later. Le Grand was waiting by the street.

"What the hell are you doing here by the pavement?" I asked.

"Had to wait and prevent any officer from entering the yard. Turned out I did the right thing. Constable Harvey passed by, asked where you were and told him you went in the yard to check if everything was under control. He felt satisfied and went on. I could have told him you went to relieve yourself," he said smirking, "but he would have run in and arrest you, don't you agree? Now quick before hc returns."

I could only smile at Le Grand.

Timmy and Le Grand went to pick up the body while I waited in the coach.

"This bugger is damn heavy," Timmy said as he and Le Grand wrapped the body in the horse's blanket and placing him at my feet. "Next time, find someone your own size," he added with a mocking smile.

"We need to find a doctor to take care of Woodrow," Le Grand said.

"No need to worry. I know where to pick up one on our way back," said Timmy.

A few blocks from Fitzgerald's home, we stopped. Timmy went down, knocked at the door, and only a few minutes after, I wasn't surprised to see Fillmore, running towards us, leather bag in hand.

"What in the name of God did you do this time, Woodrow?" he asked noticing blood stains on my overcoat.

"I slipped on a broken bottle," I said.

The expression on Fillmore's face spelled out the word 'doubt'. "And that, I suppose, is the bottle," he said kicking the wrapped body at his feet. We all looked at each other and chuckled.

We arrived at FitzGerald's home through the stable

entrance. Timmy and Le Grand helped me out the carriage and into the house.

"Be careful with what you will say," suggested Timmy. "As far as we're concerned, you got caught in a bad fight, nothing else."

Le Grand nodded, "We'll take care of the rest, do you hear me?"

"I know I can trust both of you," I said.

They carried me to my room making sure they would not wake anyone. We didn't expect Winston would be at his post, an oil lamp in his hand clearing the way in the corridor.

"I heard the coach coming and expected mister Reily would enter through the front door which he didn't," he said.

They laid me on the bed. Fillmore cleaned the wound, and suggested using ether as an anaesthetic. I refused well aware it would turn my stomach. Winston offered me a full glass of Scotch which I gulped Fillmore then closed the wound with some stiches causing me to grimace each time the needle entered my body.

"You know, Woodrow, I'm more into autopsies, but given the... huh... opportunities you've been offering us lately, and if you insist on providing us with more of them, I might as well commence right now with yours"

The room door suddenly opened. In came Elizabeth wearing a pale blue nightgown and robe jacket. Describing her as being upset would have been an understatement. Infuriated would come closer to what she was about to let us understand being. Everyone looked at her then at me wondering what would happen.

"Out! All of you, except for Doctor Fillmore," she firmly said pointing at the door.

They left the room offering her the smile a child caught with his hand in someone's wallet would wear.

We were silent.

"Is one of you going to tell me what is going on?"

"If I were you, I wouldn't suggest the bottle explanation, Woodrow," said Fillmore.

"What bottle?" she asked.

"Forget the bottle," I said, "I was attacked, and Doctor Fillmore is taking care of it."

She came closer to me. "My God! Someone tried to slice you. Did the attacker get arrested?"

Fillmore and I looked at each other not knowing what to say.

"If I may," said Fillmore, "The incident has been properly dealt with."

"This should tell you something, Woodrow," Elizabeth said.

"One thing seems to be quite clear to me," I said, "Le Grand and I talked about it before this incident happened. I'm done with the patrols."

"Honnestly?"

"Yes."

Deep inside, I knew exactly why I had to stop patrolling but preferred not mentioning it. Even if I obviously prevented a crime against a woman, it became urgent for me to avoid showing myself in the East End at the risk of falling into the hands of those who might have seen me but didn't intervene out of fear.

"Excellent," Elizabeth said, "Is he going to be well?" she asked Fillmore.

"As long as he rests for a while and the bandage is changed regularly, everything should turn out fine," said Fillmore as he closed his bag and prepared to leave.

"Thank you so much, doctor."

He saluted us with his hand and slowly went out the room.

"Now tell me what really happened, or I'll call back Fillmore and ask him to stitch you more than you would like."

I described my encounter with the assailant providing her with all the details, but I must admit that the last words I pronounced were those she preferred and had nothing to do with the attack.

THURSDAY, NOVEMBER 22, 1888

Around six o'clock in the morning, from my room on the second floor, I could hear someone banging at the door. I dressed up, picked my pistol and went down as fast as I could. Winston had already opened the door to someone he knew but didn't expect to see so early, Le Grand.

"What's all this commotion? You're scaring the whole household. Do you know what time it is?" I asked him.

"We need to move, Woodrow, move quickly," he said.

"Let's go to the library," I said as I pulled on his overcoat.

"Would you like some tea?" Winston asked.

"Tea would be fine for me," Le Grand said.

"I'd rather have coffee, if it's possible, Winston."

"Tea and coffee. Shall have it ready in a few minutes."

"Now what is going on," I asked as we both sat.

"One of our helpers in France found out that an officer of Scotland Yard's Special Irish Branch, a man named William Melville, has spotted Tumblety in Barcelone and followed him to Le Havre. The French refused to arrest him and have him sent back to London, having no probable cause"

"I knew it. I knew he would pass through Le Havre and cross over to the States. We need to stop him."

"The British officer seemed to be seeking a rather

discreet help from outsiders in having that done, if our informer understood him well."

"And if something goes wrong with the French authorities, the Yard wouldn't be blamed for a..."

"...kidnapping."

"Precisely."

"Can we do it?"

"My men are just waiting for your approval."

"Then tell them to proceed. Now what are our options if we fail get to him, and he leaves for the States?"

"Someone will have to cross also to catch him over there and attempt to bring him back."

"And I think we both know who that person shall be," I said with a disconcerting feeling we shared together.

"We will have to wait and see what happens in Le Havre."

"I don't think we should wait. If the worst-case scenario is not catching Tumblety, I might as well prepare myself immediately to leave for America in the next coming days."

"I heard that."

Elizabeth had just entered the library holding a tray with pots and cups full of tea and coffee.

"I thought you said you were over with this Tumblety hunting fantasy," she added as she banged the tray on the desk where I sat.

"The night patrols, yes, but not catching Tumblety. You even approved me wanting to catch the Ripper."

"I did indeed," she said, "And how do you plan doing that since you're not sure Tumblety is the Ripper?"

"We are making arrangements in Le Havre to get Tumblety before he crosses over to the States, and if it doesn't work, I'll be there to pick him up the moment he leaves his ship. I'll make him tell the truth. Once it's all over, I'll go to Quebec City and see how our families are doing."

She kept silent, which worried me.

"Didn't you plan to cross over in Canada in a few weeks with a group of families?" I asked.

"Yes, but..."

"I'll simply be there waiting for you," I said with a hopefully convincing smile.

"Things don't turn out to be that simple if I recall the recent incidents you've been involved in. But then, I think you have already made your mind, and whatever I might say won't make you change it."

"I swear this will be the last time I ever try to confront Tumblety."

"Consider yourself lucky. Father will not be back from the estate until Saturday. He would have found a way to prevent you from doing this."

"I doubt it." I said, not really convinced by what I was saying. "What you need to know is how much I care for you, and would not compromise our relation."

"If you don't mind, I'll try to get the boat departures for the next coming days," Le Grand said as he walked to the door and left.

Elizabeth and I continued our conversation, which shifted towards matters more intimate I would not reveal.

During the afternoon, Le Grand came back with some rather disappointing information.

"We need to talk in private," he murmured.

I was a bit surprised to see how embarrassed he was, Le Grand being known as an outspoken person.

"There's only one boat leaving Liverpool soon enough to arrive before Tumblety would. It's the Nova Scotian, and it's heading for Halifax. From there you would have to take a train to get to New York."

"Is that the problem?"

"No. All the cabins have been sold. Not a single place left, even in the steerage class."

"Damn!"

"There's still a way around."

"Which is?"

"I spoke with some officers who would accept you as a member of the crew, but..." Le Grand hesitated for a moment, "you wouldn't be with the crew. You would have to stay in the cargo hold and only be allowed to go up on the main deck during night hours."

I stood up from my chair, walked around in the library head down, crisping my fists. "I'll have to live with that. When is it leaving?"

"To-night, and if you want to make it, you need to leave by train now."

"You must be kidding!"

"Sorry, but it's the only choice you have if you want to get Tumblety."

"Wait here while I go pack a suitcase and say a word to Elizabeth."

An hour or so later, Le Grand and I arrived at the Euston Station. Elizabeth refused to accompany us. She was in tears when we left, and I figured out it would have been an emotional experience she preferred not going through.

THURSDAY, NOVEMBER 29, 1888

Trying to get to New York didn't turn out as I had expected. Although it only took the Nova Scotian seven days to reach Halifax, the voyage was rather awful. It seemed endless because of the stormy sea we kept having. As for the food, I wonder if East-Enders would have eaten it. The cargo hold was cold and damp, and even if the crew had given me blankets, I was freezing. Instead of counting sheep to fall asleep, as children would often do, I was counting rats. There were more black rodents around me than passengers and members of the crew all together.

I would walk on the upper deck late every night to admire the sea and the stars meeting other passengers only twice. I never felt so isolated in my life, and began to grasp the unusefulness of my quest Elizabeth and others tried to make me understand. It was, however, too late to stop. I had to bring it to its end.

Although I tried to take care of my wound as best as I could, cleaning it and changing bandages every other day, it wasn't healing well, and began to swell. I paid a member of the crew to obtain some carbolic soap from the medical staff which I used to disinfect it.

Once in Halifax, I felt completely weakened by the crossing but couldn't allow letting it show. I hastily passed through the quarantine officers without any problem well aware they could have prevented me from continuing my travel. I sent a telegram to Elizabeth informing her that everything was going although it wasn't really the case.

Finding a way for me to make it to New York was another cause of deception. The train would have been the logical way for me to get there, but it would have required of me to frequently change railroad lines creating unexpected delays and making me reach New York, a day after Tumblety would have arrived. Luckily, a ship was leaving for Quebec City. She was an iron paddle steamer named Druid used as a lighthouse tender, and her season having ended, she would return to winter in the port of Quebec. From there, I could take a train heading directly for New York. With her powerful motor and drawing little water, the Druid could move fast up the Saint-Lawrence river. Her Captain, Louis Plante, hesitated a little before accepting me as a passenger.

"You don't look too good, mon brave," said the

Captain noticing I was sweating. "Maybe you should rest for a while before boarding and going to Quebec."

"I need to get to Quebec as fast as I can," I told him. "We don't have any medical support on board. It's at your own risk."

"I believe I can manage it."

At least, it's what I thought I could do, but it did not work out that way. The fever kept rising, and more and more pain came from my wound leading me to believe it could be seriously infected. I hadn't shaved nor bathed since I left Liverpool, which was the first thing I did as I got to my cabin, minding my wound came second. I laid on my bed and went for a deep sleep.

FRIDAY, NOVEMBER 30, 1888

We had entered deep in the gulf. Later that evening, I went up on the deck. I noticed the Captain maneuvering the ship. He saluted me, gave the wheel to a crew member and joined me for what I hoped would be a friendly conversation.

He took a long look at me, leaned on the guardrail and invited me to for a drink in his cabin. I immediately suspected things might go wrong. "We need to talk," he said pointing at his cabin door.

It was a rather small cabin with a single bed, one large wall cabinet, table and seats. "Have a seat." He went to his wall cabinet, pulled out a bottle and a couple of glasses. "Try this."

I noticed the words De Kuyper and Geneva on the bottle. He poured me a glass, and from its awful odour I knew it was gin, the kind poor East-Enders would take to blind them from their misery, which could now shadow the pain from my wound. I sat and gulped it.

"Ewww, I never had a taste for gin, but thanks anyway."

"I'll be frank with you. You're sick, mon ami, and I have a problem knowing exactly what it might be."

"It's only a fever," I said.

"A fever is like the tip of an iceberg. It only shows what it wants to show. It could turn out to be typhoid, consumption, cholera and I can't risk seeing my crew getting sick."

"I respect your opinion. What do you intend to do Throw me overboard?"

"Elle est bien bonne," he laughed out in his French Canadian accent."

"We will arrive shortly at Grosse Isle, a quarantine station where we'll drop you off. They have an excellent medical staff who can take care of you."

"Are you serious? I have to be in New York by Saturday."

"Impossible, mon ami," he said in an attempt to share my disappointment. " I'm sure you would do the same if you were in my position, and the way you look, New York should be the last thing on your mind."

"I..., I..." I was speechless, completely devastated as if my whole life had suddenly come to an end. I had no idea of what could now happen to me given how my physical condition appeared to be, Seemingly, I shall never be able to learn the truth from Tumblety.

6 THE EVENTS OF DECEMBER 1888

SATURDAY, DECEMBER 1, 1888

My fever got worse, and I began to have this rash forcing me to keep my sleeves rolled down so it wouldn't be seen. I felt dizzy and weak, so weak I could barely make it to the upper deck. An officer noticed me and strongly suggested me to return to my room. Only minutes later, the Captain came in without knocking.

"You must remain in your room until we arrive to Grosse Isle," he said wearing a rather worried face.

"Am I your captive now?" I asked.

"Not at all. It's for your own safety. One of my men saw you walking on the deck in such a way he believed you were completely drunk. Haven't you noticed the sea? You could have been easily swept over board."

I simply looked at him and laid on my bed.

"Besides, you're getting worse," he said pointing to my face, "and I like I said, I don't want you to spread out on my crew whatever you may have. All of us may be already contaminated and if so, would have to stay on the island as well. I'll bring you some food. We should arrive in a couple of hours. I've waved up the flag requesting an inspection."

These hours seemed to have passed in minutes only obviously caused by the fever cutting off my notion of time. I could hear voices close to me, but couldn't understand what was said. I was, however, aware I'd been carried off the boat. From that moment, I completely lost track of what may have happened from then on.

7 THE EVENTS OF JANUARY 1889 (CONTINUED)

SUNDAY, JANUARY 6, 1889
GROSSE ISLE

I've been stranded here on Grosse Isle for over a month having almost died of typhus. I was quite lucky. The quarantine season usually ending in mid November had been extended a few weeks for reasons I ignore and Doctor Frederick Montizambert, the superintendent and medical director of the station, had not returned yet to Quebec City for the winter. I was the only patient of the station hence, I was placed in a private room, and Montizambert personally took care of me.

"We almost lost you a week after your arrival," the doctor had told me. "You were infected with typhus when the Captain brought you here. The crew of the ship you were on came out clear. All we needed to do was to disinfect the ship. Now where the hell did you get those wounds? They needed serious attention, and those damn rats on the ship didn't help. You're safe... for the moment."

"I believe I owe you my life," I said.

"I simply did my job."

"I need to inform my friends in London. Is there a way to do so?"

"We have a telegraph station on the island. In a couple of days, you will be able to send them a message."

It was the first thing I did once I felt my mind was clear and was strong enough to hold a pen. I told Elizabeth that I never made it to New York and had been held under quarantine on Grosse Isle with typhus. She must have been more than upset for I haven't received a response from her yet. Then again, even if she had tried, no message would have reached me, the heavy ices having recently dragged the telegraph cable against the rocky shore and broken it.

MONDAY, JANUARY 7, 1889

The first time I had a view of the island, I said to myself it was probably the last place I would have chosen to live. But it's a world within a world. The island is small, a mile long by half a mile wide and part of the Isle-aux-Grues archipelago in the middle of the Saint-Lawrence river only thirty miles from Quebec City where I expected I would have stopped two months ago before reaching New York. The quarantine station is on the western side while the locals live on the other end, most of them working at the station.

Being the only patient turned me into the island's season curiosity. Once my typhus was cured, I was invited on the west side where voyagers are not allowed for obvious health reasons. I never considered myself as a person who enjoyed sharing his free time with others, quite to the contrary. Before the East End events happened, I limited my exchanges to the minimum necessary. Such was the way I had chosen to survive when I left my home town some twenty years ago, and even if it seemed centuries, once again, survival had become my main concern. However, I had to convince myself of making certain compromises and accepted some invitations, in particular, those made close to the Christmas period. I must say I was the first one to benefit from my decision. I never could have imagined how cold and snowy this part of the world was, and many provided me with warm clothes, boots and gloves allowing me to walk around the station. It gave me the opportunity to better know and understand the people living here. The exceptional kindness everyone shows has become part of the local culture. I was told that during the immigration season, the staff was able to communicate in many languages directly or with the help of translators. The locals consider themselves part of a large family regardless of their religion, Catholic or Anglican, or their language, French or English. All were eager to explain to me what they did and have me visit the various buildings where they worked.

Those who fascinated me the most were the boatmen. They were the only link between the islands and the main land during winter months. They usually would be three boatmen on these wooden fifteen feet long canoes and learned in their younger years to cross through floating pieces of ice pushing and pulling their shallops on the ice. They could read the strong currents and winds like others read a book and followed the tides to make for a better time. But the weather conditions could change drastically, and they would drift away from the shores. Some would only carry cargo and mail while others would take the risk of adding a passenger. I asked them many times to bring me across so I could get to Quebec and find a way back to England, but they always refused even if I offered them more than required.

"We only accept passengers strong enough to handle difficult situations, and you're much too weak," one of them said to me. "Maybe another time."

I had no idea how long would I have to wait.

SUNDAY, JANUARY 13, 1889

Three boatmen decided to cross the river to-day. They left around seven o'clock this morning with the up-going tide and good winds. I gave them a message to send by telegram to Elizabeth. They would come back to-morrow hopefully with an answer from her.

I began coughing during the afternoon and thought it would be a simple cold. But fever came up followed by shaking chills. A nurse believed it was pneumonia, which was confirmed by Doctor Montizambert when he asked me if I had any chest pains and trouble breathing.

"Even if you have recovered from typhus and your wounds have healed," he said, "you are still very weak and should stay rested."

I was well aware that many have died of pneumonia in the past and that the same could happen to me. Three times someone attempted to kill me and three times I survived. I had typhus and survived. Now it's pneumonia and it, also, was trying to kill me.

"What are my chances?" I asked him.

"I honestly don't know. I will have a nurse close by all the time, but you must rest."

He left.

I've never been the kind of person who would wait for something or someone to force me to act. Nor would I deny facts such as Montizambert's conclusion. If my body isn't in its best shape, I could, however, keep my mind busy. Hence, I decided to write down everything that happened since the beginning of the East End events and asked the nurse for a pen and some paper. Doing so would probably help me put an end to this mad idea I had of capturing the Ripper instead of letting my sickness and possible death slowly making it disappear from my thoughts.

MONDAY, JANUARY 14, 1889

When I woke up this morning, a nurse was doing some cleaning in my room. Still feverish, I sat up and coughed more than yesterday. However, I was glad to be alive one more day, although I ignored if my condition would improve hence, expecting the worst. I was feeling weaker and weaker and tried not letting it show.

"Did the boatmen return?" I asked.

"I don't think so, sir. A snow storm began during the night, and it's building up. So I would be surprised if they would risk their lives."

She approached me and cleaned my sweating face with a cold-watered towel. "You must stay in your bed. I'll get you something to eat."

She walked towards the door, opened it, offered me a comforting smile and left.

THUESDAY, JANUARY 15, 1889

I keep drinking tea and coffee to stay awakened and focused on my writing. The nurses didn't agree but finally understood my desperation and let me do as I wished. It demanded a great part of my energy already quite low, but should it be the last thing I ever do, I shall do it until the end.

During the afternoon, a nurse came and told me that the boatmen had returned with a telegram for me. I would have jumped out of my bed had it not been my condition. Nevertheless, I tried to express my overwhelming feeling of joy. I was quickly disappointed for it wasn't from Elizabeth and contained words that both saddened and reassured me. It was dated January 12 and informed me that Fitzgerald had died and that Elizabeth had left England after the funerals without telling anyone where she intended to go. My hands dropped on the bed, the telegram slipping down on the floor.

"Maybe I should go," the nurse said noticing my reaction.

"No, that wouldn't be necessary."

"Is there anything I can do for you, sir."

I didn't respond and simply laid down trying to convince myself that Elizabeth maybe had decided to cross over. Regardless of what she may have thought of me, she still had excellent reasons to come to Quebec. Everyone knew that families we had sent here were expecting her hence she need not hide her intentions. I slowly began to doze off.

THURSDAY, JANUARY 31, 1889

I've been working relentlessly on my writing and managed to be up to date, but it came at a heavy price: the worsening of my already deteriorated health condition. However, I should be ending it soon either falling out of ink and paper or simply falling dead. I am completely exhausted and only wish to sleep at least one night without the drugs I've been given.

8 THE EVENTS OF FEBRUARY 1889

FRIDAY, FEBRUARY 1, 1889

I must have overslept more than usual for half the day had passed when my eyes opened. Although my mind was foggy, I recognized Montizambert's voice in the corridor.

"Let me first go in and check him out," he said, "then I'll see if you can see him."

He entered, quickly closing the door behind him and sat by the side of my bed.

"Who were you talking to?" I muttered as I raised myself up leaning on my elbows.

He did not respond. He placed his stethoscope against my chest and began auscultating.

"Breathe deeply."

I did as he told.

"Deeper. Do you still have pain breathing?" he asked.

"A little less than yesterday."

"Good. I believe your fever will be going down."

I laid back, closed my eyes still feeling weak and only wanting to sleep.

"You can come in," said Montizambert. "He appears

to be stable."

I heard footsteps. It was probably one of his nurses bringing me some food and drinks as they would do a few times a day.

"Woodrow, it's me," a voice whispered to my ears.

I was certain I was dreaming and kept my eyes closed fearing I would wake up only to see one of the nurses.

"Can you hear me?" the voice spoke out. "Doctor, are you sure he's doing well?"

I felt a soft hand on my cheeks followed by a kiss on my lips. I opened my eyes. I was wordless.

"Elizabeth!" said I, making tremendous efforts to move.

She gently covered my mouth with her fingers. "Don't say a word. Everything will be fine now. I'm with you and shall not leave without you," she paused, "never again."

"Doctor," Elizabeth said as she stood up and faced the doctor. "We need to give him better medical cares.

I'm well aware you and your staff saved his life, but it would be better if he were surrounded by a larger team."

"I agree," he said. "But he's much too weak to cross.

These heavy winds we've been having are dangerous and demand strong hands in case things go wrong."

"If I may," said I. "I prefer dying while attempting to do something than dying out of waiting."

Both Elizabeth and Montizambert turned towards me surprised by seeing me sitting on the side of the bed. "If the boatmen say it can be done to-morrow, then I'll cross with them."

They looked at each other and smiled. "Can I have a word with Elizabeth?"

Doctor Montizambert didn't say a word and left.

Elizabeth sat by my side.

"I thought I would never see you again," I said. "You didn't respond to my first telegram and the only thing I knew was that you had left after your father had died without saying where you were going. I was devastated."

"Now you know how I felt when you did the same thing to me."

"I do and I'm so sorry for everything. It's all over now. I'll never get a hold of Tumblety and find the Ripper."

"You won't have to. Before dying, father told me that the Ripper had been killed."

"Your father was such a good person. You have no idea how much I shall miss him. He was the father I never had."

"And you became the son he wished had lived."

We were out of words, only looking at each other softly holding our hands.

"I don't want to be disrespectful," I asked after a few minutes, "but did he mention who the Ripper was?"

"I don't know. Actually, nobody seems to know. He, nevertheless, wrote you a letter explaining everything."

She opened her handbag, pulled out a sealed envelope and gave it to me.

"Maybe you should read it."

The envelope had only two words on it, 'To Woodrow'. I placed it on the table close to my notebook.

"It can wait." I kissed her tenderly and felt as if I was really alive again.

SATURDAY, FEBRUARY 2, 1889

I woke up early this morning. Elizabeth and the nurse were talking together.

"Good morning ladies," I said working hard to build up a smile.

Elizabeth came close to me with a cup of warm coffee, which she gave me.

"It seems we are lucky. Nurse Turcotte here told me

that the winds were softly blowing west just the kind the boatmen like. The tide will begin to rise in a couple of hours. It means will be able to leave soon."

"Great," said I. "But I have to do something before leaving and will probably need your help if you don't mind. Can someone bring me my clothes?"

The nurse pulled my clothes out of a drawer and laid them on the bed. Both understood I needed to be alone.

When I stood up, I felt dizzy and almost fell to the floor.

In my mind, I may have believed my health was improving, but my body kept telling me it didn't seem to agree. The small mirror above the sink sent me a miserable unshaven face I hardly recognized. It was mine. I cleaned myself and shaved. It took me more time than usual to dress up. I would still have to be careful in the coming days.

I opened my room door and asked Elizabeth to come in.

"I need to talk to you," I told her.

"Is something wrong?" she said as she saw me sitting on my bed.

"I just need to sit a moment," I said trying to breathe. "Do you remember yesterday when I told you this crazy quest was over?"

"Yes, I do."

"I was serious. At one point, I can't remember exactly when, but it seemed quite likely that I could be buried here. I said to myself that if I survived, I would instead bury these past months."

I took a deep breath. "This is my past," I said pointing at my notebook. I held her hand. "I beg you, help me bury it."

"I will, but it must be done now. We're about to leave," she said shedding tears.

I picked up my notebook and noticed the un-opened

envelope probably containing Fitzgerald's last words. I took it, slowly looked at it and decided to bury it as well. I would wrap the notebook and envelope with a waxed piece of sail I used as a rain hat on the Druid and put the package in a thin copper box with brass corners probably forgotten on the table by a previous patient. To protect the content of the box, I would fill it with rice that had dried in my plate and seal it with wax dripping from a burning candle on the table. I shall shove everything in the leather shoulder bag I had and would be ready to go and bury it. Who knows? Maybe some day, my little metal coffin will be found. I had once noticed a nice bay close to the hospital and decided I would hide it there beneath the stones by the shore away from the high tides.

Let these words be my last words pertaining to my hunt of Jack the Ripper. Only months ago, before the East End events, I needed no one and had organised my life so that no one would need me. But I was wrong. I did what seemed to me to be the only task an honest man should accomplish when he becomes aware of abuses committed against others. As a young boy, I ran away from those deadly acts my father perpetrated against me, my brother and mother. Maybe Fitzgerald was right in saying I was hunting a ghost. At least, I was hunting, and hunting I shall always do should events such as those of the East End ever happen again. For it made me accept who I was, build upon it and become a better person, the sole purpose any living being could ever have.

BERNARD BOLEY

EPILOGUE

Many times during the years after I had discovered Woodrow Reily's diary, I attempted to find traces of him in Canada only to fail. Did he and Elizabeth succeed in crossing the Saint-Lawrence river and reach Quebec City? I don't have the slightest idea. Nevertheless, some ten years ago, I met a man named Timothy O'Conner, who told me his great-great-grand-father had immigrated to Quebec at the end of the 19th century, aided by a young English woman. Coincidence? Perhaps.

Francis Tumblety spent the last days of his life at Saint John's Infirmary and Hospital in Saint Louis Missouri where he died at the age of 73 on May 28, 1903.

In 1889, the Cleveland Street Scandal investigation concerning a male homosexual brothel was given to Frederick Abbeline. The British government was said to be covering up the scandal because it involved many well-known aristocrats. Abberline died at the age of 86 on December 10 1903.

Charles Le Grand who had many aliases was

convicted under the name Charles Colnette Grandy in 1889 for blackmailing and later in his life for forgery. He died the 6th December 1935.

Grosse Isle is considered among the Irish community to be hallowed ground. More than 5400 immigrants crossing over on coffin ships were buried there. I felt it was my duty to honor Woodrow Reily and decided to hide my treasure exactly at the same place I found it. Maybe one day, a descendant of his will come and visit Grosse Isle and try to find it as I did. Until this happens, let me reveal the content of the letter.

The letter

My dear Woodrow,

I would have wished being able to find a way for you not to cross overseas in pursuit of Tumblety. It was useless. "Why?" you would ask. Because, I know for a fact that he is not the Ripper. On many occasions, I tried to discourage you from catching him but couldn't reveal the truth. Even if I had told you what I'm about to say, you would not have believed me. Now the time has come for you to know how all the pieces of the puzzle fall into place.

Let me first go back years ago for you to better understand how and when all these mind-blowing events began. I am quite aware that what I am about to tell you will not only surprise you, but will also infuriate you for me not having shared this with you before. The reason was quite simple. The more you would have known, the more your life would have been at risk and it had already been seriously threatened.

Now for the whole story.

Some six years ago, after the Phoenix Park killings of Frederick Cavendish, Chief Secretary for Ireland and Henry Burke, the Under Secretary for Ireland, a group of Irish moderates met in Dublin and agreed that if anything good could happen to the people of our land, it should exclude any form of violence. These murders were the works of committed by Fenian radicals known as the 'Invincibles' and only resulted in worsening what was already unacceptable. Derrick O'Connell and I were the instigators of this group of moderates, which openly spread the word about a peaceful reconciliation only reaffirming what had been included in 1879 in the Irish Republican Brotherhood's constitution. Derrick and I maintained close contacts ever since. You can easily figure out now how he managed to be on the same train you took for Manchester. He and I arranged it after you told me Abberline had given you his name.

While I was a more secretive person, and even if everyone knew him as a moderate, Derrick was quite outspoken and quickly fell under the eyes and ears of Scotland Yard. Soon after, he met a tall and rather charming American who presented himself as a physician, but who turned out to be a person having made money selling herbs providing some positive medical results. You obviously have guessed who I'm talking about: the man named Francis Tumblety. He was well known by the American and Canadian Irish community and appeared having been helpful to them. Derrick introduced him to me, and I must say that I was rather impressed. He was excessively well-dressed and almost led anyone to believe it was a privilege of being in his presence. But when he spoke out his first words, it was almost impossible for me not to laugh. Had your eyes been closed, you would have sworn by his effeminate tone of his voice that a woman was in front of you. His distracting mannerisms were typically those a woman would have adopted. But once a certain level of trustfulness would have been achieved, one would discover a brilliant man offering an incredible mascarade and whose convictions towards the Irish cause couldn't be challenged. He was not only a person who would help out many amongst the Irish people with his own money but was also a courier who would deliver letters and packages for those he knew. His peculiar appearance and the reputation he carried would allow him to avoid any form of inspection from the customs agents an Irishman would be usually subject to. Hence, he would also carry arms in his luggage hidden under smelly boxes of medicine custom agents dared not to examine. Did you know he was asked to run in Quebec's 1857-1858 election having been favoured against Thomas D'Arcy McGee, an ex-rebel of the 1848 Young Irelander Rebellion? He refused and D'Arcy McGee was elected becoming one of the Fathers of the Canadian 1867 Constitution. Can you imagine this scenario? If Tumblety had accepted, he could have become one of those 'Canadian Fathers', and everyone would have seen him promote close links with Great Britain and the Queen when years before he was favouring the independence of Ireland. But he preferred money and the company of young good-looking men which brings me to tell you how you came to know him. It was a pure coincidence. Tumblety was looking for female organs to complete his collection and found a way to contact Fillmore. They had never met before, and you unexpectively happened to be there. Looking back at the past events, I must say that you met him precisely at the right moment, otherwise, you probably never would have hunted the Ripper.

Now for Thomas J. Fillmore. He is an old friend of mine. We lived in the same neighbourhood in Ireland for years and was one of the first persons I helped out once my financial position had been settled. A rigorous scientist and physician he is, but he's unable to have a normal conversation with anyone. I managed to obtain for him the job he holds and hence becoming your superior. I was once at the London Hospital a year ago and heard him address you with what I considered to be undeserved words after you had respectfully presented him with a case. From that moment on, having noted the way you reacted, I told myself I should learn more about you. Fillmore mentioned to me how you had brought in so many improvements he never acknowledged, but from which he very much benefited. I then thought I should hire you to assist and eventually replace my estate manager and dear friend Liam Gallagher. I had asked Fillmore to make sure he would build up a high degree of resilience in you which seemed to be lacking and was indispensable in my field of works. I honestly believe he has succeeded.

So as you can guess, our initial encounter at the pub was not a random occurrence. It had been planned. But what I never expected was how much Elizabeth became infatuated the moment she saw you. We both know how it turned out, and I must say I couldn't have wished for my daughter to have met a better man.

The outcome of the meetings Derrick and I had become an elaborate plan allowing us to neutralize as much possible Brits and turncoat Irish leaders from the moment Charles Stewart Parnell would have supported a piece of legislation introduced to the parliament by Gladstone giving Ireland more political powers. We almost did it when he presented his First Home Rule Bill two years ago. The bill was drafted without Gladstone's ministers or even the Irish members of the Parliament contributing to it. Parnell wasn't totally in favour of the bill, certain parts of it not going as far as he wished, forcing us to make him understand that it was the first step towards a free Ireland to be completed when the new Land Purchase Bill would be tabled. Tumblety and I would provide Derrick with the money he needed to accomplish whatever he deemed necessary with what had by now become his plan.

His strategy was twofold. Firstly, he would look into all the members of Parliment as well as their private allies who opposed or were indifferent to the improvements of the condition of the Irish and offer them the possibility of either disclosing their secret lives or supporting our cause. Secondly, he would create a diversion forcing the police force to move away from his main area of action, Westminster.

To do so, I helped him hire someone known for disturbing the peace without getting caught. His name, he told us, was Edgar Kinley, an Irish. He was in a habit of threatening women something we knew the City wouldn't tolerate and asked him to leave women and create havoc wherever he could. He would begin in the City and move progressively to the East End forcing the City's police and the Metropolitain police to collaborate and expand their intervention in the East. "Our adversary's bishops will follow the knight," O'Connell used to say when we played chess. We were well aware that Scotland Yard's Special Irish Branch would get involved and weren't surprised to learn Frederick Abberline was chosen for that purpose. He knew the East End like the bottom of his pockets, was known to be methodical, tireless and would cut the corners to do whatever had to be done with or without his superiors' approval.

But if the plan started well, it quickly went bad, terribly bad. When a woman named Martha Tabram was killed, we suspected our man had done it. When Mary Ann Nichols was murdered, we were sure it was him. He butchered them all, Annie Chapman, Elizabeth Stride, Catherine Eddowes and Mary Jane Kelly. We failed in our attempts to stop him and completely lost track of this man who became Jack the Ripper. Derrick had no other choice but to bring to an end, a plan we truly believed would have worked.

That's when you came in. You were a witty, brilliant young man who deserved more than what he had. I decided to help you out. But as any pig headed, passionate Irishman would, you picked what appeared to be a lost cause. At the beginning, I supported you. Given what you considered to be strong evidence, you were convinced Tumblety was the Ripper, something Derrick and I knew was impossible. But we couldn't reveal to you the whole story back then. I wasn't too sure who you were really going after, Tumblety for having deceived you, your father for having caused the death of your brother or the Ripper. This ambiguity of yours was the same kind that caused the death of my own son, which my wife blamed for me ever since we lost him. Hence, I had to protect you from yourself. Elizabeth and Derrick did the same. Even Abberline thought you were a bit foolish and told you so when he came at my house. By choosing you to become my estate manager, I had no doubt you would be the best man for the job, but more than that, I hoped it would place you on a new track making you forget about the Ripper and Tumblety. I was wrong. You kept at it and almost lost your life twice in the hands of Edgar Kinley, the man you killed while defending a poor woman's life and your own and once, helping my good friend O'Connell.

Now I don't know what would be the best way to reveal to you what I am about to tell you. Hence, I must ask you to forgive me for all the pain it might entail.

When Timothy brought Kinley's body back to my carriage shed, he found a few objects in his pockets and left them in my room. You had already left for Canada when I returned to London and looked at them, it was too late to contact you and let you know about it. The papers he had in a wallet clearly showed his real name *was not Edgar Kinley but Louis Reily from the town of Derry, your home town. A second object confirmed what I feared the most. It was a medallion, with a Celtic cross on one side and two letters on the other one, KR, the initials of name you told me your brother had, Kevin Reily.*

My dear Woodrow, the man you killed was your father, and he was Jack the Ripper.

May God have mercy on our souls.

Gordon Fitzgerald

ABOUT THE AUTHOR

Born in the town of Havre Saint-Pierre on Quebec's North Shore, Bernard Boley spent some ten years in his childhood in the United-States where his father studied surgery, mostly in New York City. Although a French Canadian, the first language he spoke was English and admits he had a hard time learning French. His career brought him constantly closer to what he aspired to become, a writer. He wrote governmental papers, political speeches and years later, given his passion for gardens, wrote a book on designing and building water gardens, a French Canadian bestseller. Always carrying a notepad and a pen, he enjoys writing about whatever he sees and hears that makes a difference.

www.ingramcontent.com/pod-product-compliance
Lightning Source LLC
Chambersburg PA
CBHW072255020726
47501CB00002B/279